Freedom of the Monsoon

Malika Gandhi

Best Wishes

M Gandhi

Published in 2012 by FeedARead.com Publishing – Arts Council funded

First Edition

A CIP catalogue record for this title is available from the British Library.

Contents

PART FOUR Change

Freedom of the Monsoon *takes place in India, during one of the most brutally contentious periods of the 20*th *century. Outraged at the Raj's ignorance of their civil rights, India's people embraced the long overdue call for a Free India.*

In August 1942, Mohandas Gandhi called for immediate independence and the Quit India Movement began.

Freedom of the Monsoon is told through the eyes of five individuals: Rakesh, Dev, Pooja, Amit and Sunil.

From the birth of the Quit India Movement in 1942, to 1947, the fall of the British Raj and the rise of two new nations: India and Pakistan; we experience the pain and anxieties but most of all their love for one another and for their mother country as they strive to survive these often cruel and murderous times of change.

PART ONE

Dawn broke and India witnessed a new revolution: Gandhi. Mohandas Karamchand Gandhi. His strong, forceful words spread to the North, the South, to the East and to the West.

'Free India'

~

RAKESH

~

One

August 1942

I jabbed at the dying embers. 'It's our turn, Dilip. Now, it's our turn.'

Dilip puffed on his cigarette and rolled out a few circles into the air. 'Are you sure? Rakesh, what about your family...about Dev?' He tapped his cigarette, letting the ash fall to the ground.

I gave up trying to revive the smouldering coals and rolled up my shirt sleeves. I snapped the stick in half and began to doodle in the ash instead.

The heightened wind extinguished the fire, allowing a rise of wispy smoke escape to the sky. The clouds chased each other across the darkness; the stars playing hide and seek. A dog barked in the distance.

'You know my history. I have to do this,' I said.

'Even if it will cost you your life? Last week, you know— Mohan was hanged. He was caught handling explosives.' Dilip said this matter-of-factly.

I shook my head. Mohan was a good man; he'd died a martyr...like so many others. 'I am not important. I can sacrifice my life to free my country if I have to. What about you? Your parents are old. You have a wife and two young children and one on the way. They depend on you. If something happens to you, then who will support them?'

Dilip looked me in the eye. 'If I die, I will be *shahid*[1]. My family would be proud. I have discussed this with Rakhi and she has no qualms. She will support me all the way and my children—I want them to grow up in a country free from the rule of the Raj. I am prepared to die to give them that chance.'

I had to respect him. 'Good. It is settled then. Who else is involved?'

He dropped his cigarette into the dead fire. 'Two other men. I will introduce them to you tomorrow.'

---

[1] *Shahid*, Martyr

11

I felt Dev's excitement and his eager smiles on my back. I'd allowed him to come, just this once. I hope he would be content after that. I call him "Chottu[2]" – my dear, younger brother. We have a close relationship and his respect to me is shown when he calls me "Bhai[3]" – elder brother. This is his love. My reluctance for him to join me in this meeting is reasonable but Dev was stubborn. My frequent disappearances had made him suspicious and his relentless questioning began. I had little choice but to bring him on the secret.

'*Bhai*, where are we going?' he asked, walking closer to me.

'I'll tell you in good time, *Chottu*.'

'Do you believe...India will have her independence?' Dev asked hesitantly.

'Yes. India *will* be free and that's why we are doing this—to put pressure on the *Raj*[4]—to make sure India is freed!' I halted and turned to face him. 'Never think otherwise. This country belongs to the Indian people, it belongs to us!'

'Yes...*Bhai*.' His face showed shock and uncertainty.

I was alarmed. Had I said too much? '*Chottu*, I can't say anymore here. If someone overhears our conversation, there is bound to be trouble. What we are about to do, is not only dangerous but unlawful. We could be arrested or maybe worse. Wait until we reach our destination.'

I was nervous. Dilip had called on me unexpectedly, he said it was urgent. He wanted Dev there too. At first, I was angry; I didn't want my brother getting mixed up in this but Dilip insisted that he could be a lot of help.

My parents had become suspicious too. Without realising it, I changed and my family saw it. During the last few months my temper flared without reason and I nearly stopped talking altogether. Doing this to my parents was awful, lying to them, betraying their trust was not something I wanted to do, but it was better than telling them the truth.

We now walked past dimly lit houses – a sign that the day was coming to an end for most. The lingering scents of sandalwood and spice drifted towards us. At the last house we passed, a cycle was left abandoned outside the gate and a mother was singing a Gujarati

---

[2] *Chottu*, Younger brother (Dev is Chottu)

[3] *Bhai*, Brother (Elder) (Rakesh is *Bhai*)

[4] *Raj*, meaning King (Raja). The British Government during its reign.

lullaby from inside. It was something Ma used to do when Dev and I were children. Even in these times, lives carried on as normal.

'*Chal*[5] *Chottu.*' I walked a little faster. Dev glanced at the unlit oil lamp I was carrying and raised an eyebrow. 'We can't risk being seen,' I answered his unspoken question.

A few cows lowed as we approached the cow house but no one was around. I breathed a silent sigh of relief. Every breath, every step and every sound multiplied in the dark. I wished we would get there sooner.

As we came to the river, it whispered its greetings. The air was still and the trees stood as if in command, allowing their leaves to do as they pleased. Only the crickets made themselves known.

We entered a long stretch of road after leaving the riverside, it was eerily quiet. We moved faster, concentrating on the moonlit road and soon a house loomed ahead of us.

'Is this it?' asked Dev.

'Yes.' I checked all around but the area was clear apart from two people by the front door. I acknowledged them and they disappeared into the shadows.

'Who are they?' asked Dev.

'I'll tell you once we are inside.' We moved around to the back of the house. Dilip and I found this place by accident, it was just right for what we needed it for. The state of the building kept away unwanted visitors and mainly the police. The windows were boarded up and the roof was tumbling down.

The door creaked as I pushed it open. It took a few moments before my eyes adjusted to the gloom. Careful to tread quietly, I passed from the first room to the next like a shadow. Dev followed.

Old unsmiling portraits of men and women hung on the walls in the second room... there was a picture of a family too but it was difficult to make out the detail.

'How long has this house been empty? Those pictures...' said Dev, coming to stand beside me.

'Could be thirty years and those pictures—they were the owners,' I said as I searched in the room.

'Why did they leave?'

---

[5] *Chal*, Come

13

'They didn't leave. It's said that this house is haunted, the family who owned it were murdered.' I pressed the north wall and knocked it with my knuckles and moved to the next.

'How were they murdered?'

'Do you really want to know?'

'Yes, what happened?'

'Some say the deaths were terrible to behold; throats were sliced and then the bodies were hanged. A farmer found them, poor man; he had nightmares until the day he died. They say he went mad. People are frightened to come anywhere near the house, they believe the spirits still wander around. The villagers still talk about it.' The space between us narrowed; I held back a smile.

'Haunted, ghosts…oh God, *Bhai* have you seen them?'

I couldn't help but laugh. 'Not scared, are you?'

'No…no, of course not,' Dev said too quickly.

This time *I* raised my eyebrows and chuckled but turned my attention back to what I was doing. I checked the other walls— pressing my ears against them one at a time.

There wasn't much in this building; a few chairs, a table, and some broken clay pots laying around that no one had bothered to remove.

'What do we do now?' Dev asked.

I lighted the wick of my lamp, casting shadows across the room. Dev shuddered.

'In here.' I pointed to an open trapdoor. The lamp illuminated a set of stairs, leading to a basement. Carefully and quietly, I closed the trapdoor behind us and we proceeded down the creaking stairway.

The basement was warm in comparison to the above floor. It contained a small, wooden round table and three chairs. In one corner, a mat and some cushions made the room cosy. A few empty beer bottles were stashed in a box and a set of playing cards lay on the table.

'What were you doing before?' asked Dev, picking the cards up. He began to shuffle them.

'When?'

'When you were pressing the walls.'

'We check if the walls are false, if they have been tampered with to trap us. We check each time we come here,' I said.

'But how can they be tampered with— if no one knows about this house, except for us?' he asked.

14

'With the Movement, security has tightened around the country, *Chottu*. All police officers are on the alert for anything suspicious. All they need is evidence—anything to catch us with. Other derelict places have been raided; this house could be on their list. We know that entrapments are used—like I said, false walls to hide in or to leave a recorder. Just be careful, *Chottu*. This house must be kept secret; it must be monitored and used with discretion. We cannot come and go as we please, and everything—every little detail must be planned.' I placed the lamp on the table.

'How is it monitored?' said Dev.

'We have people on the lookout.'

'Those two we saw outside...'

'You are sharp. Good.' I appraised him. 'Yes, Manoj and Namdev.'

Manoj and Namdev including myself and Dilip, made the group of four. Everything was done together. Dilip was the ringleader – the planner who took to foresee any problems ahead. I was in charge of printing, Manoj dealt with surveillance and Namdev supplied materials.

'Manoj and Namdev are already watching this house. If they see the police within two hundred yards, they will alert us with a wail, or they will hoot. We stay here until the way is clear.'

'Do you…are you scared *Bhai*?'

'We are always scared.' As I increased the flame a little, a floorboard creaked above. We froze into a crouch.

'*Chottu*, did you hear that?' I lowered the flame.

Dev's eyes were wide. 'Do you think it's the police?'I hesitated for a second, then slowly stood up and relaxed. 'No, it can't be. They would make a lot more noise than that and besides, our watchers would have warned us. It may have been a rat.' I returned the flame; shadows flickered across Dev's anxious face.

'Or a ghost,' he whispered, his eyes widening.

'Maybe you shouldn't have come.' I looked at Dev's tired face and thought about the hour. Dilip was surely taking his time.

'But I wanted to.'

'No, it was reckless of me, bringing you along.'

'I am nineteen!'

'Nineteen and still young.'

This time we heard a different kind of noise. We froze again.

'Is that Dilip?' said Dev.

'Let's hope so.'

'I think we should leave. Something is wrong; I can feel it *Bhai*.'

'It's too late. We'll have to wait—don't worry. Dilip said he will be here, and so he shall.' Time ticked on. I checked my watch—it was past midnight now.

'Do you think Ma knows we're not at home?' Dev asked.

'We will be home before dawn; she will not awaken until then.'

The trapdoor opened and Dev jumped. Dilip appeared.

'Good. You two are here. Sorry, I am late.' Dilip came down the stairs.

'We've been here for over an hour, Dilip, where were you?' I said.

'Look, I said I was sorry. I got held up. It was difficult getting away. You know Suresh, my eldest – he is ill. I had to get some medicine,' he said.

'I suppose—you had good reason. Sorry for—well you know, I get nervous. Anyway, what was the urgency?'

'I'll show you.' Dilip took out a piece of paper from his shirt pocket and laid it out on the table. He blew away the dust and brought the lamp nearer.

Students: Fellow Indians
Be Indian in both culture and life
Boycott schools and colleges
Send foreigners away
Boycott all national newspapers
Organise freedom movements in towns and villages
Educate All
Paralyse the Raj
Persuade Raj servants to quit their jobs
Damage lorries carrying troops and war goods
Cut communication wires and remove rails.
JAI HIND[6]!

---

[6] *Jai Hind*, a common salutation used during the Quit India movement in speeches and communications – a translation of "long live India/victory for India".

'This is why I wanted you to bring your brother. He will be able to do this with ease,' he said, directing his words to me. 'This is the first step.'

'What am I to do?' asked Dev eagerly.

'We need help in getting these pamphlets around colleges, and you are the link. Your brother tells me you are popular and connected to the right people. Therefore, this will be very easy for you.'

'It sounds dangerous,' Dev said.

Dilip looked at me in surprise. 'I thought you said he could do this?'

I took Dilip to one side and spoke in a low voice, but rather sharply. 'I didn't say anything like that but he was eager to come. You insisted!' I frowned, was I mistaken? Had I read Dev's eagerness as courage? Was I fooled to think that he too, wanted a free India?

Dilip and I returned to Dev.

'You shouldn't have come,' said Dilip. 'I was wrong to ask Rakesh to bring you. Maybe, this is too much for you to handle.'

'No, no. I will…I can do it,' said Dev.

'I'm sure your brother has told you, but I will tell you again. This operation is dangerous and if you are arrested, they won't forgive you. A lot of courage is needed, boy. Are you sure you can do this…if you are not, then I don't want you involved. It is risky.' Dilip looked at him hard.

'I am ready, I promise,' said Dev.

'Alright, you will need to start off with people you can trust and who will give you support—close friends first. No one must be connected to the authorities – no teachers, politicians, police or official servants of the Raj.

'If this,' Dilip waved the pamphlet in the air. 'Reaches the wrong hands…well, you know what could happen. You cannot afford to be careless and you must be on your guard at all times.'

'I won't let you down.' Dev tried to say it confidently but I wasn't fooled.

'In that case, Rakesh—take this to Ali and Narendra and get two hundred printed,' said Dilip. 'Now the next step, I will need to see you in private tomorrow, to finalise... but not here…I have seen the police wandering in this district; looks like we may have to find somewhere new for us to meet. I will send a note with Namdev when I know where to go, what time and what date.'

'Can I come too?' asked Dev.

17

'No,' Dilip said curtly. 'This other job is not for you. It's...unpredictable.' Then his voice softened. 'Dev, you are still young. I don't think you will be able to do this.'

'But—' said Dev.

'Enough,' I said, putting a hand on Dev's shoulder. I stared at Dilip disapprovingly.

'What?' he said.

'Why couldn't you tell us about this back at home? Why call us out here at such a ridiculous hour?'

'Rakesh, I needed to speak to Dev personally and thoroughly. The Elders are already talking about our meetings, I fear they know something. I don't trust them. We *must* be discreet! It's time to leave. Wait here, I will look if it is safe to go.' Dilip opened the trapdoor and disappeared. After a few moments, he re-opened the door and signalled. I followed after Dev.

Dev wanted to know what other things had been planned and how serious it was; his unspoken questions were large in his eyes as he stared at me. I knew he was waiting until we were alone. I hoped I could avoid answering – Dev would plead with me to not go, to not do it.

The journey back to the village was quicker. We said goodbye and each went our own way.

Two

Will there be a future?

I pretended to be asleep. It didn't take long before Dev's breathing became slow and dense. Another five minutes and I slid out from the bed. I changed and quietly made my way to the front door.

I knew what Dilip wanted to see me about—we had been planning this for many weeks. I was grateful to him for not speaking to Dev about this. It was something I wouldn't have allowed Dev to participate in, even though many others would be of his age.

Putting a shawl over my shoulders, I walked past the cow house, through the fields and along a narrow dirt road which led to *Bhai-ji*[7]'s house. He was a freedom fighter too and wrote many articles on the Raj which largely aggravated the public, much to the annoyance of the Raj servants but he kept on writing and his editor never stopped him.

I found out accidentally about this but when I did, I knew I had to see him. *Bhai-ji* and I had a long conversation and soon after; I was committed to the Quit India Movement. Tonight I wanted advice, not from a freedom fighter but from an uncle. I wanted to be sure what I was doing, was the right thing.

The lamp was still burning when I arrived. I knew he would still be awake, even at this hour. *Bhai-ji* was writing when I entered. He was crouched over an old desk which had seen better days. His moustache ruffled as he read and wrote.

Many people shied away from *Bhai-ji*. He was quite different in mind and spoke roughly, sometimes coming over as rude. His appearance was wild for he preferred to wear his long hair bunched up in a pony-tail with thick, gold hoops in both his ears. His thick moustache was his pride.

Bhai-ji detested anything foreign made, especially if it was *Angrezi*[8]. Like *Bapu*[9], Mohandas Gandhi – he preferred to wear hand-

---

[7] *Bhai*-ji, Uncle (father's elder brother)
[8] *Angrezi*, English
[9] *Bapu*, Mohandas Gandhi was known as Bapu (father) and also known as "Mahatma" meaning Great.

sewn clothing and became extremely skilled as he learnt to spin cotton[10] and sew. He lived simply; a bed was placed in the far corner and a stack of magazines and newspapers lay haphazardly on the floor next to it. Through the semi-darkness (for he only used one lamp) I made out a pot in the small kitchen.

Around this one room house, there was an extra chair and a small temple of *Lord Krishna and Radha*[11]. A devotee, *Bhai-ji* prayed every morning before he set off to do his bidding. The room was quiet apart from the ticking of the wall clock – the only grand item he owned which was given to him by an old friend. I sat on the other chair and waited for him to finish. The scratching of the fountain pen continued for a while. It stopped as I was about to drop off.

Bhai-ji looked at me, adjusting his spectacles. He didn't apologise for his ignorance.

'Is everything ready?' he said.

'We still have more to discuss, but...'

'You have doubts.' *Bhai-ji* looked away. I waited for him to speak.

'Listen, *beta*[12],' he began. 'If you don't want to do this, you don't have to. You have to do it from here.' He pointed to his heart. I could not get used to his directness; it always made me nervous.

'I know and I do want to do this. I have waited so long...but it's *Chottu*. I am worried about him. If something happens to me, then who will look after him?'

'IF. If something happens, Dev will be proud to have a brother who fought hard. *You* need to be brave if you want to do this.'

'I can't back out now.'

'Of course you can't. This country is in our hearts, in our blood. We can't let our mother down.'

I nodded. That was what I needed to hear. 'Our next meeting will be our last and then we will finalise a date.'

'Would he mind if I came along?'

---

[10] *Spinning cotton*, Mohandas Gandhi used the spinning wheel to defy the Raj, to create his own clothes. This was a unifying element for all Indians who followed his example. It was seen as economic and the boycotting of all foreign goods followed shortly after.

[11] *Lord Krishna & Radha*, Lord Krishna and his devotee Radha. Krishna is a well-loved Hindu God, who got up to mischief in his early years and later became a hero, defeating villains.

[12] *Beta*, said in the context as son or daughter.

'I think he would like that.' I was surprised; *Bhai-ji* usually did not make himself available. I left my uncle, who returned to work right away.

I met Dilip, Manoj and Namdev next, at an unused barn, one mile away from the village. This was secluded from the main road. Luckily, Dev was visiting our aunt. I thanked the Lord.

As predicted, Dilip was delighted to meet *Bhai-ji*. We worked into the night, discussing and planning. *Bhai-ji* listened and advised appropriately, perhaps making mental notes for his next piece. I had never felt so tense but the taste of anticipation drove me along.

'We march on the 2nd of February, be prepared,' said Dilip. 'Make any arrangements you need, especially you, Rakesh, since you don't want Dev to participate...are you sure about that?'

I glared at him.

'I was only making sure,' he back-tracked.

We departed around eleven, my thoughts on the impending date. I was not expecting Dev to be waiting for me; neither did I want to listen to his warnings.

'I've told you many times *Chottu*. I can't tell you,' I said in frustration as I got dressed into a vest and *dhoti*[13].

Dev was sitting on the edge of his bed, looking annoyed. 'You have to—I am your brother! What are you hiding?'

'It's complicated. Don't harass me now, I'm tired and need to sleep.'

'But *Bhai*—'

'Please *Chottu*, leave it.' I climbed into bed, turning away from him. I could feel the seething anger and frustration flare from him but I ignored it. I let sleep take over.

'What are you doing tomorrow? We all have been invited to Dilip's house,' I said to Dev the next afternoon. He was just finishing his lunch.

'Oh good! It has been a while since I've seen *Bhabhi*[14]! I will cancel my plans with Pooja,' he said, picking up his glass of water.

---

[13] **Dhoti**, White wraparound sheet worn instead of trousers.
[14] **Bhabhi**, Sister-in-law (brother's wife)

21

'You seem to be spending a lot of time with Pooja, is there something I should know?'

'*Bhai*! She is a friend. I have to go now.' Dev abruptly stood up and went to wash his hands. I smiled, my brother was growing up.

Dilip's house was small. He lived with his mother, father, his wife and his two children. He worked as a farmer during the day and spent his other time on the Quit India Movement. His passion was unfounded and his determination never failed.

I knew Dilip from when he moved here from Bombay. That was eight years ago; we studied together in St Kings College and became friends almost instantly. We found we had something in common – the love to free this country. Our initial dislike for one another disappeared.

Those years were easy. We studied hard but played too. Dilip was known to chase girls and got into a lot of trouble because of it! His beatings never taught him to stop. Then he met Neetu. He married her after finishing college. Their bond is still strong; something I envy, even now.

Ma was still packing food in a basket.

'Ma, come on. They are waiting!' I said, leaning against the door frame. Dev was sitting outside on the steps and *Babuji*[15] had his head in a newspaper.

'Wait, Neetu is with baby, she needs good food and I know she wants *Khaman dokla*[16].' Ma saw me look at the other items in her basket. 'There is nothing wrong with that!' She shut the basket and declared she was ready. I rolled my eyes and *Babuji* folded his paper.

Dilip's parents greeted us with joy. We sat about talking and exclaiming over the children who were ecstatic to see us. Dilip's daughter, Laxmiba, jumped all over me and I smothered her with kisses. Ma went straight to *Bhabhi*.

'*Beta*, are you keeping well? I have brought you some *Khaman dokla* – your *sasu*[17] tells me you are always asking for them.'

---

[15] *Babuji*, Father
[16] *Khaman dokla*, Gujarati savoury dish made with Besan flour.
[17] *Sasu*, Mother in Law

'*Shukriya*[18].' *Bhabhi's* eyes twinkled as she smiled. She made to get the basket but Ma stopped her.

'Don't be silly, I will do that,' she said and took the food into the kitchen.

The afternoon was full of activity. Dev played with Suresh (Dilip's first child) and *Babuji* played with Laxmiba. *Bhabhi* was pacing up and down whilst Ma and Dilip's mother were gossiping. *Bhabhi* seemed to be in discomfort; I nudged Dilip who was writing some notes in a small book. He looked up.

'What's wrong with *Bhabhi*?' I asked.

'Nothing, it's her last month, she is just anxious. Don't worry, Neetu is well. Here, this is what we are to do.' Dilip had been writing about our next mission. It was detailed. 'I have told Namdev and Manoj. They have gathered a few more who want a part in this.' He whispered. 'I was thinking, just let Dev...'

'No,' I said. 'He is too young.'

'He handled his first job spectacularly. He seems determined and I can see he really wants to, Rakesh. Just think about it.'

'No,' I said again with a final edge.

Dinner was announced and I was relieved. Dilip didn't say anymore on the subject as we ate but he kept on glancing at Dev, a curious expression on his face.

'Are you sure?' he said again.

'Dilip, I don't want to risk his life!' I whispered. Dev looked at me as if he heard, but then put his head down and began to eat again.

'Ma!' *Bhabhi* suddenly shouted. The plate fell from her hand and she crouched, her hands on her bulging stomach. Dilip rushed to her, holding her back.

'Ma, call Jeela *ben*[19]!' he shouted to his mother. I helped him carry *Bhabhi* to the bed.

Ma was with us in an instant and ushered us out. 'Dev, you go and get *Jeela* ben. Rakesh, Dilip – outside.' She was efficient. She and Dilip's mother soothed *Bhabhi* until the doctor's wife, Jeela *ben*, came.

'Is she alright?' I asked anxiously.

'She is having a baby,' Ma said from inside the room. 'Look after the children. Take them outside, somewhere far. I don't want them to be here.'

---

[18] ***Shukriya***, Thank-you
[19] ***Ben***, Sister

Dev was fast. Jeela *ben* went straight to *Bhabhi's* room.

'Let's go. She is safe. *Chalo batcho*[20]!' said Dilip. He scooped up his girl and Dev let the boy climb up on his shoulders. The five of us walked to the river and *Babuji* returned back home.

As the children played in the water with Dev; Dilip and I talked about the mission again.

'The General's headquarters is in Delhi. We will begin to march from the little road here.' He took out his book and showed me a map which he had drawn. 'This will ensure others see us, some may join in too.'

'What time will we get there?' I asked.

'I am estimating noon. We will begin in the morning.'

'Does *Bhabhi* know? Should we wait? You are having a baby Dilip.' I reminded him.

He shot me a look of disdain. '*Gandhi*[21] didn't wait for the 'right' time Dev. Neetu knows what we are doing. She is supporting us.'

I accepted this but still it didn't feel right. 'I don't want anything to happen to you, it frightens me...'

'You don't think I worry about you too, Rakesh? You are like my brother. I am worried too. Listen, nothing will happen. We are just going to speak to the General. Then we will come home.'

My eyes wandered to Dev. He was laughing and splashing with the children. He must have felt my gaze on him for he looked up. He grinned and I waved.

'*Bhai*! Dilip *Bhai*! Come in!' he shouted.

'Papa, come in!' the children chorused.

Dilip gave me a challenging smile and hauled himself off the ground. He jumped into the river fully clothed. I laughed and joined them.

Bhabhi had another boy. Dilip's mother cried tears of joy as Dilip held his new addition in his arms. He gazed down at him; a look of uncertainty on his face. I watched Bhabhi and Dilip from afar and wondered if their immediate future would be a happy one after the march. I felt slightly nauseous thinking about...if Dilip was killed...

---

[20] *Chalo Batcho!* Come children!
[21] *Gandhi*, Mohandas Gandhi (also known as Bapu and Mahatma Gandhi (the Great one). He was known to begin the Quit India Movement.

'If only your father was alive, Dilip,' Dilip's mother broke into my thoughts. She took the baby and rocked him in her arms. 'Let's name him Kanha, after *Lord Krishna*. He will look after all of us.'

I saw tears in Dilip's eyes...suddenly the future did not look right.

'Dilip, think about it. We can postpone this,' I said when we were alone.

'No, it is settled. We will march on that date. Don't worry, we will be looked after.' His eyes fell on his new son.

Three

Karenge Ya Marenge! Will Do or Die!
February 1943

It was fiercely hot, making the march towards the General's headquarters uncomfortable. Yet, each and every one of us, forty altogether, were determined to reach our destination.

'QUIT INDIA! We want our rights! We want freedom!'

The chant was monotonous and full of power—a union of one voice; I felt the strength of the group multiply with every step as we marched, holding a lighted torch above our heads. The area was sparse, with only a few buildings—some houses, a church and the odd shop. We began marching at seven that morning on the outskirts of Delhi. It was cooler then and much easier. Soon we came to a river where women were filling their pots with water – a morning chore. They swiftly hoisted the full, clay pots onto their heads and watched us. I imagined they couldn't get home fast enough to gossip with their neighbours as they walked away in the opposite direction.

At last we arrived. Some white folks peered over their balconies as we – brown men proceeded down the street, chanting.

KARENGE YA MARENGE[22]! WILL DO OR DIE!

Children playing in a nearby park came to see the commotion. Holding the rusty rails, they stood on the lower rung and leaned outwards to see. A small girl began to cry and was quickly picked up by her mother, who ushered her and her siblings away from the unruly, dangerous brown men.

The road leading to the General's office was an expanse of white that dazzled. We continued to march and chant until we reached the gates. Shiny black iron rails separated us from the General's

---

[22] *Karenge Ya Marenge! Will Do or Die!* The words of Mohandas Gandhi during a passionate speech when Quit India was called for: 'We shall free India or die in the attempt!'

spectacular building. A *chowkidaar*[23] sat outside on a stool, picking his teeth with a stick.

'*Bhaiya*[24], open the gates, we have come to see the General *Saab*[25],' said Dilip.

The *chowkidaar* smiled, showing his yellow rotting teeth. His eyes darted from one man to another and then he spat red tobacco into a metal bucket by his side.

'Do you have a pass?' he said wiping his mouth with the back of his hand.

'No, of course not,' snapped Dilip. He stepped forward. 'Does it look like we are here by invitation?'

Some of the group laughed.

'Dilip.' I came to stand by his side. 'Please, stay calm.'

'*Bhai Saab*, why are you making a scene? I can't let you in without a pass,' said the *chowkidaar*.

'We are not going back. If you don't open the gates, we will stay out here and chant until you are forced to let us in,' Dilip threatened.

The *chowkidaar* eyed us and knew we would hold true to our word.

'I will speak to someone,' he said. 'Wait here.' He cautiously opened the side gate but kept his gaze on us. He sidled in, barely able to get his fat stomach through the narrow opening. On closing the gate, he scuttled away as fast as his short legs could carry him. He was back in ten minutes and kept the gate open.

'You can go in,' he said, out of breath and hot in the face.

A statue of two dolphins and a stunning mermaid centred a marble fountain in the middle of the forecourt; a showcase of the wealth of the Raj, I thought grimly.

Water gushed out of the dolphins' mouths catching the sun's rays as it splashed into the pool below. My look shifted from the fountain to the General's building. I counted the windows – thirty. Ten were on the highest level with balconies. The larger balcony led from the General's office, Dilip pointed out the marble steps leading to the entrance.

---

[23] ***Chowkidaar***, Guard
[24] ***Bhai/Bhaiya***, Brother (elder)
[25] ***Saab***, Sir

The hubbub from outside seemed to vanish and we stood, entranced, taking in the exquisite surroundings but the spell was broken when an officer in white uniform came through the front doors, followed by two guards each holding a rifle.

'Gentlemen,' said the officer in a clear, loud voice. '*Namasté*[26], what can I do for you?'

'We have come to see General *Saab*,' said Dilip.

'Oh...was there an invitation? There is nothing in the diary and the General is a very busy man.' The officer looked perplexed.

'There wasn't an invitation, but—'

'How strange...I'm afraid then there is nothing I can do. Anyhow, the General is away on business. He is a very busy man,' the officer repeated, grinning stupidly. He rocked on his soles, his fingers twining and untwining.

'That is a lie!' someone shouted.

'Is there anything *I* can help you with?' He was still grinning which I found very annoying.

'We want a meeting with General *Saab* personally. We have matters to discuss. Please give that information to him,' said Dilip politely. I could see he was trying to restrain himself from hitting him. I was impressed with his self-control.

'That is impossible.' The officer put his hands in his pockets and stared at us; his grin vanishing.

'You know why we are here! We don't want your government—we want our freedom!' I said, my sudden rage flared, taking me by surprise.

The officer looked bored. 'Why are you wasting everyone's time? Do you honestly think raving and ranting like a bunch of idiots, will make the General speak to you? Absurd Indians! I am not going to say this again—the General is out of town. Now please leave.'

'*Bhaiyo*[27]! *Shuru ho jao*[28]!' Dilip shouted. 'NO BRITISH RULE! NO BRITISH GOVERNMENT!'

The group followed.

NO BRITISH RULE! NO BRITISH GOVERNMENT!
NO BRITISH RULE! NO BRITISH GOVERNMENT!

---

[26] *Namasté*, Greetings
[27] *Bhaiyo*, Brothers
[28] *Shuru ho jao*, Begin

The officer stepped back from the deafening noise. His eyes flickered to the armed guards, worry etched on his face. The guards adjusted their hold on their rifles, ready to fire on command.

'Please, be reasonable,' shouted the officer once more. 'No decision can be made like this! I can arrange—' his voice was drowned as we went into another chant.

KARENGE YA MARENGE! GO AWAY BRITISH RULE, INDIA WANTS FREEDOM! INDIA WANTS FREEDOM! NO BRITISH RULE! NO BRITISH GOVERNMENT!

The sound of the gun silenced us. 'That's more like it. I will speak to the General...by telephone. Please be patient.' The officer walked back into the building with the guards following. We were unsure of what to do; we didn't expect this.

The gunshot had attracted a few locals who stood outside the gates, trying to get a look in. The *chowkidaar* was having a hard time telling them to go away. He gave up and sat down on his stool again, popping another *paan*[29] into his mouth.

'Now what shall we do?' said Manoj. 'Should we chant again?'

'No, let's wait,' said Dilip.

A few minutes later, a car horn hooted and we turned in the direction of the gates. A white car had stopped outside and the *chowkidaar* began conversing with the man inside. He opened the gates and the car drove through, parking right outside the building. The officer came out to greet the man, who was dressed in a khaki-coloured uniform, crisp and neat. His body manner indicated this could only be the General. Did Dilip have it wrong? He was positive that today the General would not be out of his office.

'The General was not away,' said Dilip, erasing my doubts. 'This is some kind of ploy.'

The officer and the General spoke in low voices; the officer pointed to us.

'*Bhaiyo, Namasté.* I am General William Forester.' The General said coming to stand just a few feet from us. 'My officer tells me you have come here, on this fine day to speak to me.'

---

[29] *Paan*, Betel leaf

'*Namasté*, General *Saab*. We have come to voice our views and requests – we want to see changes in our village,' said Dilip.

'You were informed, were you not, that an invitation is needed to be permitted entry. I am a very busy man, Mr...'

'Dilip.'

'Right. The basic fact is that you need to write to my administration team for an appointment, then we can meet properly, have a chat, maybe some *chai*[30], eh?' He chuckled at his own joke. 'You can tell me about your fears then but today I am not available as I have a meeting to attend in a few minutes. So please gentlemen, do excuse me,' said the General.

He turned on his heel and went into the building. The officer followed, it didn't seem like he wanted to stay in our company. I smiled wryly.

'Cowards!' Dilip's eyes blazed. '*Bhaiyo*, begin chanting. We will not go until they hear what we have to say!'

We didn't need telling twice and once again we began to chant. It wasn't long before the harassed looking officer came out—this time onto the balcony of the General's office. He waved us down. 'The General and I have discussed your requirements and he has agreed to grant you an appointment. If you write a short letter to us first, noting your reason for the meeting and our administration team will respond with a suitable date.'

'Liar!' Namdev shouted, which provoked more angry outbursts. The lighted torches swung above our heads; our voices getting angrier and higher.

I felt my heart beat faster; something awful was about to happen. The officer went back inside and came out with a megaphone. 'If you don't leave now, we will have no choice but to call the police. You will be arrested and thrown in jail. This will lead to prosecution, for some of you,' his eyes rested on Dilip. 'It could mean something else.'

An ominous silence fell over us and as we looked at each other, determination replaced the anger. An understanding spread amongst us. Setting our torches aside, we sat down and linked our arms.

'Hold your head up and do not give in *Bhaiyo*!' Dilip commanded.

---

[30] *Chai*, Tea

'Gentlemen, this is your last warning. Remove yourselves from the premises,' said the officer.

No one moved.

'You leave us no choice,' he sighed.

Within a few minutes the iron gates opened. Police entered the forecourt; batons at the ready. They circled the group like angry vultures and waited for the signal. We tightened our hold.

'Will you or will you not leave? This is your last chance,' the officer said, like he was offering us one last request before our execution, but we didn't move and then he signalled.

Things began to speed up then, but to me, it all moved in slow motion. The police charged, pulling our arms away from our neighbours and half dragged, half threw us away from each other. The batons came down on us thick and fast; there was no time to run. Bones crunched as the batons cracked on hips, legs and arms. Some fell whilst others fought.

'Get your filthy arms off me, traitor!' one of the men shouted.

'Aaagh! Leave me, in the name of God!' another screamed.

Someone grabbed my arms behind my back and twisted me around. He crashed his baton across my torso and I fell sideways, twisting my leg the wrong way. I screamed. Clutching my leg, I closed my eyes and waited for another blow but it didn't come. I breathed in and out and controlled the pain...it became very quiet and I opened my eyes.

Everyone was still and staring in shock at something on the ground. My eyes followed but I couldn't see; my view was obscured. Spasms were crippling my leg but I paid no attention. Gritting my teeth, I dragged myself closer until I found a space...my breath caught; my heart turned cold. There he was, a few yards away from me, my brother, my friend. Dilip lay on the ground, his eyes glazed over and mouth open in a silent scream.

Something snapped inside. I dragged myself closer and grabbed his shirt. 'Dilip, you can't go, don't be weak! Think; think of *Bhabhi*, Suresh, Laxmiba and your baby – Kanha. Think of *Ma-ji*[31]. Think of me! You can't leave us, you can't...*Bhai*, open your eyes, please *Bhai*...' My sobs came fast. I didn't care that everyone was watching.

---

[31] *Ma-ji*, Mother (directed to another's mother, out of respect)

31

'Rakesh *Bhai*, please, let him go. We need to move him,' someone whispered hoarsely. I looked into the tortured eyes of Manoj and Namdev. I looked back to Dilip's face, unable to move.

'Please, *Bhai*,' said Rajiv, another fighter.

Before we could do anything, the gates opened and hordes of Indians charged in. In a matter of seconds, our non-violent march turned into a riot.

'Kuthé[32]!' someone yelled. He threw a lighted torch at one of the policemen.

I stood up, my damaged leg limping. My eyes met Manoj and Namdev and with the help of Rajiv, we quickly moved Dilip's body to the side. We ducked as shards of stone flew in our direction; the once beautiful mermaid was in ruins, defaced. Water exploded, drenching us all. It washed away the blood that stained the once pristine court.

Anger pulsed through my body and I charged – straight into an officer. Picking up his fallen baton, I smashed it on his head. Craze smeared my reason and I crashed the baton on him again and again until he was dead. I hoped it felt like Dilip's pain did.

The pain came in excruciating waves. My scream sounded distant; darkness pressed down on me. My mind strangely felt disconnected to my body and everything began to swim. I was plummeting into a black hole. Was I still breathing? I couldn't be sure; I let myself be sucked further in.

I groaned in agony as I tried to lift my head. Severe spasms hit me, making me fall back onto the stone floor. Rolling on my side, I vomited and then became unconscious once more.

I didn't know how long it had been—I was confused. Strong vapours of urine reached me, making me retch. The sound bounced around me. I heard someone, something? I couldn't make any sense out of it.

'Rakesh Sharma.'

A man wearing shorts came into focus.

'Who are you?' I managed to say.

'I am Haricharan, one of the jailors. The officers want to see you. But first, please drink this.' He handed me a glass of water. I drank gratefully.

---

[32] *Kuthé*, Dog

'Do you know where you are?' said Haricharan. 'This is Nilpati jail. You are in Bombay.' He pointed to a plate. 'Eat, you need your strength. It may not look nice but it is food.'

I glared at his back as he left and ignored the food. Having no strength to stand, I simply fell asleep.

The light bulb swung to and fro above my head; the bright light making me squint. I couldn't see anything. As I tried to focus, freezing water was splashed onto my face, cutting sharply into my wounded skin.

'Who is your leader?' someone demanded.

'I don't know, let me go,' I spluttered weakly. My eyes could hardly open and I ached all over.

The man slapped my face with the back of his hand and I winced.

'Why did you go to the General's headquarters? What were you doing there?' This time another man spoke, his voice wasn't harsh but more enquiring and familiar.

'*Bapu...*' I said.

'What?!' shouted the first man.

'Mansingh, he has had enough interrogating. Let him go back to his cell,' said the second man.

'No, we need answers!'

'We are getting nowhere. He needs rest.'

'Alright, Haricharan. Be it on your head. Take him away.'

Days turned into nights and nights into days. How many—I didn't know. The smell of sweat, blood and urine was high but now I was used to it. I thought of Dilip. I missed him.

The cell door opened and food was pushed through, then it closed with a clang. Without looking at the plate, I ate automatically, not tasting, just eating. I gulped down the water, and put the empty plate and tumbler near the door and went to sit back in my grey corner.

What felt like moments later, I heard the cell door open again. My eyes fluttered open; no doubt I had fallen asleep.

'You have visitors,' said Haricharan.

Visitors? Could it be *Babuji*? No, he doesn't know. Then, who? Haricharan was looking down at me sympathetically.

I tried to stand but didn't quite succeed—had Haricharan not caught my arm, I would be on the floor again. I was held rather gently which I was not used to. With grateful support, I walked with him to the hall.

'Rakesh! Rakesh *beta*!' Ma flung her arms around my neck, her body shaking uncontrollably.

Babuji's trembling hand gripped my shoulder. I inwardly winced as the pain shot through me. Thankfully he didn't notice.

'How do I look?' I asked Dev minutes later when he was able to compose himself. I smiled awkwardly feeling my bruised lips.

'*Bhai*! What have they done to you, I will kill them!' Dev said hoarsely.

'Shhh Dev, don't say things like that, it makes me nervous. I...I love you and nothing can happen to you, you hear?' I said.

'I can't see you like this, *Bhai*!' Dev's face was a mask of horror as he took me in. I could tell that he hadn't slept most nights.

I turned to Ma and *Babuji*. 'I'm sorry; please don't be angry with me.'

'*Beta*, we are proud of you,' *Babuji* said. 'Do you know—the whole village is behind you. We are so proud Rakesh, so proud.'

'You are so thin...' Ma said. 'Do they give you food?'

'The food is nothing like yours, Ma,' I gave her a watery smile.

'*Beta*, you must be strong. Don't give up, we need you at home,' *Babuji's* voice cracked. I held my tears.

'I know. I want to come home as well, Babuji. I miss Ma's *roti*[33],' I smiled again and Ma burst into tears.

'It doesn't look good, does it *Babuji*. I won't be coming home,' I said after a moment's silence.

'Don't talk like that. We are all praying for you.' But I saw the truth in *Babuji's* eyes. He too, had doubts.

'*Bhai*, where is Dilip?' asked Dev. 'I know he was with you.'

I thought I saw a shadow of hate cross Dev's face and hoped I was wrong.

'*Bhai-ji* told us...when you didn't come back home. He told us everything. *Babuji* was very angry—they argued. *Babuji* still hasn't forgiven him and neither have I,' said Dev, his fists clenched.

---

[33] ***Roti***, Leavened bread

'Don't make it hard on him, *Chottu*. He is a freedom fighter like me and well, he does things differently. It's not his fault,' I reasoned.

'He should have told us – *you* should have told us!'

'*Chottu*, please, don't hate me,' I pleaded. 'I couldn't bear it.'

Dev flung himself on me, burying his face into my shoulder. 'I could never hate you, *Bhai*. Oh why did this happen? Please, come home.' His face was wet when he let go of me; I found mine was too.

'Dilip is dead, Chottu. He was killed.' I said in a flat tone. It sounded far and distant.

There was silence between us now although Ma was still crying. I wanted to hold onto her forever and never let go.

'If something happens, *Chottu*, look after Ma and *Babuji*, won't you? Tell *Bhabhi*, Dilip was brave, he is *shahid*[34]...'

Dev's eyes were red and all he could do was nod.

Soon the jailor announced time. Ma kissed my forehead and *Babuji* and Dev clung to me. As I walked away, I glanced back and saw my family standing there, looking like death had come early...maybe it had.

---

[34] **Shahid**, Martyr

Four

Inquilab Zindabad! Long Live the Revolution!

Fists punched the air as the crowd chanted, waiting for the hearing to begin.

FREE THE PRISONERS! THEY ARE INNOCENT!
INQUILAB ZINDABAD[35]!

The courtroom was busy; reporters, politian's and the general public had come to see us on trial. I stood in the prosecution box with the others; Manoj, Namdev, Kuldip, Rajiv and Imran. If Dilip was alive, he would be standing here too...

I knew in my heart that this was inevitable. They wouldn't let us have any other sentence. For us, there was only one. Babuji said they were behind me and they believed in me...I was sorry to have let them down. I hoped that Dev would be able to fill the void that I will leave behind.

They sat together in the front row. Ma wiped away her tears and *Babuji* stared at me with tormented eyes; Dev looked angry. To my surprise, *Bhabhi* was here also with Dilip's mother. They looked hopeful, like waiting for a miracle to set us free. *Bhabhi's* eyes were red and she had dark circles under her eyes. It shadowed her pretty face. I couldn't look anymore; it hurt too much.

'Order please.' The judge came in and took his chair.

The crowd quietened and settled down in their seats. Some stood on the side with newspapers in their hands; fanning themselves vigorously in the stifling heat. The prosecution stood up as the judge declared the case open.

'Your honour, since Mohandas Gandhi began this non-violence campaign – Quit India, there has been nothing but violence. What happened in this case is unforgivable,' said Burke, the lawyer for the prosecution.

'Go on,' said the judge. He looked at me, his face curious. I smirked.

---

[35] *Inquilab Zindabad*, a Hindi phrase used during the Quit India movement which translates into "long live India".

'Is there something funny which you would like to share, Mr Sharma?' the judge said. His eyebrows were furrowed.

'Not yet, your honour,' I said.

'So as I was saying before being rudely interrupted,' Burke continued but not before he shot me a glance of contempt; I smiled wider. 'These young men aren't anything but trouble makers. They had the nerve to go to the General's headquarters, your honour!'

'We have rights!' Namdev's voice startled me.

'Your honour, I would like to question the accused please,' said Burke, pretending he hadn't heard the outburst.

'You have permission,' said the judge.

He came to our stand. 'You are Namdev Chopra, Kuldip Singh, Rajiv Khanna, Manoj Prasad, Imran Ali Khan and Rakesh Sharma,' he said reading from a list.

There was a rustle in the audience, someone sniffed.

'Who is your leader?' Burke asked.

'Our leader, our brother, is dead,' I said. 'One of your men killed him.'

'His name, please.'

'Dilip Ram Tilak,' I said in a clear voice. *Bhabhi* lowered her head and wiped her eyes.

'This Dilip Ram Tilak, was the leader of your group?'

'Yes.'

'Did he plan this confrontation at the General's headquarters? Were any of you involved in the planning?'

None of us answered. After a few moments, I spoke. '*Bhaiyo*, what shall I tell him? The truth or what he wants to hear?'

'I want the truth!' Burke shouted. 'Speak now!'

'The truth is that we had been planning this since *Bapu* announced the Quit India movement. Perhaps you are unaware...?' I winked and the room laughed. Burke looked annoyed.

'We have every right to go to any public place in Hindustan, "our" land, the soil of the brown man. What you are doing is wrong! We are very poor; it has become difficult to feed ourselves, to clothe our families...the taxes rise, taking more than half our crops. What do we have left to sell, to live on? The rich get richer and we get poorer! That is why we have the courage to go to see the General, to go to his headquarters. Does that answer your question?' Burke had gone red in the face. The audience began clapping hard and stood up. My friends patted me on the back.

'That will do. Order please!' The judge banged his gavel on the bench. Everyone quietened and sat down, once again. 'Mr Burke, please carry on.'

Burke wiped the sweat off his face and cleared his throat. 'Mr Sharma, do you agree to have murdered a policeman during the riot?'

'A lot of murders are happening, sir.'

'Please answer the question.'

'No, I did not murder a policeman,' I said.

'What other plans were made? A bomb plant? Sabotage of the municipal buildings?'

'I cannot tell you that.' I held my head high.

'You were a friend of Mr. Dilip?'

'Yes, a very close friend. We were like brothers,' my voice hardened as I thought of the way he was mercilessly killed, like he was nothing important, just another Indian. I felt the prick of tears. 'I loved him like a brother.'

Burke faced the bench. 'I don't have any more questions for Mr Sharma. But I do have a witness whom I would like to question.'

'Bring in the witness,' said the judge.

The chowkidaar looked nervous as he walked to the witness stand. His beady eyes darted to the lawyer and then to us.

'What is your name?' asked Burke.

'Ram Dayal, *Saab*,' said the *chowkidaar*.

'Ram Dayal, put your hand on the bible and swear that what you say is the truth and nothing but the truth.'

'The truth *Saab*,' said the *chowkidaar* placing his hand on the holy book.

'Ram Dayal, how long have you been working at the headquarters of the General? *Kitne waqt tum kam karte thé* General *ké pas*[36]? '

'*Das saal, Saab*.'

'Ten years, very good and have you been faithful, working hard, doing your job? *Tum kaam barabar kartethé vaha? Tumahra nokri acha hai?*' Burke asked.

'*Kuthé*,' I said under my breath. Rajiv heard me and grinned. '*Saab*, I don't understand the point of such a question,' I said aloud.

---

[36] The prosecutor will first speak in English and then in Hindi for the sake of the chowkidaar, who does not understand much of the English language. The British were well known to understand and speak the Indian language: Hindi

'Mr Sharma, please keep quiet in the room of the law. Your turn will come,' said the judge.

'Ignore him Ram Dayal, please answer my question,' Burke said calmly. I scowled.

'I *Saab*, I work good.'

'Tell me, what happened that day? *Kya hua tha woh din?*'

'*Woh General ko dekné ayé thé, aur woh uské saath baath karné jaathé thé*,' said Ram Dayal.

'So what you are saying is that these men came to see the General to talk to him. Hmmm. *Phir kya hua,* what happened next?'

'Officer *Saab né kaha ké voh nahi mil sakté hai aur Kagar jahiyé.*'

Burke walked up and down in thought and then faced the judge. 'These men were told that they needed to write to the General to be given an appointment but still, they didn't go away. The Officer who was present at the time, gave a statement that they were given explanations and chances but still they stayed. Ram Dayal, did they want to fight?'

'This is not fair!' I said. 'You are putting words into his mouth!'

'Fight...yes, they fight,' said Ram Dayal. '*Saab,* they don't listen to Officer *Saab* and they fight the police *log*[37].'

'*Shukriya*, Ram Dayal.' Burke let the *chowkidaar* go. He turned to face the judge again. 'Your honour, I have come to believe that these men are responsible for the riot at the General's headquarters as was Dilip Ram Tilak. I would like to have their punishment considered in respect to the riot and in the case of Mr Sharma, the murder of a policeman.'

Namdev came and stood in front of me. 'Whatever punishment he is given, we will have the same. If he didn't kill that traitor policeman, I would have!'

'*Chup*[38] Namdev! Don't make it worse for yourself,' I hissed.

'No Rakesh *Bhai*, we are in this together; I *will* have the same punishment,' said Manoj. The others all agreed.

Burke laughed. 'Eager for the rope, are we?'

The judge turned to me. 'Mr Sharma, do you have a lawyer?'

'No *Saab*.'

---

[37] *Log*, people
[38] *Chup*, quiet

'Do you have any questions to put to the bench?'

'No,' I said again. 'But I want to say something.'

The judge nodded.

'I want to say is that India is *our* country, *our* land! The Queen and her people have no right to it. A long time ago it was taken from us by force, but now, we want it back. We have sacrificed our land, our living and our pride. But no more! *JAI HIND!*'

'*JAI HIND!*' the others chorused and a cheer went up from the public.

'Order! We will finish for today. The court will adjourn and a verdict will be passed in two weeks from now.' The judge stood up and left the room.

In an instant we were handcuffed. My eyes sought for my family; they were sitting there, not moving.

'Ma,' I said. '*Babuji*, Dev!'

'Come along now,' a jailor pushed me forward. I turned around; my eyes flashed.

'Don't. Push. Me. I am not an animal!' My tone was not forgiving.

'Move along,' he said quietly this time.

I took one last look at my family and walked out.

'Rakesh!' Ma screamed. 'Oh, my Rakesh!'

The sound returned to me like crashing waves, accelerating my heartbeat. The verdict was final, given perhaps too easily. I stood rooted, my legs unwilling to move. I saw the judge leave his seat and the room emptying. A police officer handcuffed me and my brothers[39]. In single file we walked outside to the glaring sun and to the surging throng of people. There were hundreds of them, chanting.

'*JAI HIND! MERE BHARAT MAHAAN*[40]! LONG LIVE INDIA!'

They shoved and shouted, trying to get to the front to see us. The police were struggling to keep order and the barrier was finally knocked over.

---

[39] Brothers – used in the context of brotherhood.
[40] *Mere bharat mahaan!* Long live India!

'*JAI HIND! MERE BHARAT MAHAAN*! LONG LIVE INDIA!'

I was astounded. *Bhai-ji* had done his work, like he said he would. He'd got them; the publicity, the reporters, the photographers – all where we wanted them! This was just the beginning. I felt triumphant; I would not be around but Dev would be here to see a new India, a new government!

'FREE THE PRISONERS! THEY ARE INNOCENT! FREE THE PRISONERS!'

My attention came back to the present and a woman was screaming at a police officer.

'People like you will go to hell!' she spat in his face. 'You are a traitor! The *Raj* is our enemy, and here you stand by them like a faithful dog!'

She was immediately handcuffed and dragged to a police vehicle. I watched the chaos around me with a grim expression. Ironically, I was safe from this madness. Photographers flashed their lights at us and reporters shouted questions; no one was making any sense.

'Get inside,' a police officer barked at us when we reached the police van. I found myself pushed into the back, behind me – Namdev, Manoj, Rajiv, Kuldip and Imran, followed by two police guards. I stared vacantly inside my temporary prison, then, I saw something move against the window...I took a sharp intake of breath.

'Dev!' I was immediately there, my hands on the glass pane— trying to feel his face. A guard pulled me back just as the van began to move...I saw Dev's face disappear out of sight.

Death – it couldn't be really bad. To Hang Till Death. I paced, trying not to think about it...I saw Dev's face again – I kept on seeing it, in my dreams and during the day – the terror which mirrored my own. I closed my eyes and concentrated on breathing right until the pain could be thrown.

A writing pad and a pen lay next to me. I'd asked Haricharan – I wanted to write; to explain to Dev, to Ma and *Babuji*. I didn't want them to hate me for ending my life like this.

I flipped a page over and began to write.

I stood holding the bars, thinking about it. *Babuji* and Dev would be there...Ma would be home...knowing...watching the clock. A low sob escaped from me and I crouched, winding my arms around my body.

'Let it out, *Bhai*,' Rajiv put a hand on my shoulder. My sobs died down but the pain didn't go away. 'Remembering Ma?'

'Yes,' I managed to say.

'I have a wife and daughter and my sixty-seven year old *Dadi*[41]. Babuji passed away when I was eleven and Ma died giving birth to me. Dadi brought me up. She is proud of me...I will miss them so much.'

Namdev was sitting alone, staring at the ceiling. Manoj was asleep but fidgeted every few minutes – he called out a few times. Imran and Kuldip were lying on the cold floor, staring, just staring. We were all thinking about our families. Who knew my life would end like this? I laughed out loud.

'What happened?' Namdev said, taking his eyes off the ceiling to look at me.

'Nothing happened. I'm laughing because it's better than to cry,' I said.

The day of the execution arrived like any other day. Everything seemed normal—the only difference was the frantic beating of my petrified heart.

Ma always said to sing to the Lord is a road to sanctuary. I concentrated, calming my mind and I sang. '*Om Jaya Jagadisa hare...*'

Immediately I felt a strange but happy, calm sensation enter my body and I sang a little louder. The others in the cell recognised the song; some joined in and some bowed in respect.

It was 8.30am when the jailors came for us. The execution was timed for 9am. I noticed the jailor ordered to escort me was not Haricharan. For that I was grateful—Haricharan had become a good friend and I didn't want him to see me go like this. I looked up at the

---

[41] *Dadi*, paternal grandmother

jailor with hollow eyes, he stared back – the stillness between us speaking volumes. Handcuffed for the last time, we began our slow march.

Heads held high, we walked onto a high platform, standing five spaces apart from each other; the death rope hung motionless above our heads, like a coiled snake, ready to strike. I dropped my gaze from it.

This wasn't a private execution; a mass of brown faces under black umbrellas watched us – they stood in nervous anticipation. It wasn't quite time yet and the minutes seemed to slow.

There was a stir in the audience. People began to shift their weight and whisper – a severe chill, pin-pricked my skin that had nothing to do with the weather. I wondered if I would die quickly or would I struggle until my last breath? It was now 8.45am; the clock ticked. I could feel Dev and Babuji—they were here...I began to search—I needed to see them one last time...where were they? The faces swam – I couldn't focus.

'*Beta*!'

I followed the cry and saw them. Dev was clutching *Babuji's* shoulder, looking terrified.

'*Babuji...Chottu...*' My voice broke. They looked at me; eyes tormented. I fidgeted with my bound wrists and tried to run to them – a stinging pain threw me, motionless. I writhed as the whip came down on me again and again.

'Nai[42]!' A shill cry rose from *Babuji*. He was holding onto Dev.

Dev scuffled on his feet as he tried to reach me. '*Babuji*, let me go! I will – '

'*Nai Chottu*, don't...*Chottu*, don't come here!' I shouted. All eyes were on me now; I could feel their anticipation. Dev stopped and slumped into *Babuji's* arms. I was relieved.

'*Bhai*, get up. You can do this, *Bhai...Mere Bharat Mahan! Inquilab Zindabad! Inquilab Zindaba*d!' Rajiv spoke, purpose punctuated with each word.

Namdev, Manoj, Kuldip and Imran joined in the chant – my heart hardened and courage burst within.

---

[42]*Na/ Nai*, No

'*Mere Bharat Mahaan..Inquilab Zindabad...!*' I stood up slowly; my eyes blazing. A cheer went up from the crowd; a victory? I forced myself to look at Dev and *Babuji*. 'I will always be with you,' I said aloud. '*JAI HIND!*'

From the corner of my eye, I saw a jailor look at the time and nod. It was time. I braced myself as a black bag was slung over my head. It was rough and smelt of earth and tobacco. I couldn't see anything. The rope tightened around my neck; my heart began to react in an odd way, like it was trying to take wing; it seemed to know...

The thumping in my weak body was deafening and I wanted to run and hide. I didn't want to die like this...I took a few breaths and began to pray...my mind began to clear...I saw my family and my village...

'Chottu! Come out of the river! Ma is calling,' I shouted from the riverbank.

'Five more minutes, Bhai!' Dev shouted back and he dived under the water again, coming out at the other end.

'Don't do that! It always scares me.' Dev climbed out, grinning. I threw him a towel. 'Let's go home.'

The smell of sweet earth enthralled me as it always did after a cool swim in the river. I inhaled it deeply. We ran along the path, coming to some cows whose bells rang pleasantly. We let them pass and then moved on. Babuji worked in a crop field not far from the river. It was our next stop. I waved him over and he came, wiping his hot face with his dhoti.

'Is it time for lunch?' he asked.

'Ma has been calling,' I said.

'Good. I am very hungry. I forgot to take the tiffin. Did you two have a nice swim?'

'It was very nice Babuji, but Chottu is a little rascal!'

Babuji laughed. 'Why is that, now?'

'I was doing nothing wrong—Bhai, leave it, it was nothing!' said Dev.

'You shouldn't go under like that. Anything—'

'But it didn't. Tell him Babuji,' said Dev.

'Someday Beta, you and your brother can take over this land from me. I will look forward to that day,' Babuji completely ignored

our argument. He looked up at the sky. 'Looks like more rain. Good for the crops.

Freshly cooked chapattis, rice and okra sabji[43] enticed us when we arrived home. Ma had already laid the dishes.

'Rakesh, Chottu, and you too Ji[44], chalo[45], lunch is ready.'

'Ma, this is lovely. Do you think that my wife will cook like this?' I picked up the okra with a piece of chapatti and popped it into my mouth. I grinned mischievously.

'Chup[46]! Find a wife first and then we'll see.' But Ma was smiling too.

I hurtled back to reality. I barely had time to register what was happening and found myself falling. The rope tightened unbearably around my neck...

---

[43] *Sabzi,* Vegetables
[44] *Ji* wives did not call their husbands by their first names and substituted with 'Ji' in respect.
[45] *Chalo*, Come
[46] *Chup*, Quiet

PART TWO

Loss and Gain

~

DEV

~

Five

Bhai

Babuji held me by my shirt as I pushed and pulled to get free again but he was surprisingly strong. *'Bhai!'*

'*Babuji*, let me go! *Bhai* needs me, he has fallen!' I shouted. 'Why won't you let me go?'

'*Beta*, Rakesh is dead. He is dead.' *Babuji's* cry echoed strangely in my ears.

A man in uniform made his way to us. '*Beta*, it is over,' he said.

'I want to see him, I want to see *Bhai*!'

'I'm sorry but that is not allowed. You don't want to see his face, not anymore. Please stay calm.'

'What do you mean, what's happened?' I challenged him, ready to fight if I had to. *Babuji* seemed to sense it and put his hand on my shoulder firmly.

'There is a reason why those black bags are put on their faces; it's not nice. Let it be.' His eyes were deep, his voice tormented.

I let my hands fall to my side. 'Please, I want to see *Bhai*. We need to take him home.'

'He will be in peace now; he is no longer in pain.' The man seemed to not have heard, like he was talking to himself. He stared at the sky for a moment and then looked at me. He seemed young, yet his manner suggested otherwise. He reminded me of *Bhai-ji* and I hated it.

'Who are you?' I said.

'My name is Haricharan. I'm one of the jailors here. Rakesh and I...' He cleared his throat. 'We became good friends.'

'*Bhaiya*, how do we take him home? Should we be signing papers? I want to cremate my son as soon as possible – only then will he be in peace,' said *Babuji*. I buried my head in his shoulder and felt my sobs coming fast. He held me tight.

Haricharan looked uncomfortable. '*Kaka*[47], the prisoners are buried in the prison grounds. They are never sent home.'

I shook my head furiously. '*Bhai* is coming home with us where he belongs! He is a Hindu, Haricharan, like you and me. He

---

[47] *Kaka*, Uncle (father's younger brother) but also used to acknowledge elderly men in respect.

cannot be buried! I will go and talk to them!' My voice got angrier as I tried to get past him but he was strong.

'I will do something,' he said kindly but he looked uncertain. 'Please be patient.'

The area was empty now; only the three of us remained. I looked past Haricharan's shoulder. The executed had disappeared too. I don't know why but I remembered Dilip.

'*Bhai Saab*, there was a man – Dilip, he was murdered during the riot. Do you know what happened to him?'

Haricharan thought. 'So many Indians have been killed in these riots. The police have to clean up.'

'But what happened to his body? Was he sent home?'

'As it happened at the General's headquarters, these 'killings' couldn't be ignored but there was no one who could identify them. I believe they were all taken away and cremated, but where, I don't know.'

My head began to swim and then I violently threw up, narrowly missing *Babuji*.

'It's the shock,' said another voice. 'Haricharan, what are you still doing here? Who are they?'

Babuji was holding me down so I couldn't see the other man.

'They are relatives of Rakesh Sharma. I need to speak to you...can we go this way?' Haricharan's voice turned low and I strained to hear.

'It's their right,' said Haricharan, a little loudly than intended after a while.

'Religion does not dictate the laws in this jail, you know that better than I,' said the man loudly.

'Then it must change! Remember I am a Hindu too. I have turned a blind eye once too often in this jail and today, it's my turn. You will do it!' Haricharan voice shook with anger.

'Take it easy old sport. There's no reason for this aggression,' the other man said.

I began to feel better. With *Babuji's* support I straightened up. Haricharan was still talking to the man, although in low tones now. They were standing some feet away. The other man's face was red and sweaty. He had beady, narrow eyes – cruel eyes, I thought. I spat on the ground and the white man turned his head towards me in fury. Haricharan looked frightened.

'Let's go inside and talk,' Haricharan said quickly but with a level of authority.

'That boy just spat on our ground, Haricharan. That's against the rules!' the man shouted.

'Let it go, he's only a boy. He doesn't understand. Please, let it go,' Haricharan's eyes were wild with fear now. I didn't understand why but then I saw the man's fists and I quickly understood. My hands were also curled up in fists and I wanted to hit him, hard. Dev, stay calm, I told myself. If I am arrested, *Babuji* will not be able to handle it.

'I am sorry,' I said through gritted teeth.

Haricharan visibly relaxed as did the man and they both went inside. When Haricharan came back, he was alone. '*Kaka*, Dev, please come with me.'

Haricharan led us away from the cells but I still heard the wails, the banging, and the smell of blood and sweat; it made me shudder. We were led to a room with a table and three chairs; it looked like it was used for interrogation.

'What did that white man say?' I demanded as soon as the door was closed.

'The man you saw me with, is Officer Smith. He is one of the charges here who can help us. He does things in... certain ways.'

'You mean a bribe,' I said. 'We don't have that kind of money.'

'I'm not talking about money. Smith owes me a lot – I've seen too many things in this jail which the "white man" has abused and he is one of them. I have got him out of trouble more than a few times...' Haricharan's gaze was mixed with many emotions – worry, humiliation and dislike. I wondered what happened. 'It's now my turn. I *will* have your brother released.' He paused as if considering something and seemed decided.

'Rakesh spoke about you a lot, also of your Ma and *Babuji*. He really loved you all. After the sentence was passed, he wrote a letter. I think it's the right time to give it to you.' Haricharan pulled out an envelope from his pocket. My name was written in *Bhai's* perfect handwriting. I took it and put it in my pocket – I couldn't read it yet.

'I need to talk to Smith, will you be alright?' he asked

'Yes, but please hurry.'

I paced the floor whilst *Babuji* sat on the chair. Haricharan seemed to be gone a long time.

'Ma must be worried about us.' My voice was hollow and it echoed in this oppressive room.

'I can't bear to think about it *beta*, I just hope she is not alone,' *Babuji* whispered.

The walls were thin and I could hear the sounds of peril clearly. I thought of all the poor souls, trapped in this dungeon, through whose fault?

'Close your mind, Dev. We cannot do anything about it,' *Babuji* said, sensing my emotions right. I sat, feeling helpless.

'*Babuji*,' I said.

'Yes, *beta*.'

'Was *Bhai* tormented?'

Babuji raised his head. 'Don't do this to yourself. It will do you no good.' His was pleading; I couldn't stand the grief.

A fly zigzagged above our heads haphazardly. Restless like me; it seemed unable to stop and be still. I turned my gaze away and again, my thoughts wandered to *Bhai*. If he hadn't met Dilip, if he wasn't committed to the Movement, he would still be alive. I should have tried harder to stop him! Tears began to slide down my face but I wiped them away furiously. Just then, Haricharan returned.

'You can take Rakesh home. It wasn't easy but like I said, he owed me. You will need to sign these release papers.' He placed a form and a pen on the table.

'What will happen to the others?' I said. I began to sign the papers straight away.

'There is only so much I can do. I'm afraid they will be buried here.'

'But their families...they can't do this!'

'Dev, please...' Haricharan was agonised.

'I'm sorry.'

'I have been thinking and under the circumstances, I would like to advise you,' he said when I handed the form back to him.

'Say what you have to.' I didn't mean to be abrupt but part of me was still furious.

'Cremate Rakesh here in Bombay. Rajkot is a long way away and his body will decompose quickly in this heat. I...know of a place,' said Haricharan.

'That's very kind, thank you,' said *Babuji*.

'I would like to be there, if you will allow...I would be very grateful,' said Haricharan and I nodded. I owed this man a lot.

We cremated *Bhai* on a secluded beach, a place where no white people came. A few Indians lingered but they drifted away as the sun made its descent. The pyre was built by men whom Haricharan was familiar with. We paid with what we had in our pockets. Thankfully, they didn't ask for anymore.

We watched in silence: *Bhai's* laughter, his chatter, his beliefs – all burned away.

I must have fallen asleep as *Babuji* gently nudged me awake. The fresh smell of a new morning was refreshing. The scene had changed. *Bhai's* pyre was now a small heap of ashes... his compassion and bravery was erased; only his ashes were left behind. I looked to *Babuji*.

'*Bhai's* ashes are in here,' he said gently and showed me a pot. 'Haricharan bought one from the men who built the pyre.'

Afterwards, we washed ourselves in the sea and said a prayer. Thanking Haricharan again, *Babuji* and I boarded the train back to Rajkot. The journey was silent but our hearts were beating together in sorrow.

I was first to enter the house. It felt like a tomb; empty, grey and...lifeless. A small table was arranged in the centre of the main room and a picture of *Bhai* stared back at me – his face, a monument of happiness. A *divo*[48] was burning and Ma was sitting cross-legged next to it, praying with her beads.

'Ma,' I said softly. Her head jerked up and I saw tear stains on her face; she looked beaten. My vision blurred as she dropped her beads and took me into her embrace. Her sobs were fierce as she clung to me. *Babuji* put his arms around us and we all cried until we no longer could.

I took *Bhai's* ashes out and placed it next to his picture.

'My Rakesh! Oh Rakesh! Why did you leave me! *Maro dikro*[49]!' Ma screamed. She cradled the pot to her bosom. I made to go to her but Babuji stopped me.

'Let her be. She needs this,' he said.

---

[48] *Divo*, a divine flame used in holy Indian rituals and ceremonies. Also used to give peace to the deceased.
[49] *Maro dikro* – my son (Gujarati)

We let her be alone as she cried. I could feel her heart breaking, torn into many pieces. Eventually, I couldn't take it any longer and sat down next to her, laying my head on her lap as tears dropped down my face onto her sari. It was then that I remembered Dilip.

'Ma, I have to do something.' I said. I kissed her on the cheek and promised her I wouldn't be long.

I was on my way to Dilip's house – *Bhabhi* and his Ma had to be told about Dilip, but how, I was unsure.

I took a deep breath when I reached the house. I expected *Bhabhi* to be inside and was surprised to see her sitting outside in the courtyard. I wasn't prepared...it took me a lot of self control to not break down, for she was dressed in a white sari[50] and her face was plain, void of any vermillion and *chandlo*[51].

'Dev *Bhai*,' she embraced me. 'How are you?'

'*Bhabhi*...I am fine but look at you. Dilip *Bhai* wouldn't have wanted you to be like this – to wear white,' I said.

She smiled. 'I cannot change society rules, Dev.'

'But you didn't wear white when you came for *Bhai's* trial, why now?'

'I didn't want to believe it then...that he had really gone...' She wiped her eyes. 'Never mind that, how is Rakesh *Bhai*?'

I was confused, didn't she know...?

'*Bhabhi*, he was given death, yesterday,' I said. The pain thundered down to my heart as I said this aloud and I could hardly breathe.

'*Hé Ram*[52]!' Tears sprang to her eyes. '*Eh Eeshwaar*[53]!' *Bhabhi's* tears turned into heaving sobs and all I could do was hold her.

'*Bhabhi*, listen. I have some news...'

---

[50] Women wore white when their husbands passed away. They weren't allowed to wear any colour or any symbol of a married woman, such as bindi and red and green bangles.

[51] *Chandlo* – Gujarati name for Bindi. A red dot painted on the forehead of married women (Now it is also a fashion statement and worn by girls and women alike, married and unmarried. The chandlo now comes in an array of colours and designs).

[52] *Hé Ram!* Oh Rama (Hindu God)

[53] *Eeshwaar*, God

She looked at me. 'Have you found out about your brother?' She was asking about Dilip. As yet, she didn't know what had happened to him after he was murdered. No one would tell her...

I nodded and took both her hands in mine. '*Bhabhi*, he was cremated. One of the jailors, he told me about it. He said they all were – those who died that day in the riot. But he didn't know where. But *Bhabhi*, he is with *Eeshwaar*. He is in peace.'

Bhabhi walked to the window. Each step echoed grief, relief and calm. 'Now they both are at peace...Rakesh *Bhai* was cremated too?'

'Yes *Bhabhi*. *Babuji* and I have brought his ashes home.'

Word spread quickly and soon friends and family began to arrive. They wore white – the colour of mourning. *Bhabhi* came with Dilip's mother and with the children. They embraced Ma and sat next to her.

Pooja, Amit and Sunil came together and I saw their intake of breath as they studied my face. Pooja's warm hand found mine and she held fast, her hot tears falling down her face. I squeezed her hand as I tried to control my own tears. Amit and Sunil couldn't stop either.

Ma stood up.

'Where are you going, Ma?' I asked.

'I will be back soon.' Ma came back holding a small photograph – it was a picture of Dilip and *Bhai* together. They were smiling at the camera on their last day of college. Ma put the picture inside *Bhai's* frame.

'There, now the brothers are together.' Her smile was calm.

I picked up Kanha, Dilip's youngest and kissed his little forehead. His dark brown eyes looked directly at me. I tickled his palm and he chuckled, then his tiny fingers wound around my index finger and I smiled.

'Make your Papa proud,' I said. I glanced at Suresh and Laxmiba. They were still young but the sadness in their eyes was unbearable. I leaned over and kissed their cheeks and they buried faces in their *dadi's* lap.

To my anger, *Bhai-ji* came. I wanted to shout at him, to tell him that he was not welcome here but then I remembered *Bhai's* words.

'Don't make it hard on him, Chottu. He is a freedom fighter like me...'

I let *Bhai-ji* be but I couldn't and wouldn't forgive him. We sat united as we remembered *Bhai* and Dilip – the martyrs. The incense and *divo* calmed my mind and I felt content for a little while.

Sunil was absentmindedly playing with his handkerchief – a sign that he was hungry. I let out a small laugh. He looked at me like I was crazy. 'What?' he asked.

'*Bhai* always used to scold you for being greedy.' I half-smiled.

Sunil's mouth twitched. 'I will really miss him. Who will tell me off now?' his eyes shone.

'Don't worry, Dev and I will continue his work,' Amit said but there was no humour in his voice.

Kanha was now sucking his thumb, fast asleep. *Bhabhi* made to take him but I shook my head. 'I like him here,' I said.

'*Beta*, it's time for prayers.' *Babuji* took Kanha and gave him to *Bhabhi*. My tears began again, I tried to concentrate on breathing, to calm myself but the tears kept on coming. No longer able to hide it, I howled, launching myself onto *Babuji*, clinging to him. Every core of my body shrieked with anger, grief and abandonment. I couldn't live without *Bhai*!

Ma's arms engulfed me as did Sunil's and Amit's. I couldn't hear anything apart from my cries; the room seemed silent. Pooja's slight touch calmed me down and slowly my sobs ebbed away.

'Rakesh *Bhai* is with us. He is in our hearts. Don't make him unhappy.' She said and led me to *Bhai's* picture. I lighted another *divo* and burned incense, circling it around the picture. We sat down as the *Marajh*[54] began the prayers. I laid my head on Pooja's shoulder and she continued to hold my hand. I closed my eyes, silent tears rolling down my cheeks once again.

I lay on the floor, staring up at the indigo sky. It was peaceful here, like always. It wasn't yet quite the time of sleep nor was it the hour for visiting. I was on the roof, the place where I could truly be alone with thoughts of *Bhai*. He was always able to find me here when I hid. He seemed to know my very core. Time passed; three months since *Bhai*...

It had been another busy day and Ma and *Babuji* were downstairs with some late guests. Pooja left a while ago – I was

---

[54] *Marajh*, Hindu priest

indebted to her, to Amit and Sunil also. Pooja came frequently and helped Ma around the kitchen. Amit would sit with *Babuji* discussing the news and Sunil entertained us with jokes with his casual banter. I couldn't ask for anything more.

I yawned as the night began to draw in and rolled over to my side, falling asleep.

'*Chottu*, wake up, *beta*. It has gone eleven.' Ma's voice rang through the haze.

I groaned, too tired to move but opened my eyes. I was on the wicker bed. That's strange, I don't remember this.

'*Chottu, Bhai-ji* is here.' Ma shuffled up the steep steps, out of breath.

Bhai-ji can go to hell, I thought. *Babuji* may have forgiven him but I would not.

Ma was putting the washed clothes out on the line. 'Why don't you get up? *Bhai-ji* has been waiting.'

'For what?'

'You are going to Ahmadabad today. Don't you remember?'

'I told him I wouldn't go with him. Why is he here?'

She sighed and sat next to me. 'It will take your mind off things...you need to get out of the house *beta*.'

I shook my head.

'What *Chottu*?' she said.

I smiled at that name, *Bhai* gave it to me when I was one and the name stuck. Only he used it but now and then, Ma did too. It felt nice.

'Dev, are you listening to me?' Ma sighed. 'You don't want to do anything anymore. You don't see people and you don't want to study, you only stay up here all the time.'

'Not all the time, Ma. I go to Khan *Bhai*'s garage; I do work for him when he needs me.'

Ma looked at me sharply. 'It's been three months. Let *Bhai* go.'

'No...*Bhai* is still here, with me...I can feel him...I miss him. Coming up here brings...I don't know. I just feel closer to him.' I said this in a rush. 'Ma, there is also one more thing.'

'What is it, *beta*?'

'You and *Babuji* need to let him go too.'

'What do you mean?'

59

'*You* are always praying for him—I know you do.' Ma gave me a look of disdain. 'You sit alone in the kitchen and cry. *Babuji* has stopped working in the field. He sits idle looking outside the window or sometimes sits with the paper, turning the pages but not reading. He doesn't talk anymore. I am worried.'

'I worry about him too. I have tried talking to him but he won't answer me. Maybe he will listen to you, will you try? *Chottu*, he needs you too.'

'I will try Ma.' I sighed. 'But will you? Will you stop crying?'

'Yes, now, come downstairs and have some *nashta*[55]. You are so thin... I will tell *Bhai-ji* that you are not feeling well. Maybe you can go another time.'

I took her lined face into my hands and kissed her forehead. 'Thank you.'

Babuji was sitting in exactly the same place as yesterday.

'*Babuji*, shall I call the doctor?' I sat beside him and took his cold, thin hands into mine.

'No.' His response was automatic and it hurt. '*Mané shu thayu ché*[56]?'

'Your health is not getting better and I am worried.'

He continued to stare outside. It seemed like a very long time before he spoke. 'Rakesh has betrayed me—he said he would take over the field and let me retire. He lied to me.'

I understood and heard the denial under that false accusation. 'I know you don't feel that way. What *Bhai* did, it was for this country. You told him – you said you were proud of him. He is a martyr. *I* am proud of him and I know *you* are too. *Babuji*, I will help you get through this. I am still here and I will help you, I promise.'

'*Beta*, I thought it would be you who would fall apart. Your brother always confided in you...he was your friend, how do you do it, Dev? How do you carry on?'

'*Bhai* chose that life. He knew what would happen if...it was a risk he took. He told me this himself. I wish more than my life that I could go back to that time and that place and stop him going on that march.'

---

[55] *Nashta*, Breakfast
[56] *Mané Shu Thayu Ché?* What's happened to me? (Gujarati)

'You are so brave. Look at us. Your Ma isn't herself anymore and I am hardly here in mind. I don't know what to do.' Huge splashes wet his cheeks.

I took his hand. 'Come and have something to eat now, for me...for *Bhai*.' I helped him stand and we proceeded towards the kitchen. Ma smiled as she saw us together. We ate in silence but there was a positive change now. It was time.

Six

Dev Pooja

It was early afternoon and the sun beat down mercilessly on the already baked ground. Pooja was drawing in the red dust with a finger; her knees folded towards her. She was humming to herself – it was a tune I didn't recognise. I listened, ignoring the other two squabbling like children. Pooja stopped after a while and turned her attention to Amit and Sunil. Regretfully, so did I.

'You know the rules. We cannot play with the white *Babu*[57]. They stick to themselves,' said Amit.

'Let me ask,' Sunil said hopefully. 'Did you see how they threw the ball! I could do that'.

I shook my head and laughed. I turned back to reading the book but it was near to impossible – my attention kept on slipping to Pooja.

'I'm going home,' she said, picking up her vegetable bag. 'Ma is waiting to make the dinner. She is probably wondering where I am.' Her hair brushed my face as she got up. I took a deep breath to steady myself.

'I'll walk with you,' I said, also getting up.

'*Nai*...it's...I can go by myself,' she said colouring faintly. I turned my face, trying to hide my joy but she saw.

'What?' she said.

'Shall I tell you the truth? I'm getting bored with these two children. I like to be with you.' The last bit was true.

Pooja shrugged. 'Amit, Sunil, we are going,' she said but it seemed to fall on deaf ears. They didn't turn around and continued analysing the game. Pooja began to walk away and I stepped in line with her.

It was one of those fine mornings. Not hot, nor cold. The village was picturesque as usual but today it seemed more so. The Banyan and Mango trees looked healthy and "happy" as they swayed in the light breeze. The *Phool-wallah*[58] and the *Chudi-wallah* [59]were

---

[57] *Babu*, Man
[58] *Phool-wallah*, Flower seller
[59]*Chudi-wallah*, Bangle seller

62

talking to each other and Chandu rode by in his tonga[60], with passengers in the cart. Chameli neighed as she trotted at a low speed. We passed the pot-maker and I waved. I brought my attention back to Pooja, who hadn't spoken a word since we left the others.

'You have a melodious voice.' I watched her face as I said it casually. It was hard not to, she was just so beautiful.

'Arjun says that to me. Ma and Papa like to hear me at night,' Pooja said matter-of-factly.

'What were you singing then?'

'Just something,' she said and paused. 'Do you remember Dev, Rakesh *Bhai* used to sing a lot too? He always had an audience. I could sit and listen to his sweet voice and never tire. I miss that, I miss him.'

I stopped walking. 'Yes, *Bhai* did sing...only, I wouldn't ever hear it again.'

It was a minute before Pooja realised that *I* was quiet now. 'Oh Dev, I'm sorry. It still hurts, doesn't it?'

'I can never forget *Bhai*. He was my friend; my everything,' I said quietly. We stopped walking and stared at each other. She subconsciously leaned into me, our heads nearly touching. She looked into my eyes.

'It will get better,' she whispered.

I took her hand but she didn't pull away. 'Pooja, if I ask you something, you won't mind, will you?'

'What do you want to say?'

'It's...it's nothing.'

Pooja shook her head. 'It *is* something. What is it Dev?'

'I just wanted to say that you are...Arjun mentioned that your parents want to marry you. You are of age.'

Pooja scowled. 'Tell Arjun to mind his own business.'

We began walking and I noticed that we were near to her house. I let go of her hand and walked her to her door. Tilting her chin, I gazed into her eyes. She was unable to look away.

'Pooja! Is that you?' someone shouted from within the house. 'Have you got the *sabzi*?'

'Coming Ma!' Pooja lightly pushed my hand away and ran into the house. She looked back to see me still standing there. Her face coloured and she disappeared.

---

[60] *Tonga*, a vehicle drawn by horse or bullock.

63

I didn't realise when my friendship with Pooja turned into love. When did she grow to be so beautiful? When did she leave her innocence? Today, a girl stood before me who awakened feelings inside me no other girl could achieve.

Many marriage offers came my way but no one pulled my heart. Pooja was the one for me and yet, she was not within my reach. After *Bhai's* death, she became more important to me than anyone else could be. I wanted her and I needed her.

Pooja's fragrance was of jasmine flowers and it followed me everywhere, even at times of her absence, I could smell it. It wrapped around my mind with a powerful hold, rendering me senseless for a few moments. There was also her touch...which lingered on my skin for hours, burning me, making me ache for her...

'Dev! *Eh Bhai*! Who will do the work?!'

I snapped out of my thoughts like someone had slapped me.

'Kalu *Bhai*, I am doing it!' I felt silly and a little embarrassed, although there was no need to; he couldn't know what I was thinking. I was sitting idly with a toolkit open by my side – work waiting for me to begin. I was annoyed with myself; I must concentrate! I began with vigour and soon it was lunch time. I was exhausted, not from work but from frustration.

I opened the tiffin and stared at the contents of my lunch but I couldn't eat. My mind was too pre-occupied with thoughts of Pooja – again. I closed the tiffin. It was no good; I had to see her now. 'Kalu *Bhai*, I need to take leave –now, please,' I said to my manager.

'Why?' he said, stopping his conversation with a customer.

'I have something urgent to do.'

Kalu *Bhai* eyed me suspiciously. 'What can be urgent at this time? Get back to work.'

'Please, it is important – you don't have to pay me.'

'Khan *Bhai* will have to know.'

'It doesn't matter,' I said feeling hope. 'He will understand.'

'Mmmm. That girl, Pooja who comes here regularly, could all this be because of her?' Kalu *Bhai* said, his mouth breaking into a smile.

'Can I go?' I said, irritated.

'I suppose...yes. But you have to make up your work time...and I will not cut your pay!' he shouted after me as I sprinted away. I waved back and was soon out of sight.

I slowed down as I approached Pooja's house and walked at a steady pace. Her twin sisters were playing in the front yard, skipping.

'Is your *didi*[61] inside?' I asked.

The girls stopped their play and like my manager, eyed me suspiciously.

'Why?' they said together.

I grinned. 'Is she in or not?'

'Yes, she is inside,' said one of the twins. I had known the twins since their birth, yet I still couldn't tell them apart. The said twin was waiting for me to go, clearly bemused. I assumed she wanted to carry on playing. I tousled her un-braided hair and went inside, leaving her scowling.

Pooja was sitting on the floor with her mother, grinding wheat into flour. Her face was flushed and she had flour in her hair. She still looked beautiful. Her grey eyes flickered to me then and I stood there, mesmerised.

'Dev *beta*!' *Ma-ji* smiled widely. 'Come in.' She seemed to sense I wanted to speak to Pooja, for she was already standing up and brushing the flour from her clothes. Pooja questioned me silently with her eyes.

'Pooja, we will finish up later. You children talk,' *Ma-ji* said cheerfully and stepped out of the room.

Pooja turned to me. 'Why are you here?' she said.

'I want to take you by the river. I want to talk to you,' I said. 'I...have Chameli[62].'

'Be back before nightfall. Not too late, Dev!' said *Ma-ji* from the other room when Pooja came back out, after telling her mother.

'We will be back early,' I called.

I didn't talk to her on the way there but kept stealing glances of her. She smiled in return, at times, looking away in embarrassment. I inhaled the sweet scent of the river as we came to it and felt happy. I tied Chameli to a tree and gave her a few apples.

I led Pooja to the waters' edge. It was clear and refreshing as we dipped our feet in. Small fishes swam in and out, under and over the pebbles, causing tiny ripples where they swam. It was a delight to watch.

---

[61] **Didi**, Sister (elder)
[62] Chameli – the name of Chandu's horse (Chandu is a character in this book)

65

In the distance, trees of every shade of green brought serenity; I felt very relaxed as we lay back on the cool grass. I tentatively interlaced my fingers with hers and she watched my face.

'Why did you bring me here, Dev? What was it that you couldn't say in front of Ma? Please tell me.'

'I love you Pooja. I always have,' I said. 'Do you...feel the same way?'

'Always,' she said, smiling. 'What took you so long?'

I laughed, relieved and ecstatic. Pooja, now bashful, looked away.

'I have one more question,' I said. 'Will you marry me?'

This time she spoke with caution. 'Yes, someday but you know my family's status. I need to work to bring in money. My sisters are still in school, I don't want them to work as a maid like me. My brother is in college...Papa's wage is not much...'

'Shhh. Don't be upset. I am here, I will help – we will help.'

'I can't take your money,' she shook her head, her brown curls shaking wildly.

I sighed. 'Pooja, Khan *Bhai* has offered me a job – in Simla. I cannot turn him down and I don't want to go alone, without you.'

'Simla? That is a long way away. When are you going?'

'At the end of the month.'

'Go Dev, I will not stop you. I'll wait until you come back – ask for my hand then but I can't marry you like this, not now, I'm sorry.'

I paused and took in her words. It hurt to hear her say this and I wanted her to change her mind. 'Won't you think about it?'

'I don't know what else to tell you.'

'Promise me then, you won't marry someone else whilst I'm gone?'

'Oh Dev, there will be no one else apart from you,' she said and I felt better.

We spent the rest of the day in each other's arms, talking. I was thinking of our future.

As promised to her mother, I took Pooja home at a good hour and then went home.

Babuji was listening to the news on the radio and I sat with him for a while, listening too. We didn't talk but were comfortable in each other's company. *Babuji* yawned after the news finished and said he was going to sleep.

'You go to sleep soon, *beta*. You look very tired,' he observed and shuffled away to his room where Ma was already asleep. I walked slowly to my room. My legs were heavy and my eyelids struggled to stay open. A book was on my bed which I threw aside and without changing, fell asleep.

Bhai sang in the bathroom as he shaved. I was still getting ready.

'Chottu, come now, get ready for school. Your bus will be here.' He was holding my satchel in one hand and my tiffin in another. I took them as I ran past him.

'Dev, let's play on the swing,' said Pooja as we walked towards the tree. A swing was bound to the thickest branch but it looked dangerous.

'It doesn't look safe,' I said.

'Don't be a chicken. Come,' she pulled me as she ran.

Pooja smiled at me in her red wedding sari; she was stunning. She frowned as I was pulled back by Bhai.

'I am going Chottu, I am going....'

'*Bhai*!' I woke with a start, my hand stretched outwards as I tried to hold onto his hand. I realised I was drenched in sweat. I quickly changed into dry clothes and then sat on the edge of my bed. My dream...it was vivid. It felt real – *Bhai's* singing echoed in my mind sharply, bringing back the pain. It twisted inside me, attacking every fibre in my body.

'Oh *Bhai*,' I wished so much that he was here now.

It began to rain in sheets. The sound soothed me and a part of me relaxed, dimming the pain. With the rain, came the wind – a partnership. It entered my room through the open window; it was a welcome guest. Something fluttered and my attention turned towards the floor. It was the book that I had thrown; an envelope flapping from within its pages. I reached over and grabbed it.

It looked familiar but I couldn't remember why. Where did it come from? Why was it tucked into this book? I flipped it over. I froze as I stared at the writing – it was *Bhai's*. A faint memory of a jailor named Haricharan – he gave this to me...a letter from him. I had tucked it into this book when I came home the day after he was...I quickly tore it open.

Chottu,

I don't know where to start this letter; maybe by saying I am sorry. Sorry, to not have been there when you needed me most, sorry to have got myself in this situation, and sorry to cause you, Ma, and Babuji much grief.

This is my last letter to you and I want to say a few things. After reading this, I hope you will understand why I had no choice. I don't know how much I am allowed to tell you here...it is risky...but still, it needs to be said.

We had a good life once; we were happy. We had a crop farm. Business was good and we both received a good life and a good education. Dadu[63] was a good farmer and he was an honest man. He worked all day and sometimes late into the evening on the field with Babuji.

I remember Ba[64] sewing clothes and Ma ready with hot chai and food when they came home at the end of each day. Neither Dadu nor Babuji complained about the back-breaking work and were happy... we were their priority.

Sometime later, Dadu became unwell. That was the year the Raj raised the tax. I remember it very well.

Babuji worked alone on the fields then, but couldn't keep up with the demands. Times were hard – he pleaded with the tax collector to take fewer crops, but was only laughed at. A lot of our crops were taken and this meant we had little to sell. Money was small and our education was at risk. I didn't want your studies to suffer, Chottu, so I decided to leave school and help Babuji in the fields. He wasn't happy but I persuaded him. It was the only way.

Dadu began to get thin and everyone became increasingly worried. Ba's health began to deteriorate too with continuous worry and stress. The strain was on everyone's faces.

We carried on but struggled. A year later, the Raj raised the tax again, this time a lot higher. Dadu couldn't take it and he had a

---

[63] **Dadu**, Grandfather
[64] **Ba**, Grandmother

heart attack. He didn't survive…I will never forget Babuji's heartbreak.

Dadu was everything to him. He cried for a long time. Ba was a lot stronger, she and Ma put a brave face on things and encouraged Babuji to look ahead. He spent a lot of time thinking after Dadu's death and one day he made his decision: he would sell the crop farm and move to Rajkot. You were only small when this happened, but I was a lot older. The anger inside me was strong and I promise myself that I will never forgive the Raj for what they did to our family and our lives.

And I suppose, this is why I am here. Chottu, don't be sad. I will always be with you, even here, in Eeshwaar's place. I love you. Tell Ma and Babuji I love them too. Tell them.

Jai Hind!
Bhai.

I re-read the letter several times that night and a strange feeling entered me. I understood now why *Bhai* wanted to do this – after all this time. He was *right* to do this.

I didn't dream about *Bhai* after that night. I didn't dream at all.

~
POOJA
~

Seven

Pooja

Ma walked around the *Tulsi* tree[65], muttering prayers and promises that only God could hear. She glanced in my direction and sighed; her forehead creasing. I didn't have to guess what she asked for and I too, sighed – dramatically, splaying my hands on my forehead and sighing again. Ma shook her head in disapproval and mumbled something like 'she doesn't understand how important...' and went inside. She came back a few moments later with a *thaali*[66] of *bhojan*[67] and presented it to the Tulsi tree, bowing her head.

'*Chal*, come and pray for your future, for a good boy to marry you,' she said beckoning.

My grin disappeared and I crossed my arms, looking the other way. She waited, I huffed but didn't move. I was very annoyed. Ma didn't give up. She took my *dupatta*[68] and draped a part of it over my head as a veil. I grumbled incoherently as I closed my eyes and bowed to *Mata*[69] *(the Tulsi tree)* with my hands clasped.

'*Mata*,' I addressed her in my mind. 'You know that I don't want to get married. Please don't bring anyone to see me.' I took a flower from the *thaali* and laid it next to the plant. Ma looked pleased and went back inside the house.

The cycle bell rang loudly and I jumped. I shook my head of my silliness - it was the *phool-wallah*. The fragrance of his *gajras*[70] reached me before he did and I was already outside waiting for him to turn into my road.

'*Bhaiya, ek dena*[71],' I said as he stopped at my door. He took down his basket.

---

[65] *Tulsi tree*, a holy basil tree, sacred and worshipped by Hindus. This plant is seen at temples and in Hindu homes and is offered water and prayers. The Tulsi is likened with various Hindu Goddesses and is considered auspicious.

[66] *Thaali*, adish made of steel/brass/silver.

[67] *Bhojan*, Food

[68] *Dupatta*, a multi-purpose scarf, worn over the head as a veil or over ladies' Indian suits.

[69] *Mata*, refers to "mother Gods". The Tulsi is seen as a mother.

[70] *Gajra*, a flower garland, worn by Indian ladies in buns or in braids. Usually made with jasmine.

[71] *Ek dena*, Give one

'One *rupaiya*[72],' he said. 'What colour?'

'White, please,' I said. 'Wait, I'll get the money.'

I went to inside to retrieve my purse when I heard some giggling from the twins' room. I will deal with them later, I thought grimly. The *phool-wallah* was waiting patiently on the bottom step, re-arranging the garlands as I arrived. He was soon on his way and I went back inside, inhaling the sweet aroma. I put my cheek against it, suddenly thinking of Dev. He had always adorned my hair with a gajra. Then, it was just friendship...but I realise now, it was his love. I felt myself blush – I was glad no one was around. I smiled to myself, taking a pin out of my hair and fastening it onto the gajra, then pinning it back onto my hair.

My emerging youth came as a shock. I was no longer a child but a grown up fifteen year old, girl. I wasn't allowed to play games with the boys; it wasn't right, Ma scolded when I protested. Years passed; my features and my body became more prominent and men began to notice. They appraised me with their eyes and stopped in the street to talk to me. Sometimes, (my protectors, I called them) Dev, Sunil and Amit became overbearing and infuriating when the said man was just being friendly.

'They don't talk to you to pass the time, don't be naive,' Dev once said angrily when I had argued. I'd stomped away. The next day he came apologising and I forgave him, because my heart said so.

He proposed to me and I was very surprised. I did want to marry him, very much so but I couldn't, not yet. I wanted to take my refusal back as soon as the word "No" was out of my mouth, but I couldn't. The time wasn't right. I had hurt him deeply, I knew, but he still came to see me like everything was normal. He didn't bring the subject of marriage up again and so I played along with him; it was easier this way. Sometimes, I saw him gazing at me intently and I'd look away. The colour of my cheeks always betrayed me. Dev hadn't come my way in the past few days and that bothered me. I really missed him.

'*Didi*! Come and see!' That was Ritu, the eldest of the twins. The girls were huddled together under a blanket and were giggling.

'What is so funny?' I said my hands on my hips.

---

[72] **Rupaiya**, Rupee

Reema came out from under the blanket. '*Didi*, come here, this is funny!'

'What have you done?'

'Oh *didi*, we were only talking. Come in, it's really funny!' Ritu and Reema said together.

Curious and annoyed (I'd seen their incomplete exercise books), I crawled on all fours and entered the blanket. The girls had organised the blanket into a "tent". They had been busy doing anything but their school work - my eyes fell on two pictures. They had drawn caricatures; one was of a teacher and one of the school caretaker. I remembered the teacher as an annoying little man and I was sure he hated children. The caretaker was the joke of the school. He was constantly stumbling and tripping or dropping things. He didn't mind when the children laughed at him. In fact, he joined in.

I suppressed a smile and looked sternly at my sisters. 'It is not good to make fun of people,' I said. 'More importantly, you were supposed to be doing your school work. Why isn't it done? I see now why you come home with marks on your palms.'

'*Didi*, Mr Shah is a horrible man,' said Reema.

'I don't agree with the beatings either – that is no way to punish children. But girls, I still expect good work from you. Start your school work now and then I will let you play outside.'

The girls groaned but I knew they would complete it. As expected, they fell asleep after their school work was done.

I watched two crows hopping around each other; they danced left, then right then right and left, circling each other as if preparing for a fight. This carried on for ten minutes and I watched, amused and fascinated. I was entirely absorbed in his little dance- fight. They flapped their silky black wings and harped loudly. The "dance" slowed as one of them grew tired. It then stopped and flew away. The other crow cocked its head and then, seemed to bow. It hopped onto the wall and then also flew away. I looked over to see where it went to, but saw Papa instead, turning a corner in our *gali*[73]. He saw me and his eyes lit up. He waved to me as he hurried home. This could not be good.

'Pooja, I have been thinking,' Papa said as I took his umbrella and bag.

---

[73] *Gali*, narrow street/alley

I smiled uneasily. 'About what?'

'It is time you got married.' Papa proceeded to the wash area and washed his face and hands.

I cleared my throat. 'Have you been speaking to Ma?' Papa's guilty face gave him away. 'Why? I am fine as I am,' I said.

'You are eighteen now,' he said, like it was news.

I rolled my eyes. 'Yes, I know that but we cannot afford it, how are we going to pay for Arjun's tuition and the girls' schooling?'

'Many girls younger than you are already married *beta*; it doesn't look good for an unmarried daughter to be still sitting in her parent's house. People will talk.' Ma was sitting in a corner sorting through some *chana*[74] looking for stones. 'Pooja, Shanta *ben* came yesterday. She has found a boy for you.'

'No Ma! Why don't you and Papa understand, I can't get married now!'

Ma's lips puckered. 'It is not good to be unmarried for such a long time. Three girls from this village are already married. There is Shama, she got married at sixteen and now lives in Simla. Already, she has four children. Then, there is Jammu who got married when she was fifteen. No children yet, poor girl and also Namu. She got married at fifteen also. She lives a little out of the village and is very rich. I got married to your father when I was twelve years old.' Ma looked proud.

'But how can I leave the Chatterjis[75]?' I said out of desperation.

'We allowed you to leave school so you could help bring in some money. But now *beta*, it is different. You will be too old for people to accept you if you don't get married.'

I turned to Papa. 'I don't want to marry, not yet. We need the money. How are we to live if I stop working? Besides, we don't have any money for my marriage,' I tried.

'It is our duty as parents to make a life for *you*. We will manage with money. I don't want any more arguments now.' Papa turned to Ma. 'Jaya, talk to Shanta *ben*. We will arrange the best wedding this village has seen,' Papa declared. It was obvious that the conversation had ended.

'It is for the best,' Ma said, patting my hand.

Tears slid down my face and I turned, running to Arjun. He would understand. He will make them see that I am right. Arjun is my

---

[74] *Chana dal*, Lentils used in a soup like curry, which is served with rice.

[75] Chatterji's - A wealthy (fictional) family, high in the ranks of society.

older brother – he was getting ready when I came to stand in his doorway, playing with my bangles.

'*Shu ché*[76] Pooja?' he said. He took out a comb and slid it through his slick hair whilst looking in the mirror.

'Ma and Papa want me to see a boy – that *dayan*[77], Shanta *ben* has found a boy for me.'

Arjun didn't respond straight away. 'Is it so bad?'

'No...yes, I think it is,' I said.

'Pooja, this will be good for you.'

'But...I don't know. *Bhai*, why am I the only one who isn't excited? All of my friends were talking about getting married months, even years before they found their husbands.'

Arjun stopped combing his hair. 'Listen to me, marriage is a blessing. You will be married to a good man who will worship you. You will have lots of money too so you won't have to work. Do you think we would let you get married to a pauper?'

'Do I have a choice?'

'Don't wait until you are twenty. It will become difficult to find a suitable man.'

I narrowed my eyes as he fiddled with his shirt collar. 'You sound like Papa. When did you speak to him?'

'It doesn't matter, it is all for the best. But now, I am running late. They are showing Madhubala[78]'s film at the theatre. Sunil told me she is stunning!'

I rolled my eyes. 'Sunil says that about all the heroines.'

'You, my dear sister, are jealous.'

'*Bhai*, please, talk to Ma and Papa, please make them understand,' I said. Arjun sighed and said he would try. I was content with that. 'Go on, see the film and then I want to hear all about it when you get back.'

I waited until Arjun left the house and then used his mirror. I searched for the unique, pretty girl, the charismatic belle that everyone seemed to be talking about. Was I that girl? I tried to imagine myself married with children some day, but I couldn't. What would be expected of me? I realised I didn't know anything at all. I stared at my reflection and saw the doubts and worry. I closed my eyes and closed the door to that probable time. I won't think about it. Just, not yet.

---

[76] *Shu ché*, What is it? (Gujarati)

[77] *Dayan*, Witch

[78] *Madhubala* , a famous Indian film actress.

I was very late. I opened my umbrella as soon as I come off the bus and was instantly soaked through. My hair clung to my head, flattening it down. I wished I'd brought a shawl – I shivered. Adjusting my faded, cotton sari, I miserably walked to the Chatterji mansion.

'You are late,' Grandmother Chatterji's voice came from the dining table.

'I am r…r…really sorry,' I stammered.

'You are wet,' she stated the obvious. 'Go and change, Champa will give you a dry sari. Then, get me a fresh cup of tea. I had Meena make the tea this morning. You know I don't like anybody else's tea.' She wrinkled her nose.

'I am really sorry *nani*[79], it won't happen again.'

'Go and get changed.' This time she said it softly.

I called her *nani* when we were alone. It was our secret. Hired as a maid, I became a much valued help, to nani anyway. The money wasn't much but it was something. I saved every hard earned rupee and I was proud of that.

The mansion never ceased to amaze me. Stained glass windows were the attraction of the long corridors that led to the back of the house and to the servants' quarters. Rainbow colours washed the interior when the sun shone, bringing everything alive as it danced on the walls and the marble floor. Night-time brought a different show altogether – the moon's ghostly, pale light would illuminate the corridors instead. It was something I loved.

When I was required to stay late, I slept here, in the servants' quarters. I would wait until everyone was asleep and then tiptoe out into the dark, passing the moonlit corridor. I would go on the roof and immerse myself in the pale light and the peaceful freedom. The moon was my companion and I was the moon's.

There was only one room in this mansion that was the finest, and that was Rama's room. I veered towards her room to have another peek – this was my favourite room and I wasn't allowed to enter it but it didn't stop me from going there.

Rama was very particular about her room; she had designed it just the way she wanted – rich in reds, yellows and deep purples, reminding me of tomatoes, mangoes and aubergines. A four poster bed

---

[79] *Nani*, Maternal grandmother

was the main attraction – adorned with sequined cushions and a throw. Shimmering, feather-like, opaque curtains enclosed it beautifully, fit for a princess.

An adjoining room housed her many exquisite clothes, sandals and jewellery. It was larger than the size of my room and Arjun's room put together and it was always closed. It was accidently left open one day and I was very curious. I ruffled through the delicate fabrics and imagined myself wearing them. I was so absorbed that I nearly didn't hear Rama's heels. I hid under her bed and prayed she wouldn't notice me or see anything amiss. My heart raced as I'd held my breath. I waited for a long time and counted the minutes in my head. She went straight to her room of clothes. A few minutes later, she closed the doors, turned the key in the lock and left. I crawled out, vowing to never enter her room again.

Now, as I peeked into her room, I saw Rama – standing before a gold framed full-length mirror, admiring the effect of a new sari. The sari was pink, embroidered with small round mirrors and gold thread. She twirled around; proud of her new clothes. Her long curls swung around her shoulders as she twirled; she was just beautiful.

Then, Rama saw me through the mirror. 'Why don't you come in and then you could really have a good look.'

'I didn't mean to look, I am sorry. I shall leave, *Chotti*[80] Memsahib.'

'No really, it's not every day you get to see such finery,' she laughed cruelly. 'But ofcourse, you are just a silly little maid. You can never, even in your dreams afford...well, all this.' Rama spread her arms around the room. 'What is the most expensive thing you own? It must be that wet sari you are wearing now!'

'I believe wealth comes from the heart, a family's respect is rich, their good upbringing is rich and their love for one another is rich. Everything else becomes immaterial.' I put both hands on my mouth and berated myself silently. Why couldn't I ignore her? Why did I let her irritate me so that I answered back? I had been the subject of her anger in the past and received threats and sometimes

---

[80] *Chotti*, Young/Small. In this case, Rama is referred as the young Memsahib. (The elders are always Memsahib or Saab and the children are referred to as Chotti Memsahib or Chotté Saab).

punishment. I kept silent, not allowing anyone to know; this service was very important to me.

I prepared for her slap but it didn't come. I opened my eyes.

She was staring at me. 'You speak like you are a princess. I pity you – so pretty and yet so poor…who will marry you? You wouldn't be able to afford it. But still, there are so many poor men in the village; anyone will do for you.'

'I don't care about being wealthy,' I said, my head held high.

'Then you should. You are a fool and pathetic! Now, get out of my sight, I have to get ready.'

I blinked away my threatening tears and left, trembling with humiliation and anger.

Mr and Mrs Chatterji had three sons and one daughter. As a result, everything Rama wanted, she got. When I came to work here, she didn't like it at all.

'Did you see? She is so pretty, she has such beauty that I haven't seen in a while. *Chotti* Memsahib stared at her, like she wanted to burn Pooja into the ground.' Two maids were talking as I happened to pass by on my first day.

'Jealousy is not a good thing,' tutted the second maid.

When I heard this, I wouldn't believe it. Rama was far prettier than me and I could not compare with such elegance and it had left me in confusion as to why *Chotti* Memsahib was threatened by me at all.

The Chatterji family were having dinner, Champa[81] and I were serving. Rama was sipping a glass of juice and looking straight at me. 'Pooja, what does your father do?'

I stared at her. What was she doing? She knew everything about my family.

'He is a professor, isn't he? His wage packet must be what, a pittance? My *Babuji* earns ten times more than yours, did you know that? You come here in your old, faded saris, when I have a new one every week. You must wear clothes handed down to you,' she smiled wickedly. 'What a waste of a sweet girl.'

I burned with humiliation. Champa was about to speak; she was furious but I begged for her silence with my eyes.

---

[81] Champa, another maid and friend to Pooja.

'Rama, that was uncalled for,' Nani said sternly, placing her teacup on the saucer.

'I'm only saying what is true, *dadi*,' said Rama defiantly. 'Besides, she is only a maid.'

'She may be a maid, but she is also a daughter of a man who is most respected. I will not have you disgrace Pooja and her family like that. Now, I would like you to apologise.' Nani's tone was not one for debate. I was touched when she spoke for me but it scared me. Rama didn't like being told.

'Never!' Rama crossed her arms across her chest.

'I will not repeat it again,' Nani said.

Mr. Chatterji looked from Nani to Rama and was very uncomfortable. 'Ma, please leave it…don't upset Rama,' he said nervously.

'Puramjeet, your daughter is spoilt and rude. She will apologise. I will tolerate no more of her behaviour. She is childish and needs to learn how to behave - she *is* from a prestigious family. You will think about that Rama.'

'Still, Rama is sensitive,' said Mr. Chatterji meekly.

Grandfather Chatterji looked up from his plate and addressed his granddaughter. 'That is enough now. Rama, apologise now or be gone.'

'*Babuji*?' said Mr. Chatterji.

'No! I will never apologise!' Rama stormed out of the room flinging the contents of her plate to the floor.

I began to clear up, my heart thudding erratically. I noticed the table had become unbearably quiet which lasted a few good, long minutes. It became too much.

'I don't want Rama to apologise,' I said with my eyes on the floor. 'Please don't punish her.'

I left the stunned family and returned to the kitchen, but I couldn't relax. My heart was still racing. Rama's temper was dangerous and there was no way of knowing what she wouldn't do. Rama was a vile snake and it wouldn't be long before she struck.

It was the end of the day. As I prepared to go home, one of the maids approached me.

'Pooja *didi*, there has been an accident. Please come!'

Leaving my bag on the floor, I rushed with the maid to the servants' quarters. We stopped at the last room. I walked in and it was dark.

'Meena, there is no accident here...Meena?' I turned around but the maid was gone. 'Where are you?' my voice climbed an octave; my hands flying to my heart.

A familiar laugh echoed outside the room; I gasped as Rama came in. She wasn't alone but with two girls I hadn't seen before. What was she going to do? Whatever it was, it wasn't going to be nice. The girls grabbed me before I could run. They twisted my arms behind my back and I couldn't move. Rama lit a lamp and set it on the side.

'Don't punish Rama,' she mimicked and laughed. 'You disgust me!'

'*Chotti* Memsahib, please let me go.'

'Let you go? Do you realise how humiliating it was to have *my* grandmother tell me to apologise? And to who but a maid!' she screeched. 'She brought up *my* behaviour in front of the servants, in front of you!'

'I didn't...please...' I begged.

A wicked smile played on her face. 'Now, what shall I do with you? You have a pretty face; maybe I should ruin it a little. After all, the moon has a mark on his face...but I can hardly compare you to its beauty, can I?'

'*Chotti* Memsahib, please...don't,' I whimpered.

'I tell you what, I will leave your face alone, and we can't have dadi know about this little meeting of ours, can we, eh? Girls, take her blouse off!'

'No!' I shouted.

'Tut tut, shouting will not do, Pooja!' Rama unravelled a scarf from her neck and with disgust, gagged me. My eyes were wide with fear as the girls ripped my blouse off, revealing my breasts. Then, Rama took her belt off.

'Now, you will pay!' The belt slashed across my chest, searing my skin. My screams were useless against the gagged scarf and I succumbed to tears. Soon I could taste blood and salt.

Rama didn't stop there and her fury became worse. My back, feet and thighs were cut severely by the time she had had enough. Blood spilled, dripping down my legs. The open skin...I was dizzy... I was standing because they were still holding me. I dropped as they let me go.

'I hope this will teach you a lesson to never cross me again!' Rama snarled and left me, bleeding.

Champa blinked back tears as she spread *haldi*[82] over my stinging cuts. The blood had been cleaned.

'*Haldi*?' I said trying to sit up but Champa pushed me down.

'You have no idea how you looked when I found you...I thought you were dead..!'

I imagined what she saw: my body scrunched up in a ball...not moving...dead. My bruises - my skin no longer fair but hideous. My shock was confirmed in her eyes.

I had no recollection of her bringing me here. 'Your skin will heal – those purple shadows will fade. You were unconscious, Pooja. I couldn't leave you and I needed help to bring you home...so...'

'So?' I asked. 'Who else saw me?' I remembered my naked breasts and cringed. 'Champa, who else?'

'He didn't see you like I saw you. I covered you first and then went to call him. Suraj helped me carry you. We were very discreet and no one else saw us. I know...how important it is for you to work at the Chatterjis – your need for money...' Champa looked me in the eye. 'Suraj won't tell, he promised. He knows it was Rama who did this...and he is hardly going to give his sister away.'

I swallowed, I hope she was right. 'Champa, I need to go home,' I said.

'No, I can't let you go, not in this state...Pooja, please don't mind but I have told your mother that Grandmother Chatterji wants us to stay the night for tomorrow is a busy day – they have important visitors and there is much to do. It's only for one night.'

We were silent for a moment. I flexed my foot and ankle and thought I would try and see if I could stand but I froze – paralysed, as excruciating pain shot through my body – like I was standing on broken glass, each crystal cutting into my flesh and poisoning my blood. I didn't realise I was holding onto Champa's arm tightly.

---

[82] *Haldi*, Turmeric -an anaesthetic ingredient used in the form of powder or paste, for many purposes, including healing minor cuts and colds and used in Indian cooking such as *daals (lentils)* and *sabzi* and fried *puri* and *thepla* (like roti but deep or shallow fried).

She didn't complain and waited until my breath was back. I released her arm apologetically.

'Good, breathe deep, Pooja.' Champa had something in her hand. 'These are tablets to help you with your pain – Suraj got them from the doctor. Take them and the pain will fade away very soon.' I swallowed the tablets with some water. 'Pooja, why is that *dayan* after you? She deserves nothing better than my curses!' she said suddenly. I smiled as this was so out of character for her to use such words.

'You are a good friend, you know Champa?' My eyes began to droop – I was amazed – those tablets worked very fast. I was pleased – the pain was numbing. 'Champa?'

'Yes?'

'What if I can't stand tomorrow?'

'We will think about that in the morning. Now, sleep.'

I looked at myself in the mirror and gasped. Although the cuts were beginning to heal, I was badly bruised; black and blue shaded my skin. Champa saw me examining myself but didn't say anything. She gave me one of her saris and I covered myself, making sure nothing was showing. Champa was thorough for she handed me a blouse with long sleeves, a high back and which was long enough to cover my waist.

I embraced her. 'Thank you.'

'One more thing.' Champa bandaged my foot where the cut was quite visible. 'You will tell Grandmother Chatterji that you had a little accident at home – you tripped.'

Champa and I went to work together but we entered separately. Neither wanted to arouse suspicion.

My work was slow and my bandaged foot didn't go unnoticed either. I was naive to think so.

'What happened to your foot?' Nani demanded, coming to stand before me as I tried to go upstairs; it was proving to be quite difficult.

'*Nani*, I...I slipped last night,' I said. I couldn't look at her; she would know.

'Where did you slip?'

'On..on the stairs...'

Nani stared at me; I kept my face down. '*Aacha*[83], go now. But...be careful. I don't like to see you hurt...if you feel you can't work, Pooja – if you are in pain, you must tell me, *dikra*[84]. But first, come with me and I will give you some medicine.'

I followed her as fast as I could but she told me there was no need to hurry; she was patient. She handed me the same tablets that Champa got from Suraj.

Two months passed and nothing happened. Rama left me alone and I was relieved. I wasn't scared to come to work and I didn't have to hide from her or avoid her, well, that's what I thought.

It was one afternoon when I was washing the clothes, lathering and rinsing so many times that my arms began to tire. The house was quiet and I felt happy in the knowledge that Rama was out for the rest of the day. But then a shadow fell on me. I didn't have to look up for I recognised Rama's perfume.

'*Chotti* Memsahib, what can I do for you?' I dropped the soap. It slid into the suds.

'I need some money,' said Rama fingering her new, lace sari. '*Babuji* and Ma have gone out somewhere so I can't ask them. *Dadi* is asleep but I know she would only give me another lecture. I know she keeps money locked in her safe. I need you to go and get it for me.'

'You want me to steal?'

'Think whatever way you want, but I want two hundred rupees and quickly.'

'I will not do it.' I was aghast. 'It is stealing and if I get caught, I will be thrown out of the house. I will have no work to come back to. I will not betray Grandmother like that!'

'You will *not*? How dare you disobey me, you little cockroach!' shouted Rama. I jumped in fright. 'Have you forgotten your last punishment, do you crave for more?'

'You wouldn't...' I said in a small voice.

'Who is going to stop me?'

I knew I was going to be beaten again but I held my head up. 'Do what you have to do, but I will not steal for anyone.'

---

[83] *Aacha*, Alright
[84] *Dikra*, Son/daughter (Gujarati)

85

She waited, like a predator waits for its prey. We were the only ones in the house when she came to me – it was planned. This time she didn't need anybody else; she knew I was weak.

I was dusting the silverware, lost in my own world. She coughed and I jumped – making me drop a plate. It rolled away, clattering to a stop before her. Rama picked it up and twirled it in her hands.

'Why do you defy me, Pooja? I warned you, didn't I? I needed that money and you refused to get it, I told you that you would receive punishment. That money was important to me,' Rama's voice was rising and it shook with fury. 'I owed it to someone – now, he is angry. Do you know what that means?' She looked scared but then her face cleared, and her anger was back again.

'No...*Chotti* Memsahib,' I said, avoiding her eyes.

'Because of you, I had to...but why am I telling you that?' She laughed, it wasn't a pleasant sound. Suddenly, she threw the plate at me, cutting my left ear. Blood splattered the wall and my earring dropped– I heard it break as Rama stepped on it, crushing it.

She twisted my ear and I cried out. '*Chotti* Memsahib, please...let me go.' Tears sprang to my eyes.

'I am not finished yet,' she said calmly. 'Take your clothes off.'

I shook my head, backing away from her.

'*Kamini*[85]!' she screeched. 'I said; take your clothes off, now!'

I obeyed, hoping that this was all and she would leave me be. I unravelled my sari.

'All of it!'

I cried as I unbuttoned my blouse – I took off everything. Humiliated, I stood before her, naked. She smirked as she circled me. She pulled out a whip from under her shirt.

'No!' My scream was shrill and it echoed around the room.

The whip came down on me – a snake striking again and again, its venom puncturing my skin. I turned away, protecting my front with my arms. My back, legs and neck received the brunt of the punishment. I was relieved when she stopped.

'Now, I am satisfied. You no longer are beautiful,' she said.

I put my clothes back on; my hands were trembling. All I knew was that I had to get home before I collapsed. I covered my head with

---

[85] *Kamini/Kamina*, Evil (Person)

the end of my sari, making sure my ear was out of sight. I checked the rest of my body – I saw no more blood. I walked painfully home.

I went straight to bed and Ma looked at me curiously. I am tired, I said to her and she accepted.

'Ma', I cried automatically as the pain dug deep into me, like salt rubbed into a wound. I was covered in bruises; the blue shades turning darker by every passing minute. My hands had curled into balls as I fought to not cry.

'Pooja *dikra*, what is it? Why did you cry out?' Ma came running in. She touched my forehead. 'Pooja, you have a fever…!'

'I feel fine,' I lied.

'I will call the doctor. I will wake your father,' Ma said feverently, rubbing my hands and feet. She touched my shoulder and I jumped.

'What's this? Pooja, who did this to you?' she demanded. She let go of my shoulder like she had touched a burning flame. An angry mark flared on the skin and then dimmed.

'Nothing for you to worry about Ma, it will heal.' I tried to cover the mark, but she wouldn't let me.

'*It's nothing*? How can you say this! Someone has beaten you! Pooja, you tell me at once or - never mind, we will talk about this later. I will get some haldi for you.' Ma went to make the paste...I remembered Champa doing the same, not so long ago. I half smiled at the memory.

'*Eh Baghwaan*[86], what devil did this to my daughter?' Ma carefully applied the paste. The whip had left several purple welts around my body; some bled. Ma cursed aloud.

'I'm glad you are here,' I whispered.

'Did someone at the Chatterji's do this to you?' Ma didn't believe me when I said no, like I knew she wouldn't. She sighed. 'You are to stop working at the Chatterji's. Don't argue now, the decision has been made. I will personally go and tell Grandmother Chatterji and have a word about her granddaughter.'

I stared at her, my mouth open in shock. I quickly collected myself.

---

[86] *Eh Baghwaan*, Oh God

'Ma, what are you saying? That Rama did this to me?' I stared long and hard at her, hoping she would dismiss the thought altogether.

A look of uncertainty crossed her face. 'Then, I don't understand...she is hardly a friend of yours. I know she taunts you, dikra. The maids talk about it in the village. And you tell me, what answer will I give to your father? How will you hide this from Arjun?' Ma carried on.

'Ma, it is best if you let it go – trust me. It will be alright.'

'You won't tell me who did this?'

I shook my head. 'We are friends now; that is all you need to know.'

'I'm not leaving you tonight,' Ma said. 'I will sleep here with you. You will also stop working there as from now. Do you understand?'

'We need the money. If I don't work then how will we manage?' It seemed like I was repeating these words again and again and the answers were again no different.

'We will manage somehow, don't you worry. Your Papa will need to know about this Pooja.'

'No, please don't tell him. Give me some time and I will find somewhere else to work.' I was desperate for her to understand.

'I don't want you working anywhere. You can do something else at home; you are very good at your embroidery...'

'It won't pay enough, you know that...'

'Come now, go to sleep.' She kissed my forehead.

'Ma, promise that you won't say a thing to Papa or *Bhai*?'

'I can't,' she said.

'Please?'

'You get all your stubbornness from your father. Fine, I will not tell anyone. Now, go to sleep and tomorrow I will send a note to Grandmother Chatterji and tell her that you are not feeling well. You won't be at work.'

I couldn't argue anymore and laid my head on her lap. I gradually fell asleep as Ma began to mop my hot brow with a wet cloth, trying to bring my fever down.

Eight

Disgrace

The first thing I saw was Ma's face when I woke up. She had been crying. I hugged her close and gave her a half smile. I eased myself up.

'How are you Ma?' I asked.

'I should be asking you that question, *dikra*. You still look tired...' she said, putting a lock of hair behind my ear.

I noticed Papa sleeping in a chair. His head lolled to one side and his hands were clasped on his lap.

'Papa has been here since early morning,' she said, following my gaze. 'He wanted to know why I was here, so early with you.'

'What did you tell him?'

'Don't worry. I told him you were ill and nothing else,' she said. 'The doctor came to see you, you know? You were in a deep sleep and I didn't want to wake you. He said he will come by later to check on you.' Ma put a hand tenderly on my cheek. It felt pleasantly cool.

'Ma, can I have some water?' My throat felt dry and sore.

'I won't be long,' she promised and went away at once. Papa stirred then and opened his eyes.

'Oh Papa,' I sighed.

'You are still hot,' he complained putting a hand on my forehead, when he came over to me.

'Oh good *ji*, you are awake. You must be hungry, why don't you go and eat?' Ma said to Papa as she returned. She handed me the water; it soothed my throat. 'He has been very worried, *dikra*,' she added, turning her attention to me.

'Papa, go and eat. I am fine,' I said.

'You woke up many times. You were talking in your sleep but I didn't understand it, then you went back to sleep again. I don't understand how you became so ill, so suddenly.' He took my hand.

I tried to smile. 'Nothing is wrong with me, it happens. I am just a little exhausted, *bas*[87]. Now, go and eat, for me.'

'We will eat together,' he said with energy. 'I will bring the *thaali*.'

---

[87] ***Bas***, That's all

89

Ma followed Papa out of the room, leaving me to think about what had happened. How could Rama's hatred for me be so vicious? I hadn't done anything to offend her, then...why? We were hardly equals. We were very different; she had wealth and I didn't. She is pretty and I am plain. I could never be what she is – attractive and wealthy. A girl, who could have whatever she wants, shouldn't see me as a threat. She has power, what have I in comparison? I couldn't understand why she felt this way about me. Why couldn't she leave me alone?

I was feeling tired again and my pains were no less. I studied my hand and grimaced; my bruises looked awful. I decided I would avoid the mirror.

'Shall I come in?' Arjun knocked on the door, leaning against the frame.

'*Bhai*!'

'How are you *bena*[88]?' He sat next to me.

I shrugged. 'What are you doing here? Why are you not at college?' I was immediately suspicious and concerned, and he saw that.

'It's the college vacation, *bhuddu*[89].' He smiled and touched my nose but then he became serious. 'Pooja, who did this to you? Those bruises and the pale skin. *Kai to ché*[90].'

'I don't know what you are talking about,' I lied, again. 'Listen *Bhai*, I just had an argument with someone but now we have made up. There is nothing to worry about.'

'*Kai to ché*,' he said again.

'*Chal*, enough about me. Tell me, how are your studies, do you need more money?'
He rolled his eyes and we both laughed.

As Arjun started his story, Papa came back with the food. He put it down next to me and fed me the first bite of *roti* and my favourite – cauliflower *sabzi*. He then joined me.

As I ate, I saw Arjun sneak out and I was sure he was going to Ma. Something wasn't right here. I sighed quietly to myself; there was nothing I could do right this moment. I had to let it go.

There was always someone with me during the week. Doctor *Saab* came and checked on me as he said he would. The fever was

---

[88] *Bena*, Sister
[89] *Bhuddu*, Silly
[90] *Kai to Ché*, There is something (Gujarati)

gone but I was still weak. He saw my cuts but didn't ask any questions but gave Papa a list of medicines for me to take. I was worried; it was very long which meant a big expense.

Rama pulled my plait, dragging me to the water well. She pushed my head down, making me look at the bottom.

'What do you see?' she hissed.

'Nothing...just black water, Chotti Memsahib,' I answered, feeling scared.

She applied further pressure at the back of my head – it hurt. 'Now, what do you see?'

I gasped. I saw...myself, naked...I was dead.

My wild eyes looked at Rama. She was laughing but stopped abruptly. My heart thumped in my chest – she was changing.

Her eyes turned crimson, then her face became distorted, like acid licking her face. I screamed. The witch smiled and pushed me – I fell, spiralling into the well. I closed my eyes, ready to meet my end.

My eyes flew open. I touched my face and checked my heart – it was beating, then I was still alive.

'Oh,' I said. My throat felt parched. I looked around for some water and smiled – only Ma would have thought of it. I poured some water from the water pot. It tasted good.

'Pooja? Why did you scream like that?' Ma appeared by the door. I screamed? I couldn't remember.

Ritu and Reema woke, rubbing their eyes. 'What happened?' they said together.

Ma ignored them. 'Why did you scream, Pooja?' she asked again.

'I don't know...' I said, but I did and I wasn't going to tell her that. She tutted.

'Ritu, Reema, you will sleep in my room. I will sleep with Pooja *didi* until she is well. *Chal*, I will get your beds ready.'

The girls groaned but followed Ma, dragging their feet. I sighed. Was Rama ever going to let me go? Why did she have to harass me, scare me – even in my dreams?

The following few nights, I still had nightmares. Rama featured in them too but in different roles, like my nightmares were a stage. Ma was worried and she was thinking about calling the *Marajh*. I assured her that my "bad" dreams were going away. She seemed reluctant to believe me but she didn't call the *Marajh*.

I just had to learn to block the nightmares.

The villagers heard about me of course and soon my house became a railway station. They were curious and wanted to see me, for I had never fallen ill like this. Ma took care of things and reassured the well-wishers that I was recovering but resting now. She didn't allow anyone to see me; she didn't want me over-tired. Maybe they would like to come another time? She told them that I had fallen down the stairs. I was grateful.

One afternoon, Ritu and Reema were keeping me entertained with stories of their school. I was in bed, with a bowl of fruit next to me. I picked on my grapes as I listened. I still wasn't well enough to be doing anything else.

'*Didi*, will you be well soon?' Reema asked when she finished telling her story.

'Yes *beta*.' I stroked her glorious long, black silky hair. She seemed glad of my answer. I was lucky that neither Reema nor Rita asked many questions – they were good like that.

Two weeks later, I was still at home and it was then that I received unwelcome news.

'*Dikra*, Grandmother Chatterji is coming,' Ma announced in the early hours. She shook out my blanket and replaced it on top of me, very neatly. 'Come, let me braid your hair again.'

'Ma, I can't see her. She will know what happened,' I said panicking.

'*Aré*[91] *dikra*, she is coming to see *you*, let her be content after she has seen you are well. *Mane khabar ché*[92], you are like a daughter to her, am I right?'

'Yes Ma, but I don't understand why she feels she has to visit. There is nothing special about me.'

'*Na na*, everything is special about you,' she disagreed. She handed me a kohl pencil and some powder. '*Chal*, put this on your face. You will look less sick and feel better too.' I applied the powder to my cheeks and a little black kohl to my eyes, then Ma took my face

---

[91] *Aré*, Oh
[92] *Mané khabar ché* – I know (Gujarati)

in her hands. 'Now, you look like a heroine.' She smiled and went to do some last minute cleaning before nani arrived.

I couldn't question Nani's visit but I was curious. Had Champa said something to her? Had someone seen what happened? My heart began to thump in my chest and my breathing became erratic. *Calm down,* I said to myself, *it may be nothing.* I did calm a little but I was still nervous.

Everyone was ready waiting for *Nani* in the hour. Ma put some fresh flowers in the room and brushed the floor three times over. After all, it wasn't just anyone coming; it was *Nani,* my employer and the elder of the Chatterji mansion. I laughed when Arjun combed his hair again and pressed his clothes down once more. Reema and Ritu were dressed in new clothes and Papa and Ma too, were in their best. *This is silly,* I thought, *they didn't have to do this.*

'*Didi*! Ma! A big car is coming!' squealed Ritu, jumping up and down. Everyone promptly vacated the room.

I was hardly breathing. I was worried; could I trust myself to meet *Nani's* eyes? Would she guess correctly what happened or did she know already? If she knew, would she tell me to leave work? I didn't have more time to contemplate my worries as then, *Nani* came in.

The villagers trusted and respected nani's family as they were near to "royalty". Some Elders remembered her as a child and they remembered her grandparents – *Babuji* was one of them.

Nani was neither slim nor big, but she was sturdy. Her silver hair was always tied in a high bun and she dressed immaculately in the house and out. Her presence was merely intimidating to some but to those who knew her, she had a beautiful heart. I was one of the lucky ones who she had opened her heart to and now, to me, she wasn't an employer but a dear grandmother.

After Nani, Rama came in next followed by Ma, whose mouth was a hard, thin line. My eyes were wide in shock - what was Rama doing here!

Nani came straight to me and kissed my cheek. Her eyes were wet. She stepped back a little and took me in. She looked disturbed and I automatically looked at Rama.
I expected to see a smirk, an evil grin... but that wasn't so...she looked humbled and maybe...sorry? I must be imagining all this, surely. Rama could never be "sorry".

Her eyes fell on my ankle where she had opened my skin with her whip. The cut was healing but my skin wouldn't be the same again. Her mouth was a little "o" and her eyes were wide. I quickly covered it, hoping that Nani hadn't seen it. But she had. She wore the same expression that Ma had worn.

'Can I speak to Pooja alone please? Rama, I want you to stay.' My family vacated the room and Nani began. 'Pooja, I want the truth. A few weeks back, you couldn't work properly. You were in pain - I know. Today you have a fever. Tell me, who did this to you? Who was it?'

'Did what, Grandmother Chatterji?' I asked innocently.

'You can call me "Nani" Pooja, yes, in front of everyone.' Nani looked back at Rama and then back at me. 'You have not answered my question.'

'I just have a fever, it's the weather....'

Nani threw the blanket away from my legs. 'Then why do you have a scar like this? Someone has beaten you!' Nani stared at me long and hard. I had to think quickly.

'I fell down the stairs, Nani and...' I looked at Rama, and then averted my eyes. 'The truth is that I had an argument with someone and I wasn't looking where I was going and I fell down the stairs. I cut my ankle on a corner.' I hoped this story was more believable and I hoped that Nani would not talk to Ma or Arjun. 'The doctor has seen me and he said I will be better soon. He has given me some medicine. You don't have to worry.'

Nani looked at me sceptically and I looked away. I was never a good liar. 'You can't think of everyone and protect them, *dikra*, even if that person is close to me,' she said. 'Pooja, I can't see you like this. Your eyes are drawn and you are so pale...I...I will have the family doctor come and see you. Don't worry about the fee, I will look after it.' Nani's voice cracked. 'You are a daughter to me and I love you very much. This fever, it worries me...and this cut...Hé Ram!'

I could feel tears welling up and I really didn't want to cry in front of her. I put my hand on top of hers. 'I am much better now,' I said in a small voice.

Nani nodded but the pain did not leave her eyes. 'Concentrate on getting better and come back when you are well. There is no need to hurry, you understand?'

'Yes Nani.'

She stood up. 'Rama, let us go.'

94

Rama obediently followed Nani but glanced at me once more before she went.

Dev came to see me that evening. He hadn't known about my illness as he had been in Bombay. He came straight away when Amit and Sunil told him.

The obvious questions came first. Who did this? Why did they do it? I told him what I told Nani but he didn't believe me either, like the rest of them. To no one's surprise, Amit and Sunil decided to visit again and as they chatted, Dev became quiet and his mood became dark. Finally my other two friends had to go home but Dev stayed.

We sat looking at each other for a long moment. His eyes were cold and hard.

'You have never fallen ill, even as a child. Not even in the last few years. Now, you can hardly stand.' His tone was stern, cold and unforgiving. I shuddered at his hostility. I stole a look at my ankle and I was glad it was covered.

'Is that why you are angry? You think someone made me fall ill?' I laughed weakly.

'This is not a joke, Pooja...I love you, I can't bear to see you like this.'

'Try to be reasonable,' I said. 'I will be well in a few days.'

He began to shake his head. 'I can cancel going to Simla, Khan *Bhai* will understand.'

'No, listen to me! You have to go, for you. I am not selfish to keep this from you, don't worry about me.'

Dev took both my hands. 'The truth is that I can't be without you. I can't bear to leave you. I love you so much; it hurts to see you this way. If only you would agree to marry me...'

'Please Dev, we have spoken about this. I don't know what to say anymore...I love you too but I cannot marry yet. I am sorry.'

'If...if anything happens whilst I am away, anything – and you need me, will you tell me? I will come straight away, I promise.'

'I know you will, I have faith in you. Of course I will tell you.'

Dev and I talked into the evening – he was excited about his trip to Simla but he didn't want to leave me either. My feelings were no different. I concentrated on the present as I lay in his arms, our fingers entwined. It was nice.

'Will I see you tomorrow?' I asked.

'I am not leaving yet, I will come every day.'

That was good enough for the moment.

I didn't go back to work until mid-September and after a lot of arguing with Ma and Papa. Arjun was against me aswell. I was stubborn and refused to listen to any of them and then I won but with an ultimatum: if I fell again, however minor, I would be stopping work. I agreed readily, so eager was I to be free from my imprisonment, no matter how good it was meant to be for me.

I wanted to work again: I'd had enough laying in bed and feeling useless. My pains still hadn't numbed completely but it wasn't much to worry about. My only worry was seeing Rama again but I couldn't avoid her forever.

Nani was delighted when she saw me. She practically flew to me and kissed my cheeks. 'I am so happy to have you back. So happy! *I* missed you very much.' She took me into her bosom. 'You will work light until I feel you are well enough for anything else, you understand? Anyhow, I have asked Champa to keep an eye on you.'

'Nani, where is Rama?' I asked when I didn't see her. Uncharacteristically, the rest of the family greeted me with open arms. It was very strange. An employer has never been so close to a working maid before, nor have they cared.

Nani was not smiling now. She spoke stiffly. 'Rama is away on a hill station[93], for a vacation. Now, go.' She dismissed me abruptly. I was confused, had I caused her pain? I thought as I went to begin work.

Champa couldn't be more delighted either of Rama's absence and she wasn't afraid to voice it either. I laughed at her buoyant behaviour.

'Champa,' I said as I remembered something. 'When I was ill, Nani came to see me. Rama was there too...why?'

'She has...changed.' Champa stopped splashing the floor with water and took the sweeper.

I stopped polishing the vase I was holding. 'What do you mean?'

'Rama became subdued after what she did to you. As much as I hate to say it, she isn't overbearing anymore. You see, whilst you were

---

[93] *Hill station*, a vacation point for Indians and the English alike.

away, she and Grandmother Chatterji had a few conversations in her room. It was very private, even *Memsahib* and *Saab* weren't allowed to hear what was said. The following day, Meena and two other maids were told to leave work.

'On the day they came to see you, the tension was thick in the house. I remember it very well. No one was talking and everyone went quietly about their work and on their return, Rama was crying – I supposed she had been crying for a long time; Grandmother Chatterji looked worn. That day, she sent Rama on her vacation.'

That horrific night – Meena luring me to the servants quarters...those girls who held my arms whilst Rama beat me...I gasped. 'She confessed,' I said.

Champa shrugged. 'I don't see any other reason. I actually pitied Rama.'

I understood now why Rama came with Nani. I could still see her face – a mask of horror when she saw what she had done to me. Nani had been very discreet and she didn't once let me know that she knew. I admired that. What bewildered me was that I actually felt sorry for Rama.

'Now, *you* don't go feeling sorry for that girl!' Champa said, raising her eyebrows at me. She began to sweep the water, washing the dusty floor.

Nani always had trouble with her calves and this afternoon, I was at her bed, pressing and massaging vigorously. She sighed, content.

'Ah, your hands have magic,' she complimented.

'Ma and Papa like me to practice on them. But *Nani*, I don't understand why you don't let a doctor see you if you are in so much pain?'

Nani harrumphed. 'These doctors are no good. You keep doing this, *dikra*. It gives me peace.'

I dutifully carried on and soon was lost in my own momentum. I began to sing and *Nani* closed her eyes. It was very quiet – I was enjoying it and I knew *Nani* was too. But it didn't last as fifteen minutes later, I heard some noise downstairs.

'*Dikra*, see who that is,' she said. As she put her glasses back on, I went to the door but it opened before I could grab the handle. I saw his eyes first and I stared. He was beautiful. Embarrassed and guilty, I looked away.

He walked past me after so long, touching my hand as he did so. He had a smirk on his face. I withdrew like I had been scalded.

'Kem cho, faiba[94].' He touched nani's feet.

'Satish! Saru tu avigayo[95]! How long it has been, let me see you properly.' Nani took him by the arm and sat him next to her. She appraised him and suddenly began to cry. 'I have not seen you since you were so small. How is Papa? I miss him so much, you tell him that!' She dried her eyes with a handkerchief after a few moments of her nephew patting her awkwardly. 'Oh, I am silly,' she sniffed.

Feeling like I shouldn't be there, I slipped out but heard Satish ask Nani about me and I stopped.

'Faiba[96], who is that girl?'

'She is our maid,' said Nani. 'She is very sweet; I am very fond of her.'

'She is very beautiful...' Came his next sentence and I froze. I didn't like his tone...it was obscene. 'Is she married?'

'Now tell me, why didn't you tell us you were coming? It is very bad of you,' Nani scolded. She didn't answer his question which I was glad of and so I moved away. I didn't want to hear anymore.

Champa informed me that Satish Saab was going to stay for a month. I was not happy, I would rather face Rama. There was something about him that I didn't like and I wished he was gone.

That first week, I shied away from him but somehow, he found me. He was always there, staring at me. I changed my work duties with another maid but he still managed to irritate me with his presence. He was always there, leering, watching and trying to touch me.

It was one such morning when I was washing clothes. I was singing to myself and didn't know he had come until he spoke. My heart stopped in my chest.

'Will you wash a shirt of mine?' He held out a white shirt by the collar. It looked like it had been freshly ironed. 'I am out tonight and I need it for then.' His voice was silky and arrogant.

'Saab, the basket is over there. Leave it there and I will wash it.'

---

[94] **Kem Cho, Faiba**, How are you, auntie (Gujarati)
[95] **Saru tu avigayo**, Good, you came (Gujarati)
[96] **Faiba**, Auntie (Father's sister)

Slowly, he turned and put the shirt in the basket. He stayed where he was.

'Is there anything else I can do for you?' I asked.

'Let me look at those fragile hands. Let me soften them for you.' He sat on his toes opposite me and took my hand. I snatched my hand back and glared at him.

'Champa!' I shouted.

Champa appeared almost instantly. 'What is it, Pooja? Are you alright?' She turned to face Satish and looked back at me. 'Is everything...'

'I need to see *Memsahib*, she has called for me.' I stood up quickly. '*Saab* wants his shirt washed, can you do it? I won't be long.'

'No, it's fine,' Satish said, looking bemused. He glared at me; then stalked off.

I sat down, shaking.

'What happened, Pooja? Please, tell me,' Champa asked.

'Nothing, I am fine. You go on, I will carry on here.' Champa didn't ask anymore which I was grateful for.

'If you need me...' she said and looked at me meaningfully. Then, she walked away.

I had to make many excuses like this. Satish knew this game very well and he played along. Instead of stopping him, it excited him further. It turned into an obsession: somehow, he had to have me.

I usually helped with washing the floors before afternoon *khanna*[97] but I was given the task of serving instead. Nani thought I was working too hard.

I set the table as the family gathered. Satish took the chair next to where I was standing and slid into it. He barely took his eyes off me. Everyone was too busy to notice and very discreetly, he touched my waist. It happened very fast but to me the time slowed. I watched the bowl drop and the fruit scatter - the table went terribly quiet. My cheeks burned and I hastily apologised, bending down to retrieve the fallen fruit. To my relief, everyone began talking again.

'Let me help.' Satish's silky voice was too loud in my ear. *Please*, I begged to God, *please no more*! 'That was uncomfortable, wasn't it? Pooja, look at me. Don't hide – why all the pretence? I

---
[97] *Khanna*, Food – dinner/lunch

99

know you like me. Come now; meet me after dinner on the roof. No one will be there, it will be only us. We will have fun.'

'*Saab*, I don't like you and I don't want you to ever touch me again or talk to me.' I said through clenched teeth. He smirked and straightened up, picking up a fallen apple. I brushed away my tears angrily. Why did I let him do this to me?

When everyone had finished eating, Champa and I began to clear the table. I took the pots and plates back into the kitchen and relaxed a little. I still wasn't feeling quite right but I managed to behave normal or so I thought.

'I am going now; will you be alright on your own? Should I wait for you?' Champa asked as she brought in the last of the pots. 'You seemed very nervous this evening.'

I laughed. 'You are imagining it. Anyway, you go on home. I will be leaving soon.'

Once Champa had gone, I went back into the dining room to check and inspect the table. I nearly screamed when I saw him. Satish was still sitting in his chair. He seemed to be waiting for me. I turned back immediately.

'Pooja, you work so hard. Come to me and I shall massage your shoulders for you,' he said quietly but his words echoed around the big empty room. I pretended to not have heard him but he carried on. 'You have such smooth skin; such beautiful eyes...why cover up? You have such lovely assets; why not show them off to me? Pooja, I can give you whatever you want, anything you want. All I want is you.' Lowering his voice, he came towards me. My heartbeat quickened and my breathing became fast. 'What can I do for you to like me? All I want is to hold you and make you feel better, to soothe your aching body. What is wrong with that?'

'Everything is wrong, *Saab*. I think that you are forgetting that I am a maid here. It is wrong, please, I beg you, please leave me alone or I will....'

'What will you do Pooja? Scream? Let me tell you, that we are completely alone. All the servants have now gone home, yes, I paid them to leave early.' His smile widened. 'Everybody else has gone also, they had a party invite this evening, did you know that? Oh, they won't be back until after midnight.' He laughed – an edge of wonting in his tone. 'You are such a sweet and silly girl.' He leaned against me, touching my cheeks and lips with his index finger. I felt sick.

'Please let me go,' I begged.

'Ah, you make my heart flutter. How can I not have you?' he ran his finger down my neck and rested at my cleavage. He flicked my sari away, revealing my blouse. 'Don't be scared. I will be gentle my love.'

Suddenly, he grabbed me and completely unravelled my sari, spinning me away from him. I screamed, covering myself with my arms. He laughed again and crossed the room to me in two strides. Snatching my arms, he twisted them around my back, not letting go. With his free hand, he grabbed my face and kissed me, his rough mouth pressing down hard, his urgency tearing at my lips. He finally released me and then I screamed and screamed. Someone had to hear me, someone just had to. But no one came. He slapped me and laughed, then tore off my blouse.

'You are mine.' He pushed me down onto the floor. He licked his lips; his eyes hungry. He grabbed my petticoat[98] and undid the string. It dropped to the floor. He covered my mouth with one hand and with the other, parted my thighs aggressively. Pieces of my last garment were thrown into the air. I felt sick as the horror became too real.

He groped me, handling me with brute force, pinning me down. I screamed again, this time more shrill as he crushed himself to me. I felt a rip. I felt dizzy and nauseous...I was bleeding and I was going to die...

'Satish *Bhai*? Is that you?' a familiar voice said. It sounded so far away. 'Who is that? Oh! What have you done? WHAT HAVE YOU DONE TO HER!'

Rama, she was here. How strange for her to be here.

'Pooja - oh my God. Satish *Bhai*, what have you done to her! How dare you!' I felt her warm hands on my arms and then she lifted me so I was sitting. 'Pooja, open your eyes. Please...' I thought I heard her crying but I was probably only dreaming for the darkness never lifted.

The smell of incense was nice. The pain, the disgrace wasn't there anymore. Dev smiled as he took my hand. We were at the temple, our

---

[98] **Petticoat**, an undergarment tied at the waist, for saris to be kept in place.

101

lives were to be joined in a matter of minutes...we were to be wed...he started to fade...Dev was going...the pain was coming back. It was worse, I frowned: it wasn't supposed to be like this. Darkness returned and I couldn't breathe again. Satish was in front of me, he was pulling my clothes off me. His fingernails scratched my waist and arms. I could smell blood. I couldn't see, I couldn't move...I wanted him to let me go. Dev, where was he? Why is Satish here? No....no....

'Pooja, wake up, please.'

I wrinkled my nose; I didn't like that smell, what was it? Was Rama still here? Was she crying? I felt tired; I was hurting. Oh. My eyes fluttered open.

She was here. I looked around; how did I get here? I thought I was dying? But I was in hospital.

'You nearly died. If I didn't bring you here in time...I can't bear to think about it.' Rama wiped her tears with a handkerchief. 'Satish fled, you know. I don't know where he is now, I think...he is scared.

'The doctor has said you will heal but he wants to keep you in overnight, to check on you. He said this could be a police case.' Her eyes met mine.

I knew Rama was feeling remorse but what Satish did, it wasn't her fault. But I couldn't tell her that; I felt terrible for it. Forgiveness is a strange thing and I hoped that my heart would be strong enough to melt one day and I could release her from the hatred of herself.

'Rama.' She didn't seem surprised that I didn't call her *Chotti Memsahib*. In fact she smiled.

'I like that,' she said.

'I want to speak to Amit. He lives in the village – Amit Kothari. He will know what to do.' My voice was lifeless. Then I looked at her. 'Thank you for not letting me die.'

~
AMIT
~

Nine

Amit

My relationship was confusing to the villagers. They couldn't understand it; who was I close to: Dev, Sunil or Pooja? I already had an answer. I replied, they are all dear to me in different ways. To Dev, I am a confidant. To Pooja, I am like a brother and to Sunil; I am a friend who he can joke with. But what about love, they said?

Love did not interest me; I was much too interested in curing illnesses and being a sympathetic ear. It was what I did – my livelihood. I could cure colds, flu, headaches. I could clean up grazes and cuts. I could take time to listen to the many woes that they complained of whilst being treated. My home was open all the time to the villagers and we turned no one away.

I say "we" because Ma and Papa were my allies in the business. We mixed spices and ground plants into paste or powder; medicines strong enough to cure many ailments. This work took most of my time so falling in love wasn't a possibility.

I cannot say that I had many admirers, for my appearance was quite normal. I wasn't as tall as Dev who was very handsome nor did I have the endearing quality of Sunil, who was all the time surrounded by girls, and nor did my glasses do any justice to my face but dear Pooja, dear, dear Pooja, insisted I looked like a hero as she pointed out – in her words – my dark, intense brown eyes and curly hair.

As the only son, I was relied on to achieve well. I studied first and then joined Ma and Papa in the home business. So, my life circled the only three things that mattered to me: my family of friends, Ma and Papa and my work.

Life was simple until *Gandhi* announced the Quit India movement. After Rakesh's murder – yes, murder because that was what it was, I saw India in two different lenses: the rich and the poor. The first lens showed the rich Indians playing in the hands of the white man willingly and the second lens showed the poor Indians forced to play in the white man's hand.

The "white man" or *goré*[99] as Indians preferred to say, was the main topic of talk amongst the villagers (amongst other things inflicted on them by their very own families). They complained and I listened. So it came as no surprise when Dev came to me for some advice, soon after Rakesh's death.

It rained again that day, adding more water to the weather beaten roads, filling up the pot holes too quickly. I watched from my front room window as Dev fought his way through. His trousers were folded up but his knees were still deep in dirty brown rain water. A man was walking his dog on the other side of the road; both looking drowned. I opened the door as Dev was about to knock.

'I saw you coming.' I ushered my water clad friend inside. 'Wait here and don't get anything wet.' I came back with a towel and some of my own clothes. He raised an eyebrow. 'They should fit,' I said.

Dev looked worried but went to change anyway. He was grumpy when he came back. 'The trousers are short,' he said.

'Well, at least you are dry now,' I said cheerfully. 'Anyway, why are you here?'

'I need some advice.'

'I thought you looked distracted the last few days.' I sat down and folded my arms. I waited for him to begin.

'I can't stop thinking about what *Bhai* wanted...' said Dev.

'What are you talking about?' I said. 'Sit down Dev, you are making me dizzy.'

He sat promptly, but began to wring his hands. 'I am talking about the Quit India campaign. I should be part of it.'

'The Quit India campaign,' I repeated. 'You came here – in the rain, to talk about that?'

'It is important.'

'Is it really that important? I understand why you want to do this, but Dev, just think. For a moment, think of your parents. Isn't losing one son enough for them? Do you want them to lose all hope when you die too?'

'You sound angry,' said Dev, furrowing his eyebrows.

'I *am* angry! Dev, you don't have to do this.'

[99] *Goré*, White (man)

'I want to…*Bhai* wanted this. It was his dream for a free India.'

'But it's not yours.' I walked to the kitchen and Dev followed. He watched me put on some water for *chai*.

'I don't know,' said Dev truthfully. 'I am so confused.'

'So let others do it. Why are you so quick to give up your life?' I added *chai* granules, sugar, milk and *chai masala* to the water and let it boil.

'Don't you think that is selfish?' Dev asked.

'Not at all, what is selfish is you giving more grief to your remaining family. Forget what Rakesh wanted – that was in the past. Focus on the present and support Ma and *Babuji*. Give them something that they can carry on living for. Two dead sons are no good to them and I would not like to lose a best friend.'

'I know you are right but I feel restless. What am I meant to do in this life, Amit? *Bhai* had a focus, I have nothing.' Dev reached for two glasses and set them down. I poured the *chai* and we went back to the front room.

'What about Pooja?' I said.

'Pooja won't be interested in the Movement, she has other responsibilities,' Dev said missing the point.

I shook my head in disdain. 'Dev, you are in love with her and she is in love with you. I see it. If you truly care for her, then you have to think about her future too.'

'This is not about Pooja. Amit, don't you feel an obligation towards our country…don't you want freedom? I love Ma and *Babuji* but freeing our country is important.'

'My friend, I love this country as well as many others do, but my ideas are different. India has been under the influence of the *Raj* for many decades. Whether *Gandhi* achieves this freedom I don't know. I wonder if he has had doubts too. We have grown up under the British governance for so long...what they have done has been positive. You know what is right for you; I can only give you advice. Just, don't make any decisions for a while.'

Dev looked out the window; the rain was relentless. He sipped his *chai*. I stared out of the window also.

'I would like to see a change for India,' I continued. 'But I don't like the violence which has claimed so many lives already. Your

107

family has had a bad time with the *Raj* and I understand, but think *yaar*[100], is this really what you want to do?'

'I don't know... 'I'd better go home; Ma wants me home early today. I will think about what you said.'

'Dev, Rakesh was like a brother to me too. Don't think I am not hurting...but we have to see things from the head and not the heart. You understand what I am saying, right?'

Dev came and embraced me. 'You are a true friend, you know?' He turned for the door.

'Dev, wait!' I gave him my umbrella. 'Try and stay dry.'

Dev smiled taking the umbrella and was gone.

I watched her as she slept. Her fair complexion radiated against her red, wavy hair, fanned out across the pillow. People were already talking about the "white Memsahib" I'd brought home but I didn't care.

She was unconscious when I found her on the road. Her face was flushed and her lips were dry. I took out a newspaper I had in my satchel and fanned her but she didn't stir.

'*Memsahib*, can you hear me?' I said, close to her ear.

'So thirsty...' she croaked, placing a hand on her throat, eyes still closed.

'*Memsahib*, please wake up.' We were nowhere near a river or a shop. I needed water. The dry, hot road stretched in front of me, with no break of trees or buildings for cover against the unforgiving sun. The sky was a mass of blue, the clouds gone. The air was stagnant and unbearable.

I couldn't leave *Memsahib* here like this...where was her family? Did she come with a friend? I turned my head this and that way, but I couldn't see anyone. I wondered what she was doing here, all alone. Her bag lay next to her and I picked it up, hauling her up next, onto my shoulder. It wasn't difficult; she was very light.

I walked for fifteen minutes and my shirt began to stick. Oh, I so wished we were walking towards a river or a well! I came upon a patch of grass and put *Memsahib* down. She was no better. I sighed,

---

[100] **Yaar**, Friend

wiping the sweat from my face. I took off my shirt and slung it over my shoulder.

What should I do? I couldn't walk anymore and *Memsahib* needed to be seen by a doctor. I could only hope that God would help me. I sighed, deciding to walk a little more in the hope that there may be someone on the road who could help.

I picked *Memsahib* up again and began my slow walk. A few paces later, I heard the galloping of hooves and the drum of wheels.

Oh thank you, God! I waved the *tonga-wallah*[101] down and he stopped in front of me.

'Chandu!' I exclaimed.

'*Yaar*, what are you doing here? Who is she?' Chandu stopped before me – my friend and fellow villager. I chuckled, he didn't miss anything. The horse neighed.

'Hello Chameli,' I stroked her mane.

'Who is she?' Chandu asked again, raising an eyebrow.

'I will explain later. Right now I need help, can you take us back to my house?'

Chandu helped me put *Memsahib* in the back of the tonga and we were off. Once home, we made *Memsahib* comfortable on my bed.

'You look after *Memsahib*, I will call the doctor.' Chandu was very good. Whilst he was gone, I managed to give her some water with a spoon and laid cold compressed towels on her forehead. She began to look better in a few minutes and some colour had returned to her face.

There was nothing to do but wait – maybe the doctor was busy. I decided to sit outside after a while. People glanced towards me as they walked by. I smiled and waved; I was sure they were trying to peek in. This continued for a while and soon I was fed up and went back inside. Memsahib was sitting up looking confused.

'Oh my,' she said when she saw me. Her right hand fluttered to her neck.

'Hello.' I was awkward.

'Who are you and where am I?' She jumped off the bed and backed away from me.

'*Memsahib*, please don't be afraid. I won't hurt you. I am Amit, I found you on the road and you were unconscious.'

'Gosh...how long?'

---

[101] ***Tonga-wallah***, Tonga driver

'I don't know...forgive me, but I couldn't leave you like that. I brought you to my home, please don't mind. I have asked my friend to call for the doctor.'

'That's very kind of you,' she said. She hesitated a moment but then thought better of it. 'Would you mind if I asked for some water?'

'I already have some on the table beside you, *Memsahib*.'

She drank long. 'Thank you so much, but I think I should go home now. My family will be worried.'

'*Memsahib*, may I ask...did you come alone to town? I didn't see anyone with you...'

'I came here on some business. When I finished, I didn't realise what time it was and the heat! Well, I suppose I fainted.' A blush appeared on her cheeks and she looked at her hands. 'Anyway, I must thank you for rescuing me and now, I must be going.'

I didn't like this idea; I wanted her to stay a little longer. 'Perhaps you should wait for the doctor, *Memsahib*.'

'No really, I should go... you have done a lot already.' She stood up and swayed, and sat down abruptly. She laughed weakly. 'Maybe I *should* wait for the doctor.'

'Please, take some rest.' I gestured anxiously to the bed. 'I will bring some tea. The spices will help.'

Memsahib was looking through a book of mine when I got back. It was my poetry book...seeing *Memsahib* read it – it made me smile. I even liked it. I cleared my throat.

She looked up and blushed, again. 'I'm so sorry, I had no right...' She put the book down and took the *chai* from my hand. She inhaled the aroma appreciatively. 'I hope you didn't mind me reading your work. It was just so beautiful.'

'Did you like any of them?'

'Yes, the one where you describe the mountains, the valley and the wandering peacock. It was quite romantic.'

'That is one of my favourites.' I picked up my *chai*.

'Have you had anything published?'

'No *Memsahib*. I...write for myself. No one would be interested.'

'I must disagree. You are a fine writer and I should know. I have grown up reading literature – mainly poems ironically. Have you heard of Shakespeare?'

I nodded enthusiastically. 'Yes, I have read his work! *Memsahib*, would – '

'Please, call me Mary. I really do have bad manners – I should have introduced myself!' She laughed. It was musical.

'*Mem* – er…Mary *Memsahib* – will that be alright?'

'If you think so,' she laughed again and I joined in.

As we talked, we hardly noticed the time slipping by. I had also forgotten about the doctor and Chandu. When they came, I was startled and embarrassed. In followed Sunil, I shouldn't have been surprised.

'Sunil, what are you doing here?' I was annoyed. I didn't want anyone to crowd Mary, especially nosy friends like Sunil.

He winked. 'I came to say hello to your guest.'

'Hmm. Say hello and then leave,' I whispered.

He ignored me and extended his hand to *Memsahib*. 'Hello, I am Sunil. Amit's best friend. I hope he has looked after you.'

'Absolutely, he is a gentleman.'

Sunil raised his eyebrows at me. I felt heat rise to my face.

'Well, I will let the doctor do his job, it was nice meeting you,' Sunil said and left but not before giving me a meaningful look. 'We will talk later!' he grinned.

'So, my dear, how are you feeling now?' asked the doctor. 'Chandu tells me you collapsed?'

'I remember I was feeling dizzy, everything was hazy and the sun was very bright. When I woke up, I was here,' said *Memsahib*.

The doctor nodded as he checked her eyes, felt her pulse and checked her tongue.

'*Memsahib*,' he said. 'You have nothing to worry about. It seems you have fainted from heat exposure and dehydration. The only medicine for this is rest and to drink plenty of water, and not to go wandering in the sun! You seem fine otherwise. Amit, here has looked after you well.'

'Oh Doctor *Saab*,' I said, embarrassed again.

'No no. Don't be modest. I believe you have given *Memsahib* some spiced *chai*? That's why she has colour on her cheeks. Well done, *beta*.'

I showed the doctor to the door and paid him his fee, then went to join *Memsahib* back in the front room.

'How much was the doctor's fee?' *Memsahib* checked her purse.

'No, please *Memsahib*. You don't have to.'

'Now, that will not do. I cannot let you pay for me – this is outrageous. Tell me, how much did he charge?'

I reluctantly told her, although considerably less and hoped she wouldn't notice. She counted the money and handed it to me. I put it aside without looking at it.

'Amit, it really is time I went home, would you mind calling me a *rickshaw*[102]?'

Just then Ma and Papa came home. They stared at *Memsahib*, who smiled, a little shy.

'Hello,' she said.

'Who are you?' Ma asked, dropping her bags on the floor.

'Ma, this is Mary *Memsahib*.' I told them about the afternoon.

'*Namaste Memsahib*,' said Ma. 'I'm sorry for my rudeness, I didn't expect – anyway, have you had any food?'

'Ma, she will be going home soon,' I said.

'Amit, I am not asking you. *Memsahib*, I will cook something quickly. Once you have eaten, you will feel much better and then you can go home. A guest cannot leave without having eaten.' Ma bustled into the kitchen, banging pots and pans. Papa resigned to his chair and lit a cigar, sitting down to listen to the All India radio station.

Memsahib couldn't stop complimenting Ma's cooking and Ma was very happy about that. It was time for her to go home but before that Ma presented her with a gift.

'I have no daughter and so these pleasures are rare. It may seem unnecessary but I would like you to have this sari. It is not always, a young pretty *Memsahib* like you steps into our home. Please, wear it with pride.'

Memsahib hugged it close to her and thanked Ma profoundly.

Memsahib lived in a large bungalow just outside of Rajkot. I called on Chandu and we took her home in his tonga. As we reached the gate, the ground lights came on guiding us in. The smell here was very different, fresh and fragrant. *Memsahib* led us to towards her house.

'*Memsahib*, thank you for inviting us but we should say goodbye and go home,' I said.

---

[102] **Rickshaw**, this has many meanings – a two-wheeled vehicle pulled by a man; a cycle-rickshaw or an auto-rickshaw. In the days of the Raj, the first two was common.

'Nonsense. After the hospitality you and your friends and family have shown me, I can hardly let you go without a proper thank you. Please, after you,' she said, gesturing to the grand door.

'Mary? Mary, is that you! I was so worried!' A man came forward, grabbing Mary and embracing her tightly. He was wearing a nightgown and slippers and his hair was dishevelled, like he had just woken up.

'Tom, it is alright. See – I'm fine,' said Mary. She clasped her hand around his. 'I fainted and then these two lovely men rescued me. It was Amit who actually found me.'

'Are you sure you are alright? You need to see a doctor,' said the man, Tom.

'I already have. Listen Tom, it was Amit and Chandu who took me to their village, to Amit's house. The village doctor saw me and told me I was well.'

Tom noticed us then as we respectfully stood just inside the door. 'Thank you so much for what you have done for my fiancée.' He shook our hands. 'If there is any way I can repay you...'

'Fiancée?' I said.

'Tom and I are engaged, we are getting married next year,' *Memsahib* said proudly.

'That's very good!' said Chandu when I didn't speak.

'Yes...' I said. I felt a nudge in my ribs.

'I have to thank you for looking after my Mary, I was so worried.' He kissed her quickly but I burned. It was a strange feeling; I had never felt like this.

'It was nothing. We have to go now.' I began to lead Chandu back through the front door.

'Are you sure? Why don't you have a drink first?' she suggested but I was shaking my head. 'Sorry, you don't drink. Well, some tea then?'

'*Memsahib*, thank you but it is really late,' said Chandu. 'My father will be worried.'

'Will you come and visit?' she asked.

'You want us to?' I was surprised.

'I'd like to think we can be friends, isn't that right Tom?'

'Yes, please do visit us,' Tom said jovially.

'Goodbye *Memsahib*...*Saab*,' I said.

Chandu gave me a sideward glance at we drove back. 'What happened to you?'

'What do you mean?'

'*Yaar*, when *Memsahib* introduced Tom *Saab*, your expression...you are jealous!'

'Chandu, don't talk nonsense. That is ridiculous.'

'No, you are in love,' he grinned.

'Just drive home,' I said but I wondered if that was true.

That night, I lay in bed thinking about her. She had awakened feelings inside me which had not happened before and I didn't know what to do about it...maybe, I will see her again.

Ten

The Vacation

I had heard of '*goonda-giri*[103]' – a gang of thieves and murderers out on the rampage, looting and killing the innocent or guilty, the rich or the poor – whichever, it didn't matter to them. Their only motive was to take or kill. I didn't believe they existed until I saw it with my own eyes.

It was Thursday, our day of vegetable shopping at the largest vegetable market near Rajkot.

'We must not forget the aubergines,' Ma said. 'Your father cannot go without his aubergines.' She worked around us, clearing the table of Papa's newspapers and my books and generally tidying up before we left. 'Amit, have you written that on the list?'

I showed her the list which she made me write every week. She stopped and scrutinised it before seeming satisfied.

'Amit's Papa, we are going now. Don't call that Pardeep around; he is useless and don't gamble with him either. I don't like it. And if that Brimla comes around, tell her that I am out and I will see to her legs another time. God knows why she comes – I keep telling her that there is nothing wrong but no, still she comes! And you will need to go and talk to Manoj – his son, he makes the devil look good – he keeps throwing potato peelings in our field and runs away with his useless friends when I chase after him. I am fed up of clearing it every day!'

Papa and I shook our heads when Ma turned the other way.

'*Mari Ma*[104], stop now. Go or you will miss your bus,' said Papa, picking up his paper and opening it with much, unnecessary noise.

I laughed. 'Ma, tell me, do you like antagonising the village children and running after them with a stick? Chal or we really will miss the bus.'

'*Chal*,' she said, resigned.

---

[103] *Goonda-giri*, a gang who like to terrorise, steal and fight – sometimes leading to worse victim endings.
[104] *Mari Ma*, My mother – said in the context of being sarcastic, like 'Yes, my dear!' (Gujarati)

115

The bus didn't go all the way to the market so we had to hire a tonga afterwards. By eleven, we reached the bustling market.

Coming here was always enjoyable. I relished in the smells and colours of the different fruits and vegetables and I loved the sellers hollering. Some stall holders showcased their bright red, plush tomatoes and delicious looking, fresh greens, side by side. It was a great display and it worked. I immediately bought fresh chillies. I walked away with my first purchase.

Not all stall holders were particular about their goods, for their fruit was either too soft or their vegetables too old and wrinkled, probably from last week's batch. Ma passed those stalls, wrinkling her nose in distaste. I stopped at a stall which sold mangoes of all varieties; my eyes instantly focussed on the lush, orange ones. The scent of the uncut fruit was sweet; I wondered if the taste was even better. I bought five.

As I paid, a *Memsahib* asked the seller for a dozen mangoes, but which were not yet ripe. He gladly filled her basket with orange ones with a tint of green on the skin. The lady gave me a smile, moving to another stall...and then I thought of my Mary. A sigh rose from my lips as I remembered her smile, her grey-green eyes and her exuberant red hair...my heart ached to see her again...

'Amit! Amit!' I snapped out of my reverie. Ma was waving her hand in front of my eyes. 'What's got into you? Are you listening? What do you think about these aubergines, will your Papa like them?'

'Ah...yes, he will.' I nodded.

Ma gave me a curious look but then turned towards the seller. '*Bhaiya*, give me five aubergines.'

The seller selected five and put his hand on another one. '*Bena*, do you want six?'

'No, only five.'

'I will give you good price.' He was quite persistent.

'Six is too much. Five will do, *Bhaiya*,' Ma said. She counted out the correct money.

The seller handed Ma five aubergines with a sour face; a battle lost. Ma and I went to another stall and a similar process began. By the time we stopped at the seventh stall, I was tired; my attention ceased.

'*Choro*[105]! Get off me!' Someone screamed; jolting me alert.

---

[105] *Choro*, Leave me

116

I turned in the direction of the startling shriek. My feet felt like lead, heavy and unable to move as the macabre scene unfolded.

They descended upon us like vultures. Dressed in black clothing and masked – they came with knives and swords. Their eyes were...frightening.

'Give me your necklace and your earrings!' one growled at a terrified lady. He snatched the jewellery off her and then laughed, placing a finger on her cheek. His eyes followed from her face to her breasts – I felt cold hatred ripple through me. With his other hand, he slashed her blouse off with his sword and pushed her to the ground. The woman screamed and the man licked his lips.

'That is my wife!' A man pushed the masked man away, but his fury didn't quite match that of the monster. The masked man did it so quickly; I nearly didn't see it. The man went down, his front slashed from neck to torso, blood spilling like a river. I recoiled.

The market was no longer a happy, hum of noise - screams and cries filled each corner. Fresh blood stained the ground and the sellers cowered under their livelihood. People were dying and I watched. I couldn't do anything. I was a ...coward.

There was havoc; people were running. Ma took me by the arm and pulled me with her, repeating the lord's name under her breath.

'*Beta*, come let's go,' her calm whisper shocked me. She was fast but that didn't stop me from seeing everything. I passed dead people; some were young girls and some were old men. Women were still being raped by the shameless murderers. Their husbands, brothers or sons who had tried to defend their honour, were lying dead next to them.

We managed to jump on the last tonga leaving. '*Jaldi ben-ji*[106],' the *tonga-wallah* said. 'I don't want them catching up with me!'

The *tonga-wallah* drove off as fast as he could. I looked back and saw a bleeding man coming towards us. He fell and died. I turned to face the road, my heart thumping madly.

The paper lay in front of me, staring and accusing - coward! The photographs were very real. All the victims were named. Those who survived gave accounts of their sickening ordeal. It was big news. Gujarat had not seen large scale of murders this size in years.

---

[106] *Jaldi ben-ji*, Quickly sister

Where did these men come from? What were their motives? Who was the leader? The masked men had fled before they could be caught and left devastation for the police to witness. The scene so shocking that it would never be erased from their minds.

I picked up the newspaper and looked closely at the photographs. Why hadn't I noticed it before? They didn't come to murder the Indians! They came to kill the white people! Not one victim was Indian. *Eh Baghwaan*, is this what we Indians had succumbed to? Were we the villains now? Gandhi's Quit India movement was about *Ahimsa*[107] and non-violence. He didn't want this! Why wasn't India listening? I put my head into my hands and closed my eyes, trying to make sense of it all.

'Put that away, Amit.' Papa appeared at the door. He sat next to me. 'How many times are you going to read that? Look at you. You are not well....*beta*, these things happen. You mustn't suffer for it.'

'I stood there and watched, Papa. Why didn't I help? I am ashamed.' I hung my head.

'Why didn't you help? Answer these questions for me and then I will answer yours. Why didn't anybody else help, why did *they* all run away? Where was the police? What took them so long to get there? Why haven't they yet, caught the murderers? You see *beta*, these are questions no one can answer. You were not the only one who couldn't help...you could have been killed.'

My head began to ache. For days I had been feeling like this – nightmares ruled me each time I tried to sleep, even when I was awake, they wouldn't leave me. At times, Rakesh *Bhai* entered my dreams. He'd scold me for not taking action, for running – being a coward, and then there were dreams when he told me I was right to leave, that even if I wanted to, even if I did try and stop those murderers, I probably wouldn't have made any difference and I may have died...the angel and the devil, both made sense and yet, left me confused.

Rakesh *Bhai* was as much a brother to me, as Dev was. Perhaps more. His wisdom, his knowledge and his comradeship was what I had admired about him. He would give up his time to listen to any of us – Pooja, Sunil, Dev and myself. He would suggest and advise – but never lecture.

---

[107] *Ahimsa*, to not harm body/mind/soul

I found out about Rakesh *Bhai's* involvement with the Quit India Movement when one day, Dev came to me, inconsolable. A letter had arrived from the jai, a letter written by Rakesh *Bhai*. It was brief, telling us he had been arrested in Delhi. He didn't say why. Dev and his parents applied for a visiting pass straight away but when they came back after seeing him, it was not good news. Dev told me about the torture – how he had looked and the pain. I could only hold onto my dear friend as he cried.

I began to doubt my views on the *Raj* – were they really our enemy? I felt anger pulsate in my blood and rise in throat; Rakesh *Bhai's* injustice clawed at me. Dev's pain was my own. We waited hopefully, for his release but the news came, instead, of his imminent death.

Later, I would lay in bed, night after night, thinking of how he died and why. The march in Delhi was a non-violent one, then who forced it to become violent? Was it the fault of the Indians who refused to leave the General's premises or was it the fault of the officer who ordered the police to take them? The answer to me is still not clear.

I look at other people and I see they are different. They don't shy away from the violence but voice their anger and take action against the threat. Rakesh *Bhai* was one of them and Dev is too – his wanting to avenge Rakesh *Bhai's* death was perfectly understandable and when he came to see me, to hear my thoughts on his decision to follow in his brother's footsteps, it was really a plea for permission. I couldn't do it. Although I'd told him he shouldn't – for his parents, the truth was that I was petrified of losing another friend. I didn't want him to die like Rakesh *Bhai*. In front of him, I was indifferent, more of an advocate than a friend. Inside, I was trembling in fear. Losing Rakesh *Bhai* was very hard but if I were to lose Dev too, I wouldn't have been able to bear it. It was a blessed relief when Khan *Bhai* assigned him for work in Simla, away from all this – away from troubled temptation.

And now, were those Indians right to rape and murder the white *Memsahibs* and *Saabs*? What was *their* fault - that they were British? They were just innocent people, buying vegetables and fruit – why were they targeted for such horror? I pressed my forehead.

'*Beta*, take these pills. They will help your headaches,' Papa said.

119

'The pills will not help me, Papa.' I sighed, looking at the pills on Papa's upturned palm. I lay back on my bed. My eyes felt heavy with tension.

Papa was quiet and seemed lost in concentration but spoke after a while.

'Amit, it may be good for you to visit your aunt and uncle, in Goa. Go for a vacation...it will help you forget about all this...what do you think? I will arrange everything. A long vacation is a good idea. Don't worry about the business, Ma and I will look after it,' Papa urged. I saw the worry in his eyes; I was making everyone else miserable.

'That's sounds nice.' I tried to sound enthusiastic.

Papa patted me on the shoulder. 'Good. Take rest now,' he said. He seemed to have found relief. My eyes finally gave way to sleep when he left.

I walked through the rambling avenues and wide, plain streets. A bus and rickshaw passed by but the public seemed to prefer cycles as transport. The upper class *Anglo-Indians*[108] or the English drove in fabulous motorcars which shined splendidly. The air was tinted with the casual smell of motorcar gas and of busy city dwellers. I felt very far from home.

Papa arranged my stay with a distant uncle and auntie. My uncle was Papa's uncle's sister's son who married a Christian named Sheila. Yes, it is confusing and I told Papa as such. It is the Indian culture, he reminded me. Distant families are like extended relationships – it is always a good idea to keep in touch.

'We are so delighted to have you, my son,' uncle said proudly on the day I arrived. 'Oh, you look just like your father!' Uncle converted to the Christian faith after he got married, as was the rule of the Portuguese government. He and auntie had eight children who were married, studying or working in various states of India.

'The Portuguese government?' I asked as he took my small suitcase into the house.

'Yes son. Let me tell you a little history. Goa is not ruled by the *Raj*, like the other states are. Goa has been under the rule of the Portuguese for over four hundred years,' said Uncle. 'No faith apart

---

[108] *Anglo-Indian*, People who are from mixed Indian and British descent and British people who were born or living in India during the times of the Raj.

from Christianity is allowed, so in order to live here, one must convert. I was a Hindu but I fell madly in love with your aunt. She didn't want to leave Goa and I can see why – the beauty of it! I didn't want to lose her and so I decided to convert.' Uncle said this with pride.

'But uncle, if India wins her Independence...?'

'That will not affect us, sadly, but we hope it will make the Portuguese government consider leaving Goa...'

'If India has her Independence, then Goa will not be free even though she is "part of" India. Does that not upset you?' I asked.

'Why should it?' said auntie. 'Let me tell you one thing about the Portuguese government. You see our skin – it is brown, yes?'

I nodded.

'Unlike the *Raj*, this government have never referred to our "colour". They have never discriminated against us on account of that.'

As I took that information in, auntie led me to the kitchen where she had food prepared for me. I ate the fruit first – fresh coconut and then rice and curry. The taste was quite unique and so very different from the Gujarati flavours I was used to, but I thoroughly enjoyed it. I was unable to stop licking my fingers.

'It was my mother's recipe,' she beamed when I asked for more. 'It is an old Indian-Portuguese mix of ingredients. Your uncle and I prefer seafood but I know you are a vegetarian. You don't eat fish at all? Are your family all like that? I don't know how you do it. I cannot live without my freshly caught fish, cooked in the flavours of coconut and milk. Do you know – '

'*Bas*, Sheila. Will you stop talking? The poor boy will have a headache,' uncle said, cutting into his fish with a strange looking knife.

'Thank you so much for having me,' I said, between mouthfuls.

Auntie happily piled a third helping onto my plate. 'We will have you looking healthy in no time. You are quite thin,' she said, still smiling.

That night, I lay in my bed thinking about Goa; it's ruling under the Portuguese and not the *Raj*. It was strange, to see a state, although part of India, was not. Like an individual looking at its neighbour, hearing and seeing it's loss and destruction but never feeling its impact...and to hope to see his own home free one day...

The next day, I headed towards Benaulim beach, along the southern coast of Goa. I travelled by bus. It was very colourful. Passengers of different caste, taste and character were on board. I distinguished a few languages: Portuguese seemed the most common – I understood a word or two, which I picked up from auntie and uncle. Some conversations were in English but there were some people who came from other parts of Goa and spoke in their local dialects - *Marathi* and *Konkani*. I didn't understand it but recognised the descending and ascending accents and found it marvellous to listen to.

The bus stopped at the last pick-up point and an English man came on board. He sat in the last remaining seat, which happened to be by me. He wore ridiculously short trousers and a bizarre half-sleeve shirt in an array of multi-coloured patterns.

'Hello, I'm Stuart,' he said, extending a hand towards me.

I nodded and took to stare out of the window.

'First time in Goa?' he asked.

'Yes, it is nice.'

'I agree, I've been here many times. Do you know, the English prefer to go to Simla when the temperatures soar – they say it's a nice coolant but I enjoy coming here instead. My sister and her fiancé think I'm mad. It's the sea-air you know, it refreshes me. I like to travel by bus too, although I have my own motorcar. I have met so many wonderful people.'

The man droned on for a few more minutes and I began to get irritated. I turned to him and said as politely as possible, 'If you will excuse me, I'm a little tired and would like to sleep.'

'Sleeping is good. Don't mind me, I'll just read a book.' I was incredulous; he actually did have a book in his bag!

I turned my face towards the window once again and closed my eyes...my thoughts wandered to Mary. It was easy to think of her, here as mine. This vacation was surreal, it didn't exist, so imagining her as not engaged to be married was not a bad thing. There was no guilt and I was blissfully happy.

The bus jerked to a stop.

'Ah, we are here!' Stuart announced loudly, which left a ringing in my ear. 'Well, I hope I see you again. Have a lovely time.'

He got off with the other travellers. I waited until he was out of sight and then vacated the bus. I didn't follow the throng of people going away from the beach, which I presumed was the shopping area. I went straight to the beach instead.

I walked on the edge where the shallow, warm water lapped leisurely on the golden sand. There was hardly anyone here and I preferred it that way. I saw a young couple. They looked like they were on their honeymoon – they held hands constantly and stared in each others' eyes. I smiled. I let them get some distance before I followed the same route.

This was beautiful. The sun flooded the sand and sparkled on the sea. To one side of the beach, an arrangement of brown, grey and white rocks and stones lay against a backdrop of blue sky. Palm trees lined this stretch and I found a sufficiently leafy one to sit under. I cooled instantly in the shade. After a while, I decided to sleep a little, and I dug my toes into the sand, drifting away.

'By golly, it *is* you! I thought so. It was difficult to be certain when I spotted you from afar but I'm rarely wrong. I never make mistakes in recognising someone, no matter how far they are from me. Now, I'm not saying that I can see from a great distance – that would be amazing, don't you think?'

I knew straight away that the man chattering was none other than my bus companion, Stuart. I opened my eyes and squinted. I was surprised to see the sun quite low in the sky. Some lights had come on and a small fire burned in the distance, some people were sitting around it, laughing and talking. How long had I been asleep?

'Hello...again.'

Stuart sat down next to me. 'Do you know, I don't know your name?'

'I am Amit.' I extended my hand and he shook it.

'So, why are you here, alone?'

'Excuse me?' I said, bewildered. 'That is a personal question.'

'Generally, being alone means that you are unhappy. Something is wrong. Did you have an argument with your wife?'

'I am not unhappy nor am I married – but that is none of your business. Why I am here is my business and I don't want to talk about it!'

Stuart seemed to observe me. 'I believe that's a fair answer.'

'Why are *you* here?' I said grudgingly. Why was I talking to this man? I thought grimly. He was annoying and didn't seem to respect ones privacy – especially mine. He was a funny man, to ignore my protests and my obvious dislike of him, to still stay and chat like

123

we were friends! Ha! But the thing that was really irritating was that he looked familiar and I didn't know why.

'I'm on holiday, one of many,' Stuart said proudly. 'Listen, I'm famished. There's a little place just over there, will you join me?' He pointed to a small building across from the beach. It resembled a hut, with a straw roof and poles holding it up. Chairs and round tables were scattered about with people eating and drinking. Music flowed from a group of entertainers. My stomach grumbled in response.

I laughed weakly. 'I think it is a good idea.'

I ordered coconut curry and rice and Stuart had a fish dish. As he talked, I scrutinised him but I still couldn't place where I may have seen him before. Steadily, the sky darkened outside.

'What time does the last bus go from here?' I asked.

'Where do you live?' Stuart asked as he was about to eat another spoonful of rice.

'I am residing with my aunt and uncle at the moment in Panaji.'

'Panaji...I'm afraid the last bus has gone then. That's very unfortunate,' he said, sincerely.

'Yes, it is.' I was thinking how I was going to get back home. It was silly of me to not keep track of time.

'Listen,' said Stuart. 'I'm staying just a little way from here. You can come and stay with me, if that doesn't make you feel uncomfortable.'

I thought about it and I really didn't have much choice. 'That is very kind of you.'

'No problem, I like to spend time with friends.'

Friends...is that what we were now?

Stuart's house was large, with maids, a cook and a gardener. He told me it was a place where he could get away from his too often, stressful life.

'My father bought this house when my sister and I were only so high and then he died tragically in an accident. He was on a steamer – it crashed into some high rocks. It was a gruesome night. The weather was chaotic and out of nowhere a storm hit the seas. The steamer had no chance. I forget how many people died that night. The steamer was transporting passengers from India to Southampton, in

England. My poor mum was devastated but she had us to look after. God bless my father – he passed this house to me in his will.'

As Stuart talked, I noticed he was never still and his hands were constantly busy, doing something. His passion (one of many) was his love of plants and flowers, for around this beautiful home, were more than twenty pots, arranged around rooms or in windows, creating serenity all around. He tottered about watering, rearranging, dusting leaves or pruning. But this was not all. Outside, his large garden was landscaped to perfection. Immaculate borders, bright green grass shoots cropped to a good size and an assortment of flowers displayed an explosion of colour.

'Amit, treat my home as your own. I'll just be a moment. In the meantime, I will ask Maria – that's my housekeeper – to bring you a juice.'

I felt silly sitting idle and decided to go and look at the framed photographs which hung on the staircase wall. There were many of himself – on a horse, by the sea as a child, with his father and mother, with his dog and then there were others of his family. I was looking at the one with him and his two brothers and two sisters – I presumed their ages were between three and six.

'*Saab*, your juice,' Maria came with a tall glass of fruit juice.

'Thank-you,' I said.

Stuart came back. 'Ah, I see you're admiring my collection of photographs!' He was smiling.

'They are very interesting...but I don't see a recent photograph?' I said.

'No you won't here – they're all at my house, back home. I keep my most precious memorable ones here.'

'Oh,' I said. I sipped my juice.

'I think I'll have one as well,' he said and disappeared again.

I began to like this Stuart character – someone who loves his family and cherishes his plants, cannot be anything but good. Perhaps I had been too judgemental.

Stuart and I had a lot in common and a lot to talk about. He was most interested in my business as I was with his lifestyle. Stuart was a police officer. His position in the ranking system, meant he had the power to call in favours, he said. He didn't elaborate on that and I didn't ask.

I yawned and he didn't miss it. Stuart generously gave me his bed whilst he insisted on sleeping in a hammock. 'I love sleeping in the open air,' he said, sincerely. 'The mosquitoes here don't quite like my blood!'

I roared with laughter, and it felt good. I realised I'd missed that feeling.

The next morning, chai was ordered and we drank it in the fresh air. I wished I could stay another day but uncle and auntie would be worried; I was supposed to be home yesterday. Stuart walked me to the bus stop and waited until I got on. 'I really do hope we meet again, Amit.'

'I hope so too,' I said and this time, I really meant it. 'Thank you for everything.'

'Anytime,' he said.

I waved goodbye as the bus moved away.

Papa was right. Vacation in Goa was exactly what I needed. My recent angst melted away into relief and happiness as I spent time with uncle and auntie. Uncle loved to walk and I'd accompany him on his morning strolls – sometimes on the beach or sometimes on the hill top cliffs.

Auntie and Uncle were devout Christians and they encouraged me to go to church with them on Sundays. I was reluctant but they assured me that I would be embraced and not shied away from. God invites everyone in, even Hindus! Auntie winked and I laughed.

It was a memorable experience. I was introduced as their nephew from Rajkot and as auntie said, they embraced me with open arms into their community.

Evening time, uncle would read a book and auntie would sit with me, engrossed in my funny tales of the patients I cure with my home made medicine. She especially liked my tale about a lady who comes to see me on a regular basis – everyone knows there is nothing wrong with her – but she would come anyway, complaining of a stiff back, pain in her legs, stomach troubles etc when the truth is that she comes to chat about her seven daughters, trying to marry one off to me! And I tell her – when her daughter reaches maturity, then come to me! By then, I will be old enough to be their uncle. Auntie would laugh and laugh!

Sometimes, we would sit for hours discussing various properties of the herbs I used and how and which one would cure which ailment. In return, auntie agreed to teach me how to cook

126

vegetarian Portuguese food, especially her coconut curry. She couldn't be more delighted.

Uncle worshipped his books and read anything. He was mostly proud of Goa's Central Library and took me on a tour of it. I was amazed at the great architectural building and inside, it's enormity. When auntie and uncle were busy, I would sometimes go there and browse through the books on horticulture. I felt happy and peaceful.

The beauty of the sea, the cliffs made me forget about my troubles. Even the people smiled more. But like any vacation, mine came to an end when Papa sent a letter to say that Ma wasn't well and she needed me. It was my cue to leave. It had been three months.

Auntie cried when I hugged her and I shook uncle's' hand, who had a tear in his eye. He took me into his huge frame and patted me roughly on the back.

'I have packed some rice and curry for you, it's in the tiffin,' auntie sniffed. 'Come back soon, won't you?'

'I will auntie,' I said over the noise of the steam and the babbling passengers. Today, the train station was more busy than usual. I kissed auntie's cheek. 'Take care of yourself,' I said.

'Take care, son!' uncle said. I waved and settled down in my compartment.

I watched India rush by my window; the most colourful land and yet, the most dangerous. *Gandhi's* movement had no claim on Goan life and I had been left blissfully out from its troubles. But now, I began to *see* again.

I witnessed marches through villages and towns. Police trawled platforms, their batons at the ready. I heard shouting and whispers of anger and frustration from the passengers. The relief I had felt the past months faded, fast. A newspaper had been left on the seat next to me. The front page pictured the four most influential leaders – Nehru, Jinnah, Gandhi and Patel. They were smiling and standing beside a tall bookcase in an office. I cast the paper away; the train travelled into the night and I slept.

'*Chai lélo*[109], *chai lélo!*'

I woke up, wrenched from my sleep. We had arrived at a station and it was now morning. A couple of passengers left my carriage.

'*Chai lélo, chai lélo!*'

'*Ek*[110] *chai*,' I said to the boy passing by. He was laden with a tray of small glasses and a pot. He stopped by my window. Finishing the scalding but satisfying tea, I handed the glass back.

'*Shukriya Saab*,' he said and went to the next carriage.

I realised I hadn't eaten anything since I left Panaji, when my stomach did a funny somersault. I remembered auntie's rice and curry and delved into it as the train began to move. Home wasn't so far now.

Sunil was my first port of call after Ma and Papa. Dev was in Simla now and Pooja...I would see her soon after. Sunil hugged and slapped me on the back and his face showed profound relief. I could only guess that he was worried about my mood pre Goa.

We chewed on pieces of sugar cane and shared our stories. Sunil listened attentively as I described my vacation. He liked Stuart and said so.

'He was alright...later on,' I said. 'Now tell me, have you had any news from Dev?'

'Dev sent a brief letter and he is doing well,' said Sunil. 'Without the two of you here...I didn't like it.'

I nodded. 'How is Pooja?' I asked.

'Amit, I don't know. She won't talk and seems to be away – in mind. She doesn't eat much and has gone thin. I don't understand what's happened. She won't tell me. But you are here now, maybe she will tell you.'

I turned my attention to the mango I was eating, avoiding his gaze on my face. I hoped it didn't show my discomfort on the subject.

Sunil nudged my shoulder. 'Amit, look.' Excited, he pointed to a group of English men. He walked a few paces forward and then came back again. He repeated this twice.

'Will you stop that? It's embarrassing,' I said, looking around.

'Amit, don't you realise who they are?'

---

[109] *Chai lélo*, Take some tea (young boys and girls roam the streets and train stations trying to sell tea for a   living).
[110] *Ek*, One

128

'Should I?' I raised an eyebrow.

He tutted. 'Look carefully, they are the same men who were playing that game of...what do they call it...yes, cricket.'

I thought back...I vaguely remembered a lazy afternoon. Dev and Pooja were with us. Sunil and I were arguing the fact that only the white *Babu's* were allowed to play the game, not us – Indians...and then I remembered, even more vaguely, Dev and Pooja leaving together...I felt something had happened between them that day...

'Amit! Let's say hello to them!' Sunil said taking me away from my reverie.

'Yes...' I said and then I saw her. I saw Mary.

Her white and yellow floral dress flowed with her as she gracefully walked towards us. She held yellow roses in one hand; in the other, she held a white cotton-frill umbrella. Her rose-tinted complexion glowed from under a pretty bonnet and I found myself sighing, wanting to caress her cheeks.

My heart thudded evenly but with a passion that I wouldn't have believed I possessed had I not seen her. The wind changed direction; loose hair escaped from under her bonnet, framing her beautiful face. A peel of laughter chimed from her lustrous lips and I felt myself melt.

She saw me then and her smile broadened; her exotic eyes glinting with surprise and delight...oh! I was in love!

'Amit, what are you waiting for? Come on!' Sunil all but pushed me forward for I had forgotten how to walk.

'I'm coming.' I composed myself and followed him.

'Hello, Amit. How are you?' Mary said.

I was astounded, she remembered my name. 'I am very good, *Memsahib*. How are you?'

She laughed. 'It's so nice to see you, both. These are my friends, Jenny and Raquel. Jenny has come from New York and is visiting. She adores India! Raquel is from England.'

'Hello,' I said politely.

'*Memsahib*, do you remember me?' Sunil asked.

Mary thought for a while and then laughed. 'Well, ofcourse. You are Amit's good friend, Sunil. Am I right?'

Sunil bowed before her and the other ladies. I shook my head – what a charade!

'What lovely manners these gentlemen have, Mary. I'm quite impressed,' said one of the ladies.

'Yes, I agree. Amit rescued me; do you remember me telling you?' Mary said. The ladies nodded which I think, was in approval.

'*Memsahib*, do you know them?' Sunil pointed to the men in front. They had stopped talking and were watching the exchange between us. One of them was looking at me; his face was scrunched in concentration. He looked very familiar...my eyes widened...it couldn't be...

'Stuart?' I said, feeling silly.

'By God, it *is* you!' he laughed loudly, startling an old Indian woman. She scurried away, muttering obscenities under her breath. 'What are *you* doing here?'

'I live here, Rajkot is my home,' I said. I was proud.

He shook his head and laughed even louder. 'Now, this is fascinating! Mary, this is Amit, the one I met in Goa – a wonderful chap!'

'And my brother, this is the one that rescued me from my fainting fancy!' Mary said, smiling.

Brother, I thought...so that's why Stuart was so familiar. I laughed, Mary and Stuart were related! I felt instantly better but then, why didn't I recognise her in the photograph in Stuart's Goa house?

'Is this true?' Stuart cut into my thoughts. 'Well, then this is a cause for celebration!' 'Introduce me!' Sunil said in a loud whisper. The ladies giggled.

I rolled my eyes. 'Stuart, this is Sunil – my good friend. He...er...this may sound silly but he has been fascinated by the game you play in that field, cricket.'

Stuart seemed pleased. 'Well, why don't you and Sunil come over on Sunday for lunch and then we can have a game. Yes, it will be fun! I will invite my team. Do you know how to play?'

'No, but I learn fast,' said Sunil.

'Very well. Come along on Sunday, 12 noon sharp! I'd better get back to my chaps now. It was great meeting you!'

Mary and Stuart said goodbye. I was in extremely high spirits – I was to see Mary again. Sunil was a little smug; he had just proved me wrong – even an Indian man can play the white *Babu's* game. Maybe, life wasn't so bad after all, I thought.

~ SUNIL ~

Eleven

Sunil

'Thank-you for coming.' I said goodbye to the last guest. It had been a long day and I was very tired. I wasn't surprised to see the sky closing in – rolls of black cloud pressed through and a ferocious wind howled down the narrow streets. I shivered involuntarily. The storm had arrived.

'*Beta*, come in,' said Ma from somewhere inside.

'Coming,' I said, barely a whisper. I watched a streak of lightning light up a couple's horror-stricken faces as it danced; the rumble of thunder followed. I waited for the rain.

At first, it felt like tiny needles bouncing off my skin and then it hurled down in slanting sheets. I spread my arms and lifted my face towards the heavens. The rain drenched me –releasing me from my troubles.

'Sunil!' Ma shouted.

I sighed and turned to go inside but not before catching a glimpse of the couple hurrying away. The street was now empty.

Ma's expression was disappointed and a little concerned. 'That was not responsible, Sunil. Go and change and then we will talk.'

I kissed Ma on the cheek and gave her a small smile. Back in my room I rubbed a towel over my wet hair and changed my clothes.

'Why is it so hard, why can't the pain go away?' I said, staring at the mirror.

'Time will heal, my son. The good Lord will help you. Trust in him,' Ma spoke from the door frame.

'The Lord shouldn't have taken him away, Ma,' I said a little too roughly but she didn't show surprise at my behaviour.

'It has been a hard day, on all of us. I...will let you be for a while.'

I sighed when she went. I shouldn't take this out on her, it wasn't her fault. Ma needs me as I need her. I should go and apologise.

I made to go but my eyes fell on a framed photograph of Govind. His picture was placed on a small square table and a candle and a divo burned before it. I blinked and tried to fight back the tears but I lost. Today was the anniversary of my father's death.

Govind fell in love with Suzanne at a party. He was one of a selected few to be invited to the annual ball, held at the *Maharaja* Hotel and only because he had been promoted to Chief Pilot. Suzanne, a young girl of eighteen had the attention of many admirers, dressed in a lilac gown; her auburn, wavy hair tumbled down to her waist. Govind was unable to take his eyes off her. They courted for a few months and then he proposed. But there was a problem.

Suzanne was a Christian, an Anglo-Indian. Born and grown up in India, she felt like this land was her home and that she was part of it. She'd always known she would marry an Indian man. When Govind entered her life, she knew she had found him. Telling her parents was the hardest thing she could have done.

'But why Mother? I love him with all my heart!'

'Darling, he is an Indian and not even a Christian. His parents will be against this ridiculous love as we are. They cannot and will not accept you. Be reasonable, you already have many suitors of our calibre, why not court them?'

'Mother, how can you talk like that about caste? It is wrong!'

Her mother put her hands up. 'Do whatever you like darling. I give up; just remember that your father is against this too. He and I will have nothing to do with you if you go ahead and ruin your life!'

Suzanne's mother was right. Govind's parents were averse to this "idiocy" as they put it. His father stopped talking to him and his mother gave him sad, frustrated looks. Who heard of an Indian man marrying a white Memsahib? The whole town would talk! They would be laughed at!

'Ma, Suzanne is Hindustani. She will learn to make *achar* and cook Indian food. She will wear a sari – just as you want. I love her and I am going to marry her, *bas*!' Govind said this with finality. 'I don't care what the world thinks about our relationship. We are getting married in two days at the temple. I would like it if you would give us your blessing.'

Govind's father turned his back on his son just as Suzanne's mother had refused to see her again.

They married in a temple with a couple of their friends present. Neither of their parents witnessed the marriage. They were disowned. The newly married moved to Rajkot and began a new life. Only a handful of people lived there at the time and amazingly they accepted this strange union. Eventually the children came and then, so did their parents.

It was 23 July when my life turned around, although not for the better. I was playing a game of hide and seek with Meera when I saw Papa walk up to the gate. He looked tired and his body seemed to sag.

'Meera, wait here,' I said.

'Why?' She followed my gaze. 'Papa, oh Papa, you came!' she squealed as she ran to him. He picked up my five-year old sister and twirled her around, laughing heartily.

'My little angel. Just look at you, a foot taller and more beautiful!' he said.

'Papa, your leave isn't until December.' I embraced him, very surprised. 'What's wrong, are you ill?'

'I miss my family, *bas*.' Papa gave me a smile. I knew there was a lot more behind his masquerade but I let it be, for now.

Working for the Indian Air Force, meant we saw him only months at a time. It was a celebration when he came home and we would spend it together on a vacation. Meera loved going to the Hill Stations so that was where we always went.

I took Papa's bag and followed him and Meera inside.

'Where is Ma?' Papa pretended to look behind Meera who giggled.

'She's not behind me, she is at the bazaar! Come with me now, I have something to show you. Uncle Sebastian gave me a new dolly!' Meera said excitedly.

'Meera, leave Papa alone, can't you see he is tired? Go and play with Kavita. Papa, Ma will be back by two.' Meera stuck her tongue out at me.

Papa knelt down beside her and kissed her cheek. 'Let me have a quick wash and something to eat, and then we'll play.' Meera went away; satisfied that Papa would still be here when she got back.

Three hours crawled by as we waited for Ma to come home. Papa fidgeted and glanced outside many times, impatient for her, impatient to tell us the real reason why he was here. His forehead was creased in worry and it made me uneasy. I, too, was fidgety and couldn't sit for long. We talked a little. I asked about his work and he asked about my studies and my friends. When I told him about Amit, Memsahib and Stuart, he became interested and I was able to distract

135

him for a while, but soon, our conversation dried out and Papa began to wear the same expression as before. I sighed inwardly and went over to Meera. She had come back from Kavita's house.

'It is boring,' she said and began to play with her dolly.

'Come and talk to us, little one,' said Papa.

Meera became animated at once and chatted away as we listened. Papa asked her questions about her doll and her friends and she answered, her eyes lighting up. Time ticked on.

'Meera! Sunil! Come and take these bags from me.' Our heads turned towards Ma at the same time. She froze – her attention straight to Papa.

'Govind?' she said. Papa took her into his arms and twirled her around. He kissed her and hugged her again.

'I missed you,' he said.

'But...Govind, is everything alright? Why are you here?'

'I'm fine, just fine. I missed everyone, that's all.' Papa was looking at Meera and me. I thought I saw a flicker of pain or sadness. I couldn't be sure.

Ma smiled tentatively. 'Well, I'm glad you are here. I've missed you so much, you know. Have you had anything to eat?'

The atmosphere mellowed then. Meera demanded Papa tell us stories of his "travels" and he plunged in with enthusiasm. Ma listened for a bit, sitting next to Papa, holding his hand. When my stomach grumbled, they laughed. Ma went to cook, shaking her head in amusement. I watched Papa from afar, pretending to be reading. I knew there was more to this.

Finally at eight, Meera fell asleep on Papa's lap and he carried her to her bed. The time had arrived – the time of truth. I wanted to stay and hear it but Ma and Papa needed to be alone. I made an excuse to study for a paper. There was silence when I walked out; they were waiting to be alone. As soon as I was in the shadows, they began to talk. I stood still, guiltily listening.

'You are wondering why I am here – home so early? You won't ask until I say something...you have such patience, my dear,' Papa said.

'I knew it was important to you to wait. The children, especially Sunil – he is so perceptive.'

I smiled grimly in the dark.

'Yes, he has been watching me all afternoon but he hasn't probed or harassed me for answers. Even now, he is pretending to do some studying, just to leave us alone. He is such a good boy.'

'Govind, tell me the truth. I don't want to be kept guessing anymore now, it's killing me.' Ma's voice broke and I heard a sniff.

'Suzanne, oh my Suzanne. Please, don't cry.'

'What is it, Govind? Is there another woman?'

Papa chuckled darkly. 'They are drafting me to England, Suzanne. I am to fly the planes in the war.'

There was silence and it stretched on for a long while. It was Ma who spoke next.

'Why you?' It was just above a whisper.

'What God decides, what they decide, there is no difference. If not me, then another. They chose me, Suzanne.'

'When do you have to go?'

'In five days.'

My gasp was sharp and painful. Five days, that was all I would have with my father? That's all Ma will have with her husband?

'No, you can't go so soon. How can you come home and tell me this? What about Meera and Sunil, how are they to live without you? What if...Govind, I will never be able to...you will have to tell them that you can't go.'

I heard Papa sigh. 'Darling nothing will happen to me. Listen, I will be back. The war can't go on forever.'

I went away, refusing to understand his reasoning. I paced in my room; trying not to think but my mind wasn't cooperating. I tried to sleep instead but it didn't come. I waited in the silence, a silence broken occasionally with Ma's sobbing.

It was a relief when I woke up. The chirping of the birds was all I could hear, otherwise it was quiet. It was unsettling. The brightness outside indicated a full sun and I wondered what time it was. I got dressed and cautiously made my way to the kitchen.

'Sunil, good, you're awake now.' Ma's smile didn't seem quite real.

'Where are Meera and Papa?' I asked looking around.

'Papa has gone out for a while and Meera is out in the back, playing...' Ma was staring away from me.

'Ma?'

137

'Would you like some breakfast?' Ma took out a pan and some other things which weren't necessary. She was trying to keep busy.

'Yes, a little then.' I sat down and watched her put my breakfast together. She talked idly as I ate; her mind obviously on the conversation yesterday. I put my head down and finished my breakfast.

Papa came home sooner that I thought he would. He called all of us together to the family room.

'Sunil *beta*, Meera, my angel, I have something to tell you.'

Ma turned away, her eyes looked sore.

'You're not staying, are you?' I said abruptly. Papa was startled but answered my question, changing his expression to resignation.

'No, I'm afraid not. Well...here it is – '

'Don't worry Papa, I heard it all last night,' I said. I pushed my chair back and stood up.

'Oh...then, I am glad that you have had time to think about it.'

I looked at him, surprised and confused. 'You are not angry with me?'

'No, you should be angry with *me*, *beta*. You have every right to be.'

'Papa, what are you and *Bhai* talking about?' Meera asked.

Papa bent down and held her hands. 'My sweet darling, my sweet angel...your Papa has to go away again, this time it will be for a long time.' He looked at Ma and then, cleared his throat. 'I don't know when my boss will give me another vacation.' He didn't say "if I come back" but we all understood it.

'But you just came back, Papa.' Tears began to run down Meera's cheeks. Papa took her into his arms. Ma put her arms around them and cried too. I stayed, rooted.

'Sunil?' Papa said. Ma took Meera away to another room. I turned towards him.

'I understand this is hard. I thought you would understand...'

'I do, Papa. It's my heart that is rebelling, not my mind. It is... painful not knowing if I will see you again.'

'Let's go for a walk,' Papa said.

We sat on small hill, which overlooked the rice paddies. I could see Neha's house a little way from the fields. I smiled.

138

'Is there something amusing?' Papa said. Then, his face cleared. 'She is special, isn't she?'

I nodded but was embarrassed. Papa seemed delighted.

'I brought you here...so I could show you where your future will be, *beta*.' He pointed to the house. 'It will be where that girl is. I like her and I like her family; they are nice people. I know how much you like that girl also and I give you my blessing, to one day, marry her.

'I know that my future is uncertain and I hope to God that he will spare me to see the day that you marry. Meera is still young, she will come to terms quicker if...well, you know. And your Ma, I love her very much. If I had a choice, it would be to stay with you.'

Tears filled my eyes. 'Papa, do you have to go?'

'I'm sorry Sunil. But I will write to you every month, I will keep that promise,' Papa said, his eyes bright, He held me tightly.

Papa died in an air-collision. The two planes spiralled down into mountain peaks, killing all four pilots. Ma cried for days; she would read his letters which he'd sent over the year – yes, he'd kept that promise. His wedding ring was now around Ma's neck. For me, it left a hole in my heart which could never be mended.

Time carried on as it was supposed to. So did I, not understanding how a year could pass by without my father...

'Happy Birthday, Papa.' I blew out the candle.

Neha rested her head on my chest as I absently played with her fingers. The air was crisp, I was happy and calm.

'I saw Papa in my dream last night. He said thank you for the birthday gift,' I said.

'Birthday gift?' Neha lifted her head.

'Yes, *you* are the birthday gift. He said you are just right for me.' I moved a tendril of hair from her face. 'I wish Papa could have met you – properly. He would have been so proud. He told me, before he went...that he wanted to see you as a daughter-in-law...and...Ma and Meera like you...'

'I like them too.' Neha smiled. 'What are you saying, Sunil?'

'Do you remember when you asked me if I wanted to marry you?'

'Yes, that was a long time ago and you didn't answer me then. Papa was concerned, he wanted to know if you were serious,' Neha said.

'Well, he should be concerned,' I said, laughing. But she wasn't smiling.

'Papa thinks all girls should be married. I am seventeen; he thinks it will be difficult finding me a suitable boy who will take a grown girl like me.'

I took both her hands and we stood up. My laugh was replaced by anxiety.

'Neha, will you marry me?' I said.

'Sunil, be serious!'

'I am. Will you?'

Her eyes widened. 'You *are* serious. Oh Sunil, I don't know what to say...saaché[111]?'

'Are you saying no?'

Neha flung herself onto me, wrapping her arms around my neck. She buried her face into my shoulder.

'You don't know how happy I am,' I sighed in response.

'I have something to show you,' Neha smiled with a tinge of sadness. 'Come with me.'

Neha lived with her father Shankarji and sister, Anjali – away from the centre of the village. Her house stood on a hill overlooking the rice paddies and a little river. Wild yellow and white flowers blossomed around her house; their fragrant scent filling the air.

'When I think of Ma, when I miss her, I come here. She used to make clay pots right there on this veranda, in that corner.' Neha pointed to the spot. 'Anjali and I would sit on the swing and she would sing to us as we watched her work. She was part of us.'

'I can believe that.' I thought of Papa.

'I wanted to show you this.' Neha opened her palm to reveal a box. The lid was embossed in silver with an image of *Lord Ganesh*[112]. It was a miniature chest made of wood and brass; it was stunning. Neha opened the lid and delicately took out a silver necklace. The

---

[111] *Saaché,* Really (Gujarati)

[112] *Lord Ganesh*, a Hindu God – the Elephant God - worshipped at the beginning of Hindu rituals and when commencing new beginnings – a protector against bad tidings.

pendant was skilfully crafted – a circle of small stones surrounding a sapphire.

'Ma gave this to me a few days before she passed away. It was the night of *Diwali*[113] when she went. She lit the last divo and went peacefully in my father's arms, holding mine and Anjali's hands. She was smiling; she had no fear. It was as if she was sleeping.

'She told me she wanted me to wear this necklace on my wedding day. She told me she would be there too. I didn't understand at first – of course she would be there. Ma knew though, she meant she would be there in spirit.' Neha became quiet as she gazed into the distance.

'I think your Papa will be honoured to see you wear it at our wedding,' I said.

'And I will *beta*.' Shankarji appeared.

'Papa!' Neha's face turned crimson.

'Sunil is a good boy. I give you two my blessing with all my heart. Your Ma will be happy too.' Shankarji took Neha into his arms. 'Why didn't you tell me?'

'Sunil asked me today,' she whispered.

'I am glad to hear it,' said Shankarji.

'I'm sorry sir, I should have asked in the traditional way. Please forgive me.' I felt guilty. It was a wonder he didn't throw me out of the house.

'I've known for a long time that you wanted to marry my daughter, Sunil but I wasn't sure when. I was worried you would leave her...but now, I can relax. I know you will do right by her. I am very pleased.' He turned to Neha. 'Why didn't you tell me about the necklace?'

'I was embarrassed Papa. I wanted to, I really did,' said Neha.

'*Beta*, I will be honoured if I can adorn you with the necklace on your special day, will you let me?' Shankarji asked.

'Of course Papa, I would like that.'

Anjali came bounding in. 'Why is everyone happy?' she asked, taking a bite from an apple. 'Has Kaki Rangma died? Well, that is a relief!'

Anjali, Neha's younger sister by a few years, looked exactly like her but she was very hard work.

---

[113] ***Diwali***, a Hindu festival celebrating the return of Lord Rama & Sita to Rama's kingdom after fourteen years of exile. A path was lit to welcome them home.

'Anjali! That is not a nice thing to say!' scolded her big sister. 'Anyway, we have some good news. Sunil and I are going to be married.'

Anjali's eyes went wide 'Sunil is going to be my *jijaji*[114]! Thank-you! Thank you!' She threw herself onto me.

'Thank you?' I laughed.

'Yes, that Kajulal has been eyeing my sister for years now and I was scared he was going to take her away. I am glad she has you, you are much better!'

'Who is Kajulal?' I raised my eyebrows at Neha.

'Just someone – not important.' She had a twinkle in her eye.

Naturally Ma was overjoyed when Neha showed her engagement ring. The two ladies danced around the room. Shankarji watched with amused eyes, occasionally shaking silently with laughter. Anjali and Meera were ecstatic; they were going to be sisters! Shankarji and Ma talked about the wedding preparations and laughed at old stories.

'But *Bhai Saab*, I will not take any dowry. I don't believe in it. Govind would not have wanted it either,' Ma said.

'But I have the money. For my two daughters, I have saved,' Shankarji protested.

'You can use that for Anjali's education. It's my final decision.'

We celebrated that night with good food, friends and family. Pooja kissed Neha on the cheek and welcomed her as a future sister-in-law but was subdued...again, I couldn't understand why. Amit embraced me whilst Pooja pulled my cheek.

'I am very happy for you both,' she said. I hugged her closely but felt something wrong.

'Pooja, is something is not right, you would tell me, wouldn't you?' You are happy?'

Pooja answered too quickly. 'I am always happy, silly Sunil. Now, stop worrying about me, Neha *Bhabhi* is looking for you.'

I hugged her again, something was bothering me about her and I wasn't happy about it at all. I would talk to her later. 'Ma, I am going to do some errands,' I said, getting on my bike.

---

[114] *Jijaji*, Brother-in-law (sister's husband)

142

'If you are going to the post-office, please take the envelopes from the table and send them for me,' Ma said. She cleared her throat and gestured me over.

'Yes Ma?'

She kissed me on my cheek. 'I am very happy!' she sang. I rolled my eyes.

'I love you Ma.' I smiled and was away.

The weather had turned windy and dry. I rode my bike furiously in the red dust. The hot air blew into my face, making me squint. I was nearly there.

The post-office was a small wooden box that stood near the railway tracks. This was where the letters were sent and received and where a letter writer sat, every day, writing for the villagers who weren't able to for themselves.

They would line up for the service, either wanting one line or a paragraph written to be sent as a letter. As they waited, they talked amongst themselves. Some boasted that their son was a barrister in Bombay and some boasted they had a doctor in the family. Some cried that they had to sell their livestock to pay for their daughter's wedding and some cried that they were not rich enough. There were no secrets in the village.

Today the post-office was empty of customers. '*Bhaiya*, these letters need to be posted.' I dropped some money onto the counter. 'Where is everyone?'

'Today is a slow day Sunil *Bhai*. I will be going home soon. Oh but – I heard you are engaged. That is very good!' said the post man.

'*Shukriya*,' I smiled. '*Chalo*, I will be going now.' I got onto my bike again. I had left the post-office far behind in a matter of minutes.

The wind was fierce now and I shielded my eyes. The dust swirled around me, causing me to come to a stop. The air was a mass of red and brown particles flying in all directions. An old man struggled on the other side of the road. He too, was fighting his way through the hazardous dust. I didn't pay much attention until two men in dark clothing ran across the track. They came to the old man and pushed him to the ground.

'Eh!' I shouted. I began to cycle again, trying to catch speed.

One of the men threw a bag down next to the old man and then the two ran off. That was strange but also suspicious. The old man seemed hurt – he was curled over. I cycled faster. I called out but the wind carried my voice away.

Before I could reach him, a police car stopped at the old man. Two policemen got out and seemed to be trying to converse with him. I kept my distance, trying to hear. The wind raged on, making it impossible to do so. Then, it suddenly stopped, like someone had closed the doors: it became quiet. It was finally clear and I recognised the man. It couldn't be. I must be mistaken. I rubbed my eyes. I shook my head...I couldn't believe it...it was Shankarji...

'*Saab*!' I yelled but they didn't hear me. They lifted Shankarji and put him in the car. In a cloud of dust, they sped away.

Twelve

The police station

I saw images of torture, of pleading even. The man was old and frail, who used a walking stick for support. He was a kind man who loved his two daughters. One who was going to be married. Yet, this man was in jail, away from everyone he loved.

The train caught speed as my mind did. My thoughts could not stray away from my future father-in-law and the injustice. I watched Neha who had fallen asleep, her head resting against the window. I made her comfortable and covered her with a blanket – she slept peacefully, something which she hadn't done since her father's arrest. It had been two long months...

I'd cycled straight to Neha's house on the day they arrested Shankarji. It had just begun to rain but I managed to get to the balcony before the downpour. I shook my jacket off and slung it on the chair before going inside.

Neha was embroidering a sari when I entered. She was wearing her black-rimmed glasses, paying close attention to detail. Her hair was back combed into a high bun and her face was a mix of intensity and loveliness. I hated what I was about to do next.

She saw my expression and immediately put the needle down. Before she could stand up, I had already taken her hands into mine. I crouched before her, looking into her indigo-black eyes. I told her what I'd witnessed. Comprehension slowly dawned on her face – I waited, patiently.

'But....Sunil, Papa is innocent. How can they take him away, without proof?' Sudden tears rolled down her cheeks.

'They found a bag next to him,' I gently reminded her. 'I know it wasn't his but think what they saw – an Indian man with a bag that looked suspicious.'

'Are you saying it's Papa's fault?' Neha's eyes flashed. I quickly back tracked.

'I'm not saying that. I am on your side. Look, *Papaji*[115] was there at the wrong time,' I said.

---

[115] *Papaji*, Sunil calls his father in law – Papaji. 'JI' associated with respect.

Neha wiped her tears. 'What do we do now? I want to see him, Sunil.'

'We will,' I said. I looked around. 'Where is Anjali?'

'She is at a friend's house. She won't be back until eight...why?'

'I don't want her to come home and not find you or *Papaji* home. It will worry her. I think it would be best if you stay here – '

'No, I am coming –'

'Neha, listen to what I have to say first,' I snapped and instantly regretted it. Neha's eyes brimmed with tears again and I cursed myself, silently.

'I'm sorry, I'm sorry. I didn't mean to get angry.' I took her into my arms but she pushed me away. 'Neha, I said I'm sorry.'

'My father is in jail, Sunil. I am going to the police station with or without you.' Her face was turned away from me, her arms crossed against her chest.

Oh God, I raked my hands over my hair. I waited for her anger to subside. I didn't speak but let her be. I cursed myself again. How could I have been so thoughtless? Her father just got arrested!

Ma warned me of my anger. She told me to hold onto it, tight, and to think before I speak. It was one of my worst faults. I was getting married now and I have to begin taking responsibilities. Well, this is a good start, I said to myself.

I looked at Neha then and was surprised to see her watching me.

'I –' I began but she shook her head.

'I'm sorry, Sunil. I shouldn't cut you off like that. Papa told me to control my impatience.' She looked at me from under her eyelashes. We both smiled.

'We will both go to the police station. I will ask Ma to be here before Anjali comes home – she will explain everything.' I went to her and kissed her cheek. 'Now, let's not argue any longer and wash your pretty face – *Papaji* wouldn't want to see you like this, right? Go, get ready.'

Neha was really quick. I took her hand and we left for the station.

Rajkot didn't have a police station and the only nearest one was in the next town. I could only assume Shankarji was taken there. A twenty-minute journey felt like an hour.

The station was newly built and it stood on a *nuker*[116] of two roads. A bicycle repair shop and a *Paan* shop stood on either of side the stone building. People walked up and down the road; some entering the police station and some loitering around. Tall trees swayed in the breeze, sunlight filtering through – casting patterns on the brickwork.

The owner of the repair shop was not there today. Instead, a small boy was taking custom. He was fixing a bicycle chain. I noticed his clothes were blackened with grease and he was painfully thin, but his attention was focussed on his work. In contrast, two men in clean, crisp shirts stood at the *Paan* shop, chewing on betel leaves. They were showing each other their sparkly watches; they didn't look friendly. I ushered Neha into the police station.

I looked around, trying to get some attention. Everyone was busy and no one stopped to look in our direction. There were three empty seats by the window.

I indicated those to Neha and we sat down when a man was brought in. He looked to be in his twenties; his hair was unkempt and he was unshaven. The man's eyes were wild with fear, the colour of his face blue and black. A section of his cheek was criss-crossed in red. Neha turned her face away.

'*Saab*, please let me go, I didn't do it. Please, I have five small children... my wife…they will worry. Please, *Saab*,' the man pleaded.

'You can tell the court,' said the policeman. He unlocked the prisoner's handcuffs and shoved him into a cell and then locked it.

'No, *Saab*! Please. I didn't set the municipal building on fire. It was them. I can give names!'

This caught the policeman's attention. 'Is that so? You will be interviewed later today. For now, keep quiet.' He turned his back on the prisoner and went away to deal with something else.

'Can I help you?' The voice came from a desolate corner of the station. The man was in the shadows and I couldn't see him. I took Neha's hand and we walked up to the desk. Some files lay in a pile

---

[116] *Nuker*, Corner

dangerously, like they could topple any second. A plaque sat beside the pile, which read "Constable Rai." This, Rai, turned on his lamp. I was surprised to see a constable so young, not many years above my age. His face was tired and dark circles shadowed his eyes.

'*Saab*, we are here to find someone,' I said.

'Is he lost or missing?' asked the Constable, taking a pen in his hand. 'Sit down, please.'

'It's my father, Shankarji Mukherjee,' said Neha. 'He has been arrested. *Saab*, do you know where he is?'

Rai observed us for a moment and then spoke. 'He was arrested, why?'

'We don't know,' I said.

'I see.'

'What do you mean? Is there a problem?' I asked.

Rai rubbed his eyes and then drank some water. He stretched and yawned.

'*Saab*?' I prompted.

'I'm sorry; it has been a long forty-eight hours. Shankarji Mukherjee - your father. I have no record of such a person.'

'He was arrested. I saw it myself. If he wasn't brought here, then where?' I demanded, banging my fist on the desk. Rai raised an eyebrow. 'I'm sorry...about that, but you have to understand. Surely someone knows...doesn't someone have a responsibility to inform the family?'

'It is not so simple,' said Rai. 'There are procedures we have to follow, administration work – a report has to be written and filed – '

'I don't care about any procedures, Constable Rai. Just tell me where my father in law is kept prisoner!' I was shouting and I realised I may have overstepped the mark – all noise ceased and everyone turned to stare. Rai looked bemused. I cleared my throat and spoke in a low volume. 'Please, help us.'

'Everyone get back to work,' Rai said and once more there was a hum of noise. He looked at me. 'Mr...'

'Please call me Sunil.'

'Sunil, in a police station, you must control your temper. Take care to remember that. In the meantime, fill in this form with both of your names and address. I want you to write down everything you saw, every word, understand? Now, I will go and make a few enquiries. Please excuse me.'

Whilst he was gone, I wrote down my statement. He came back just as I put my pen down. He looked at our names on the paper and then at Neha.

'I have found your father, Neha *ji*. He is currently in Nagarwal jail but will be transported to a jail in Bombay- this will be in the early hours.' He scanned the form.

'*Saab*, why was he jailed?' asked Neha.

'The charges against your father are serious. He is seen as a class 1 prisoner – he was caught with a bag of criminal material. Sunil, you say that the bag was "thrown" at Shankarji?'

'Yes *Saab*,' I said.

'Thankfully, it didn't go off. The items in the bag were highly explosive. This is something which is not taken lightly. If we were to capture these men, would you recognise them?' Rai directed the question to me.

'I'm afraid not.'

'Neha *ji*, without evidence that Shankarji was not part of some plan to immobilise the *Raj*, killing innocent civilians, there is not much I can do.'

'My father is a noble man, *Saab*. A well respected man. It is absurd to even think he would do such a thing.' Neha's eyes seemed to burn in disbelief.

'Neha *ji*, many noble men, like your father can change. This does not mean his is evil but that he may be a great believer in this war for Independence.'

'You are assuming he is a criminal, Rai *Saab*. My father is the headmaster of the village school. He teaches good behaviour, respect and obedience to the children. How can you say that he would be involved in something ridiculous as a plan to sabotage the *Raj*?' Neha was incredulous.

'It's the facts, whether you want to believe it or not.'

'*Saab*, I want to see my father,' Neha said.

Rai seemed to think about this for a moment. 'I will try and arrange it as soon as it is possible but under the circumstances of his arrest, I cannot tell you when that will be. You will have to bear some patience.'

Neha wanted to argue I was certain but I cut in before she could utter a word. 'Thank you, we will wait. If you could send a note when you have a date.'

Before me, Shankarji lay in a bed of white flowers. His eyes were vacant of activity as he stared at the ceiling. Neha crouched before him, her body heaving. His thin, bruised body seemed like it could crush...

'Neha,' Shankarji's wafer-thin, papery voice spoke. He turned to look at me, his eyes suddenly ablaze in red.

'*Jijaji?*'

'Argh!' I shouted.

'Oh, did I scare you?' Anjali said, matter-of-factly.

'Anjali, what do you want?' I clutched my heart.

'Auntie wants you,' she said, meaning Ma.

'Tell her I'm coming.'

People normally had disturbing dreams in the night but I had them in the day! Sitting idle was hazardous to my health, for the "dreams" would come to me, with no warning and no provocation. If I had these thoughts, then did Neha?

Shankarji was a proud man and truthful. He believed in *Gandhi's* morals – to be truthful and wise, to love your friend and foe. He taught this to his pupils but to be involved in such a crime was unspeakable. Neha was right, it was ridiculous!

I persuaded Neha to stay at my house, Anjali too. Anjali agreed right away – she missed her father terribly and didn't want to spend any time in her home without him. Neha, however, was reluctant.

'For how long, Sunil? And what will the villagers say? We are not yet married.'

'You think too much about what the villagers will say,' I said gruffly. I was disappointed with her reaction. 'I don't like you or Anjali staying alone. It's not safe.'

'Please *didi*, listen to Sunil *Bhai*,' said Anjali.

Neha's expression changed from confusion to uncertainty. There was doubt in her eyes.

'I will stay at Amit's house if it will make you feel better,' I said.

'I don't want to make you leave your own house, Sunil!'

'Neha, I don't want any arguments. Pack your bags, you both are coming home with me,' I said with finality.

Ma greeted Neha and Anjali warmly. Meera tagged Anjali away to play and Ma sat with Neha. I wasn't sure if I should go or stay. I decided to stay.

'You are very welcome, my dear,' said Ma. 'I want you to be comfortable here. This is your home too. I don't want you to worry about anything. Meera will share with Anjali and you can have Sunil's room. Sunil will stay at Amit's house for a little while. I have arranged it all with Amit's mother so don't worry about it. She understands. And Sunil,' she said.

'Yes Ma,' I said.

'You are not to lie around Amit's house, I expect you to help without being asked. And don't eat all the food tonight, leave some for tomorrow.'

Then, Neha laughed. It was a good sound.

'Amit knows I get hungry,' I protested.

It had been a long day and it was time for sleep. I said goodnight to Ma but she sensed that I wanted to be alone with Neha; she made an excuse to check on the girls.

'I know this is hard on you but I want you to understand that you are not alone. I love you and I will always be here when you need me.' I kissed Neha's forehead. 'Now, try and sleep and I will see you in the morning.'

As I turned to leave, Neha grabbed my hand. 'I love you. Thank you so much.'

I put a finger to her lips. 'I love you too.' I touched her nose and left.

Over the next few weeks, Neha tried to do as much as she could at the school. She took over the jobs that Shankarji did and I looked after the accounts. She put on a brave face and taught the children but the spark was gone. The children knew it too and soon their parents began to get concerned.

I was in the school office going over the figures and Neha was marking some work. Another teacher – Hemant, was preparing for his class. We all looked up when Shushmita *Ben*, a parent of a very observant boy, Narendra, came knocking on the door.

'Please, come in, Shushmita *Ben*,' said Neha, standing up. 'How can I help you?'

151

She came straight to the point. 'I am worried, Neha *ji*. Narendra came to me yesterday and he said he doesn't want to do his school work anymore. I asked him why and said because *didi* is upset.' She paused then carried on.

'Neha *ji*, I understand that you are trying your best what with *Masterji*[117] not here...but I don't think you should teach, for the moment. The children are not happy and they are picking up this negativity from you. It's not only me, but the other mothers' feel the same. Forgive me...but maybe you should...leave for a while.'

I couldn't believe what I was hearing. I put my pen down with force and gave her a steely look. 'Neha is a very good teacher, Shushmita *Ben*. The children love her and all the other teachers respect her and are supporting her in her time of need. I understand your concern but she will not stop teaching.'

'Sunil...maybe she is right,' Neha said in a small voice.

'No Neha, you are not doing this,' I said.

'Neha *ji*, Sunil is right,' said Hemant. 'We will all help. If you want, I can take over some of your classes.'

Neha smiled, sadly. 'It is very good of you to do this but I think Shushmita *Ben* is right. I can't do this to the children.'

Shushmita *Ben* looked smug. 'Then I shall be going,' she said. I glared after her.

Neha didn't go back to school as I hoped she would. Instead, she listened to that witch! Neha stayed subdued and helped Ma around the house but Ma was sharp. She took her under her wing and decided to teach her some cooking, which she learnt from my *Dadi* and the cooks from my *Nani's* home.

Being Anglo-Indian, Ma had grown up watching two cooks – one was an Indian woman and the other was a white woman. The two, although so different, worked side by side amiably; Ma never heard an argument. It was a very unusual setting. Sitting cross-legged, on a stool, she would watch them advising and teaching one another and that was how Ma learnt too. After her marriage, she experimented and Papa loved it. He grew fond of her cooking and his requests were never ignored. Now, Ma was passing this knowledge onto her future daughter-in-law. I liked it, very much.

---

[117] *Masterji*, Professor

A few weeks passed and still we had no news from Rai. Neha was becoming increasingly agitated and on many occasions, I found her sitting by the window, looking out, in search of Rai – I presumed. She wouldn't admit it when I asked her about it but she didn't want to talk either. I sat with her sometimes and tried to distract her but sometimes I felt like I was invisible. My patience wore thin at times and I had to stop myself from saying something that would cause her more hurt.

One day I couldn't take it any longer.

'Come with me.' I took her hand and pulled her towards the door.

'Where to? Sunil, let go of my hand!' Neha slapped me.

I stood, frozen, surprised and hurt. Neha looked at me with wide, apologetic eyes.

'I'm sorry....please Sunil, I didn't mean to....it just happened...' She began to cry.

I couldn't speak. I was too shocked. Neha, the lovely woman who I fell in love with and am still in love with – was gentle and kind, she would never do this. She wasn't right in the mind, I could see that. I must forget what she did, it was not her! Then, why was I feeling like I didn't know her anymore?

'Sunil, please forgive me.' Neha was crying openly now.

I shook my hurt away and walked slowly to her, taking her into my arms. My hands caressed her back as she sobbed into my shirt. I decided to speak to Ma. Neha had finally succumbed to sleep. I crept out, closing the door quietly behind me. Ma was reading beside an oil lamp when I came to her.

'Ma, can I speak to you?'

'Yes dear, what is it?' Ma put her book down.

'I am worried about Neha. She has changed...she...I don't know, but I think we need to do something about her behaviour. Sitting by the window, staring out, is not healthy.'

'*Beta*, there was a time when I would worry about your father, when he was away in England. I prayed to Jesus and *Ganesh* when I thought I would crumple with grief. Take Neha to God, Sunil. Let her feel lightened. That's all we can do.'

I took Neha to the temple. We offered flowers and fruit and bowed our heads at Ganesh's feet. I prayed for Shankarji's release, to be safe and happy. I could only guess what Neha wished for: to see her father again.

Our prayers were answered.

Rai arrived with some news the next day. Ma and Neha were cutting vegetables and I was humouring Anjali and Meera with my jokes. There was a knock on the door.

'May I come in?' Rai said.

'Constable Rai,' I said, for a moment, bewildered. 'Oh, yes, please come in. Ma, Neha, come and see who has come!' I called. They came quickly.

'*Namaste* Ma-*ji*, Neha *ji*,' said Rai.

'*Namaste*.' Ma gestured to a chair.

Rai looked at Neha, who now, leaned against the wall; she was shaking. I went and put my arm around her and she instantly relaxed, but her eyes were wide.

'What's the news, Rai *Saab*?' I asked.

'I have news that Shankarji was taken seriously ill and has been admitted to hospital.'

'Dear Jesus, is he...alright?' Ma asked.

'He had a heart attack but he has recovered.'

'*Hé Ram*!' Neha cried, her arms dropping to her side. I held her tightly.

'I'm sorry to give you such news but you will be pleased to hear that he has been granted visitors – it was his wish to see Neha and Sunil a lot sooner...now they have agreed.'

'What about Anjali?' asked Neha.

'Shankarji doesn't want her to see him. He feels she is too young and wouldn't be able to bear it, so just you and Sunil. I have arranged the train tickets. It will leave in one week's time, at nine in the evening. Your visiting hour is at two in the afternoon, on the day you reach Bombay.'

Neha broke down. '*Bhaiya* – thank you so much...'

'I understand how you feel; to lose someone and wait hopefully for their return...I hope your father comes home, I really do.'

'Who did you lose?' I asked.

'My brother. He was jailed for robbing a rich man's house. He didn't do the robbery, I am certain of that. They took him and he never came home.'

'What happened?' I asked.

'I can't talk about it,' said Rai. I saw something more in his eyes and understood. His brother was killed. Rai stood up to leave. 'I must go. Don't miss your train.'

'Won't you stay for some food?' asked Ma.

'It's very kind of you to ask me but I'm afraid I won't be able to. Thank you.' Rai left promptly.

He was an unusually good man. Not many would go to such lengths as he had for us. God bless him, I thought, watching him walk down the narrow dirt road.

PART THREE

Love and Pain

~
DEV
~

Thirteen

Jail
January 1944

It was not yet seven in the morning when the jailors came for me. The cell door opened and Mansingh – the jailor who usually paired with Haricharan – ordered me to stand up. Another jailor, whom I didn't know, was outside. I wondered where Haricharan was.

'I said, let's go!' shouted Mansingh when I didn't stand up on his command.

'Another beating session?' I said, wryly.

'Do as you're told, then there will be no beating. Get moving!'

I was handcuffed and Mansingh pushed me in the direction of the torture cell. That's what we all called it for no one came out of it, untouched or undamaged. I let out a humourless laugh.

'Don't you get tired of the same routine, time and time again, Mansingh? Tell me, what do the white people give you in return? Special pleasures?' This time my laugh was black. I shouldn't provoke him but I couldn't help it. I hated the sight of him! Mansingh looked at me murderously. I held my breath – I could feel his wrath coming...

Mansingh kicked the back of my leg; my knees gave way, making me drop to the cold floor. I was pulled up roughly.

'*Kuthé*!' I yelled. 'Coward, traitor!'

'Now, now, Dev. Control your tongue.' He began to take his belt off. 'Strip him from the waist down!' he ordered his juniors. I swore loudly and he laughed.

My trousers and pants were pulled down and I stood there, naked, for everyone to see. There were no jibes, no calling, just silence. The terror of what was to come had silenced all. Mansingh sneered and kicked me hard between my thighs. My eyes watered; I bit my lip.

He threw his baton aside. I closed my eyes.

Five torturing welts cut deep into my lower body. I, now, crouched before him, my face at his boot – my shriek echoed down the hall. It lasted for one minute but the damage had been done. The jailors dragged me back to my cell, no longer needing the torture cell. Blood streaked behind me – a nice job for another sorry inmate...

'Never cross me again,' Mansingh snarled.

The clang of a cell door alerted my dearest friend. I briefly saw his horrified face before I collapsed.

'You are not doing yourself any favours, Dev. Why don't you tell them the truth? Why do you aggravate Mansingh like that? By now, you should know his anger,' said Haricharan. I saw frustration in his eyes as he dabbed me with ointment. It was midnight and he'd sneaked in my cell, in the dark. I couldn't understand why he took risks. He shook his head. 'You are so much like Rakesh.'

That stung. '*Bhai* wasn't anything like me. He was a much better man.' I winced. 'Haricharan, I have tried to tell them, they won't listen. I want to go home – I have done nothing - I wasn't part of it! I keep telling them!'

Haricharan patted my shoulder. 'Take rest, Dev. Someday, very soon, you will go home, alive.' He closed the cell on his way out.

The grey cell was stuffy and suffocating. It was still dark when I woke up. The stench of urine reached me but I ignored it.

'This is not right,' sighed my dearest friend and my cell partner, Shankarji. He sat with his back to the wall and his arms around his thin frame.

'What can we do? We are powerless,' I said.

'Maybe so…do you know why I am here, Dev?'

'It wasn't your fault, Shankarji. It was a cruel thing to do – that bag wasn't yours.'

'No, no. I am not talking about that.' Shankarji shook his head. 'I believe God brought me here for a reason Dev, and that is to look after you. You are a good person, I know that. You have done nothing wrong. You have survived this jail unlike so many others. But you have a weakness, Dev. You don't believe in yourself. You can be strong and if you learn to control your temper, one day you will leave here and be a free man. God has brought me here to guide you, to help you from yourself.'

I thought about what he said. 'Shankarji, the truth is that if I didn't have you here with me, I would have been dead. I have noticed – how you take care of me, offer me words that are soothing, that heal my heart from within – I am thankful to you. But you ask me to believe in myself; that is impossible.'

162

Shankarji looked sad. 'What happened to you Dev?'

I looked at him – the headmaster of my village school. He should be home, with his daughters, teaching in his school. Instead, here he was, a frail man, his life uncertain. How could he believe in God and his goodness?

'My brother was hanged, Shankarji,' I said ruthlessly and devoid of emotion. 'They just killed him. That's what happened to me.'

'Yes...Rakesh had been a bright student of mine...it was very unfortunate...he was a good boy. But Dev, what happened to him, won't happen to you,' said Shankarji.

I watched a rat scamper across the floor. Even he was a prisoner here. You will find no food here, just heartache, I thought. I faced my wise friend and took his hand in mine.

'I am scared...so scared. I want to get out of here. I want to go home,' I said.

'And you will *beta*. There are people out there who love you. You are not alone. Dev, does your Ma or Papa know that you are in jail?'

'They don't know.'

'What about Sunil, Amit or Pooja? You all were very close.'

'We still are good friends. They are my family.'

'Dev, do you know, Sunil is marrying my daughter, Neha? I am so happy. I saw them on Monday...I wanted to tell Sunil about you...'

'Sunil and Neha are getting married? That's good news.' I went to embrace him when pain from my thighs stopped me. Shankarji's arms came around me instead. I breathed deeply until the pain passed.

'Dev, oh Dev, what else can I do?'

'Thank you Shankarji,' I smiled.

Shankarji laid me on the thin blanket. I closed my eyes.

'Shankarji,' I said.

'Yes *beta*?'

'Thank you for not telling Sunil I am in here. No one knows and I can't tell them. They will hate me. They will think I did something to avenge *Bhai's* death. Shankarji, there was a time when I did want to do just that. I wanted to be rebellious and murder those white foreigners! I wanted to bring justice to *Bhai*...but a friend stopped me...'

'And yet, you are here,' said Shankarji sadly. 'Dev, you must tell your family or someone. It is my request that you do.'

There was movement outside the cell. 'No talking!' A jailer rapped his stick against the bars on the next cell to ours. Shankarji and I went quiet.

'Shankarji, I want you to know my story. Do you want to hear it?' I said when the jailor had gone.

'If telling me unburdens you, then it will be my pleasure.'

And so I began to tell my dearest friend, from the time *Bhai* died to the present.

Fourteen

Vacation in Simla

Bhai was the great one, the wise one. He took me to school when I was young and taught me everything I know today. I would constantly harass him with questions on life and he would never tire of answering them. He didn't know what anger was but he was stern when I said too much.

    Bhai was a patient man and very clever. It's not in my nature to be like him – I am too impatient and immature. Ma and *Babuji* adored him and they called me a trouble-maker; but I didn't mind because *Bhai* always watched my back. He always covered for me.

    Once I took Ma's *chapals*[118] and hid them. She went round and round the house looking for them. When Ma found them, she was livid. *Bhai* took the beatings that weren't his. I'd cry afterwards for the hurt I caused him and he would console me – I didn't deserve it! Ofcourse Ma found out the truth and instead of beating me like she should, she wouldn't speak to me – that was her punishment. No matter how many times I said sorry, she would shake her head in disappointment. I was sorry and I wished I could be sensible like *Bhai* was and not be a devil! I wish they could look up to me.

    'It's not too late,' said Shankarji. *'Your parents have only you now, and you have to be the one to lead them forward and to unburden them. Tell me about your childhood. I remember you left school at a very young age – twelve years old, I think.'*

    I had no interest in education, with no skills or certificates, my chances of getting work were slim. But there was one thing I knew about – the mechanics of automobiles. *Bhai-ji*, was an enthusiast. He loved engines and speed. This was before he joined the socialist newspaper, before he became a freedom fighter.

    I used to watch him work on his Saab's motors. Even from a young age, he allowed me to help him work on an engine. *Bhai-ji* educated me on the automobile industry –in practice and in theory and my knowledge and interest grew.

---

[118] *Chapal*, Sandal

It was when Khan *Bhai*, *Bhai-ji's* good friend, opened up a garage that I began work on a regular basis. Starting with small jobs only until he was confident that I could take on bigger things. Years passed, and then *Bhai*...well, my world was bleak after. I refused to go to work for a while until I saw *Babuji's* health. That was when I realised that even though *Bhai* was not around, life still carried on – I began to work again, if only for Ma and *Babuji*. I had to bring back life back into my home.

The morning of 15th July 1943, it happened. I left for work early that day, I remember it well. It was a beautiful day – clear and warm. The world suddenly seemed exciting again and I was happy. I sat down in the garage, at mid-morning. I tuned into the All India radio station as I drank some *chai*. They were talking about the Movement – more riots and arrests. It made me think of *Bhai* – I changed the channel to the sounds of *sitars*[119] and *tablas*[120] instead. I didn't notice Khan *Bhai* coming in and sitting down a few feet away from me - my eyes closed, my mind concentrated on the melodious music.

He said it quietly but I heard it clearly. 'Dev.'

Khan *Bhai*! I opened my eyes. 'I'm sorry – I should be working.' I was still holding my *chai* and hastily put it down. I scrambled to turn the radio off.

Khan *Bhai* chuckled. 'It's alright Dev; even you are allowed to have a break. Leave the radio on, I like the sounds too.' I left the radio on.

'I have a couple of new cars coming in for repairs today. Mr. Kulkarni and Mr. Johnston. They should be here around one. When the cars have been booked in, I want you to stop working and take the afternoon off. I will take over,' said Khan *Bhai*.

'Why sir?'

'You need a long break, Dev. You have been working very hard – yes, I have noticed and appreciate it very much. You have done well here,' he said when I gave him a surprised look. 'I have heard great praises from our customers about you; I am pleased. Very pleased. But now, you need a vacation. So from today, you will stop working until I say so.'

'I don't want to stop working Khan *Bhai*. What will I do away from here?'

'You will go to Simla.'

---

[119] **Sitar**, an Indian string instrument made of gourds and teak.
[120] **Tabla**, Indian drums

'Simla?' I was astonished.

'Yes, in Simla you will do nothing but enjoy the scenery and relax. After you have repaired your body and mind and have had enough of your vacation, I wish you to start work there. You are to open a new garage for me and be my manager.

'You know the industry well Dev. You know the mechanics of a car very well; you understand it more than I. I know you will make a very good manager. You have shown me your capabilities, you have a strong head, your tact with the customers is beyond my admiration of you and also you are good with figures. Who better than you? Need I say more to convince you?'

I couldn't argue with Khan *Bhai* and I admit I was excited at the prospect of a new start in my life. When I returned home, I told Ma and *Babuji* about Simla. They were not at all surprised but Ma began to cry.

'I know I am selfish but I am also a mother. How can I see my only son leave?' she clung to me.

'Usha, this will be very good for him. He needs to do this. I will miss you dearly *beta*, but what a great opportunity, this is a wonderful way to go forward!' *Babuji* was pleased but I saw the sadness in his eyes.

'I can stay if you want me to,' I offered knowing that they wouldn't agree. I was right.

The time came too soon for me to say goodbye. My bags were packed. Ma gave me enough *achar* and *roti* for my journey, even some savoury foods. Khan *Bhai*, Amit and Sunil were there to see me off but not Pooja. I could guess why not – I wouldn't have been able to leave otherwise. The last thing I saw was *Babuji* waving, a forced smile on his face and Ma crying copiously into a handkerchief.

'Tell me, what happened in Simla.'

'Many things happened, Shankarji.' As I said this, my body went rigid as knife-like pain stabbed my thigh. Ever since that Kuthé Mansingh smashed my leg with his boot, the pain came – the last one more severe – sometimes immobilising me or rendering my leg numb for a few minutes.

I bit my fist to stop from crying out but Shankarji was already there.

*'What can I do for you? How can I help?' his distraught eyes
sought mine. I breathed deeply as the damn pain subsided – for the
moment.*

*'Rest Dev beta, you can tell me your story another time,'
Shankarji said anxiously.*

'Nai, nai.' I smiled. 'Let me tell you...'

Stepping off the train transported me to a beautiful place. Simla's hills,
mountain views, fresh air and sweet scents greeted me. I couldn't help
but feel as if a heavy load had been lifted away.

A man stepped forward to take my luggage – at first, I was bewildered
and clung onto it tightly. I thought he was a thief! But it was a
coolie[121] – the uniform is different- I didn't recognise. So anyhow, I let
him take it. Then, another man came forward who extended his hand
to me. I recognised him at once. He wore a tweed woollen jacket,
black trousers and a white shirt. He wore a black hat too. It was
Gunwant-ji.

'Good morning Gunwant-ji.' I shook his hand.

'Good morning to you.' He smiled and slapped me on my
back. I nearly toppled over.

'Who is this Gunwant-ji?' asked Shankarji.

*'He is Khan Bhai's closest friend and business partner. I owe
him a lot. Gunwant-ji has helped me in more ways than one.'*

'He sounds like an interesting man.'

'Yes, he is very well known.'

Gunwant-ji works in the car parts industry as well as partnering with
Khan *Bhai*. I was to stay with Gunwant-ji at his residence – that way I
would learn a lot more about Simla and the business.

'This is my daughter, Payal.' Gunwant-ji introduced a pretty
girl, when we reached his motorcar. She was standing there, quite shy.

'*Namaste*,' I said.

'*Namaste*,' she replied but kept her eyes on the ground.

The *coolie*, who had been following us, put my bags into the
boot. Gunwant-ji paid him, and he bowed in thanks, moving away
swiftly.

---

[121] **Coolie**, Indian porter

'*Bapuji*, I am going to Gita's house,' Payal said. She glanced at me and left.

Gunwant-ji put his arm around my shoulder. 'Let's go. I am sure a good breakfast is waiting. You can freshen up and then we will talk.'

We travelled through small lanes. Colourful shrubs and hedges lined the sides and the sun cast a happy feel about the place. As we travelled further in, I saw many people were on foot or were riding a bicycle. *Memsahibs* and *Saabs* walked here and there, going about their business, whilst locals carried on with theirs.

Gunwant-ji stopped the motorcar at the top of a hill. He got out, indicating I do the same. He pointed to the picture below. I looked over to see a little lake; it sparkled like diamonds. I was mesmerized.

'Beautiful, isn't it?' said Gunwant-ji.

Yes, it was. It was also very inviting and I wanted to take a dip right there and then. *Bhai* and I used to swim in the river a lot. It was one of our frequent past-times, especially when the sun was too hot.

'You can never tire of a good swim in the river. I used to be exactly like you. I had eleven brothers and one sister. We were allowed to swim but didi wasn't and she used to complain to my mother. She was a year younger than I,' Shankar-ji had gone into his past. It was nice to hear about his life.

'Do you see her often?' I asked.

'Not as much now. She was married when she was ten years old and now has eleven children of her own. They live in Calcutta. She comes to see us when there is a celebration...the last I heard, one of her boys was jailed. It was because of the Quit India Movement.'

I remained quiet for a while as I thought about what Shankarji said. It was very near to what my story told. 'I'm sorry.'

'Never mind about that, tell me, did you swim?'

I didn't swim but I remember seeing small houses dotted around the lake. Some women were washing clothes on big grey stones – beating them with large wooden sticks, taking out the grime and sweat of hard work. Ma says that it helps when you are angry; Babuji sometimes could be very tiresome!

Children splashed in the water, laughing and having a good time. Then, somewhere nearby a bell from a temple rang.

'That is the Goddess, *Laxmi's* temple. Every day people from the town offer the Goddess sweets and fruit to thank her for their happiness or to ask for a certain wish. The community is large here and a collection goes around for the maintenance and upkeep,' said Gunwant-ji. 'They say it is lucky to be present when the bell rings, wishes come true.'

We arrived twenty minutes later at Gunwant-ji's residence. I was struck by the vastness of it – standing at the front of the house, his family greeted me like an old friend. I was overwhelmed.

'Come and meet my family – My wife Jhanvi, my two sons, Ramesh and Ballu, my daughter-in-law, Sita (she is married to Ramesh) and my daughter Payal (is she back yet?). And we can't forget my sweet little granddaughter, Rakhi.' I smiled at everyone, forgetting their names instantly. Gunwant-ji picked up his granddaughter who came running to him and kissed her cheek. Everybody began talking at once; I couldn't make head or tail of it! But Gunwant-ji rescued me.

'Sita *beta*, let's have something to eat, Dev here, must be very hungry!'

'Ji,' said Sita Bhabhi.

We all sat down and Sita Bhabhi served us hot *jalebi*[122], milk, *parotha*[123] and *achar*, amongst other delicious items. My mouth waters now just thinking of it. Rakhi sat on her grandfather's lap and ate the *jelabis* whilst chatting away. Gunwant-ji listened attentively to her morning schedule of play as he tucked in. Her talking never stopped and it was endearing to see so much love. Near to the end of breakfast, Payal came home. She stopped at the doorway and watched us silently until Jhanvi *Bhabhi* spoke.

'Where were you? Wait there – go and wash your hands and face first.'

'She is Gunwant-ji's wife, remember?' I said as Shankarji gave me confused look.

'Ah yes. There are too many people and too many names. Sita is one of the son's wife and Jhanvi is Gunwant-ji's wife.'

'Yes.'

---

[122] **Jalebi**, a sweet delicacy made of flour and water, dipped in syrup.
[123] **Parotha**, Indian flat bread (shallow fried).

Payal was obviously hungry for she went to eat straight away. 'Ma, I was at Gita's house. I told *Bapu*. Let me eat now.'

'Why? Didn't Gita give you food? Humph!'

'I didn't eat there, her cooking is not nice. I very much like Sita *Bhabhi's* cooking,' Payal put her arms around her shoulder.

'Payal, do as Ma says. Wash your hands and then I will give you something to eat,' smiled Sita *Bhabhi*.

Payal tutted and sulked away to wash, muttering under her breath. She caught my smile and scowled. Then she coloured red; I quickly diverted my eyes.

Gunwant-ji took me to a room on the upper floor. 'This is where you will be sleeping.
This is Payal's room – don't worry, she is happy for you to use it. Now, I will leave you to get some rest. Khan *Bhai* tells me you are on vacation – so go, explore and enjoy Simla. We will talk business at a later time.'

I lay on the large four poster, thinking of nothing else but the comfort. Oh, it was nice. A chilly breeze blew in from the open window and I went to close it when my eyes fell on the splendid scenery before me. A range of snow-capped mountains stood in the far-distance, with the sun setting behind. Down below, a river snaked itself around them. I'd never seen snow before, it was wonderful. Another sharp breeze and I shivered. I closed the window and looked back at the bed. I was soon fast asleep, waking then, in the evening.

Inviting aromas reached me and my stomach grumbled – I had been asleep for too long. I peered out the window and saw it was dusk. Many houses were already lit. Following the tantalising smells, I went downstairs. Payal was standing at the foot of the staircase with a surprised, yet shy expression on her face. I found it...endearing. She acknowledged me and let me pass. I smelt roses.

'Ah Dev, you're awake. Good, good. Hungry? Your *Bhabhi* has some food ready for you. I'm afraid I need to be somewhere else at this time, but Ballu will keep you company.' Gunwant-ji put his glasses on and checked his pockets. He took out some keys. 'So, I'll see you,' he said heading for the door.

I felt out of sorts but Ballu made me feel welcome. 'Come and sit, I was just about to start. Ramesh is out with Sita *Bhabhi* and Rakhi.

171

I will be glad of your company.' Ballu and I got acquainted and I found him to be quite an interesting man.

Later, he took me to the see night-time Simla. We walked instead of using transport. Ballu said that was the only way to appreciate the city. He was right, as we reached the main part of town; a positive charge filled the air. I felt alive. Primary coloured lights lit up the walkway to the shops, which were heaving with activity. Food stalls sent out intoxicating smells and we bought some samosas and onion bhajis and ate them in quick succession, washing them down with a refreshing drink. The air turned cooler; I was glad I'd listened to Ballu to wrap up.

'This is where everyone comes at the end of the day; it is a popular place. We have a very good theatre – do you like plays? There is a cinema here also. Every Tuesday, a film is shown - a popular pastime. The tickets are sold out quickly.

A couple of Ballu's friends joined us. They wanted to know about me, they were intrigued– where I lived and what I did. I told them about my life in Rajkot but leaving out *Bhai*. I wasn't ready to talk about that yet. We chatted for some time and departed, promising to keep up a correspondence which I knew neither of us would follow through.

When we went home, it was past eleven. I suppose I was having such a great time that I didn't realise the evening going quickly. It was nice, you know?

During the next three weeks, Ballu and Ramesh were away on business a lot of the time and Gunwant-ji was busy as well. Those days I explored Simla. My favourite place was the lake and I'd go and visit the temple of Laxmi. I would sit there for hours enjoying the air and listening to the bell chimes. When did four weeks pass, I didn't know but then I was itching to get back to work. I decided to end my vacation.

'I have drawn up a list of tasks which we will complete. This project should not take more than six to nine months. Today, I will take you to the site where the garage will be built. It's a great location,' Gunwant-ji explained the next morning as we were having *chai*.

We travelled by rickshaw to the location. We rolled over sweeping hills, where red and yellow flowers bloomed in adjacent fields…when I close my eyes, I can still smell the fragrant scents. I remember the sky was very blue. Small white clouds drifted and the morning sun was refreshing. Ramesh warned me beforehand that it can get quite cold in the mornings and I must wear woollen sweaters. We came upon an area which was plain and bare.

'Take a good look at the plot and remember it. I believe the way to good business is to be clear. Take your time, walk around. Take in the surroundings,' said Gunwant-ji.

I walked around. The garage, once built, would have faced a road which leads to Bombay and many other towns and cities. It would have been a good location for the business. Khan *Bhai* had indeed made a wise choice.

'Was to be? Wasn't the garage built?' asked Shankarji.

'It wasn't built Shankarji but many things happened before that and two specific things to stop it.'

Shankarji stretched his legs. Some inmates in the other cells could be heard snoring and some were talking in low voices. The pain was still there but it was now dim – I could ignore it.

I leaned against the wall, placing my injured leg so as to numb the throbbing pain. It worked and I enjoyed a moment of relief.

'Lights will be out in ten minutes,' came the voice of an unseen jailor.

Shankarji put his fingers to his lips to warn me. We pretended to be asleep as the routine check was completed. We lay in our positions for a while and when we were positive that the jailors had gone, I returned to the story.

'What happened with Payal?' Shankarji whispered. 'I gathered she thought of you quite highly, she wanted to be something other than a friend?'

'You are perceptive,' I complimented. I sighed. 'Payal...she was something I didn't foresee.'

For the first few weeks, Gunwant-ji and I worked. We made plans and wrote reams of notes. Payal was always in the background, I don't think I took any notice of her. One night, as were packing up, Payal came in.

'*Bapu*, there is a telephone call for you.'

'It must be Veeru. Dev, you continue. When I arrive back, we can have something strong to drink. I think we deserve it.' He patted me on the back and went.

173

Payal and I were alone for the first time. We stood facing each other; I felt awkward and I am sure she felt out of place too.

'How are you?' I blurted out feeling silly.

'I am fine...and you?'

'Fine also...fine...' Our eyes met and we burst out laughing.

After that, the ice was broken and we chatted easily. We didn't realise when Gunwant-ji returned, but he was too absorbed to see anything different. Payal walked away quietly.

'Dev,' Gunwant-ji rubbed his head. 'That was a call from Veeru. As I feared, we have some bad news. Sit please,' Gunwant-ji poured some whisky into two tumblers and handed one to me.

'Sir, is everything alright?'

Gunwant-ji took a gulp and shook his head. 'No, all is not right. The plot which Khan *Bhai* had bought for the garage has been seized by the Raj. I don't know the reason but I suspect foul play is at hand.'

'Are you sure, there has been no mistake?' Gunwant-ji didn't say anything to deny this. 'But will Khan *Bhai* get his money back?'

'I don't know. I will need to make some enquiries. I will go to the government offices tomorrow. I would like you to accompany me.'

'Of course,' I said.

'Good, good,' said Gunwant-ji.

'Sir, how bad is it?'

'When Khan *Bhai* bought the land, the seller assured us it was a legal sale. But you see, something inside me said otherwise. I tried to warn Khan *Bhai* but he believed this man. Now, I fear I was right.'

We passed most of the evening discussing the issue and what we could do about it. But even after five hours, we came to no conclusion. We would only get information tomorrow.

The government offices were based centrally. As we waited to be seen, clerks went in and out of the rooms. Local farmers, businessmen, families and alike waited to be seen like us. Soon, our number came up and we were ushered into a wood-panelled room. Two clerks were seated at desks on both sides of the room, and another man who looked to be the man in charge, was seated at the top desk. Painted portraits of former senior officials hung on the wall behind him.

'Please, take a seat,' said the clerk. 'How can I help you?'

'We are here to enquire about Plot 23,' said Gunwant-ji.

'Yes.' The young man clasped his hand together in front of him and looked enquiringly at us.

'It's been seized and we want to know why,' I said.

'I see.' He disappeared under the desk and began to rummage through a pile of files which were stacked in a box. He finally emerged with a file, named Plot 23. He flicked through the first few pages and then looked at us.

'Yes, you are quite right. This plot is the property of the government now. Is there anything else I can help you with?'

'The plot wasn't bought illegally. It shouldn't have been taken from us!' Gunwant-ji looked furious.

'It was bought without permission and without the correct paperwork, which makes it illegal. I'm sorry but that is the truth. You see – '

'But the man who bought it checked it was legal to purchase. He has all the correct papers and they were all signed by the seller. I don't understand,' said Gunwant-ji.

The clerk pulled out a contract and began to read its contents.

'Yes it was a legal sale but this plot didn't belong to the seller – a Mr. Sameer Kolkota. You see, he was in debt. He owed the government money and a lot of it. The ownership therefore, falls to the *Raj*. Mr. Kolkota was sent a letter detailing his debt in full. He did not pay in the time given, thus all his assets, including land, was seized to recuperate the monies owed.'

'But will Mr. Khan receive his money back? This was not his fault.'

'Mr. Khan was the buyer?' He looked back at the file. 'Right, Mr. Khan. According to the procedures, Mr. Khan will need to make a claim for this. But I must warn you that payment, if eligible, will not be immediate.'

'That's not right, he must be paid. His loss will be absolute…this is no way to treat an innocent man!' said Gunwant-ji, now standing.

'I'm sorry sir, my hands are tied. I am only a civil servant doing my job Unfortunately, I cannot change the law. Here is the address, where Mr. Khan needs to write to.' The clerk handed the address to me. 'If you have any other matters to discuss, please do call in again.'

'Sir, surely you must be able to arrange it so he is paid back some money at this stage. Can't you do anything?' I asked.

175

'Sorry,' the clerk pointed to the exit.

We didn't know how to break the news to Khan *Bhai*. Poor man, he was devastated when we called him. The loss was too great.

'There must be something we can do, Khan *Bhai*. I will go back there tomorrow and appeal, whatever it takes,' I said.

'The *Raj* is strong and we cannot do anything about it. Don't worry Dev, somehow I will get my money back,' said Khan *Bhai*. 'I should have listened to Gunwant-ji, he didn't trust that man.'

'What do you want me to do?'

'There is nothing you can do. Anyhow, I need you here, when can you come?'

'I will come as soon as I can arrange it,' I said. 'I am sorry that this happened, but I promise you, I will work harder and bring enough business in to cover your loss.'

'You are your father's son,' said Khan *Bhai* and put the phone down.

My train to Rajkot was arranged for the following Saturday, so I had a week here in Simla. The family were distraught at this news but they tried to keep the mood light. Payal and I spent a lot of time together in that week; she showed me a lot of the sights that I had missed. She was really trying to distract my mind from my worries. We became close but always avoided talking about my going away. I didn't understand at that moment until one evening.

We were sitting on a bench and watching the sunset.

'I love you Dev,' she said to me, turning her face towards mine. Her words caught my breath – she looked beautiful. I smiled and she laughed in happiness, putting her arms around me.

'Payal.' I took her arms off me. 'I'm sorry, you have misunderstood me...This is not right. I am already tied to someone else.'

'Who is it?' There were tears of embarrassment in her eyes and I truly felt sorry for her.

'She is Pooja and I love her very much. Please, don't take offence.'

Payal stared at me like I had betrayed her. 'I need to go home Dev.' She stood up abruptly.

'Payal, I am sorry. I didn't mean to mislead you.'

'Just take me home,' came her cold retort. And so I did but from then on, she avoided me.

Two days before I was due to leave for Rajkot, Gunwant-ji and I were sitting outside. We had a fire going and were drinking hot chai.

'Sita *Bhabhi* is an excellent cook,' I said. 'I will miss it very much.'

'She has magic in her fingers. Don't tell your *Bhabhi* but I think Sita is a better cook! So, Dev, it was nice having you here. If things had turned out for the better...' he shrugged. '*Beta*, there is something I have wanted to ask you...about Rakesh...'

'Yes Gunwant-ji, what did you want to ask?' I said.

'Did he tell you that he had met Mohandas Gandhi?'

I looked at Gunwant-ji, wide-eyed. 'No...but how do you know?'

'I used to live in your old village once. Khan *Bhai*, I and your father were very good neighbours. It was 1930 – the great *Salt March*[124]. Mohandas Gandhi walked from Sabarmath Ashram to Dandi – to the sea. It was a stand to stop salt tax. We didn't join the several thousand who decided to follow him, but we followed his pilgrimage by radio. *Bapu* was going to march through our village with his followers. We all stood in a line waiting to see him. Rakesh was maybe ten or twelve then, I don't know but he was very excited. *Bapu* stopped at Rakesh, who gave him some water. *Bapu* touched his head in return and said something to him. I saw something in Rakesh's eyes then – something fierce and I wondered about his future. I turned cold when I heard about his death...it shouldn't have happened. He was so young...'

'I hope so, sir, that one day, *Bhai*'s spirit will be free and then, he wouldn't have died in vain.' I hid my face from him, hoping that he didn't see my tears.

We were quiet after that, each in our thoughts. Then he asked about Payal and me.

'You and Payal have become very good friends,' Gunwant-ji said. His tact of changing the subject was very fast but strange.

'Yes, she is nice.'

---

[124] The Salt March – see notes

'Payal is taken by you very much so. I see her watching you when you work – it is adoration. Dev, I don't want to see her hurt.'

I just stared ahead. I didn't know what to say.

'Dev, will you marry my daughter?'

'Oh...Gunwant-ji,' I said. I looked away – afraid to meet his eyes. 'I'm sorry but I cannot. I know how she feels about me and I did not encourage her, believe me. Please do not be offended but I am already committed to someone else. She is waiting for me in Rajkot. She is the one I love. Payal is aware of this.'

It was Gunwant-ji's turn to be embarrassed. 'Please accept my apologies, Dev. I thought wrongly. Only I don't like seeing her so sad...'

'I will talk to her Gunwant-ji. I promise,' I said.

The next morning, I took a stroll, thinking of Payal and Pooja. I thought of Khan *Bhai*'s investment and his loss – what was happening? I walked to the park and sat on a bench, watching a crowd gather.

'Are you coming?' someone stopped to ask me.

'Coming where?' I asked.

'*Bhai* Saab, you don't know? In a few moments, Laxman Pandey – a strong headed freedom fighter is going to talk to us. We are all excited. Come and join us.'

I was intrigued and indeed went to join the throng of people. Again, I thought of *Bhai* and if he would have approved.

'Brothers and sisters, today we have come here together, to make changes. India is rightfully ours and we must claim it back! Already, a lot of Indians have taken action, regrettably in violence. But we must follow *Bapu's* lead: non-violence!' the freedom fighter began. Everyone clapped. 'We must all take charge of the situation; make them understand the importance of a free India!' The crowd roared with enthusiasm.

'But what if they put us in prison?' a man asked.

'So what if they do?' shouted a stout woman. 'What is more important? Don't be a coward!'

'I don't know, the risks…' the man said.

'Then sit at home and wear bangles! Let us women to the real work!'

There was a loud cheer.

'Brothers and sisters! We are not talking about fights or rioting. We are talking about boycotting schools, municipal buildings and transport systems. We will protest in non-violence. Why should we succumb to the laws of the *Raj*? Why should we pay excessive taxes for food, clothes and land? We must give our support to *Bapu* – who has done so much for us already and still is fighting for us. So, are you with me?' the freedom fighter shouted into his megaphone.

There was a murmuring in the crowd. I could feel the electric excitement.

'Are we going to do this!' he shouted even louder.

'YES!' came a definite answer.

He was about to speak again but stopped. The wail of a police vehicle came closer and it stopped at the park. Like me, everyone turned around to see what was going on. It happened so fast. They charged into us with batons. I was pushed over and kicked. A sickening pain made me scream – blood seeped from my head down my face. But this was not enough for them. The baton went down on my knee – I heard a crunch and my shriek should have made them stop. My head began to swim... I don't know when I blacked out.

When I regained consciousness, I found I was in a cell, crammed with many others. Some weeks later, I was transferred here.

The sky was getting lighter. It was dawn. I hardly noticed the pain now but I was careful. I used to play "kabadi[125]"with Amit, Sunil and some others on the dusty, village grounds. I'd managed to rupture my leg muscles at least twice during the games. It took a few weeks to completely heal and for the bruising to subside. That pain was similar to what I was feeling now and I could only guess that here, I would have to let my leg heal naturally, even though it could mean waiting through the excruciating pain. I doubted Mansingh would let me see a doctor. I laughed silently but grimly.

My eyes began to feel sore – I needed to sleep. The heaviness seemed to overwhelm the pain and I let myself seep into it.

I was woken up by Shankarji shouting in agony. My eyes flew open to see his hands clutched over his heart, his eyes shut tight. I

---

[125] **Kabadi**, an aggressive Indian game played by men, seven on each side. The goal is to tag or wrestle the player sent from the opposite team before he reaches their home base. Tagged members are out. When all members of a team are out, the other team wins.

179

banged on the cell bars and shouted for help. Within minutes, Shankarji was taken to hospital.

The following evening, I was told Shankarji had survived his second attack and that he wouldn't be coming back. He would be sent home.

'Then God has listened to some of my prayers,' I said.

'Yes. He was lucky. A Constable named Rai came at the right time. He had his release papers. That's all I know,' said Haricharan.

Whispers travelled around the prison, of surprise and happiness. Some say money had exchanged hands, but I was content now. I missed my good friend and decided to write the delayed letters like Shankarji said I should.

~ POOJA ~

Fifteen

Bombay

I stared back at my reflection. The bruises were deep purple and my mascara had run, too, leaving black streaks behind. Taking a wet cloth, I wiped away the signs of abuse from the corner of my mouth. I took out a compact from the antique dresser and fought to cover the bruises with my scalded hands, then I brushed through my already knot free hair. It was then that I stopped crying.

Gingerly I adorned my hair with a butterfly clip and stood up to examine myself in the full-length mirror. I looked better now; the bruises didn't show up as much.

'It's alright *beta*, things will get better, I promise,' I whispered. I put my hands on my stomach. 'You're Papa didn't mean to. He is a good man.'

I walked from room to room, overlooking the cleaning of the house. The servants were busy today; Amar was expecting guests. I must try and present myself well...

'Meenakshi, how is the dinner coming along?'

'Very well *Memsahib*,' Meenakshi, the chef's wife assured me.

I was satisfied and moved on. Everything must be perfect today, Amar must have no complaints. I passed the drawing room – something wasn't right. The cigars!

'Laxman!' I shouted.

'*Ji* Memsahib.' Laxman, who overlooks the housework, appeared.

'Laxman, the cigars. Fill the cigarette holder and quickly. *Saab* must have it full,' I said. As I watched him perform his duty, the big clock struck seven. The guests would be here soon with Amar. I steadied my breathing and went to my bedroom to get changed; maybe a little more powder will be good. I opened the wardrobe which contained over two hundred saris. I searched for something suitable and settled on a pink and silver. I hoped Amar would approve. Glancing in the mirror, I noticed there was something wrong with my hair. It was the hair-clip. Amar didn't like butterflies...he would be so angry. I changed it to a flower design – yes, that's better.

'My firm is thinking of promoting me. A higher salary, bigger car and a bigger house,' said Amar. We sat next to each other but he was too busy leering at his lady friend, who was the wife of a wealthy Commissioner. They arrived together in a luxury motorcar and were Amar's special guests for the evening. How special – I found out during the dinner.

The husband was fat and balding and didn't care for his host or his wife. His shirt buttons seemed to strain against his body as he took another long swig from his drink, slumping into his chair. His beady eyes appraised my body eagerly and greedily. I shivered and refocused on my husband but he was turned away from me. Amar leaned into his lady friend, dropping his hand under the tablecloth; he began to stroke her thigh as he kissed her throat. The lady's husband didn't seem to notice. I averted my eyes and pretended to be occupied with the flower arrangement on the table, determined to not show my burning.

'Your house is so pretty, who chose the colours?' asked the lady, giggling. She sipped some more wine.

'Just someone,' Amar looked at me; a cruel smirk on his face. 'Sir, care for some more?' He poured the husband another glass.

I silently finished my dinner and listened to the chatter. These parties were really only meant for Amar's friends, I was just an accessory.

The dinner was coming to an end. 'Would you like some sweets?' I offered a silver dish of sweetmeats to the guests and instantly regretted it.

'Did I grant you permission to speak?' Amar said in a steely voice. His eyes flashed and without warning, he kicked the chair I was sitting on. I fell backwards, taking the plate with me, spilling the contents over my sari. Amar picked up the bottle of wine and took a swig, wiping his dripping mouth with the end of my sari. He laughed and brutally kicked my stomach. I coiled into a ball, fighting the extreme pain that wanted me to cry. The baby, I thought...please let her be alright. I clutched my stomach.

'What do you think you are doing, you foolish bitch!' shouted Amar. 'Get up and clean yourself up!'

I did as he said, rushing to my room to change my clothes and wash quickly. When I came back, the chair was still on the floor and Amar was kissing the lady on the lips; the husband had fallen asleep. Amar heard me approach and stopped his humiliating act.

184

'Oh, you came back.' He looked at the fallen chair. 'Pick that up and pour us more wine.'

The wine bottle was empty. 'I'm sorry...' I said. Amar slapped me across my face – the stinging burn lingered. My eyes watered.

'Then go and get another one!' he shouted. He turned back to the lady, his eyes heavy with lust. This time, his hand travelled under her blouse. As I ran out of the dining room, unable to stop my tears, I heard him laugh. 'Sorry darling,' he said to her. 'Now, where were we?'

I stayed awake, just like the other nights. This wasn't the first time Amar had humiliated and belittled me in front of his woman friends. I should be used to it now...but no...it still hurt.

I lay, curled up under the covers but sleep was nowhere near. I stared at the ceiling. Downstairs, the front door closed – the husband was sent home. Steps – heavy and light, made their way upstairs and stopped at our room – the breathing was heavy. A high pitched laugh was let out, followed by a ringing silence.

'The illiterate wife is asleep,' said Amar. 'Come darling.'

They moved on. I heard the fumbling of a door knob and then them entering the room next to mine.

'Oh Amar,' the lady cried.

Some scuffling, a shoe thrown, then another; I imagined their clothes hitting the floor. The bed creaked and obscene sounds began. I cursed the thin walls, my husband and that woman!

Eventually, like every night for the last three months, I cried myself to sleep.

'Crying again?' Amar sneered as I joined him at the breakfast table. He was already having his *chai*.

'Amar, I need to talk to you, please.'

He ignored me and rattled the paper he was reading.

'Amar, please,' I begged.

'What is it?' he snapped.

'Please don't embarrass me in front of your friends...your obscenity...do you have no shame? You touched and kissed her...in front of me, in front of your wife!'

Amar threw his glass and it smashed on the wall. He lashed out and smacked me across the face, tearing my skin. Blood ran from the corner of my mouth but Amar didn't show an ounce of remorse.

'How dare you question me? I am your husband, understand that! I can do whatever I want, if I want to bed another woman, I will. You are nothing to me anymore, but since you are here and of course you can't go back to your small village – live with it!'

Amar grabbed his briefcase and left the house. I sat where I was for a minute, stunned. Then, I slowly went to the sink and cleaned the blood off my face, then sank to the floor.

I rocked back and forth holding my knees. I didn't know what to do but I was sure of one thing: this had to stop. I was a good person, then why did these awful things happen to me? Choking back tears I began to sweep the smashed glass, my tears finally falling. Dark hands flashed before me, pushing mine gently away whilst someone else took care of my face. Laxman cleaned up the mess and Meenakshi took me to my room and laid me down upon my cushions. I stared at the ceiling...I still remember that night clearly; the rape that ruined my life...

I needed Amit – he would know what to do. I couldn't face my family alone...or the police...I was thankful to Rama. Maybe not a friend yet but she was someone who came through for me – I didn't expect that. I lay on the hospital bed, not sure if I was going to live. I still felt the pain inside and the doctors said that the bleeding...they tried to stop it but now it was up to God. The question is: do I want God to help me? Do I want to be kept alive?

Rama keeps on crying, why is that? Does she feel she is to blame for my fate or is it because she tortured me out of jealousy and hate? I sound spiteful, something which I abhor. I am not like that – I can forgive. But forgiving Rama is very hard, even though she brought me here.

'Pooja,' she said. 'I have called for Amit. I sent my driver and he is coming. Just...don't cry.' She began to cry again.

'That's good.' My voice was empty. 'I want to sleep now Rama.'

She left me alone and I slept.

I was awake when Amit arrived. He didn't look so good. His handsome face was wrought with worry. He took my hands and kissed my forehead. I looked over him and saw that Rama was leaving.

'Don't go Rama,' I said. That was odd, why did I say that? She sat down again.

'Amit...you are a good friend...'

'Oh Pooja...' he said. He looked like he might cry.

'Perhaps it was God's decision. *Hé Ma*[126]!' The pain twisted inside me, burning, stabbing.

'Pooja!' I thought I heard Amit and Rama shout together. Blackness began to descend upon me.

Tubes were attached to me – I could feel the tugging on my skin. There was no pain now. I heard low voices, murmurs. Where was Amit? I needed to speak to him but the fog was refusing to lift...

Someone was mopping my brow. I felt hot. A hand on my cheek.

'Ma,' I breathed and opened my eyes. A tear fell on my cheek. 'Don't cry.' But she did, a lot.

Papa and Arjun came into focus. They touched my hand – they had been crying too.

'I promise you I won't be a disgrace to you any longer, Papa. I am so sorry. When I die, I promise your grief will be no more. I won't be a burden on you any longer.'

'Oh *Dikra*! Why do you say such things?' Papa cried into my palm.

'Papa, please...' He wiped his face but looked miserable. I detested myself – what kind of a daughter was I? I shouldn't let my father cry.

'Papa, where is Amit?'

'Here *beta*. He has been here all the time, even Rama. They have not left the hospital once.'

Why not? They shouldn't worry about me! 'Ma, tell them to go home...'

I began to drift again. The voices dimmed.

---

[126] *Hé Ma*, Oh God (referring to female Gods such as Sri Laxmi, Durga Ma, Sita, Saraswati, Parvati) – calling them Mother.

187

I thought I would die but God wasn't so generous. The doctors told me the bleeding had stopped and I was healing. Everyone was relieved – even Rama. Somehow, she had become part of my "family". Amit was already a brother to me as Arjun. I couldn't ask more from him.

I had been in hospital for three weeks. It was Amit who told Ma and Papa what had happened. They wanted to get the police involved but Rama disagreed. They were angry at first with her but she'd explained – I would have had to go to court and the court would ask for proof of the rape. They would want me to show them where the monster had inflicted the pain – where he had touched me – my thighs, my chest, my legs; they would want to see the bruises as proof. Rama would never let me go through more disgrace – Ma said; her tone full of admiration.

'But I will not let him get away with this! He will pay his dues!' vowed Arjun.

'No *Bhai*. Leave it be. He will get his dues – his punishment will come. I don't want you to go to jail.'

Arjun scowled but didn't say anything more. I hoped he would listen to me.

I was allowed to go home. I don't know if I was happy but one thing occurred to me.

'Amit,' I said when I was alone with him. 'Please don't tell Sunil or Dev about this. I don't want them to worry. Dev will come rushing back and I don't want that. Sunil, well he would wallow in misery.' Amit promised to keep quiet.

Gradually I began to heal. The villagers thought I had been ill again and didn't probe further, thankfully. Arjun returned to Bombay for his studies and Papa, reluctantly went back to the college where he was a professor.

But Sunil was worried – he couldn't just let me be. He wanted answers and I couldn't give them to him. I told him I would tell him if something had happened...if something was wrong – on his engagement party, but I think he felt like I wasn't telling the truth. I didn't say more.

I was alone some days and those days were bad. I thought about my service, about *Nani*, why hadn't she come to see me? I felt neglected. Ma sat with me sometimes but she had work to do, the girls to look after, Papa's tiffin to see to and other jobs around the house. I was selfish and I did want her to stay with me, talk to me but she told me gently that I needed rest.

Suddenly, everyone had something to do. Ma had her work, the girls, their school, Arjun – his studies and Papa, his teaching. I was by myself. I was confused; did no one want to be with me anymore? Was I such a disgrace to be seen with them? Were they ashamed of me?

I laughed to myself – how could anyone want to be with me? I *am* disgraced. Even Dev wouldn't want me now...I had become an untouchable. And there was only one thing I could do to erase that.

It was afternoon and nobody was around. I put on my *chapals* and went out the back. I knew where I had to go. Covering myself with a shawl, I crept out.

The sun was shining, bright and happy – but I saw black clouds and despair instead. I wished I'd never been born. I was a dark mark against society; a black burden on my family.

My aunties liked to taunt me when I was a child. I had grey/green eyes; my skin was the colour of sweetened milk – a light hue on my otherwise fair colouring. I had brown eyes. I didn't look like the other children or my family who had dark brown-black eyes, black hair and a dark brown complexion. I was different and they called me so – I wasn't like them – I was a foreigner, a European girl. Ma told me they were jealous of my beauty and Papa said I was far better than anyone. He dreamed I would find a *Rajkumar*[127] and would marry him and the villagers would eat their chapals! He made me laugh when he said that...I was naive and young then, what did I understand? No one would want to marry me now, be it a *Rajkumar* or a normal man.

My bad luck kept following me. My short school years (girls were not deemed important to be literate) didn't pass without more taunts and jeers. The girls didn't want me to join their groups and excluded me from their play. I'd sit on the bench, watching them – an outcast. The boys called me names and pulled my plaits.

But I made friends, who were more my protectors. They fought my battles and anyone who called me names, were warned severely. They were my family – Amit, Sunil and Dev. Still, my fate was not in my favour and I had no way of stopping it. Each time I surfaced from

---

[127] *Rajkumar*, Prince

the dark depths of desolation and misery; able to breathe the fresh tint of happiness that had succeeded in reaching me, the claws of dread and horror took me back to the place where I could see no light. I know now, I should have done this a long time ago...I should have closed the doors to the degradation, to the taunts, to the horror of the beatings and the rape. I should have closed the door to my life.

People whispered as I passed them. Of course, they were talking about me. I carried on walking. The well wasn't far now. I glanced around me but no one was following. My thoughts of a new life, a good reincarnation kept me walking. My shawl fell from my shoulders and that was when I noticed I wasn't alone. They were not near me and I walked on. This was my destiny.

'Bhagwaan[128], keep my family happy,' I said a silent prayer and took a deep breath. The well was inviting me. I closed my eyes and took a step on the brick wall. I thought of Dev.

'Please forgive me.' I whispered and took another step, my foot hovering over the gaping hole.

'What are you doing?!' someone screamed. My arm was pulled and I landed backwards onto the grass. I struggled to get up but I was caged – arms held me tightly around my waist.

'Let me go,' I screamed.

'Not until you promise to stop your stupidity.' The voice was calm and familiar.

'Let me go!'

'Promise me!'

'Alright, I promise.'

The arms released me and I stood up, breathing hard. Rama stood in front of me. I gasped.

'Why are you determined to kill yourself?' she said in disgust.

'But what am I supposed to do? My life is worth nothing now!' I said. 'Nothing!'

'Your life is not your own, Pooja. It is part of your Ma and Papa's – they gave you your life, you have no right to take it away. Have you thought about what you are doing? Do you want them to die with you? You need to go back home, Pooja. They will be worried.' Rama handed me the shawl I had dropped. I took it without saying a word.

---

[128] **Bhagwaan**, God

'Pooja, I am truly sorry for what I did to you. I am truly ashamed and hate myself for it. I know you don't like me and I understand that. I don't expect you to befriend me nor do I want you to forgive me. But Pooja, I will not let you die.'

I was suddenly reminded of *Nani* – she had the same expression when she had come to see me when I was ill. Again, I wondered why she hadn't come to see me.

'Rama, does *Nani* know anything at all – about Satish?' I asked.

'Oh Pooja,' she broke down.

'Rama?' I was feeling uneasy.

'I knew she was close to you. I'd always known it. Your pretty face and your innocence. Dadi never looked at me the way she does cut you. What is it about you? Why are you so nice? That's why I hated you so much.'

'*Nani* came last time to see me last time...well, when I was unwell.' I didn't meet Rama's eyes. 'Why hasn't she come to see me?'

'When Amit came to see you, I went home for a while. I needed to tell *dadi* what happened. I was lucky, for they were home when I arrived. I told *dadi*, Ma and Papa everything. *Dadi* wanted to come straight away but I stopped her. I didn't know if you wanted her to know...she waited for a week when I requested it – telling her you will be out of hospital in three or four days. So she waited but by the second week, you were still there. We were coming to see you....when....'

'When what, Rama?' I asked.

Rama took a deep breath. 'Satish came back. There was a big argument and dadi threw him out – she never wanted to see him again and she threatened him with the police. Satish fled. Then...*dadi* had a heart-attack, Pooja. She survived but I don't know...she is asking for you, she wants you.'

I made myself walk home. As I arrived, hands hugged me, held my face and touched my head. My family had surrounded me.

'Where were you? We were so worried!' Ma cried.

'I went for a walk.' I sounded far and distant.

'Why didn't you tell anyone? Tch!' Ma said.

'Ma, can I speak to you alone?' She took me inside and made me sit in the kitchen. She poured me some hot milk. 'Rama came to find me,' I said, taking a sip of the scalding liquid. The sweet milk tasted good.

'She is a good girl, we are indebted to her – she saved you.'

'She did save me.' Twice, I added in my head. I felt foolish, Rama was right – what had I been thinking?

'Ma, *Nani* had a heart attack. I need to see her, Ma.'

Ma didn't argue.

Nani seemed asleep. Her face was grey and drawn. I put my cheek against hers, my tears dampening her face.

'Pooja,' she opened her eyes. 'You came.' Her voice was raspy and fragile.

'You are everything to me, *Nani*,' I managed to say. I put my hand on her hot head and stroked her thin, grey hair.

'I don't have much time left. Let me speak –' she said as I was about to protest. 'Rama told me everything...I am so sorry. I can only pray that he has not blighted your sweet life.'

'Don't talk like that, *Nani*. I can't bear it. Please...don't leave me.' My sobs were fast now and she waited until I was able to calm myself.

'It is God's decision, *beta*. It is my time.' *Nani* pressed something into my hand. 'This bangle belongs to me. I want you to have it.'

The gold bangle was simple, yet it was heavy.

'No, I cannot take it.' I was shocked and surprised. This should be passed down to a member of her own family. 'Rama would like this, let her have it.'

A shadow of pain crossed her face. I gripped her clammy hand.

'It is my last wish for you to accept it. I have given Rama other things of mine but I kept this especially for you. Please don't say no.'

I folded my fingers over the gift. 'I won't say no.'

'*Dikra*, I have no right to ask you this but I hope you can forgive Rama one day. She has changed, I know it.'

'I don't hold any grudge against her; it's all in the past.'

'You are a good girl.' A jolt of pain stopped her from speaking. Her breathing became dense. When it passed, she looked at me. 'My work is done here. *Eeshwaar* is calling. Be good to yourself.' *Nani* closed her eyes and her hand went limp in mine. I sobbed, my frame shaking. I felt Rama pull me away and Ma took me home.

Nani's passing away left a hole in my heart and I couldn't think of anyone except for her. She was my *nani*. My appetite left me, making Ma and Papa anxious. Arjun would bring me delicious foods which I declined. My sisters came to play with me but I couldn't.

'Maybe we should call the doctor,' said Ma to Papa one day. I was pretending to read.

The doctor saw me but found nothing wrong. 'She just needs some time to deal with this. Death is something that takes time to be accepted. She will be alright.'

A few days later, Papa came to me with an expectant expression.

'I have some good news, Pooja.'

'What is it?'

'Satish has been arrested and is now in jail. Officer Stuart – Amit's friend, personally saw to his arrest. He was found hiding just outside of Rajkot. *Beta*, I have something else I want to say.' I stared at him with vacant eyes. He looked away but carried on speaking. 'I have found you a husband.'

This information did not shock me, it was inevitable. I remained silent.

'He is a lawyer and lives in Bombay. He is a very wealthy man; you won't have to work anymore. He will treat you like a queen. But *beta*, he is twenty-nine years old.'

'Eleven years older than me,' I said.

'The whole village and the neighbouring villages found about you, *dikra*. No one is willing to marry their son to you.' Papa's eyes filled up but for once, my eyes remained dry. 'It's my fault; I should have married you a long time ago. I was selfish.

'He is a widow. His wife died a few years ago and he has...three children. Rani, Kamla and Veer. They are still very young.'

My eyes were hard and uncaring outside but I was crying inside. 'It's not your fault, it is my blackened fate that has brought me here Papa,' I said with a bitter expression. 'You had to do what you had to do.'

My marriage was small. No one apart from my family, Amit, Sunil and Neha were present. We married in a temple and my husband took me to his home in Bombay.

'Ma, I am feeling cold.' Veer, the youngest of the three and only four, cuddled up to me in the bed.

'Where are Rani and Kamla?' I asked, rubbing his arms and legs. I felt his forehead – no fever. He shrugged his shoulders and leaned into me. I kissed his cheek fondly.

'Will you sing me the Gujarati lullaby?' he asked. His eyes drooped and he was soon fast asleep by the time I finished.

'Is he asleep?' Kamla whispered as she came in. She was eleven years old. She kissed my forehead.

'Come,' I moved over and winced.

'Papa hurt you again, didn't he?'

'It's nothing, *beta*.' I smiled. 'Where is Rani?'

Rani was the oldest, she was seventeen. Just one year younger than I. She wasn't happy when her Papa married me and so she kept away.

'Ma, you know her. Why worry? She must be out with one of her friends!'

'Shhh. Don't speak like that about your sister. She is older than you, have some respect.'

Rani was a difficult girl. She resented me and after all, I was only one year older than her, how could I be her mother? How dare I take her mother's place!

'But Ma, she doesn't talk to you and always – '

'She will be my friend soon, like you.' I touched her nose.

'You are not my friend but my Ma.' Kamla snuggled in close with me and Veer. She soon fell asleep but I stayed awake, caressing my unborn child, holding and cradling my stomach lovingly. She would be beautiful, I could feel it. I knew it would be a girl – I could see her sweet, dimpled smile, feel her chubby fingers around my one finger. Her hair would fall in soft spirals around her waist. Her laughter would sound like music and she would be loved by everyone...but...I feared for her life...I had to get out of here before Amar killed her.

Sixteen

Pooja's Flight

'Laxman, see who it is,' I called as I finished braiding Kamla's hair. 'Off you go now and be careful.' Kamla blew me a kiss and skipped out of the door. I busied myself with tidying up her room and then went downstairs.

'Who was it Laxman?' I froze when I came to the last step. I couldn't believe what I was seeing.

'Hello Pooja.' Sunil stood in the doorway and gave me his mischievous smile. I flew into his arms.

'This is a wonderful surprise!' I said.

'Ah, my arm, Pooja,' he said, laughing.

'I'm sorry.' I relaxed my hold on him but didn't let go. I was still smiling. I saw that he was scrutinising me and I absently pulled my hair over my left eye. 'Why didn't you write to say you were coming?'

His smile vanished as he touched my cheek. 'You look pale.'

I forced a laugh. 'Don't be silly, it's nothing. I fell over something and hit my face on the corner of the cupboard. I'm so clumsy.' I played with my bangles.

'*Nai*, you are hiding something from me.'

'Let it go, Sunil,' the girl beside him tugged his arm.

I hadn't noticed her and my embarrassment coloured my face. 'Oh! I'm so sorry!' I took Neha's hands and embraced her. '*Bhabhi*, please forgive me, I didn't see...'

'*Didi*, please don't apologise. I understand,' she said.

'I don't know where my head is! Please, come, come in.'

'You are living well,' Sunil commented taking in the main room. 'I am almost jealous.' His eyes twinkled.

'This was the first room Amar brought me into when we arrived after our marriage. He gave me free reign over this particular room and told me it was mine – I could do as I pleased. It became my baby and I decorated it and cared for the littlest things...' My face may have shown sadness for Sunil's face looked worried. 'Tell me, what brings you to Bombay?' I said quickly.

'It's not a happy reason, *didi*.' Neha folded her hands on her lap and looked down. 'My father was arrested. It wasn't his fault but they took him. He's been in jail for some time now but we come to see him each month. Sunil has been a great support.' Neha looked into Sunil's eyes and I saw the love that he gave back. I was jealous.

'*Chalo, Eeshwaar* is with us. I will pray for your father. He will listen,' I said gently, squeezing her hand. 'Will you have something to eat and drink first or do you want to rest?'

'Papaji's visiting time is 2pm. A little *chai* would be nice,' said Sunil.

I ordered the *chai* and we talked about Rajkot. Sunil told me about Amit and his *Memsahib.*

'Amit has fallen in love with someone? I can't believe it! Our Amit!' I said, shaking my head.

'It's true,' laughed Sunil.

'*Aacha*, tell me, have you heard from Dev?' Instantly I regretted it. If Amar found out that I'd asked...he didn't know about my love for Dev and if he ever found out...

'We don't know. He hasn't written to me or Amit in a long time,' came Sunil's casual reply. I could see there was more to this that he wasn't telling me.

'He must be busy,' I smiled wilfully.

The *chai* arrived with some savoury snacks. We ate whilst talking about Bombay city. Soon, it was time for them to go. As Neha went to freshen up, Sunil cornered me.

'You can't lie to me.' He put a firm hand on my shoulder and with the other hand; he gently lifted my chin, moving my head both ways, having a thorough look at my beaten face. 'How did you get those bruises?'

'I told you it's nothing. I'm clumsy, I tripped over, and that's all.'

'You are hiding something from me.' I looked away pretending to busy myself with the end of my sari.

'I'm ready Sunil,' Neha announced as she appeared. I gave a silent sigh of relief.

'I will have my driver take you,' I said avoiding Sunil's eyes. I went to talk to the driver. When I came back, Sunil and Neha were whispering.

'What are you two talking about?' I asked suspiciously.

'We need somewhere to stay tonight,' said Neha. 'I hope you don't mind, but if we can we stay the night here?'

'My house is your house. You are very welcome to stay and...you will be able to meet my husband.' I was glad that they were staying but whether Amar would welcome them, I wasn't sure. I instructed the driver to take them to the jail and I eagerly awaited their return.

It was 4pm when the doorbell rang. I was expecting Amar but to my delight it was Sunil and Neha. Neha had red rims around her eyes and Sunil looked tired and unsettled. I made the *chai* myself this time and we all sat down again in the main room.

The sky was an indigo grey and black clouds threatened heavy rain. A chilly breeze blew across the room. I closed the shutters. Veer came to me with his colouring book and pencils and sat down beside me. Not minding Sunil and Neha, he began to colour and soon got lost in his own world. I stroked his head fondly.

'This is Veer, he is four,' I said. 'I also have two other children, Kamla is eleven and Rani is seventeen. To the youngest two, I am their mother now but Rani, well, she still hasn't adjusted to me. It will take some time.'

I felt the shocked silence but I pretended not to notice.

'But Pooja, a mother, so soon?' Sunil said, clearly shocked. 'Did you know about this when you got married?'

'Yes, Papa told me before my marriage.'

'You knew this and still got married?'

I wondered if Sunil knew about my rape. Would Amit have told him? No, he had given me his word. I looked at Sunil. 'I am not sad or angry. I love these children like they are my own.'

'You are very brave, *didi*. I don't know if I could be strong enough to take on children, especially someone else's,' said Neha.

Fate doesn't let you choose, Neha, I thought. If what happened to me, happened to you, you wouldn't have a choice either.

'*Bhabhi*, how is your father?' I asked. This distracted them, I was glad to see.

'He is not very well. Being in jail has taken some life out of him, but he is strong.' Neha looked deeply into her *chai*.

'I have some news,' Sunil said abruptly.

Both Neha and I stared at him. Neha tried to stop him from speaking with her eyes and that made me even more curious.

'What is it?' I asked.

'Dev... is here, in Bombay.'

Silence followed and then I laughed shrilly. What absurdity. 'Impossible Sunil, Dev is in Simla.'

'He is in Nilpati jail,' Sunil said seriously. 'Sharing a cell with *Papaji*.'

My face fell and I was no longer laughing. 'But after Rakesh *Bhai*...no...he wouldn't do it. He wouldn't get involved with the Movement. He couldn't!' I said loudly.

'It is true. Papa told us. They share the same cell,' said Neha.

But I was still shaking my head. How could this be? Why would he put himself in danger? What about his family, what about me? Then I stopped. What was I thinking? I am a married woman, Amar is my husband. I shouldn't have these thoughts about Dev, I shouldn't care about him anymore...but no matter how many times I tried to reason with myself, I couldn't stop loving Dev...even though it was wrong. I looked at Sunil with wide, fearful eyes.

'Pooja, I am sure he will be freed. He won't die like Rakesh *Bhai*.'

'I'm fine,' I said. I began to pick up the finished cups of chai but Neha took them from me.

'Please, let me.'

Sunil put his arm around me and I began to cry on his shoulder.

'It's just a shock. I'm being silly.' I hastily wiped my face. I could feel Neha talking to Sunil with her eyes – he shouldn't have told me.

'No *Bhabhi*, it's good he has told me. This is something I had to know about. Amit, I, Dev and Sunil – we have known each other since being children and we are family. It is right that Sunil told me.'

'I'll take these into the kitchen,' said Neha kindly.

'You have found a good wife, a good companion,' I said as Neha left.

Suddenly a voice bellowed from the doorway. 'WHO IS THIS?' I jumped.

'Ma?' Veer's sleeping frame stirred and I took him into my arms.

Amar was holding a half-drunk bottle and his eyes were wild with rage. 'Well, who is he? Your lover?'

'You have drunk too much. You don't know what you are saying...shall I get you your dinner, you must be hungry. I will put Veer into his bed and then I will set your plate,' I said quickly.

'No, stay. Meenaxi Ba!' he called.

The servant came running. 'Ji Saab?'

'Take Veer to his bed,' he barked at her.

'What's all this shouting?' Neha came running and saw Amar – his hand around a half-drunk bottle and Sunil who was guarding me from my husband, pushing me away from him.

'This is my f...friend Sunil. He is engaged to Neha.' I said but my heart was thumping.

Amar's eyes roamed appreciatively over Neha's body, lingering where they shouldn't. She didn't waste time getting behind Sunil. I was very embarrassed.

'*Bhai Saab* that is my fiancée you are ogling at!' said Sunil rather sharply. 'I can forgive you as you don't know what you are doing. I suggest you go to sleep.'

'Who are you to tell me what to do in my own house?!' roared Amar. He took a swing at Sunil who ducked out of the way. Neha screamed.

I was afraid that Sunil would try to hit him back. I pulled Amar's arm and tried to lead him into the kitchen. He slapped my hand away with such force that I cried out.

'That was unnecessary.' Sunil took a step towards Amar, his hands clenched.

'Sunil, please,' I begged. 'It's late and Neha must be tired. I have made up your rooms, Meenakshi will take you up.'

'That's a good idea,' Neha's voice trembled slightly, taking Sunil's hand and following Meenakshi, our help, upstairs. Sunil went reluctantly, looking at me all the while. I dismissed him with my eyes.

It was only Amar and I now and I was even more frightened. He quietly went to the kitchen where the dinner was already served. The steam was rising from the plate. The cook nodded and left us alone. Amar sat down.

'Is he your lover? Were you with him before or after our marriage, or both?' Amar's accusing voice was harsh. He toyed with his spoon.

'He...he is a friend,' I whimpered.

'Why was he alone with you?'

'Ne..Neha went...'

'SHUT UP! SHUT UP! You are a filthy, disgusting whore!' He smashed a plate off the wall, shattering it to pieces. I missed the shards by inches, crawling under the table just in time. My heart was hammering against my chest. Amar grabbed my ankle. I screamed as he dragged me out.

'You cannot hide from me, bitch!' He kicked my stomach and I doubled over, breathless. My baby...oh my baby...

'Get up!' he pulled me to my feet and slapped me. Tears streamed down my face, I looked at him, pleading. I saw he wanted more. He took off his shoe and came towards me.

'No Amar, please, don't.' I heard some movement upstairs. He froze too, looking up at the ceiling. 'They will hear, my friends will come – '

Amar put the shoe down quietly then crushed me to his body, gripping me tightly with one arm. It hurt. He brought my face near to his roughly, his breath reeked of alcohol. With his free hand, he clamped my mouth.

'Now you listen to me,' he said. He looked up at the ceiling again and then back at me. 'You will suffer in absolute silence, otherwise...' He slid a finger from the nape of my neck, down to my waist where it rested for a moment. I held my breath. Then he pinched my flesh and twisted hard. I held back my cry. 'That's a good girl...looks like your lover and his whore decided to stay put. Wise of them.' Amar released me. I tried to leave but he pulled me back by my hair.

'Not yet, I want you to satisfy me – my beautiful wife.' His eyes were drunk with lust and hate.

I sobbed quietly through his roughness, his incessant roaming – biting and pinching and slapping me when I turned my face away. He lifted me onto the table and pulled my sari up, baring my thighs...oh God...please, no....

I was trembling – dirty from soul to skin. Amar sank into a chair and lit a cigar, watching me put my sari on properly. I hadn't yet finished when he took the end of my sari and twirled it around my neck, applying pressure. I could hardly breathe. He released it a little and I gulped in air.

'Scary, isn't it?' he breathed his hot breath in my face. 'The feel of death...hopefully this will teach you never to cross me again. I am your husband and I will not have you belittle me! You understand? I will not have a whore as a wife! Amar hovered his lit cigar over my face and smirked. 'Such a plain but beautiful face...it would be a shame to ruin it, wouldn't it?'

My eyes travelled to his cigar – he saw my fear. 'Do you know why I married you? It's because you were already damned, you were already used. Did you think I didn't know about your past? Tragic, wasn't it? I needed a servant and someone to look after my children – I got one. I never loved you; you are just a stupid, village girl - someone to feed my lust.' He laughed and then ground the cigar into my shoulder, slamming the door as he left.

I sank to the floor; I was too shocked to cry anymore. Damn Amar! I wished I was dead...but no, I had to think about my unborn. Oh my baby...she has to be alive, she must. God may punish me as much as he wants but I won't let him take away my baby!

I rocked back and forth. I shook uncontrollably – horrible images of my baby – dead – flashed through my mind. I now wailed, clutching my stomach and praying, praying that *He*[129] must keep my baby alive!

'Pooja! Oh Pooja.' I looked into Sunil's face. I hadn't heard him come. Sunil kneeled before me, taking me into his embrace. I clutched his shirt.

'*Didi*, I'm sorry...' Neha wiped my face with a cool flannel; her eyes were wet. 'We should have come earlier...I am so sorry.'

'I need to sleep,' I whispered.

Sunil lifted me into his arms and carried me upstairs. It was comforting to feel secure. He gently put me into my bed and I closed my eyes, feeling oddly relaxed. My eyes were heavy...I felt Sunil's hand leave mine as I drifted away.

The following morning, I washed my body. I daren't look at myself in the mirror; I was too scared of my appearance. When I was dressed and slightly comfortable with myself, I went down to find Sunil and Neha packed and ready to leave.

'Our train leaves soon, *didi*,' said Neha. She kissed my cheek ever so gently, like I was a porcelain doll that might smash under the slightest pressure.

'Please don't mind Amar, he isn't usually like that– ' I said.

---

[129] *He*, God

'Spare us. This isn't the first time he has hurt you, is it?' Sunil's eyes were full of loathing. I lowered my eyes. 'I thought so.' His tone was clipped. 'So, we have decided that you are coming with us today, back home.'

My eyes were wide with horror. 'I...can't. I can't go back home, Sunil. *Bhabhi*, you must understand.'

'We have already packed some of your things, *didi*. Please come with us.' She came to take my hand but I pulled back sharply.

'I have to think of the children,' I said desperately.

'They are not your children, Pooja. You are not living with this monster anymore. You are coming home,' Sunil's voice was raised a little. His face showed no sign of sympathy, like it was set in stone.

'I can't shame my family by coming home. Amar will calm down and see his mistake. Please believe me.'

'*Didi*, how can we leave you when we know what happens here?' said Neha.

'Please, I'm begging you, let me be. I will handle Amar. He will not do this again.' I needed them to understand. 'Give me one more chance. My marriage is important. I love Amar.'

Sunil snorted. 'Another lie...if we can't persuade you to come home then I want you to promise one thing. If he does this to you again, then you will tell us. I will bring you home. Just remember that.'

I nodded, tears brimming my eyes. 'Please don't tell anyone at home.'

'If that's what you want.'

'It is.'

Neha embraced me but Sunil walked out of the door. Neha looked at me apologetically before she left too.

The baby was safe, the doctor told me. 'But you must be very careful, Pooja. Running around in the early days of pregnancy is not safe, for you or your baby.' He watched me over his spectacles, examining me from head to toe. He shook his head. 'Pooja, if there was something wrong at home, you would tell me?'

'Ofcourse, doctor *Saab*.' I couldn't look at him; I was a terrible liar. He didn't seem satisfied with my answer but said I was fine to go home but he would come to see me regularly.

My right-hand help, Meenaxi Ba, showed the doctor out. She was like my *dadi* and she disapproved of me.

'I have told you to leave, *Memsahib*. I curse that husband of yours a thousand times! I'm sorry,' she said when I gave her a look of contempt.

'Meenaxi Ba, you know Amar's anger. It will subside. He is a good man, deep inside, he loves me.'

'*Memsahib*, just try and be careful around him. Your baby is precious and I want to see the little one born.'

I smiled and she embraced me. 'I will get the food brought up to you.'

'Thank you,' I said. I took to looking out of the window after she was gone.

Amar's drinking worsened over the weeks. His womanising continued with no shame or guilt on his part. I tried to not see, to not hear and hurried out of the house when he came home with someone on his arm.

I was unlucky sometimes and had to bear the humiliation as he wooed, touched and kissed the women before me. When I tried to speak, he became angry – my punishments not far between. It was game to him and he enjoyed it.

I was four months pregnant now and my bump was visible, at least to me – I wanted her safe...yesterday it got all too much.

Amar was drinking straight out of a bottle in the early hours when I approached him. He seemed relaxed – that was a good sign.

'Amar, I need to make up a room. I will need some money,' I said, thinking of the baby's room.

'Why do you need to decorate? For whom – your lover?' he laughed, amused by his own joke.

'Please Amar, I need you to listen. You will be pleased.'

He looked at me like I was dirt – something he wanted to get rid of. I carried on. 'I'm pregnant, Amar.'

He looked at me, surprised but didn't smile. 'Get rid of it. I don't want a child of yours.'

I gasped. 'How could you say such a thing? Are you not pleased?' I was hurt, ofcourse I was.

'I already have children – worthless as they are. That thing –' he pointed at my stomach. 'It's not mine. It can't be.' Then, without warning, he slapped me, throwing me down. His eyes flashed. 'It's your lover's child, isn't it?'

Amar moved towards me, the bottle swinging dangerously in his hand. The drink sloshed inside like an angry sea. He took a long drink.

'Amar, please believe me, the baby is yours. Amar, please!' Amar grabbed my hair and pulled me up from my cowering position. He flung me against the wall and I fell to the floor. I screamed – the horrendous pain! I rolled around, clutching my stomach. I saw Amar's foot above my stomach and instinct told me to turn. Before I could, the door bell rang.

'*Saab*, someone has come to see you,' said Laxman, bowing his head but not before I saw the shock on his face.

'Who is it?' Amar barked.

'*Memsahib* Jenny and her husband.'

'Show them to the guest room. I will be there in a moment.'

'Yes *Saab*.' Laxman went away. Amar turned to me. 'Get presentable, now! I expect you to be on your best behaviour. Will we deal with *that* later.'

I packed a bag for myself and a bag for Kamla and Veer, as Amar slept in the next room with his lady. I was trembling in fear – what if he woke up? Would he stop me? Would he kill me, trying to stop me from leaving? I had no choice. I had to go, for myself, for my baby.

I would leave in the morning when Amar would be at work – Kamla and Veer will be happy to come. There was only Rani. I will speak to her tomorrow...

I halted at the door. My children stood beside me holding a small bag each, waiting expectantly for me to do something.

'Ma, where are we going?' Veer asked.

'We are going to Poona. Rama *maasi*[130] lives there, we are going for a visit.'

'Can we play there?' he asked.

'You can play as much as you want there and you will get a lot of sweets too,' I smiled, ruffling his hair. He smiled back; he seemed

---

[130] *Maasi,* Auntie (Mother's sister)

satisfied.

Rama and I kept in touch after *Nani's* passing. As *Nani* requested, I tried to forgive her but some things weren't easy. Rama wrote letters to me frequently but I didn't reply. After a few months, my heart melted and I began to forgive her. Her next letter was full of happiness.

Rama sent a wedding invitation and that was the day Amar and I had our first, violent argument. He tore the invitation to pieces and threw them into my face.

'Ma isn't Rani *Bena* coming?' asked Kamla.

'She is unable to come today but she may later,' I said.

'I know why she isn't coming Ma, you don't have to cover for her. She doesn't like you – she doesn't see what is happening here...to you...she is selfish!' I was surprised at the sudden outburst. I had never seen Kamla so angry...and what did she mean by saying she doesn't see what is happening here, to me – how much did she know? I would need to speak to her as soon as we reach Poona.

'*Beta*, you must not say such things about your sister. She has a right to feel how she does...give her some time. She will like me one day,' I said. Kamla shrugged but crossed her arms, looking the other way. I sighed.

I looked at my watch. Should I wait any longer? Rani wasn't coming – I had to admit it. Veer tugged my sari. 'Is Papa coming?'

'No *beta*, now enough questions. Let us go or our train will leave the station without us.' I looked to the stairs, still hoping to see her. I sighed and opened the door.

'Pratap *ji*,' I said to the driver. 'Give this letter to *Saab*. I am going away for some time...I need you to drive us to the station.'

He looked forlorn. 'Saab has treated you badly. We all see and hear but we are afraid, *Memsahib*. We couldn't help you and we are sorry. I will miss you.'

My throat constricted; I felt tears prick my eyes. 'This is not anyone's fault,' I said. I took an envelope from my purse. 'Here is some money, share it out amongst everyone.'

Pratap *ji* nodded numbly. Taking our luggage, he stored it in the back of the motorcar and drove us to the station.

I felt free – in so many months...it was just me now and my two children. I couldn't leave them in that big house with that beast. I hoped Rani would have understood, hoped that she would agree to come with us. I shouldn't have been surprised when she refused.

I'd entered her room merely hours ago. She was sitting quietly by her window, staring out at the garden. I stood beside her bed and waited for her to speak to me. But she continued to ignore me.

'Rani *beta*, please look at me,' I said softly.

'I don't want to talk to you.'

'Please Rani...I wish you would accept me – not as a mother but at least as a friend. I don't intend to take your mother's place and I never will. We can be good friends instead of mother and daughter, can't we?'

Rani let out a frustrated sigh. She stared at me with dark, cold eyes. 'Why did Papa marry you? Why someone so young?'

'I don't know Rani.' I couldn't tell Rani the truth – the truth that I found out only recently...Rani looked at me scornfully. 'Your Papa wanted you to marry my Papa for his money. He is a rich man, he could have had anybody. Why you?'

'Does that matter now?' I sighed. 'Listen, I am going away for some time. I am taking Veer and Kamla and I would like you to come with me.'

'You are taking Veer and Kamla? Where to? No, I will not allow it! They are not your children, you have no right!' Her rage vibrated throughout her body. 'Does Papa know about this?'

'By law, I am your and their mother now. I will take the little ones with me and your Papa will know about it. I am leaving you my address...if you change your mind.'

'I will never come! I will tell Papa, he won't let you go!' she screamed.

'It's your choice but I am going,' I said calmly. 'Look after yourself, Rani.'

Before I left, I wrote a brief note to Amar and left it in his office.

The train left the station and soon my children were aleep. I was right to do this; they would be away from a drunken, womanising and out of control monster. I imagined his face – full of rage and disbelief – when he opened my letter. I shuddered. I was glad that at least, Kamla and Veer were with me.

Entering Rama's house was like stepping back to the past, a house, simple, yet beautiful. I felt I was back at home, in Rajkot. I half expected Ma to be jostling around in the kitchen, Papa listening to the radio or entering figures in his book, Arjun combing his hair and looking in the mirror and my sisters, running around the courtyard. My heart skipped a beat as I thought of them. I missed them very much.

The front door was open and I glimpsed in to see a man tending to some plants. He didn't look like a gardener but someone who lived here. He was smartly dressed in a white shirt and brown trousers. Something about his demeanour told me he was a good man. I tentatively knocked on the door and the man looked my way. His face spread into a wide grin.

'It's so good for you to come at last!' he said as he came to the door. 'We have all been waiting for you.'

Waiting for me? But they didn't know that I was coming...had I got the wrong house?

'Is this Rama's house?' I asked.

'I am Rama's husband. You are Pooja, aren't you?'

I nodded, very surprised.

'Come, come inside,' he ushered us through the door and I stood awkwardly in the courtyard, with the children.

'I am Shivraj and this is my mother. Everybody calls her Mangal Ba with love.'

Shivraj introduced a short, round woman with warm, twinkling eyes and a kind smile. She was quite dark and had prominent lines on her face and hands.

'*Namaste*,' I said.

Mangal Ba clasped her hands to her mouth, making her metal bangles clang.

'Pooja?' she looked at her son, then at me and beckoned me to sit down next to her. Veer and Kamla followed in my step. Mangal Ba looked at them.

'They are my children, Kamla and Veer.' I pushed them gently forwards. '*Pai lago*[131],' I said to them.

'*Nai, nai*. That's alright. My blessing will always be with you,' she said putting a hand each on their heads. 'They are very good and behaved.'

'Is Rama here?' I asked looking around.

---

[131] *Pai lago*, an action to touch one's feet to show respect.

'It's been very long; Rama has cried over you many times,' said Mangal Ba. 'She has longed to see you. You have changed her life.'

Shivraj came with *chai* and *puri*[132] and some juice for the children. 'She will be home soon; she has just gone next door. The daughter has just had a baby girl and she is helping look after her.

I nodded and without thinking, put my hand on my stomach. I yawned.

'You and the children must rest after you have eaten. It will be good for your baby too,' said Mangal Ba.

'Sorry, what did you say?'

'Your feet are heavy[133], *beta*. How many months are you along? No more than four?'

I gasped. 'How did you know?'

'A mother always knows. It will be a girl. When *Ma Laxmi* enters your life, you will become very happy. She will unburden you life.'

I wondered how she knew so much. I'd certainly not told Rama in any of the letters about Amar, good or bad. I smiled and pretended to look around; I was still feeling quite unsettled. I observed there were no servants here. Nothing was elegant or extravagant.

'It is simple here, I like it,' I said.

'We are not wealthy people. We believe in simplicity. *Paisa*[134] is a fiscal thing...it is important of course. We must use it wisely, for clothes, food and a roof over one's head.'

'But Rama...'

'She has changed very much, but I will let her tell you. You must have known a very different Rama,' Mangal Ba stated.

'She likes all this?' I was startled.

'Yes, it was her idea,' said Shivraj. 'When we married, she only brought sentimental items with her. Her dadi's things – a sari, a necklace, a ring, a photo and....I will let her tell you.'

Could Rama have changed so much? I looked around to see if there was a photograph. I spotted a framed picture of a happy couple on their wedding day.

'May I?'

---

[132] *Puri*, fried Indian bread

[133] *Your feet are heavy*, a saying in the Indian language, meaning you are pregnant.

[134] *Paisa*, Money

Shivraj handed me the frame. Rama was standing next to him, smiling shyly at the camera. She was beautiful. With flowers in her hair, she wore a pretty bridal sari which bore small, embedded stones. A glistening border ran along the edge of her sari. Shivraj was dressed in a shiny Kurta suit; he looked very important standing straight, his head held high.

'How did you meet?' I asked.

'It was not arranged – I saw her at a friend's wedding. She came from the groom's side and I was from the bride's side. We got married without her parent's permission but Mangal Ba was delighted. They have accepted us now but sometimes I still wonder...well, anyway that doesn't matter now.'

'Ma, I'm tired.' Veer came to me, rubbing his eyes.

'Pooja *beta*. Go and rest. The children are tired too. We will wake you when Rama comes home.' Mangal Ba showed us a room with a large bed. The room was nice and comfortable with a picture of baby *Lord Krishna* hanging on the wall. She left us be. As soon as I got the children to sleep, my energy waned and I slept soundly.

I don't know what woke me but my sleep vanished and it was replaced with a serene, familiar face, yet, maybe altered a little.

'You finally came,' Rama said, tears splashing her cheeks.

We sat outside on the swing. Shivraj was inside with Mangal Ba; they were looking after my still, sleeping children. Clouds had gathered and rain began to fall softly. We were safe under the swing's canopy.

'I'm sorry I didn't...wasn't at your wedding,' I said. Flecks of rain hit my face, it was nice.

'I waited but when you didn't come, I had a feeling something was wrong. The Pooja I knew would come, I was sure about that. I even argued with myself to wait. The *marajh* was getting impatient – the *maurat*[135] was slipping away. We couldn't wait any longer. When you didn't come at the end of the wedding, I was very disappointed. And the strange thing was that I was nervous, for you.'

'Yes, Rama. There was something wrong,' I said. 'My life in Bombay is very different to my old life in the village. Once I lived in a

---

[135] *Maurat*, Holy period of time.

poor house, now I am the *Memsahib* of a mansion. I marvelled at the marble floors, the carpets, the drapes and my large bed with the curtains. The funny thing is my bedroom now resembles yours at the Chatterji house. I had not owned such wealth. Amar had many servants. They treated me with respect, with honour.

'The first few months of my marriage were full of happiness. Amar took me to all the high society parties, to the theatre and the cinema. I even learnt some English,' I laughed. 'Saris, bangles, *chapals*, *bindis* – Amar chose them with care and love. I didn't wear the same sari twice. I was living your life Rama.'

'And the children?'

'Veer is so young. He called me Ma straight away. Kamla was hesitant and shy but she liked me. I became their mother. Rani, she is the eldest and only one year younger than me. She still hasn't accepted me.'

'Tell me about my brother-in-law,' said Rama. 'Does he love you?'

'Amar,' I said bitterly. 'He soon became bored of me, his wife. He got in bad company and began to drink heavily. He forgot he had a wife who waits for him at home, to come home, alone at the end of the day.'

'What do you mean?'

'He brought other girls home; in front of me...my husband is a violent man, Rama. He sleeps with other women and humiliates me.'

'*Hé Ram!*' She looked at the sky. I saw her eyes were wet.

'Our *kismet*[136] is our own,' I said. 'You are very lucky to have such a nice husband. I envy you.'

'What's this?' She slid one of my bangles aside to reveal a black mark. Amar had held my wrist and twisted it three days ago when his anger peaked again. It could have been worse had Kamla not walked in. Amar threw me aside and walked away.

Before I could give Rama an answer Kamla came into our midst and settled beside me. I kissed her forehead. 'Ma, does that hurt a lot? Why did Papa do that to you, why was he so angry?'

'Amar did that to you? In anger? What else has he done?' Rama said rather sharply.

I was hoping to avoid these questions. 'Kamla, go to Veer. I

---

[136] *Kismet*, destiny

think he has woken up.'

'Ji Ma.' Kamla nodded and was away.

'He beats you and you keep quiet. Why didn't you come to me? Why did you suffer all this time? It's my fault. If I hadn't treated you like I had, if I hadn't beaten you too...I am no less of a monster than he is. I am really sorry, Pooja. I am so ashamed.'

'It's all in the past - and I don't want to think about it. I have my husband, Rama. He won't be hurting me again. Now, I want to ask you a favour.'

'Anything,' said Rama. Her tortured face sought mine and she held there for a while, probably trying to find some happiness in my eyes. 'I have met no one like you, I doubt I ever will. Dadi was right, you are so different. Beautiful, from the heart. Beautiful from outside.' She wiped away her tears.

'Rama, can I stay here until I find a house to rent?' I asked.

She suddenly embraced me, squeezing me hard. 'You are always welcome here, my sister. Always.'

We rocked back and forth on the swing, our minds alike. I was at peace.

~ AMIT ~

Seventeen

Secrecy

Time and time again, I was given the opportunity to see Mary.
Sometimes, it was Stuart who invited me to their house and sometimes
it was Mary who needed help and sometimes Tom surprised me too.
He called me the "medicine man" and relied on my herbal remedies
and called me over for colds and the odd aches and pains.

Stuart wanted my companionship and we would talk for hours
about politics, the climate, London and Goa, of course. Mary, oh my
lovely Mary...she liked me for my knowledge on many subjects. She
loved to wear saris – ever since Ma gifted her one, she has been in love
with this simple garment. But she didn't know how to wear it so I
asked Ma to show her. She was very happy to do it and as before,
didn't let Mary go without eating.

Mary would ask me specifically – how do you make *roti*, what
is the correct price for a dozen mangoes, what colour sari would suit
her – the last question suited a husband to reply but I was more than
willing. It is blue, I said. The colour of the ocean and the sky.

But what she loved the most, were my poems and she would
request I recite them for her. I could never refuse. During lazy
afternoons, when there was nothing much to do, she would ask me to
come and teach her to write beautiful verses. Yes, life was a great
thing right now.

It was the mango season and I picked two dozen by hand, especially
for Mary. I asked Sunil to accompany me to Mary's house. I wanted to
surprise her.

Chandu dropped us off at the bottom of the steps and we
slowly walked up, reaching the gate, quite out of breath. Sunil was
nearly dying – I had to laugh. We opened the gate to a heavenly scene
– the lawn, immaculate and lush green, the trees, standing tall and
important and the flowers, the fragrance divine. I inhaled
appreciatively. Mary also had a dog – *Rajkumar*, they called him. As
he came bounding to greet us, Sunil hid behind me, praying for his
survival. *Rajkumar* leapt up on his hind legs and licked my face. I
laughed and patted him on the belly. He was a gentle dog but poor

Sunil, ran. *Rajkumar* thought it was a game – Sunil was running for a long time.

'*Rajkumar*, stop!' To my admiration, the dog stopped on command – Tom's command. He had just come out of the front door. Sunil relaxed.

'Well, I am impressed,' I said.

'He has been trained well, by me,' said Tom happily. This is what I liked about him – he was not over-confident, nor did he think he was above everyone else. I saw no smug looks, no air of importance. And that was what made it hard for me to dislike him.

'Did you want to see someone?' he asked.

'No, we thought we would come by and drop off these mangoes – we are going to the *Mela*[137]. Is *Memsahib* around?' I asked.

'No, I'm sorry you missed her. She just popped out but Stuart is inside. It's his day off. He will be pleased to see you.'

My smile wavered but he didn't notice. He got onto his bicycle. The driver came forward but Tom waved him down. 'Thank you, Shyamlal, but I prefer to ride the bike today. It won't take long to get there. When Mary arrives home, do tell her I won't be back until late this evening. Goodbye,' he said to Sunil and me.

We waved Tom off and went inside. It was quiet apart from the ticking of the big clock.

'Maybe we should sit and wait somewhere,' Sunil suggested, looking dubiously at a long, white settee. He patted his clothes down but then decided to sit on the floor. I walked to the window which faced the garden. The wooden shutters were opened wide and an amiable discussion was taking place between Stuart and a man I didn't recognise.

'They are considering my posting elsewhere, a secondment, maybe in Calcutta,' said Stuart.

'That's a big move,' said the other man. 'Do you have a choice in this?'

'Under the current climate, the commissioner is considering many things. The Quit India Movement has somewhat quietened down but the threat is still there. The Indian population are restless. It has come to an understanding that a lot of planning and secrecy, in Calcutta and the North, has been in action. Gujarat seems to be in

---

[137] *Mela*, India fair

control and we haven't had any reports thus so far...' Stuart trailed off; his thoughts seem to be elsewhere.

'But even so,' said the second man. 'Surely, there are Officers in Calcutta. I don't see why they want to send you. It seems absurd.'

'George, it's a dilemma. But what can I do? The senior inspector has seen my work here. Like I said, things are in control. He feels I will be able take charge in Calcutta – take down the Indians who are retaliating against the *Raj*.'

'Stuart, do you want to do this? If you do find the culprits, what would you do? Shoot them?' said George.

'Not at all. But I would find an alternative way to make them understand...well, let's see.' Again, Stuart seemed to go away from the present.

'Is there something else you want to talk about? You seem bothered, somehow. Go on, spit it out.'

Stuart sighed. 'I'm worried about Tammy. She is so far away from her mother; she was supposed to be here by now. Cindy is looking after her but it's not right. Oh – I'm glad that she is away from London – the air raids...'

'Mother tells me London is in ruins. Wherever you look, there is rubble and dust. People, whose homes have been demolished by the bloody Germans, are now squatting with other families who still have a home or are living in the Underground tunnels. It's safer, they say. Tammy will be fine, don't worry unnecessarily,' said George. 'What about Mary, how does she feel about her?'

Who was Tammy? Mary had never mentioned this name before. Who was Tammy to her, why would she care? Perhaps it was another Mary they were talking about; after all, it was a common name. But that didn't make sense either – how many Mary's did Tom know of?

'You see Mary – she is –' Stuart stopped talking as something smashed.

'Oh! Sorry, sorry!' exclaimed Sunil. Damn Sunil! Why did he have to be so careless?

'Who's there?' Stuart said from his chair, his hand shielding against the glare of the sun. I quickly backed away from the window, reaching Sunil in two strides. A servant was already sweeping the broken vase and picking up the yellow flowers. I hit Sunil over the head.

'Ouch!' Why did you do that?' he complained, rubbing the spot where I'd hit him. I gave him another for good measure. 'Will you stop that?'

'Why do you have to be so stupid?' I hissed. Sunil looked at me like I had gone mad.

Just then, Stuart came in, followed by the man, George. 'What was all that commotion?' He saw us standing near the "accident" spot.

'Amit, what brings you here today?' he asked. He looked at the broken pieces which the servant was holding in the dustpan. 'Mary won't be pleased, that was her favourite vase.'

Oh no, I thought. I wanted to hit Sunil again.

'I'm sorry *Saab*, it was my fault,' Sunil said sheepishly.

'Sorry Stuart, we will be going now,' I said. 'We only came by to drop off some mangoes...I will leave them with the cook.'

Stuart glanced from me to Sunil and back again. He looked confused and very distracted. It was strange. Never had I seen him like this – could this be because of the person called Tammy? Stuart shook his head slowly, like he was clearing his head. It was our time to go.

'Well, goodbye Stuart.' I nodded to the other man who looked as bewildered as I was with Stuart's behaviour. I took Sunil by the elbow and nearly dragged him away. I almost forgot about the mangoes – quickly giving them to the cook with a brief message for Mary, we left.

Even though I have known Stuart for a short time, I got to know his behaviour – which was normally carefree and light. It was disturbing to see him like this. Sunil was talking all the way home but I wasn't listening. I wanted to know why or what was making Stuart behave in such a way. It was making me uneasy. I planned to ask Mary the next time I meet her. Yes, she would tell me.

'What is it?' I said as we walked down the hill.

Sunil has been brooding over something for a couple of days and today he decided to tell me.

'I am worried about Pooja,' he said. 'I want to talk to you about her.'

'Has something happened, is she alright?' I couldn't understand Sunil's anxiety. He shook his head dismally and told me about his trip to Bombay – the way she looked, the beatings and the children. I couldn't speak for a while...Amar had children? He was married before? And...Pooja was getting beaten...Oh God!

'She won't leave him,' said Sunil. 'I asked her to come home but she was concerned about leaving the children. She said Amar would not beat her again. But Amit, I have seen his temper and I have seen what he can do to her.'

'We have to bring her home,' I said. 'But we cannot force her. A girl to come back after her marriage – under whatever circumstances – is a taboo subject. Everybody in the village knows about her past now, she will be taunted and her family would not be able to bear such humiliation. Pooja believes in her marital vows, she was brought up like that. She will try and make her marriage work before making any decisions – I know that much. We have to tread carefully...'

'But what about in the meantime? What if her husband beats her again?' Sunil was very angry and frustrated.

'I don't know...let me think about it,' I said.
We were near the *Dhaba*[138] and we stopped for some juice and something to eat. We sat down as the boy went to get the beverages.

It was a cool evening, the red and orange ball was shimmering in the sky. A dog scooted across the way and disappeared into the bushes. A cow walked with her owner – her bell tinkling around her neck.

I thought about Pooja, could it really be as bad as Sunil said? I hoped not but I needed to see her for myself. I picked up my juice and took a long drink.

'I have more bad news,' said Sunil.

'What else could there be?' I asked wearily.

'Dev is in jail, Amit. He is in Bombay.'

'Don't be silly, he is in Simla,' I said but Sunil shook his head. 'But there hasn't been any letters, no word. Sunil, he promised he would stay away from trouble – he said he would stay away from anything to do with the Quit India Movement – he said he wouldn't try and avenge Rakesh *Bhai*'s death!'

'What makes you think that's the reason he is in jail?' asked Sunil.

I shrugged. 'I can't foresee any other explanation. Tell me, have you spoken to him?'

---

[138] **Dhaba**, a small restaurant which sells "quick" snacks and refreshments such as chai/juice aswell as hearty meals.

'Not yet, but I mean to.'

'Then how did you find out?'

'Neha's Papa told us,' said Sunil, pausing over his food. 'They share the same cell – ironic isn't it? *Papaji* told me that Dev chose not to tell anyone.'

'Well then he is stupid!'

'What are we going to do?' asked Sunil.

'First I will speak to Stuart. When we go to see Dev, then we will go and see Pooja.'

'That sounds like a good plan.'

Sunil and I finished our juice and left the *Dhaba*.

I wanted to go alone to see Stuart – it would be a quick discussion, I was sure. Sunil said he had to see to the school accounts anyway.

Stuart was at the police station. The shadows of distress and worry that I had seen earlier in the past few weeks were not there, much to my relief. He listened intently as I explained Dev's situation – as much as I was able to.

'Do you know why he's in jail?' Stuart asked.

'No, not at all.'

Stuart leaned back into his chair. 'Do you think he was involved in some kind of Quit India action? Maybe a march or a speech?'

'Maybe. There was a time when he was thinking of joining the Movement and I thought I had dissuaded him but now I am not so sure.'

'Amit, we need to know what actually happened. The more accurate, the better. You are good friends with him, he will tell you. I will arrange a visiting time for both you and Sunil – I presume he would like to go with you?' Stuart smiled warmly. 'In normal circumstances, one doesn't have to apply for a visit but in some cases, it is necessary. For Dev, it may be. I will look into it.'

'Thank you,' I said. I paused – should I ask him about his worry? I decided I would risk it. 'Stuart, I want to ask you about something that may be...personal. I would like to think that we are good friends?'

'That we are, Amit?' he smiled. 'What's on your mind?'

'I hope I wouldn't be overstepping the mark by asking you if everything was fine at home. You have been worried and distressed.'

Stuart's smile vanished. His forehead furrowed, he looked at me. 'Why do you say that?'

Oh no. 'I overheard your conversation that day with your friend, George. I didn't mean to, I am really sorry.'

'How much did you hear?' Stuart seemed to be angry.

'Something...about someone called Tammy...I'm sorry, Stuart. Please forgive me. It is not my business.'

'Oh dear Lord.' Stuart stood up and paced. 'Here is the thing, Amit. It is a shame that you heard our conversation but there is absolutely nothing to worry about. It is a private matter of mine.'

'I understand,' I said. I felt awful. I stood up to go but he put a hand on my shoulder. His anger had vanished.

'I'm sorry I was harsh. It's not your fault that you overheard and I shouldn't take it out on you.'

'If you need my help...anything...'

'I will bear that in mind. You are a good person, Amit. I am glad and thankful to God to have kept that seat empty, on that day, on the bus.' Stuart cleared his throat. 'I will see to your request for your friend.'

On my way home, I couldn't stop thinking about Stuart; what was it that he wasn't telling me? The dry soil crunched under my feet as I walked on, my mind too occupied with thoughts on Dev, Pooja and Stuart. It was all such a problem!

I trusted Dev; I believed that he was innocent. I hoped he had not gone against my advice and done something silly. The reason to go to Simla was to forget all about his troubles. Khan *Bhai* told me himself - that was the reason why he had sent him. But why hadn't Dev written to us about his imprisonment? He hadn't even told his Ma and *Babuji*.

Maybe I should tell them...*nai*...I will wait until I have seen him. That would be the right thing to do.

Pooja, Pooja, Pooja...my dear sister – why did bad luck follow her? She is a good person and she doesn't deserve this. Not at all! I thought of her husband - *Kuthé, Kamina*[139], *Ullu ka Patha*[140], selfish son of...I took a deep breath...calm, Amit. Yes, I thought, I will calm

---

[139] *Kamini/Kamina*, bad person
[140] *Ullu ka* Patha, Fool

down – so when I see him, he will not know his own name! *Ullu ka Patha*!

'Amit!' I heard a cycle bell ring shrilly in my midst and the next thing; I was lying in a ditch – mud all over me. Then I heard the most beautiful sound – Mary's laugher. I sat in the mud, mesmerised. There she was, sitting on her bicycle; her pretty fingers gripping the handlebars as she leaned back, laughing. Today, she wore a blue floral dress; her hair loose, playing around the nape of her neck...

'Oh Amit, I'm sorry.' She wiped her tears – of laughter. 'It's very rude of me. I am not good at this, but I thought I would give it a try. I did ring the bell – you were obviously not paying attention. And look at you, covered in mud!'

'That's alright,' I stood up. 'I can wash.' I looked at her face and she was watching mine. Our eyes met and held for a long moment. She broke away first.

'I'd better go,' she said.

I remembered Stuart's behaviour. 'Mary *Memsahib*, can I ask you something?'

'Ofcourse.'

'I am worried about Stuart *Saab's* behaviour. He seems disturbed and worried. I overhead – by mistake – a conversation about someone called Tammy. He mentioned you – *Memsahib*, where are you going?'

'I'm sorry, Amit. I have to go!' She looked horrified and cycled away furiously.

What did I say? Something strange was happening and for some reason, I was being kept in the dark. What was the secret?

Eighteen

How could this be?

Our visiting date to see Dev was fixed. I asked Stuart if he had any information on Dev's imprisonment.

'He was arrested during a speech from a freedom fighter, in Simla. Other than that, Dev hasn't said,' said Stuart. 'The jailors tried their best to get him to speak but he was stubborn – he said he was innocent and that he didn't go there to listen to a speech, that he accidentally came across it.'

'Ofcourse he is innocent!' I exclaimed. 'Dev is telling the truth.'

'I want to believe you, Amit but the odds are against your friend. Find out more from your friend if you can.'

So here we were – Sunil and I, on the train to Bombay. It was uneventful and we passed the time playing cards or sleeping. It was eight hours into the journey and night had fallen. The train chugged past villages where only spots of lights twinkled in the distance.

Sunil lay on the top bunk with a hat on his face and I sat cross-legged on the seat opposite. Eventually, I heard snoring and the odd incoherent word from above. I drifted in and out of sleep but not dreaming of anything.

I was irritable when I woke up, feeling sleep deprived – Sunil kept a safe distance from me. He flagged down a tonga when we stepped out of the station. Soon, we were at Nilpati jail.

Dev walked towards us, slow and maybe uncaring. I breathed in sharply as he came closer. A similar sound echoed from Sunil.

A drawn face; pale, his complexion almost papery. Bruises shadowed his once, happy face which was now pensive. His clothes hung off a skeletal frame. He sat down facing us, his hands on the table. I couldn't speak.

Then he smiled. 'I look dead, don't I? Are you scared of me?'

'Ofcourse not, my brother.' Sunil, I and Dev rose all at the same time and embraced, our arms over each other's shoulders.

'Dev,' I said. 'Why didn't you tell anyone? Why are you

punishing yourself?'

'I didn't want to worry anybody,' said Dev, quite calmly.

Sunil cut in. 'Dev *Bhai*, you should have told us, we would have done something – anything to get you out of here.'

'*Bas bas*, Sunil.' Dev's tone was grave but he smiled. 'If it was that easy, then Shankarji would not have been here this long. But thank you, it's nice to know you believe me.'

I stared at him. 'What happened in Simla?'

'I was intrigued...a large gathering took my curiosity. It was a speech, innocent and non violent. The police arrived and here I am.'

'Was that all? Dev, we need to know exactly what happened,' I said. 'I have a friend who is an Officer. He might be able to help but you must tell us everything.'

Dev told us about the speech – what was said and that everybody was listening. The police didn't give anyone a chance and they used *lathis*[141]. He didn't remember anything much after that.

'But the speech was innocent,' said Sunil.

Dev shrugged. 'There was no instruction to sabotage or attack. There was no malice.'

'Will you speak to Officer Stuart? You can trust him,' I asked.

'I will always tell the truth,' he said.

I was relieved. Dev had not intended to kill – to avenge his brother. He'd kept his promise.

'Have you told Ma and *Babuji*?' he asked.

'No, but they have to know.'

'Does Pooja know?'

Sunil and I looked at each other.

'Dev, so much has happened...I don't know if I should tell you...maybe she should be the one...' I said.

'I don't understand,' said Dev.

'After you left for Simla, she was... raped...at the Chatterjis,' said Sunil. 'Her father married her to an older man; he has three children. The oldest is one year younger than her; the others are six and eleven.' I didn't know if Dev needed to hear the details but I for some reason, felt he should know.

Suddenly he grabbed Sunil's shirt. 'Tell me you are lying!' His eyes were wild and then he turned to me. 'Tell me, Amit!'

---

[141] *Lathi*, Baton

'Dev, let him go,' I said calmly. 'Unfortunately, it is all true.'

'What's going on here? Stay away from the prisoner!' A jailor came towards us. 'What did you give to him?' he accused Sunil. The jailor forced Dev to stand and was searched but nothing was found. 'Be careful,' he warned. 'We don't allow contact!'

'Pooja,' whispered Dev when the jailor turned back. 'It's my fault. If I had stayed in Rajkot, I would have married her...she should have been mine.' His face crumpled. I began to put my arm around his shoulder but stopped, remembering the jailor's warning.

The bell rang.

'You will be released, Dev. Don't worry about Pooja, we will look after her,' I said.

Dev didn't seem to have heard us, for he walked away, keeping his head low.

'What do we do now?' asked Sunil.

'We visit Pooja.'

We arrived what seemed like moments later on Pooja's doorstep. A servant opened the door and recognised Sunil. He looked scared.

'*Saab*, *Memsahib* is not here.'

'Where is she?' I asked.

'She is not here, *Memsahib* has left us. *Saab* will be home soon. He does not like visitors...' the servant's eyes flickered to Sunil. 'You must leave.'

'Pooja doesn't live here?' Sunil asked. 'Where has she gone?'

'I don't know. Goodbye,' he said and closed the door.

How could Pooja just go, without a word to anyone? If she had told her help, then why didn't they tell us? He recognised Sunil – he knew he was a friend, not a stranger – then, why the secrecy?

'I am sure she is happy, wherever she is. She finally understood the danger here – did you see how scared that servant was? Like that beast was going to come home anytime soon...what would have happened? I could beat him with just my palm!' said Sunil.

I shook my head. 'Don't try and be a hero. Pooja will write to us when she is ready. She is a strong girl.'

'Let's hope so.'

I added the last of the masala bags into the box, which I was taking to Mary. Papa walked in, holding a pipe to his mouth.

'What is this?' he enquired.

'Only a few things,' I said. Papa peered into the box.

'Is that right?' he raised his eyebrows. 'Going to see *Memsahib*?'

'*Ji* Papa.'

'Be sure to give her my regards. By the way, Amit...you have been spending a lot of time with her. She is engaged, doesn't her fiancé mind?' Papa asked. 'Be careful *beta*, this is a matter of the heart.'

'I know, Papa.'

'I am worried about you, that's all. You care for her, maybe even love her but it is dangerous for both of you. I hope that she is only a friend.'

'I know my boundaries, Papa. Someday my marriage will be to an Indian girl, suitable to be your daughter in law. I understand that.'

'Nethertheless, will you be able to let her go in your heart, when the time comes? Will you be able to love your wife when you marry?'

I didn't have an answer for that. Papa took my silence as a no and walked away, leaving a cloud of smoke behind.

Mary was trying to cool herself with a hand held fan, sitting underneath a canopy as I arrived. She was dressed in an all white lace dress; a black belt was tied around her waist. Her cheeks were red and her lips parched. She reached over and took a sip from her glass.

'Oh, this heat is terrible,' she complained loudly, fanning herself vigorously now. She drank more juice. 'The electricity has gone so the fan is not working. The weather is dismal, oh my head!'

I looked up at the beautiful plain blue sky; there was not a cloud in sight. It was a lovely day.

'Good afternoon, Mary *Memsahib*,' I said as I drew up a chair and sat down next to her. 'Who are you talking to? There is no one here.'

'Amit, I am so glad that you came.' Her smile shone as she took off her sunglasses. You must think I am mad talking alone. Tell me and be honest, how can you stand this heat? How do you tolerate it?'

'We are Indians *Memsahib* and we have lived in this climate for centuries. The sun is our in our blood.'

She looked at me strangely like she was seeing me for the first time. A flicker of uncertainty crossed her face but it was gone in an instant.

'Would you like some juice?' She poured me some. I settled down, taking the juice from her and enjoyed the garden.

'Do you like the sculptures, Amit?'

Before me, a range of stone statues stood in the garden of naked men, women and of creatures which I had not seen before. I did recognise a single one.

'Is that a *Parie*[142]?' I asked.

'A what?'

'She comes from above; from heaven...they come to here, to help the troubled people.'

'Angels...oh, *Parie*. Do you believe in angels?' she asked.

'We believe in reincarnation,' I said. 'Jainism is an old, powerful religion which worships the soul. It is a privilege to come back as a human, to come back into the Jain religion. And angels – it would be nice to know if the existed. If an angel is one who can make someone happy, show love and help in times of trouble, then I believe they exist.'

'In that case, Amit, you are *my* angel,' Mary said. Before I could react she was alerted by one of the servants.

'*Memsahib*, there is a message for you,' he said.

'Please excuse me, I will be back soon.' Mary stood up. 'Please have another drink. I shan't be long.'

As I waited, I thought of what she had said – I am her angel. I smiled and wanted to dance, to touch the sky with my bare hands. I wanted to tell her I loved her and maybe she would tell me that she loved me too...

As I waited for her return, the beautiful blue sky was suddenly replaced with dark, grey clouds. A wind howled as it picked up, throwing the chairs over. Mary's half full glass shattered on the ground. This was a bad omen. Clutching my glass, I hastily moved inside to see the servant running to me, his eyes wild in fear.

---

[142] *Parie*, Angel

'*Saab*, it is *Memsahib*! She has collapsed!'

It felt like someone had put ice on my heart. I heard nothing more, only the pounding of my blood. My eyes sought for her.

She was lying on the sofa, muttering something. Her eyes were closed. Two women were fanning her; one had brought her water. I bent over her and patted her cheek. Her face was thick with perspiration and her hair was damp. I used my handkerchief to wipe her face.

'Has anybody called the doctor?' I shouted. 'I need a blanket, quickly!' I couldn't stand to see her like this.

A servant came back with a blanket and I put it on Mary. Her shaking slowed slightly.

'The doctor is on his way, *Saab*,' said the servant.

I took off Mary's shoes and rubbed her feet and hands.

'Tom...I need Tom.' Mary's eyes fluttered open and looked at me. She reached out for me...she wanted me, she needed me...

'I need Tom,' her voice was below a whisper but I heard her clearly. 'Go and get him, Amit. I need him.'

I pulled away like I had been burned. Mary looked at me confused and hurt. Taking my eyes off her, I walked to the window and watched the rain and wind dance around outside like a malicious show.

Mary wanted Tom, ofcourse she did. Who was I? Nothing. I had no right to think of her, to love her...she could never love me. I knew this, then why did I not listen to reality, to Papa?

The door flew open and for a while, the noise of the wind and rain was deafening. Loose papers flew around the room then settled as the door closed. Stuart and Tom were here; the expression on their faces nervous and worried. They went to Mary at once.

'What happened darling, why are you so upset?' Tom took her hand.

Mary began to cry and clung to him. I turned away.

'Sweetheart, it's alright. Please tell me,' he said.

'It's Tammy. She has taken ill with the fever. The doctors cannot do anymore...she needs her mother.'

She needs her mother? Who is this Tammy again? I didn't understand but I felt like I was intruding, it seemed like I shouldn't know. I should go home.

Tom stayed with Mary whilst Stuart made a phone call. When he finished he instructed the staff to do different things at once but I

228

did not pay any attention. My mind was a thousand miles away from the hubbub of the room and I heard Mary's name from a long distance...I thought back to what she had said..."She needs her mother"...the last piece of the puzzle locked in.

Mary has a child. Why didn't she ever mention it to me? Did she forget or was it not important to her? I was a fool. It was dark outside and no one cared if I stayed or not; no one would miss me. Pushing back my angry tears, I slipped out. I needed to be away from Mary, from Tom, from everyone in that house. I walked home, not caring about getting wet and the questions came.

Was the child Tom's? But they weren't married yet; did they have the child out of wedlock? No, Mary isn't like that...but then the child was someone else's child. Perhaps she had adopted this Tammy. I shook my head. It was none of my business. Whatever happened, whoever that girl was to Mary, I shouldn't care.

I was soon back home. This is where I should be - with Ma and Papa. This is my life, my reality. I must forget Mary. I was naïve...I had loved.

It was a week before I saw Mary again. She came and found me.

'Where did you go, Amit? Why did you go away?' This was her first question.

'I had something important to do, *Memsahib*.' I didn't look at her. If I did, I would fall...'Why are you here?' I asked.

'You are angry with me, I see that. You have a right to be.' She sat by me, putting her bag down.

I concentrated on the river's pace – it seemed to be in a hurry, not waiting for anything. It washed over stones and rocks, around children playing in the far end.

'I'm really sorry, Amit. I should have told you,' said Mary.

This time I looked at her. She was pale and her face was subdued. She also had dark circles under her eyes.

'I went to your house and your mother told me you were here.'

I nodded. I liked it that she cared enough to find me.

'*Memsahib*, you don't have to say anymore. Please forgive me, I have been very silly about everything...but...I have been wondering...'

'Who Tammy is and what relationship I have with her?'

'Yes *Memsahib* but it is your business and not mine,' I said but I didn't smile. 'Tammy is really Tamara – she is my daughter.'

It was true then – I was right. My heart began to race. 'Is she Tom's daughter too?' My voice was shaky.

'No, Amit. Tammy is not Tom's. She is the child of David and I. Let me tell you about my past life, a time ago in England. Will you hear it?'

I nodded.

'David was my husband before I met Tom. He was a sweetheart and he loved me so much. If I was upset, he would be and he would fight every man who came within a yard of me – David was very protective and a little over zealous. But that was one of the things I loved about him.' Mary's smile made me burn but I kept a straight face. 'He died two weeks after Tammy was born. He was a gentle soul and was very excited to see his baby. Tammy had a weak heart; it was a matter of life or death but she pulled through. We couldn't be any happier. Just as it seemed things were getting better, David was taken away.

'Tammy had good and bad days but she was a little survivor. I still think of David sometimes and I believe he is looking over us.'

'And Tom?' I asked, curiosity getting the better of me.

'I met Tom a year and a half later. We were friends for a long time. Tammy became attached to him and she began to call him "daddy". Mary brushed her tears away. 'Everything had happened so fast. Tom proposed and we were set to be married. Then Tom was seconded to work here, in India. I couldn't refuse this great opportunity but I couldn't bear not to be with Tom and I needed Tammy with me.'

'But you did leave her.'

'Yes Amit, I did. At the time, the circumstances were quite dire in London. A lot of children were moving away to the country to foster parents. Tom and I had decided to take little Tammy to India with us but my brother intervened. He said he would look after her until we could come back for her – he loved her as his own child and I knew she would be in safe hands...Tammy had a bad turn and she had been quite ill for a few months; my baby was in hospital a lot. I had lost hope – again...had it not been for Tom, I would have fallen apart. Tom promised that once we were settled in India, we would bring Tammy.'

230

'You once told me that you arrived here two or three years ago,' I pointed out. 'Why haven't you brought your daughter here yet?'

Mary looked guilty and again, tearful. 'I have no answer to that Amit. I love my daughter, I really do. I know I have neglected her, I am truly ashamed.' Mary wrung her hands.

'Why are you telling me this?'

'You are a good friend, Amit and good friends have a right to know.' Mary took out a small box from her bag. She opened it to reveal a silver watch. 'This is for you.'

I took it into my hands and turned it over. I handed it back. 'I can't accept this.'

'I am not taking it back.' Mary stood up. 'Please don't hate me so much. Amit, our train leaves at seven, today. We are going to England on the morning ship.' She bent down and kissed my cheek. Her sweet, warm lips lingered for a moment. 'Take care and be sure to write. There is an address inside the box. I am going to miss you very much.'

My hands closed over the box and tears splashed down my cheeks. I watched her get into the car and be driven away.

It was never to be and I should have known. But still, I couldn't stop loving her. It was six. The clock ticked...Mary would be boarding the ship soon and I would never see her again.

I flung the covers off and jumped out of bed. Without another thought I pocketed the watch which had been lying beside me. I shouted something to Ma about coming back soon and rushed out of the door.

I ran and ran. People stared at me; they shouted - why hurry? Who's been killed? I didn't stop to answer. I didn't have time. I ran faster; my chest was heaving and tightening but the station was so far away. I ran to Chandu's house, grateful that he was at home. I didn't have time to explain.

'Chandu, please, take me to the station now.' My good friend didn't disappoint me. Chameli galloped as she had never galloped before; my heart thumping with the beat of her hooves.

'Please God,' I prayed. 'Please, please...'

We got to the station just as the whistle was blown. I jumped out, running onto the platform.

The train had begun to move. I ran alongside it, clutching my side, trying to find Mary's compartment. I was nearly too late...but I saw her.

'Amit, what are you doing here?' she said, looking startled.

'I needed to see you...to tell you...'

The hoot of the train drowned my voice.

'What?'

The train was speeding up.

'Mary, I love you!'

Her face showed no sign of surprise. She knew. I crumpled to the floor, still watching her beautiful face.

The train was nearly out of the station. I watched, my heart drowning in sorrow.

'Amit!'

I looked up to see her hanging out from the open carriage. She took off a bracelet, kissed it and dropped it.

It fell onto the platform, turning in circles until it settled to a stop. I reached it, tears streaming down my face. Mary was crying too. The train left the station, taking my Mary away from me.

~

SUNIL

~

Nineteen

The Girl
January 1945

I looked out of the window as the bus rambled on. Some village girls were attending to the morning chores, filling their pots with water by the river. It reminded me of a certain girl who was once exactly like that. She was free and happy until she married...but now vanished...I wished that Neha hadn't stopped me that night. I could have saved her from that monster...

> *'Let me go, Neha!'*
> *'No, it will be much worse later if you go downstairs,' Neha said holding onto my hand tightly.*
> *My heart thudded angrily as I listened to Pooja's muffled screams and cries. I felt helpless.*
> *'No Neha, I can't stand this. I am going to kill the dog!' I wrenched my hand away from her and threw myself down the stairs, ready to tackle the beast. The door of the kitchen was slightly ajar. There was no noise; I pushed the door but I was too late. Neha was right behind me, her eyes wide.*
> *We stepped into the kitchen and saw devastation. Smashed glass scattered the floor. Pooja was sitting on the floor, amongst the glass, her head in her arms. I took her into my arms and tilted her face towards mine.*
> *'Pooja! Oh Pooja.' I took her into my embrace. Her red, scratched hands clutched me.*
> *'Didi, I'm sorry...' Neha wiped Pooja's face with a flannel. 'We should have come earlier...I am sorry.' Neha looked at me, asking for my forgiveness but I was angry with her. She shouldn't have stopped me. But I was a fool – I listened to her when I knew what was happening to Pooja. I was ashamed of myself.*
> *'I need to sleep,' Pooja whispered. Her eyes were swollen and she had a sharp cut on her chin and her right cheek. Her bottom lip was bleeding.*
> *I took Pooja into my arms and carried her upstairs and gently lay her down on her bed. She smiled at me and began to drift away. I let her sleep and prayed that she be left alone tonight – I will kill that bastard!*

'What do we do now?' Neha asked.

I watched Pooja sleep. I sighed and stroked her hair. 'We let her rest but tomorrow she is coming home with us.' Neha nodded. She took Pooja's hand in hers and began to cry.

'I am so sorry, I shouldn't have stopped you before,' she said between tears.

I touched a hand to Pooja's cheek Pooja's cheek. 'Sleep well.'

My eyes opened at the break of dawn. Neha was awake and ready when I knocked on her door.

'I couldn't sleep,' she said. 'I couldn't stop thinking about Pooja didi.'

'I have been too.'

'I have also been thinking about Pooja didi. Will she agree to come with us?'

'She doesn't have a choice. She will come.' Pooja wasn't in her room and I guessed she went for a wash. 'Pack some clothes, quick before she comes back. If she sees we are serious for her to come with us, she won't refuse.'

'No,' Pooja said. She was adamant that she would stay with her husband. It was only right; she told us.

How could I make her see that it was safer for her to leave and come back to Rajkot? But there was nothing I could do or say that would change her mind. In a state of despondency, I didn't argue. Pooja had made her decision.

Neha put a hand on mine; her eyes told me to let go. They were sad but understanding. My Neha, who had her worries and her own problems, shared mine. She did understand – maybe I was a bit harsh on her last night. I nodded and smiled and she visibly relaxed.

I said goodbye to Pooja but wished she didn't have to be humble and modest of her duties as a wife and mother. If only she could see that she deserved better...

'Sunil, where are you?' Ma said aloud in my ear. I jumped.

'Sorry Ma, did you say something?'

'It's nothing. You look tired,' Ma said.

'I think I will rest for a while,' I said.

236

Ma, Meera and I were going to Jaipur, to see my uncle and auntie and for shopping – for my wedding clothes. Ma had this planned quite a few months ago and this morning, we packed for a week's stay. Wrapped up warm, we ascended the bus steps, on this cold, but sunny day.

Papa's older brother and his wife – my *Tau* and *Moti Ma*, moved away from Rajkot five years ago. From the time I can remember, we were 'their' children for they were not blessed with any of their own.

I was excited – I wondered if Tau had changed. The last time I saw him, he was a little overweight and only wore *Kurta-Pyjamas*[143].

It wasn't an easy journey. The bus drove slowly, bumping over loose stones and then, crawling over pot holes. Meera, however, jumped up and down in delight each time the bus jolted. I ceased to understand why.

We soon came upon a narrow dirt road which meandered through woodland. Large trees stood on either side, the branches and leaves overlapping one another as they followed the snake-like road. The branches scraped the top of the bus as it rattled past. Meera now cowered next to Ma, I laughed and she scowled.

'Oh thank God,' said a woman aloud when the bus left the road. Others made murmurs of agreement.

Even though we had left the intimidating road, our troubles had just begun. The number of pot holes increased on the next road. Long cracks swept the length, making it very uneven. The bus swayed from left to right. Some of us screamed or held tight onto our seats. Ma began to pray.

Eventually, the bus began to climb steeply. It struggled and slipped back. The women screamed louder and the men shouted. Meera held onto Ma's arm, her eyes closed tight. Ma prayed faster.

We were unlucky – the bus came to a stop but was stuck – in a deep ditch. The driver revved the engine but the bus was not moving.

'Look *Bhai*,' Meera pointed out. Without warning, it began to rain.

The windscreen was a blur of water in a matter of seconds. 'Driver,' I shouted. 'Please, you must do something!'

'*Kya*[144]?' shouted the driver over the drumming on the roof. He was watching the rain with a worried expression.

---

[143] *Kurta Pyjama*, a long shirt and pyjama style trouser worn by Indian men.
[144] *Kya*, a Hindi word which translates into "what".

237

'The rain is filling the road. We need to get out of the bus, *Bhaiya*. If we wait, it could be too late,' I shouted back.

The driver faced the passengers. '*Bhaiyo, bena*, take whatever you can and leave the bus.'

'Why? We are safe here!' said one woman.

'The bus cannot go on – it is deep in mud. The rain is not going to stop and soon the bus will be in flood water. We need to leave now!'

'Where are we to go?' she said.

'We will find shelter somewhere else, somewhere safe. Come now everyone, we must leave!'

'Ma, take Meera, I will take the bags,' I said.

We all splashed into the already knee-deep water. Some carried luggage on their heads and some held it close to their chests as they treaded carefully through the rapidly rising water.

'I'm scared,' said Meera, clutching my hand.

'It will be alright,' I said as calmly as I could. 'Stay close.'

Somewhere in the distance I saw two lights bobbing. The rain made it extremely difficult to make out any detail. The lights vanished as did any hope of rescue. We had reached some high ground now which was free of water but there was no shelter.

'My bag!' a woman shouted. A bag floated downhill in front of us.

'No, it's too dangerous!' a man shouted and pulled her back as she tried to retrieve it.

'My money, clothes - I have to get it back!' the woman cried. 'I have to get it back!'

'*Maasi*[145], you must leave it! It's too dangerous!' I repeated.

We saw her bag disappear out of sight. Meera took her hand and smiled.

'I will give you my money, *maasi*,' she said. 'You can come with me.'

The woman sniffed but took Meera's hand.

We began to walk towards some dense trees which seemed safe. That was when I saw the lights again - they were lamps which two men were carrying. One was holding a black umbrella but he was soaked through, like the rest of us.

---

[145] *Maasi*, Mother's sister. This word is used to address ladies, even though not related. Sometimes also called "Kaki" in respect of them being elder.

'Is everyone alright *Saab*? We have come to help,' said the first man. 'We saw the bus.'

'Is there anywhere we can stay until the morning?' asked the driver.

'Yes S*aab*. You can stay in my house; the village is not far from here.'

We all followed the man and his companion through the trees and along a narrow dirt road.

The trees protected the road from the rain a little but we were all cold and wet when we reached the man's house. Ma had thoughtfully packed a blanket which she wrapped around Meera, who was shivering.

'Please come in. You are all welcome to stay here.' The man was kind. 'My name is Ram Prasad.'

'*Bhaiya*, I will be back with some blankets,' said the second man. He nodded to us and left swiftly.

'Santu, we have guests,' Ram said as he opened the door. A woman appeared whom I guessed was his wife. 'N*asta layaw*[146],' he said.

I clasped Ram's hand. 'Thank you.'

'It is nothing, *Saab*. We are happy to help. My brother, Balraj – he was the man you saw with me – he saw your bus in trouble and alerted me and in good time. Please, sit and make yourself comfortable.' Fifteen minutes later, Ram's wife came back with water and food.

'*Bhai Saab*, it is very kind of you,' said Ma gratefully.

Ram's wife had made a tower of *roti* and enough *sabzi* to feed us all. While we ate, the second man, Balraj came back with more blankets. After our fill, we sat dozily on our makeshift beds. Meera had already fallen asleep on Ma's lap.

'We are going to Jaipur. My son, Sunil is to be married soon. We will be shopping for his wedding clothes and for my daughter-in-law too. She is so beautiful,' Ma told a woman proudly who was looking at her intently.

'Are you English?' she said.

Ma laughed. 'I am Anglo-Indian. I was born here but my family are English. Sunil's father was Hindu.'

---

[146] *Nasta layaw*, Bring some refreshments.

'Was? He is no longer alive?'

'He died fighting for England, he was a pilot.'

'I'm sorry,' the woman touched Ma's hand. 'May God bring him peace.'

It was the same woman whom Meera had befriended. 'You have a good child,' she stroked Meera's hair.

'Without my two children, I don't what I would have done,' Ma said.

It was quiet now and mostly all had fallen asleep. I too, drifted off.

The piercing scream tore me from my sleep and I jumped to my feet; my heart thumping.

'Ma, Meera?' I said aloud.

The house had woken up and everyone looked around for the noise.

'What happened?' someone asked.

'Did someone shout?' said another.

Bleary-eyed, we tried to make sense of the frightening scream.

Ram came into the room with a lamp. 'Come quickly, I may need help,' he said calmly but with an air of urgency.

'But what's happened?' I said.

'Someone has jumped into the well.'

Ram, myself and a few other men headed into the centre of the village. The well sat in the middle of a square. I looked over and to my shock; I saw a face, a hand?

'Take this rope,' Ram pressed the end of a thick rope into my hand. 'Hold onto it tight.' The others held other parts of the rope.

'I am going in.' Ram tied the other end around his waist. 'When I shout, pull us up.' Ram wasn't a young man but he was strong and angular and with a swift jump, he splashed into the well. We held on with all our strength.

He shouted his signal and we pulled them up. When they were out, Ram put her down on the hard ground. She looked barely sixteen.

'Is she breathing?' I panted. I was anxious; she must be alive! For ten minutes, Ram tried to revive her. All the water was pumped out of her stomach, but still, she was unconscious. He bent down and put two fingers against her neck and then he tried her wrists. He shook his head. 'She is dead.'

There was a ringing silence.

'We have to tell her family,' said Ram when we failed to speak.

I stared at the girl. Her blood stained clothes were torn and she had marks and bruises on her arms and neck. Before me, I saw a dead girl who didn't have to be.

'My daughter! Where is she? Sarika!' A thin woman pushed past us and stopped at the feet of her daughter. She crumpled and sobbed, cradling her girl. We stepped back respectfully giving her space. The woman kissed the girl's hands and face and shook with grief.

Most of the village had arrived for now there was a crowd. Tears and wails filled the sky. More of the girl's family had arrived and they knelt by her.

'Sarika!' the father's bereaved moan sent a chill down my spine; I didn't stop my own tears from spilling now. The girl's sisters' hugged their mother and simply stared at their sibling.

The brother was the last to arrive. 'Who did this to my sister!' he roared. 'I will kill him!'

Someone mumbled something which I didn't catch.

'What did you say? How dare you!' the brother seized the man's shirt and pulled him towards him, his eyes blazing.

'He is telling the truth,' said another villager. 'You letting that white man come into your house. You have grown-up girls in your family. Didn't you think? Not only me but everybody has seen the way he stares at them and now look at your poor sister now! Look what he has done to her!'

'He always had an evil eye; I never liked him since the day he arrived in our village. What business did he have here, to come and disturb our peace? Who made him the guard of our crops, who was he to tell us what we can grow and what we cannot? *Khabar che*[147], he would come when the women and girls take a bath, when every man in this village knows not to be near the river at that time! He was told but he still would leer at the women! *Ram Ram*[148]!' one woman carried on.

'If this is true, he will not be alive by morning!'

---

[147] *Khabar ché?* Do you know? (Gujarati)
[148] *Ram Ram*, saying Lord Rama's name "Ram Ram"

'No, *beta*, come back!' cried his father but the boy had already gone.

'*Bena*,' Ram's wife stepped towards the girl's mother. 'We have to cremate Sarika's body. Come, my husband will take care of things,' she said. She led the poor mother and the sisters back to their house. The other village women followed, leaving the men to do what needed to be done.

It was past midnight now: the rain and wind had stopped.

'Go back to the house, Sunil S*aab*,' Ram said.

'Can I help?' I offered.

'You are kind but this is something the village men have to do.'

I nodded and walked away, taking a last look at the dead girl.

I couldn't sleep. After I had told everyone of the horror, the house was awake. No one could sleep after this and the news became a point of conversation. The children, aware that something had happened but couldn't understand, slowly went back to sleep. Some of the men, including myself, stood outside, waiting for Ram. Finally, he came near dawn.

'There will be prayers in the house for Sarika's peace. She will be cremated afterwards. You are all welcome to stay,' he told us. He was tired and solemn and seemed disturbed.

'Did the brother find the man, was it him?' I asked when I was alone with him.

'The white man has not been found,' he said bluntly.

'Ram, how can you know it was him? It is a big accusation.'

Ram watched me for long moment. 'You are still young; you don't realise or understand...'

'Understand what?'

'Before *Gandhi* envisioned the Quit India Movement, before he was even born, Hindustanis fought to free India from the *Raj*. Have you heard of *Mangal Pandey*?'

I shook my head.

'He was a great *sepoy*[149], a soldier. A great *Hindustani*. He was one of the first fighters who wanted justice for our mother - our land

---

[149] *Sepoy*, a native of India employed as a soldier during the Raj.

and for all the *Hindustanis*, whether Muslim or Hindu. He fought valiantly but Mangal Pandey, the great *sepoy*, was hanged. He was *shahid*.'

'Why?' I thought of Rakesh *Bhai*. 'Why are you telling me this? I don't understand.'

'They coated the top of bullets with the fat of the pig and the cow, which the *Hindustani* and the Muslim *sepoys* had to bite off to be used. They knew that we Hindus worship our cows and Muslims do not touch pigs, it is against their faith. Still, they tried to humiliate our beliefs.' Ram carried on, in his trance.

'Forgive me, Ram, that was many years ago, why are you blaming that white man for the death of Sarika? And what is Mangal Pandey's story in relation to all this?' I asked.

'Because nothing has changed. They are all the same; didn't you listen to that woman? They take from us. Sarika was just another girl to him, another village girl, whom he took. Another puppet to him and he used her like the *Raj* used the *sepoys* for their amusement. She was an innocent fifteen year old girl. She had a future of marriage and children, she was supposed to grow old and see her own grandchildren. He took that from her!' Tears were shining in Ram's eyes. 'She was my brother's daughter; a daughter to me also. I want that man killed.'

Ram buried his head in his hands and sat down on the ground.

'Ram.' I took him by the elbow and he allowed me to pick him up. 'If there is anything I can do, I will.'

Ram patted my shoulder and walked into the house, drying his face with his hands.

The sun was full now in the bright sky and it was then that I witnessed the beauty of the village. White homes stood side by side along narrow streets which only pedestrians or cyclists could use. There was no room for motor cars or tongas.

Fruit trees grew in the courtyard of these houses. I imagined children playing and men smoking their pipes and women drying chillies. It was a welcoming place; how could such a dwelling bring such bad tidings?

Sarika was dressed in new clothes and garlands of flowers were bestowed upon her. She was beautiful - serene in her new world. Her mother sat by her head, crying copiously as she held her daughter's hand.

'She was supposed to leave this house a married girl, with a *mangal sutra* [150] around her neck. *Kankoo* [151] and *chandlo* [152] and red *chudlas* [153] on her soft wrists...whose evil eye was upon you, *beta*?' she berated. 'Her marriage was arranged, *eh Baghwaan*, why did you take her away?' Sarika's mother began to slap her chest. '*Mari chokri, mari chokri* [154].'

Ram's wife held her sister-in-law and gently prised her away. 'It was God's wish,' she said, tears glistening on her cheeks.

The priest said the prayers and Sarika was carried away on a bed of flowers to the crematoria by the river. Soon, the fire burned the girl's body to ashes, whose life had been cut short, whose life had not yet begun.

'Ram, you have been very kind to us, we cannot thank you enough,' I said.

We stood in a semi-circle around Ram and his wife, ready to depart. I took out some money.

'We would like you to have this,' I said. 'Please accept it. It's from all of us.'

Ram looked at the wad of notes. 'It is generous of everyone but I didn't ask for payment. You all are my guests. *Bhaiya, shukriya* but I cannot take it.'

I put the money into his hands and closed his fingers over it. 'It is not payment but a gift. Share it with your family and with Sarika's family. This is yours.'

Ram took me into his embrace. Then, he and his brother walked us to our bus, which now stood, not in mud but on dry road, thanks to the help of the villagers. It was early evening and everyone was tired. We climbed aboard and our journey began again.

---

[150] *Mangal Sutra*, a necklace worn by married women to symbolise their marriage, whose husband is alive.

[151] *Kankoo*, red powder – vermillion. Used as a symbol of marriage or for holy Hindu rituals.

[152] *Chandlo*, Bindi – a red dot painted on the forehead of married women (Now it is also a fashion statement and worn by girls and women alike, married and unmarried. The bindi now comes in an array of colours and designs).

[153] *Chudla*, Gujarati word for Bangle

[154] *Mari chokri*, My daughter

Our journey to Jaipur was quiet; some slept and some stared out the window. I, myself couldn't shake off the image of Sarika's dead body by the well. For what reason did she die? Her mother had said her marriage was arranged, was she raped out of jealousy? It was a mystery, one that probably wouldn't be solved but blamed on a man who was probably innocent. I was certain that the white man would not be showing his face in the village again.

Ma noticed my silence. 'This happens, Sunil. Don't let it burden your heart,' she said.

'It shouldn't have happened.'

'Try and think about something else. Jaipur is a lovely town; it will take your mind off what has happened.'

I continued to stare out of the window.

The first thing I saw in Jaipur was colour. Splashes of bold, primary colours were worn by the locals and draped over animals and objects. Women peeped from under their veils, wanting a glimpse of us. Men and women alike sat in front of their baskets of fruit and flowers, waving flies away with their dark hands. On the far side of the bus station, men sat with their camels and waited patiently for customers, as they chatted to their neighbours. It was a lively place and I began to forget the past few hours. It didn't seem real.

'Ma, can I ride on a camel?' Meera asked.

'Not now, maybe your uncle can take you later,' Ma said. She scanned the road for *Tau's* motorcar.

'Ma, look!' Meera squealed. A white, shiny Ford car drove in amongst the chaos. I stepped nearer to look at the wonderful motorcar as it stopped, literally in front of us. The door opened and Tau stepped out, beaming. I laughed – he wore a white *kurta* and long *pyjama* style trousers.

'Look at you!' he bellowed in his deep voice. 'It's so good to see you!'

Meera hid behind Ma; her head buried in her waist. Ma tried to push her forward.

'Say hello,' she said but Meera wouldn't let go of Ma's clothes.

'*Bhai-ji*, how are you?' Ma said, embracing Tau affectionately.

'I am very well,' he said but he frowned. 'But what have you done to yourself? You are so thin!'

245

'It's nothing like that *Bhai-ji*. Chalo, tell me, how is *Bhabhi*?'

'She is waiting for us at home, let's go.' *Tau* didn't like to waste time.

'*Tau*, do you own this car?' I asked, full of admiration.

'Yes, I bought it last year. Worth every rupee. Now, come on. We can chat on the way.'

Tau drove fast through dusty roads, up steep hills – we soon arrived at a large white house. *Tau* had the house built exactly as he wanted – a large house for a large family. Unfortunately, his life didn't turn out the way he wanted.

Moti Ma was already standing outside; she had a wide smile on her face.

'*Bhabhi*,' Ma smiled and the two women embraced.

'It has been so long,' Moti Ma said. 'After *dever*[155] passed away, we have only seen you once.' She knelt down beside Meera. 'Will you come to me?'

To our surprise, Meera went to her straight away. I touched her feet and hugged her.

'My children, you have grown up before your time,' she said sadly.

'Now, we will have none of that, *Bhabhi*. There will be no crying,' Ma mock scolded her.

Moti Ma wiped her tears and we all went inside the house.

After an enjoyable day, Meera had fallen asleep and Ma and *Moti Ma* were talking in the main room. Tau took me to his private room, where he spends time reading or working.

'How was your trip, *beta*?' *Tau* set himself down on a comfortable chair.

'Not good,' I sighed and began telling him of our journey and the death. He seemed lost in thought after I finished. He went and brought out some strong drinks and placed them down in front of us on a small glass table.

'You have had quite an adventure,' he said, talking a sip of his drink. I followed his example and choked. 'First time, eh?' he chuckled. 'You will get used to it. You are a man now, Sunil. When I

---

[155] ***Dever,*** Brother-in-law (The wife calls her husband's younger brother "Dever")

246

saw you last, you were only a boy. *Beta*, I have been observing you...since Govind died...you seem different now.'

'No *Tau*, I am the same. I just have more to think about now.'

'It is your wedding time, Sunil. So from now, you will think of nothing but that, understood? These few days will be important and busy. Your wedding and your bride are important, yes?'

I saw Neha in my mind and smiled.

'Yes, that's good,' said *Tau*. 'A shy man is a healthy man! Is she beautiful? Ofcourse she is, nothing else will do for my son, eh? Now tell me, have you ridden on a camel? No, then you will.'

I yawned involuntarily.

'It's time for bed, for you and me.' *Tau* ruffled my hair. 'Come with me, I will show you your room.' I followed him, not caring about anything else but sleep now. It was like yesterday didn't happen.

PART FOUR

Change

~ DEV ~

Twenty

Dev's Release

The sun blazed on my back as I struck another small gash on the unforgiving rock. Every muscle ached and my throat was painfully dry. I searched for Haricharan – the only jailor who was friend and family to me. Since Shankarji left, Haricharan was the only one I could talk to, who gave me hope, for the future. I was proud to be his friend.

'Dev,' he said one evening. 'Don't fight with the white man. They don't care about us. We are nothing to them. Keep your head down, work hard and then when they see that they can't hold you here any longer, that they have no real reason to keep you here, you shall go home.'

'Haricharan, if you feel so strongly, why do you work here?' I asked. 'You can work anywhere?'

'Someone has to work here, why not me?' He shrugged and that was all he said.

We weren't allowed water during work time. It was not permitted. But I couldn't bear it, my throat was screaming for water – and the only man who would let me have some was Haricharan. But I couldn't see him. I only saw jailor March, a mean and spiteful man who loved to see the Indians suffer. I sighed, I had to ask him.

'*Saab*, please, I need some water,' I said.

March didn't pay me any attention. He continued talking to a fellow officer who looked at me, like I was a mosquito. He fixed his eyes back on March.

'Please, I am really thirsty,' I said again.

March finally acknowledged me. 'Can't you see I am talking to an important man? It is not time for a break. Go back to work!'

'But *Saab*, I am in pain. I need just a little please.'

'Fine, stand there in that corner.' March went away and came back with a pot of water which he handed to me. I was about to drink when he laughed. 'Drink,' he said.

I was immediately suspicious. I looked into the pot and almost vomited. It was full of flies. '*Saab*, this water is dirty. I cannot drink this,' I said.

'It's what you lot deserve, you stinking brown men! Now, drink!' he commanded.

'No,' I said and March's face contorted in anger.

'Maybe then I shall assist you. We can't have you dehydrated, can we? The papers would love it – another Indian dead in jail,' he laughed. He grabbed my arms and made me lay down. I knew what was coming; I sealed my mouth.

'Get the tube!' he barked at someone. Other inmates had gathered to watch now but no one attempted to help. My jaw was wrenched open and the tube was stuffed down my throat. I thrashed my head but strong hands kept them still. March filled a bowl with the infected water. I closed my eyes as he was about to drop it in.

'Stop!'

My eyes flew open.

'Let go of him!'

The tube was wrenched out and I was free. March's face was convulsed with fury. 'How dare you!'

Haricharan!

Haricharan helped me get up and told me to go but I stood where I was.

'He was refusing to drink!' I could tell by March's face that he felt humiliated; I felt justice was done.

'If you give water that was infected with flies, nobody would drink it, March. I see how you treat the Indians and your people differently – a fine division.' Haricharan spat on the floor. 'This 'incident' will not go unreported.' He kicked the bowl of water.

'These Indians are cockroaches, they deserve what they get!' said March.

Haricharan went up to March and stood nose to nose. 'I am an Indian, remember that, won't you? *Chal* Dev.'

He took me inside and gave me clean, drinkable water. I drank until my thirst was quenched.

'Won't you get in trouble?' I asked afterwards.

'I have known worse jailors, Dev. March is a mouse compared to them, so don't worry about me. But are you alright?'

I nodded non-committed.

'You should go outside now. Don't worry about March, I will deal with him. You keep your head down and work hard.'

The work was done for the day and now I lay on the grey floor. It was a pleasant feeling; the cold stone soothed my aching muscles.

I turned around and saw my new cell partner staring at me with vacant eyes. I nodded and smiled but he just turned away. Haricharan appeared and rapped the bars with his baton. He was smiling.

'Is everything alright Haricharan?' I stood up and went to him.

'I have something that will make you happy. I have letters for you today, from your village. They arrived a while ago but I had no way of getting them to you without being noticed.'

'Have they been opened?'

'I got them before anyone else could. Don't open them yet. Wait until after the morning work tomorrow and all the jailors are busy elsewhere.'

'I...thank you Haricharan.' I put the letters safely away under my thin blanket. I couldn't wait until tomorrow.

I opened the first letter. It was from Shankarji; he spoke of the impending marriage of Sunil and Neha and how proud he was. His also said his health was not so good and he hoped he would live to see it before God took him away. I prayed that God would spare my dear friend.

The second letter was from Amit and Sunil: funny and informative about the village people. However, there was no mention of Pooja which I was expecting. The third and last letter was from *Babuji*. Dried watery blotches splattered the page.

'*Beta*,

After all this time, you have chosen to write to us. We are disappointed in you *beta*, that you couldn't tell us that you were in jail. I don't know the reason behind this...was it to spare our grief? Your Ma has been crying all the time and I don't know how to console her.

Beta, we have applied for a visiting pass, that day will come soon. We are with you and we love you. Khan *Bhai* has been very helpful and he has lent us some money – he blames himself as the reason you are in jail...if only you stayed away Dev. Why did you do this? Why did you follow Rakesh?

I must sound angry...and I am sorry for that. I just want you home and safe. If it were not for Payal and Gunwant-ji, your Ma and I would have fallen apart.

Dev, we will come to you soon.

Babuji.

255

Babuji is angry with me – just as I thought he would be. I was a bad son and one who deserves nothing but punishment. I was stupid and didn't think once of my family. I should have walked away from that speech and not stopped to listen! I am truly ashamed...I wiped my tears as I read the letter again and again but the ball in my stomach did not go.

Payal and Gunwant-ji were there, what had happened at home? Why were they in Rajkot at all? I re-read the letter but there were no clues. I took out a fresh page from a pile which Haricharan had given me and quickly wrote back to *Babuji*, apologising and promising him that I would be a good son and wouldn't disappoint them again. I paused as I thought of asking about Payal...maybe this wasn't the right time...

I sealed the letter, ready to give to Haricharan.

'Dev Sharma,' said a loud, authoritative voice. I looked up from my dinner.

'Dev Sharma,' he said again.

'Yes *Saab*.' I stood up.

'Come with me,' said Haricharan.

I walked past the other inmates who were staring at me with curiosity. Questions were asked silently. I had a question too. Haricharan didn't say anything until we were standing outside the Superintendant's office and he beamed.

'Well,' I asked.

'You are going home, Dev!'

'What are you saying? Really?' I hoped he wasn't lying. But I knew Haricharan and he only told the truth...

'The Superintendant just needs you to sign a few papers for formality, then you are free to go home.'

'I don't understand, just like that?'

'The answer's inside. Come on, let's go in.' Haricharan opened the door to the office. 'Sir, I have brought Dev.'

'It is unnecessary to tell us Haricharan. We see he is here, but good,' said the Superintendent. 'Dev, I have good news for you. We have the release papers for you, sign here and you are free to go back home.'

'It is true then? I can go home? May I ask why suddenly?'

He turned towards the two men standing next to him. 'Dev, this is Officer Stuart Amcotts and Constable Anand Rai. Your friends Sunil and Amit have been campaigning for your release for some time now and requested the help from these noble policemen who are based in your district.

'See, the thing is, the officials couldn't find anything on you. Your record here is clean, no *goonda giri*, no fights and you are a hard worker too. Then, when Officer Amcotts and Constable Rai turned up, it was imminent that you were going to be released. I regret that it took a long time.

'Amit and Sunil have been coming to us nearly every day. They are relentless. You have very good friends.' Officer Stuart smiled and slipped a fat package towards me. 'Here are your wages – real money along with your original clothes. Please, if you can sign this form.'

I signed and took the package.

'Good luck Dev,' said the Superintendent.

'*Namaste Saab*,' I said. Haricharan lead me to a room to get changed where he left me alone. I thought of home, I couldn't believe it, I was smiling. Oh home! I couldn't wait to step on the old, red soil, smell the rich earth and feel Ma's hand on my cheek. I wanted to feel the familiarity of *Babuji*, to hear the rustle of his papers. I wanted a lot of things...I had forgotten what life was but now I was given a second chance, a new life. Warmth crept from my toes towards my heart. I was happy as I should be.

Haricharan accompanied me to the gates. We didn't talk much for we both felt the weight of our hearts. We were near the gates when two men, handcuffed, crossed our path. Their hands were tied behind their backs and they wore ankle chains. One of the men had a bloody hand and a bruised eye. The other man was limping. His trousers were torn and I glimpsed an ugly, black wound. Both of the men held their heads high – they were proud.

We let them pass but I was unable to move. I had forgotten in my recent wild happiness, just for a moment, that there was still a war happening outside of these walls. Innocent Indians were still being imprisoned. They were being tortured...turned mad perhaps.

A scream. A shiver ran through me.

'No! I will not eat dead animals! I am a Brahmin[156]! A sacred caste, you hear? Do not force...Aaaargh!'

Four jailors were huddled close to the man. They were going to force feed him. He had refused food; he said he would rather starve than eat their filth. The jailors stuck a tube down his throat and passed meat soup through it. The Brahmin's body shook and he made indistinguishable noises. He was choking...in a few minutes he was dead. The jailors, bewildered, stepped away. My scream never left me...

Countless, many others went this way. Lives ruined, forever.

'We cannot help them,' said Haricharan. 'Look ahead *beta*.'

We were outside the gates. I didn't realise I had moved at all. There were lots of people, it was very busy. People shouted, one or two motorcars rambled past, children screamed and laughed as they chased one another. This was the India that I had forgotten within the walls of the jail.

Haricharan gave me a fatherly embrace. 'Don't worry about what happened to those men and everyone else. Look after yourself and think of your family. Don't think about jail, try and forget...I know it will be difficult. Goodbye Dev. I will miss you a lot...but I don't want to see you here again.'

'Will I see you again?'

'If it is God's wish.'

'Thank you for everything. I couldn't ask for a better friend,' my voice cracked.

'God be with you.'

I left Haricharan, I left the jail and now, I was going home.

A sigh rose from my heart as I stepped onto the platform but I was scared too. No one knew I was coming home – I didn't have a chance to tell them... would Babuji and Ma want me? Would the villagers laugh at me? I shook my head – I couldn't think about that; I was going home.

---

[156] *Brahmin /Brahman*, a Hindu caste ranking the highest position in the hierarchy of Indian society/Hindu caste system.

I sat on the familiar rattling bus that bumped along the small lanes, over uneven surfaces and pot holes. I saw *"Bhai"* as we passed the 'ghost' house; my first meeting with Dilip. It seemed so long ago...

'Last stop,' said the driver. He stopped the bus a good distance away from the village. I would have to walk the rest of the way. I passed some people but no one paid any attention to me – did they not recognise me? Had I changed? I was beginning to feel tired and I wished for a tonga. I walked some more, then heard wheels and hooves. The tonga slowed down as I waved frantically.

'Where do you want to go, *Saab*?'

Chandu didn't recognise me either.

'Chandu, don't you know who I am?' I said.

'I don't think so *Saab*. Should I?'

'It is I. Dev Sharma!'

Chandu stared long and hard, he scratched his head as he looked me over, scrunching his face. Then without warning, he jumped from the tonga and crashed into me, knocking me down.

'*Oh re, my baap*[157]! Dev Sharma. You are Dev!' Chandu was now jumping up and down. 'But by God, you have changed *yaar*!'

'Chandu, will you take me home? Take me to Ma and *Babuji*...it's been very long.'

Chandu's face lit up. 'Dev *Bhai*, you are a hero here!'

He slapped my back and pulled me up. I climbed onto the back of the tonga in sheer elation. The ride back home was anything but quiet. He wanted to know everything, but I only gave selected answers and finally the village came into view.

'Dev is here! Dev Sharma!' Chandu shouted to everyone we passed. I laughed. It felt good to be home.

I saw green and brown fields – villagers working, earning their daily bread. Houses were dotted around the village – soon a small cluster of buildings. We were going through the centre of the village.

'Chandu, my house is other way,' I said.

'Please forgive me but *Bapuji* wants me to collect his medicine. I won't be long.' With Chandu gone to the medicine shop, I decided to stretch my legs. In the next moment, I was surrounded.

---

[157] *Oh re my baap*, an exclamation in Hindi or Gujarati – oh my, my father – also meaning 'Oh my God'.

'Dev? Is that you? Welcome back,' said the postman.

'Dev *beta*? You are back! Shanta *ben*, look here, our Dev is back!' said another lady. I was hugged and kissed; my hand was shaken as more and more people gathered around me. I was overwhelmed. Chandu came back, pushing his way through the crowd.

'*Chalo, Chalo*, go and do your work. Dev will be here tomorrow,' he said, dispersing the crowd. Some were wiping their tears and some were shaking their heads in disbelief.

'Thank you Chandu, I didn't know if I would be able to get away. But how did they know – recognise me? You weren't able to.'

Chandu chuckled. 'Dev *Bhai*, news travels fast, have you forgotten?' We moved on.

News had reached Ma and *Babuji*. They cried openly, pulling me from the tonga and crushing me to their chests. Eventually the tears dried up but Ma and *Babuji* didn't let go of me. *Babuji* held me by the shoulder and Ma had her arms on mine. They led me into the house. They stared at me like I was a mirage and would be gone in one blink.

'*Babuji*, it is really me. I am here,' I said.

'Oh *beta*, I can't believe it!' he shook his head. 'But how did you get out? Did they release you?'

'You can ask him questions another time, *Ji*,' said Ma to *Babuji*. She turned to me. '*Beta*, your face is so thin. The food must have been terrible there. Nothing like your Ma's cooking, eh? I will bring some *roti* and *sabzi*.'

Ma brought out the food and I realised I was famished. Ma fanned me whilst I ate and Papa talked about Khan *Bhai*, his garage and that he had begun work on the fields again. I expected him to talk about Payal but he didn't. Oddly, I was glad. Ma filled my plate until I begged for her to stop. I yawned after.

'Rest, *maro dikro*. We will talk later,' said *Babuji*.

'Nai Babuji, I don't want to waste any more time. I want to live my life now, with you and Ma.'

It was with no surprise when Sunil and Amit burst through the doors fifteen minutes later.

'You're back! You're back!' shouted Sunil, ruffling my hair.

'Welcome back,' said Amit. 'We missed you *yaar*.'

I grinned. 'It's good to be back...thank you for releasing me from jail,' I said after the excitement had worn off.

'We couldn't let you rot in there for long, could we?' said Amit. 'When Sunil told me you were in jail, it was all I could think of. I wondered too...if you were avenging Rakesh *Bhai*'s death...but you can tell me another time. I see you are tired.'

'No stay, it's been so long since I have seen anyone. I want your company.' I yawned.

'No, you don't,' Sunil laughed. 'Today we will let you spend the day with your Ma and *Babuji*, and then we will see you tomorrow.' Sunil grabbed a banana on the way out and I laughed out loud.

We went for a long walk and I told my friends everything that had happened to me in jail – the near force feeding, the incident of the dirty water and how Haricharan rescued me and the ill treatment only reserved for Indians. The white prisoners were treated like *Maharajas*. But I didn't tell them about my beatings.

Sunil and Amit had their arms around my shoulders and listened quietly. They knew I needed to speak.

'I had a letter from Pooja,' Amit said a while later after I finished.

'What did she say?' I asked.

'She has left her husband and is now living in Poona. She is not alone for she lives near Rama. She is also pregnant.'

'But why is she not here, with us?' I asked. I was still bitter about her marriage and still blamed myself but just hearing her name, made me feel happy.

Amit shrugged. 'God is playing a mysterious game.'

Suddenly, I remembered the letter from *Babuji* and about Payal. I hadn't seen her at home, where was she?

'Payal and Gunwant-ji are back in Simla,' said Amit. 'Has your father told you? He has agreed to make Payal his daughter in law. You and Payal are getting married.'

My marriage to Payal? No, Amit has heard wrong. I can't get married to Payal, I love Pooja. Gunwant-ji and Payal know this.

'I need to speak to *Babuji*. I will see you later,' I told Amit and Sunil and went straight home.

261

'*Babuji*, why didn't you tell me? I can't marry Payal,' I protested.

'Why not, *beta*? She is a nice girl; she has good manners. Your Ma likes her and so do I. She is perfect for you,' said *Babuji*. He took his glasses off and cleaned them with his shirt.

'How did you meet?' I asked. 'Gunwant-ji and Payal live in Simla.'

Babuji looked at me gravely. 'When you didn't go back to Gunwant- ji's house, they were worried. You just vanished. They searched the hospitals, asked around the town and then went to the police. It was too early to give information of your arrest. Gunwant-ji spoke to Khan *Bhai*, who confirmed that you hadn't come here.

'We were told, ofcourse. We waited for a long time for some news from you but none came. We nearly gave up hope – we thought we wouldn't see you again...then Payal came to Rajkot. She looked after us and Ma began to rely on her. She is a daughter to us, Dev. It was Ma's idea – she wants Payal as a daughter in law. She wants you to marry her. Please, don't say no. It will break Ma's heart and even Payal's.'

I couldn't argue with that. I couldn't let down Ma and *Babuji* again – I owed them some happiness. I agreed to marry Payal.

~
POOJA
~

Twenty one

No regret

What *bewakuf*[158] was banging on my door at this time of the morning? I checked my clock and it was 5am. I groaned as I made my way to the door.

'Don't you know –' I was ready to shout a thousand things at the *bewakuf* but she stopped me. We both stared at one another, one of us shy and timid and the other confused and amazed.

'Rakhi?' I said. 'What are you doing here?'

'Oh Ma,' Rakhi dropped her bag and threw herself onto me. She was sobbing; I didn't know what to do or what to say. This was strange...I rubbed my eyes, maybe I was still asleep. I opened my eyes but she was still standing there.

She called me Ma, something I thought would never happen and yet here was the one daughter who had refused me as a mother and hated my existence. It was extraordinary hearing that word from her.

'Rakhi, what happened? Did your Papa...' I stopped myself. How could I ask her this? A father would never hurt his own daughter. What has become of me? I looked around her. 'Where are your bags?'

'I only have this,' she picked up the one bag.

I stepped aside and smiled, my sleep vanished. 'Come inside.'

She stepped into my one bedroom house which I had been renting for the last few months. It was my decision although Rama assured me that I didn't have to do this. Nethertheless, Rama asked her neighbours and luck was on my side. An elderly husband and wife were moving temporarily to Calcutta where their son lived with his wife. She was to have a baby soon and would need looking after. They agreed to rent.

I could see she was tired. Dark shadows under her eyes told me she did not sleep well...was there something to worry about?

'Is Papa alright?' I asked. I don't know why I asked that but now my anger had subsided, I realised I cared about him.

'He is, yes, in some ways,' said Rakhi.

'What do you mean? Is he hurt?'

---

[158] *Bewakuf*, Idiot

265

'Ma –'

I placed a hand on her arm and smiled. 'It is nice to hear that word from you. Anyway, I see you are tired, do you want to sleep?' I changed the subject quickly. I wasn't prepared to hear about Amar just yet and talking on the doorstep was not a wise thing to do. People were already staring even at this time. I shook my head in disgust.

Rakhi yawned confirming my thoughts. 'Just a little bit,' she said.

'How did you find me?' I asked as I took her to my bedroom. The children were still sound asleep. I smiled for she hadn't noticed and was already climbing into my bed.

'I went to Rama *maasi's* house and she told me you were here.'

I smiled. I liked it that she had met Rama. 'You go to sleep now and we will talk later.'

'But Ma, where will you sleep?'

'I am not tired and I have lots to do,' I reassured her.

Poor girl was obviously really tired for she fell asleep straight away. A few strands disturbed her face and I brushed them away. I felt happy; my daughter had finally come home.

'Ma, a baby is crying,' Rakhi woke up from her four hour slumber. I picked the baby up and walked over.

'Meet your little sister, Radha.'

'Ma, is this...'

I nodded, beaming. 'I was expecting when I left.'

Rakhi put her hand on her mouth, her eyes wide in wonder. 'She is just beautiful...like you. Can I hold her?'

I gently put Radha into her big sister's' arms. Radha's tiny fingers curled over Rakhi's thumb and she gurgled.

'She likes me,' said Rakhi. She played with her for a few minutes then asked the question which I knew would come.

'Ma, does Papa know?'

'What makes you think I haven't told him?'

'Because then he wouldn't have let you go. Maybe he would have treated you more like his wife.'

Oh Rakhi, I thought. If that was true then I would gladly have stayed...but your Papa thinks the baby is someone else's. Oh! How much did she know – did she see the beatings or the bruises? Had

266

she along with Kamla and Veer seen Amar hurt me? Was I blind to not realise they were witnesses to my pain?

'I have seen and heard everything, Ma. I'm so sorry,' she said as I searched her eyes for answers.

'If you know, then Kamla and Veer?' I already had the answer.

'Kamla knows but is helpless. I think that was why she wanted to come with you, to protect you – she loves you very much. Veer is still very young, if he saw something – I hope he will forget about it. And as for me – I saw what he was doing to you and like the last time, I was a coward. I couldn't stop him.'

'What do you mean? What happened last time?'

Rakhi fidgeted with her bangles and looked down. 'When Ma was with us, Papa beat her like he did with you. Even then, he went with other women and his drinking...one day it all got out of control. It was an accident. Ma was standing on the top step of the staircase and they were arguing. Papa lost his temper and slapped her. Ma fell, rolling down the stairs – she cracked her skull on the pillar. Papa took her to the hospital but it was too late. Ma was dead.' Tears streamed down my face, matching Rakhi's and I embraced her. 'I saw it all...and then he married you. It was like he never loved her. I saw you and hated you – you were taking my mother's place. Then I saw him beating you and the arguments...I didn't care and I thought you deserved it...I was bitter but now I know I was wrong. And I am truly sorry for that.'

'Oh my daughter,' I sighed, stroking her hair. 'I don't blame you at all. I wiped away her tears. 'I'm just glad you and I are friends now.'

'No, we are not friends, Ma,' she said. 'We are mother and daughter.'

It was midday and Veer and Kamla came back from school for their lunch.

'Has *didi* woken up?' asked Veer. 'I want to play.'

'Is that Veer?' Rakhi hugged her little brother tightly. 'You have grown! I have missed you so much!'

'Then why didn't you come with us?' Kamla said sharply. 'Why did you choose to stay with Papa? I hate him!'

'No, *beta*. He is still your father. You mustn't say that,' I said gently. Kamla crossed her arms and looked the other way.

'You have a right to be angry, Kamla, but there is a reason. Let me explain,' said Rakhi.

'I don't want to hear it!' Kamla stormed out. I started behind her but Rakhi stopped me.

'I'll go.' She put Radha into my arms and kissed Veer. 'We can play later, yes? I need to speak to Kamla.'

'Veer *beta*, come and help me make *rotis*. You can roll them out,' I said, taking his hand. 'Rakhi, be gentle with her...don't be too upset if she doesn't understand.'

I thought of Amar as I had done since the day I arrived. There were many questions I wanted Rakhi to answer – how was he? Did he eat well, does he look after himself? But why do I care about him? Because he is your husband, came the answer again. Yes, I agreed, because he is my husband.

I asked Kamla to take Veer over to Rama's house; she agreed too quickly. She wasn't yet happy with Rakhi. Please God, please take this indifference away.

Rakhi and I sat in the front room, facing one another. I saw she had grown more beautiful.

'Tell me, why are you really here?' I said.

'Ma, Papa needs you. I have come to take you home – we need you. Ma...Papa has changed, he is not the man you knew.'

I shook my head. 'It's not possible yet.'

'You said "yet". Does that mean you will come...one day...' Rakhi's eyes were hopeful. 'Ma, I heard you cry nearly every day. You have a right to be angry at Papa and hate me. I let him carry on and for that I am ashamed.' She came to sit by my knee and laid her head on my lap. 'I am really sorry, Ma.'

'It's in the past, let's forget about it. But do you know,' I tilted her chin towards me. 'You are like me in some ways – forgiving and kind – I imagine your mother was the same. As for coming home; I need more time.'

'I don't think Papa has more time...he has fallen apart without you,' Rakhi said.

'Fallen apart? How so?' I couldn't imagine Amar weak and vulnerable – I nearly laughed at the idea had I not seen Rakhi's face. 'Tell me.'

268

'He cries every night for you. He hasn't touched the drink in many months and his friends have stopped coming.' I knew she was talking about his "women" friends. 'Ma, remember the portrait he had painted of you?'

I nodded. Amar had made me sit for hours whilst the artist painted me. He told me it was a gift from him. That was days after we married. It was a good time then.

'Papa stares at your portrait and talks like you are there, right in front of him,' Rakhi carried on. 'When I come close to him, he pretends he is happy. He doesn't let me see him sad.'

I gasped; I didn't expect this at all. Had Amar really changed so much – has he begun to love me? I looked at Radha who was playing with her fists in her crib. She has a right to know her father and Amar has a right to know his daughter.

'Why didn't he come here to bring me home? Why has he sent you?'

'Papa doesn't know I am here. He thinks I am on vacation with some friends. He...forbade me to ask you to come home when I spoke about you. He said he didn't deserve you.'

I took in what she said and I wasn't ready to think about it. The clock ticked to nine. 'It's getting late,' I said. 'Let's pick up your brother and sister.'

Shivraj entertained the children and Mangal Ba was with Rakhi. I took Rama outside – I wanted to speak with her. She held Radha.

'Amar is in a bad way. Rakhi wants me to come home,' I began and told her everything Rakhi told me.

'Do you want to go home?' Rama asked. She rocked Radha who had fallen asleep with a smile on her face.

'If Rakhi thinks he has changed, then maybe he has. She wouldn't lie,' I said. 'I'm scared, though, for Radha. What if he doesn't accept her?' I remembered his cruel words...*it can't be mine*...

'Rakhi has accepted her new sister, then so will Amar. If you believe that Amar is a changed man, then I agree with Rakhi, that you should go home. But I will miss you very much, my dear friend.'

'So shall I. You have been like a sister to me these past few months. I don't know where I would be if...'

'Think of it as my penance for all my sins.'

We looked at each other and laughed.

269

'I have an idea,' she said.

'What?'

'Shivraj has always wanted to visit Bombay and this is our chance. We will all come to Bombay a week or so after you leave from here. We will see how Amar is with you...if he loves you, otherwise, you are coming back home with us. Agree?'

I couldn't contain my gratitude and flung my arms over my friend. 'I agree.' I said. 'Rama?'

'Yes?'

'I wrote to Sunil and Amit and told them where I was and that I was happy. Did I do right?'

'They are your friends and they care about you. You did absolutely right.'

'It's Sunil's wedding in two weeks. Will you come with me to Rajkot?' I released her from my embrace and searched her eyes. I needed her; I don't think I could face going alone if things with Amar had not changed.

'I can't wait to tell Shivraj,' her eyes twinkled.

We told everyone of my decision and Rama told her husband and mother-in-law about their trip to Bombay and Rajkot.

'*Na*, you children go,' said Mangal Ba. 'Why would you want an old lady like me to come with you? *Na na.*'

I put my arm around her shoulders and crouched slightly to reach her height. 'I love you, Mangal Ba and I will always want my grandmother with me.'

So it was decided. I was scared but excited. We packed and I gave the house keys to Rama, who would be seeing the old couple before she comes to Bombay. I had written a letter of thanks, put the remaining rent money in the envelope and left it on top of a box of sweetmeats.

We didn't cry over our farewells for as Mangal Ba said, we shall see each other very soon.

I stood at the gates of my house, holding Radha close to my chest. I looked through the rails and saw a house that didn't look like the home I had left. So much had changed; it felt strange.

'Shall I tell Papa we are here?' Rakhi said it softly but it still startled me.

'Give me a moment.' I opened the gates and walked through. The front garden was unkempt; the paving stones had not been washed and black dirt marked the grounds. The flower beds were dead and weeds grew in their place. From this, I understood the gardener had left and had not been replaced.

Radha began to cry and I tried to soothe her without success.

'Ma, let me.' As soon as Rakhi took her sister, Radha fell quiet and began sucking her thumb. I was amazed.

'Ma, are we going inside?' asked Kamla. 'Is Papa home?'

'Ma, I'm hungry,' complained Veer.

I took their hands. '*Chalo*, let's go home.'

'*Memsahib?*'

'Pratap *ji*?' It was the driver.

'You came back! I knew you would. I kept telling the others but they wouldn't believe me. I told them you would...you are staying, aren't you *Memsahib*?' he asked.

'Yes, I am,' I smiled.

'*Memsahib*, so much has happened, some for the good and some for the worse...but things will be alright now.'

Before I could speak, he ran into the house and called everyone.

'*Memsahib*! You are back,' they exclaimed in delight. The servants embraced me and cried. It was a while before I could speak to them.

'It is really good to see you and I mean it from my heart. I am happy you stayed for *Saab*. No matter what happened in the past, he still needed you. It's good you stayed,' I repeated.

'Oh *Memsahib*, he has really changed. I never thought he would, his mother would have been so proud had she still been alive,' said Laxmi, the cook's wife, wiping her eyes with the corner of her sari. 'He is a better man.'

Meenaxi Ba nodded, her eyes wet.

'Where is he?' I asked. My heart began to race – I had never felt so nervous.

'He is at work,' said Pratap *ji*.

Radha began to cry. 'I think she is hungry,' I said.

'Memsahib, is she your...' asked Meenaxi Ba.

271

'Yes, your *Saab's* and my child.' I didn't have to explain to everyone but didn't like them to think otherwise.

'She is very beautiful, like you Memsahib,' she sniffed. '*Chalo*, let Memsahib come in. Radha *beetiya* is hungry.' Meenakshi Ba made space for me to enter.

I looked around my room as I fed Radha. It was just as I had left it. I could have just woken up yesterday and...I checked myself. What was I thinking? The last few months did happen. I have Radha to show for it...Amar's and my daughter...Amar, what did he look like now? I looked down at our daughter – she had his eyes – dark and mysterious, but she had my smile and dimples. Radha fell asleep immediately after her feed and I put her down. I asked Rakhi to look after her whilst I went downstairs. I had a lot to oversee.

It was eight in the evening when Amar came home. He looked dishevelled and his clothes were creased. This couldn't be the Amar I left, who was always smart. I was in the main room with the children when he came in. He stood in the doorway, unsure to come in.

'Pooja?' he said.

I stopped combing Radha's hair. 'Hello Amar.'

'You are back. You really are.' He began to walk towards me; his hands slightly raised but he stopped. He looked uncertain.

'How are you?'

'I missed you...'

'Kamla, Veer – go and say hello to Papa.' Veer flew into his arms whilst Kamla stayed with me. 'Kamla, please.'

She went but didn't embrace him.

'Looks like I have a lot of explaining to do,' he smiled weakly. He hugged both his children. 'I have missed you so much...' When he let go, Kamla ran out of the room. Amar looked at me.

'She will come round,' I said. 'Rakhi, can you take Veer?'

I was now alone with him and Radha. He looked at me with hopeful eyes, tears hidden. He saw Radha in my arms but didn't say anything.

'This is Radha, our child – *your* daughter,' I said.

His breath caught and tears finally spilled. He touched her cheek, so gently that she may have been a china doll. 'I'm so sorry...for everything. I didn't mean what I said about... I believed you when you said the baby was ours. But I was angry...I am a monster!'

272

'Rakhi tells me that you have changed, can I believe that?'

'She is a good girl, Rakhi. She is sensible and kind...I have hurt her a lot.' Amar seemed to be far away, probably thinking about his first wife. He smiled. 'She came to me two weeks ago, pleading with me. She wanted me to come to Poona to bring you home. I didn't deserve you – I forbade her to go.'

'But she came anyway,' I said. 'Tell me, Amar. Do you want me back? Do you – have you ever loved me?'

'I admit – you were only a wife to me when I married you. A mother to my children and I didn't love you, but I did care about you. I know it's not enough. After you left, I realised what I had lost. I cursed myself over and over...Pooja, I love you with all my heart.'

'Did you love your first wife?' Amar's shock echoed around the room. 'Rakhi told me everything.'

Then Amar broke down completely. 'Asha was my life, my love. She was my children's mother. I don't know when all that changed – perhaps when I stopped drinking –and then I killed her.' Amar cried louder and without thinking, I took him into my arms. He sobbed into my chest like a child hugging his mother.

'It wasn't your fault,' I said. 'It was an accident.' I brought Radha to him and put her in his arms. Amar smiled through his tears. I saw confusion, sadness and torment behind them. I realised there was a lot more to talk about but now wasn't the right moment.

I took a deep breath. 'Amar, I want you to promise me.'

'Anything, I will do anything you say. I owe you that much. I love you so much and I promise you that I won't hurt you again.'

'Will you stop drinking?'

'I already have and there are no longer other women in my life,' he said sincerely.

I felt a lump in my throat. 'That's enough for now but I have a few things I have to say. I cannot be the wife that you married. I am not that woman anymore. A lot has happened in my life, in the past and present and I will not have that repeated again. Radha has made me a stronger woman and I will not succumb to anything or anyone. I cannot love you readily. It will take time.

'But I will try and be a good mother and wife. Your children are my children as Radha is ours. They will share our love as Ma and Papa and all I ask from you is that you promise to be a good, honest father and husband.'

'Yes, I promise. It's all I want.'

'Another thing, we will sleep in separate rooms until I feel ready to be a wife to you.'

'I understand...I am really sorry, Pooja.'

'It's getting late,' I said. 'I need to sleep.' Radha was already asleep and Amar gave her to me. I saw a fatherly longing in his face which I had not seen before. I didn't know how I felt about it. 'We will see you in the morning.'

Amar's pained expression made me sad but I had to do this. I had to be sure for me and the children.

In the next week, Mangal Ba, Shivraj and Rama came to stay and Amar showed his hospitality respectfully. He was a good host. With me, he was polite and gentle and didn't over step his mark.

Rama, who had never seen Amar and had only heard about him from me, could see the way he behaved towards me and was happy. Shivraj was tough and asked him questions about me and his relationship like he was my big brother. Amar was shamed. I felt like justice was done. He needed this, to feel like I had felt.

During the next week, Amar brought me flowers or surprised me by making me *chai* with no help. I knew he was trying very hard to win me back but like I said, it would take time. This was a new Amar but I couldn't yet trust him enough to love him.

One evening, I told Amar about Sunil's wedding and again, he surprised me.

'It was very wrong of me to think of you like that...I know you are pure. I am sorry to have embarrassed you in front of your friend. Pooja, I have no qualms of you attending his wedding with the children.'

'I want you to come too, Amar.'

Amar's eyes shone with happiness and gratitude. 'Thank you.'

~

AMIT

~

Twenty two

Mary's letter

I was a fool – I loved a *Memsahib* who was far from my reach, someone I couldn't have but my heart said otherwise. I tried to forget her but it wasn't to be. In literature, myth and reality – forgetting one's first love was near to impossible so what chance did I have?

    '*Pyar*[159]? Beta, what is love? You need to get married now, that is the solution,' Ma would tell me from time to time. 'There are lots of girls ready to get married in this village! Should I talk to Neelu *ben*? She has five daughters and wants to marry them very quickly. Her eldest daughter is very pretty and she knows how to cook well...Amit? What do you think?'

    'I don't want to get married Ma.'

    'But *dikra*...'

    'No Ma.' She would walk away mumbling to herself. 'That *chokra*[160] doesn't know what is good for him, there are nice girls waiting and he just wants that *Memsahib*...tut tut...'

Sometimes I would walk along by Mary's house only to glance from afar. I no longer went to the house – knowing she is not there anymore...I couldn't stand it. I would see other *Memsahibs* and I'd see Mary's face before me; I'd long to talk to her and to hold her hand but now I only have memories of her lingering scent and the touch of her kiss on my cheek.

    She was my passion, my amour. She made me happy – she took away my woes. The day I found her on the road was a gift from the Gods and I fell in love with her from that first sight, although I hadn't understood it then. My heart fluttered when I saw her and it hurt when she was away.

    Mary had given me a watch and her bracelet – I was special to her; a symbol of her love. I sometimes wondered about "our life" had she not married David and had a child or if she hadn't met Tom – perhaps then we could have been together.

---

[159] *Pyar*, Love
[160] *Chokra*, Boy (Gujarati word)

277

Bewakuf, it is because of Tom that she came to India at all. It was a coincidence that you met her and your bad luck that you fell in love.

It is not bad luck but my good fortune that I had a chance to meet such a beautiful and caring *Memsahib* – forget about her past, Mary will still be my first love.

But what about your future? My future – I don't know where it will lead. I may get married someday but I will not be able to give my heart to my wife; I may begin to love her but it would be empty and would never compare to the love for Mary.

You are a bewakuf. Yes, perhaps I am.

Sunil and Dev are a good distraction. Dev, now back from jail has committed his time between his Ma and Papa, Khan *Bhai* and the garage and between myself and Sunil. Sometimes we would talk about the Quit India movement, *Bapu* and the other leaders – Patel, Jinnah and Nehru and their politics. Other times we would talk about Payal who has come to stay with her *Kaki*[161]. Dev and Payal were engaged two days ago. It was a fine ceremony. I asked my dear friend if he loved her but he said not. She was someone who he could spend his life with – she was wife material but he could never love her: his love was Pooja.

Sunil was a busy man. With his *lagan*[162] at the end of the month, he hardly had time to stop and chat but he always made time for me. I would see him running errands, sometimes with me in tow. Neha, his love, was the centre of his life and with Shankarji so ill, he would look after her and her family as well as his own. My friend had grown up.

The one friend I did not expect to see was Pooja with her baby and with her husband, Amar. Like Sunil, I was angry. 'What is he doing here? How dare he show his face?' I said.

'Amit, he is not like that anymore...he has changed. I am happy,' Pooja told me. I looked at the baby she was carrying. 'This is Radha, my child. Amit, forget the past, this is the present, the good life I had always wanted.'

---

[161] *Kaki*, Auntie (Father's younger brother's wife)
[162] *Lagan*, Wedding

I wanted to believe her and I had no other choice but to do so. 'You deserve to be happy, Pooja,' I said. But I wasn't sure that her happiness would last, not with that man.

Pooja still hadn't met Dev but it was only a matter of time and I wondered what would happen then? Did she still love him as he still loved her? Would Dev be able to let her go once he sees that she has a complete family?

'Amit!' Stop daydreaming! We have some guests!' Ma's voice shouted from down below.

I sighed and got off the wicker bed. I looked down from the rooftop, hoping it wasn't someone I didn't want to see.

'Amit!' shouted Ma again.

'Avu chu[163]!' I went down slowly; I was in no hurry. My heart skipped a beat when I saw him, the one person I had been avoiding.

'Hello Amit.' Stuart's wide smile washed my thoughts away and brought one image to my mind: Mary. 'Phew! It's so hot in the village, how can you stand it?'

'We are used to it,' I said. 'What brings you here, Stuart Saab?'

Stuart raised an eyebrow. 'Saab? Since when do you call me that? We are friends, aren't we?'

I had to smile. 'Of course, Stuart.'

'That's what I like to hear. Before we sit as you so kindly have not asked us to...' his eyes twinkled and I knew he was having a joke with me. 'Let me introduce my fiancée, Sara.' He gestured to a breath-taking lady who was standing next to him. She had rosy cheeks and bright green eyes...she reminded me of Mary...the same complexion, the same beauty...

She was elegantly dressed, wearing a full-length yellow and white floral dress with matching hat and sandals. Stuart looked comic in comparison. He wore his usual attire of brightly coloured floral half-sleeve shirt (which was matching to what his fiancée wore) and knee-high shorts and sandals. I smiled as I thought of the bus trip in Goa when I had met him first – he had worn the same shirt.

---

[163] *Avu chu*, I am coming (Gujarati)

He looked well and happy but I saw a shadow underneath. Looking closer, I saw his face was tired and pale but he glanced lovingly at Sara *Memsahib* from time to time – it was endearing to see such affection.

'Amit? Where are you?' Stuart said, waving a hand in front of me.

'Sorry, I was just....congratulations, to you both,' I said. '*Memsahib* is just right for you.'

Ma, who was sitting in a corner working on her embroidery, put it down. 'Stuart *beta*, Memsahib, would you like some *lassi*[164] with a little salt and coriander? It is very refreshing in this weather.'

Sara looked at Stuart.

'Amit's mother doesn't see me as a *Saab* but as her son,' explained Stuart.

Sara smiled. 'That is sweet. Amit's mother, I would love some,' she said. 'Actually, I am very fascinated by the village and its people. Would you mind...can I come into the kitchen with you? That's alright, isn't it dear?' she turned to Stuart who nodded his approval.

'If it is fine by *Ma-ji*,' he said.

'I would be delighted, *Memsahib*. You do remind me of Stuart's sister, Mary.' My heart sank – why did I have to be reminded of her so much? 'You look so much like her,' Ma continued. 'She was a wonderful girl. Anyway, I am also making potato *bhajiyas*[165] and *samosas*. I will show you how I make them. In the morning, the heat isn't so bad and so it's easy to fry, but in the afternoon, *eh Baghwaan!*' Ma's voice faded as they went further into the house and then it was only Stuart and I. He watched me which I found to be uncomfortable.

'Amit, have you ever fallen in love?' he asked suddenly.

'Sorry?'

'Yes, love. Have you ever fallen in love?'

'No. I cannot say that I have. Why do you ask a funny question?'

Stuart stood up. 'Come, let's go for a walk. It is such a beautiful day.'

'What about *Memsahib*?'

---

[164] *Lassi*, *a sweet or salty yogurt drink.*
[165] *Bhajiya*, Savoury vegetables coated in Gram flour (made from ground, dried chick peas) then fried.

'Sara is well looked after, we will only be a few minutes. Come on.' To my bewilderment, Stuart went to the door. 'Shall we?' 'Are you serious?' I found this all very strange and surreal.

'Amit, I am always serious. Now, come on, will you!' He mock threw me out of the house by my shirt collar.

'Where are we going?' I laughed. It felt good to see Stuart and I was ashamed to have avoided him.

'I like the river, let's go there. How long will it take to walk there, should we call for a tonga?'

'There is only one tonga in this village and Chandu drives it. He is at a wedding today, besides this is a small village and so the river is only ten minutes away.'

Curious villagers stared at us; an unlikely pair walking and chatting amiably, like there was no war between the white man and the brown man. We talked as old friends and laughed at our own jokes. He told me how he met Sara and about their courtship. They were engaged three weeks ago. As I listened, I sensed that he was biding his time to tell me something and it wouldn't be good news; it made me nervous. I didn't rush him and let him ramble on.

The sweet smell of the river reached us before we arrived. The smooth sound of the rush over pebbles and stone, the chirping of the birds, and the feel of the cool air...I would not change a thing - it made me feel free. Stuart appreciated it too.

We sat on a large, flat stone and watched the river for a while. Down the way a little, children threw in stones and splashed each other as they waded into the water, waist high. I called out to be careful.

'We will,' they shouted back and swam to and fro to show me it was safe.

'Amit,' said Stuart. 'I want to say something.'

'I was wondering when you would. It was playing on your mind all the way here, wasn't it? You brought me here for a reason.'

'You know me well.' He hesitated for a moment. 'What has happened to you, Amit?'

'I don't know what you mean.'

He stared at me. 'I've noticed the change in you. You don't come to the house anymore. You are nowhere to be seen. I have sent you letters but you chose to ignore them. I wondered if I'd done something wrong or something to offend you, my friend. But then I realised – you weren't angry or upset with me. You were upset with Mary...you loved her...'

'You are very observant, Stuart,' I was impressed. 'You are not angry about that?'

'But why should I be? Your infatuation with Mary was obvious from when you first came to the house with Sunil. You were talking to me but your mind was elsewhere. You wanted to talk to Mary and be with her. When it was time for you to go home, you were sad. You hovered, perhaps thinking of a reason to stay. Do you remember? Your face lit up each time she spoke to you and when she laughed – you became animated.' I stared at him in disbelief – how could he know all this? 'Amit...I have to say how impressed I was with you – how you held yourself around her, knowing she was engaged to Tom and still your love for her brought you back time and time again.'

'Why are you telling me all this?'

'Because I never want you to think that you should forget her...she was special to you, to your heart. And that should never be erased...there is a connection between us and between you and Mary and that can never be broken and never be sullied by distance or silly wars.' Stuart took out an envelope from his pocket and handed it to me. 'From Mary.'

I held the envelope in my hand, my mind asking a thousand questions.

'I'm glad you rescued her, Amit,' Stuart said when I failed to speak for my eyes were wet. 'I'm glad I sat next to you on the bus in Goa.' He then laughed and I looked up, quite embarrassed. He pretended to not notice. 'You were a funny person – you ignored me through the whole journey and even went the other way when we all descended, I think trying to avoid me? You're not like the others. you don't befriend easily but that's what I like about you. You're not pretentious like so many ....but I managed to win you over.'

I laughed. 'I thought there was something very familiar about you and as much as I tried, I couldn't think why. I went to your house and saw the photographs but still – nothing, until I saw Mary again in Rajkot with you.' I shook my head. 'It is an amazing coincidence.'

'It sure is,' said Stuart.

'I'm sorry to have ignored you; to not come and see you and not send replies. I hope you can forgive me.'

'I wouldn't be here talking to you otherwise, my dear friend. I have missed you greatly. Now, don't be a stranger anymore...Mary was fond of you, you know. On the day she left for England, she told me that you were a true friend to her and that she would miss you very much. She wanted me to keep a look out for you...I think she knew that you loved her.'

'Thank you very much,' I said in a near audible voice. We watched the children playing in the river for a while. A bird flew above. I sensed there was more to come and I was right.

'Amit, my post has been seconded to Calcutta – it was on the cards. I will be residing there with Sara and we shall be leaving in two days.' I vaguely remembering the conversation by the window – the day Stuart began acting strange around me...a few days before I knew about Mary's daughter.

'I will miss you,' I said. I felt tears prick my eyes again. Was it because of the letter or because Stuart, my one link to Mary and friend to me – was leaving? I suppose both...

Stuart put his arm around my neck. 'I will miss you certainly,' he smiled sadly. He cleared his throat. 'Now, let's get back to your house. I think Sara and your mother will be worried where we have got to. Besides, I quite fancy some *lassi* and those *bhajiyas*.'

I managed a small smile and folded the envelope, pocketing it. 'Let's go home.'

That night when everyone was asleep, I went to the roof and lit an oil lamp. The crickets gave me company as they called each other across the field. I brought the lamp near to the letter.

29 September 1946

Dear Amit,

I write to you in good health. We arrived in London safely. The seas were calm most of the way but it became frightening when the storm arrived. Poor Tom had to stay in the sick bay. He does detest the sea journeys.

On our arrival, mother greeted us at Southampton. She was ever so pleased and relieved. We wasted no time getting home. Tamara, my beautiful child, had grown more and I cradled her. I never wanted to let her go. I thought she had forgotten but she never did, she called me "momma". My dear little one walked to me on her unsteady legs. I cried unashamedly into her ringlets and kissed her face, again and again. Oh, how could I have left her?

Oh Amit, let me tell you about London, for it is so different. I feel threatened almost every day, not by the people but by the unknown. In some streets, houses have been demolished by bombs and have left desolate streets full of rubble and dust. Many children have been evacuated to the country. Mother wanted little Tammy to be sent too but she was too ill. We are all going to Leicestershire tomorrow and will reside there until the war is over. By the time you receive my letter, we will be safe in our temporary house.

Amit, maybe you don't know this...it is very hard for me to confess, for my heart flutters each time I think I can say it. I am a coward – I couldn't tell you in person. I hope you will understand when I tell you now.

The day I met you, you were charming, caring and loveable. Your heart was beautiful and your attitude to life admirable. I began to grow fond of you and I waited eagerly for your next visit. I saw a great friend in you. I don't know when I began to love you – there, I've said it! I have loved you.

But don't misunderstand me – this love for you is different to my love for Tom. I love him with all my heart but Amit; you are my special angel – my "parie".

Tom is aware of my adoration for you and he doesn't mind, can you believe it? He knew from the beginning but he couldn't be angry with you, for you engaged him. You made him like you. He saw no threat to our "relationship" but saw devotion, something like your Hindu story of Radha and Krishna[166].

---

[166] **Radha & Krishna**, a story of love and devotion between Lord Krishna and his devotee Radha. Lord Krishna is known by many names – Kishen, Gopal, Murali and Kanhaiya being some of them. Their story is known by generations of Hindu worshippers and relayed in plays and books around the world.

Amit, I'm truly blessed to have you as my friend – my angel. Thank you for coming to see me at the station – you had forgiven me. I miss you greatly and I hope one day I will see your sweet and generous smile again.

I hope you write - I wait eagerly.

With all my Love,
Mary

I stared at the word "love" and kissed it. I had found my Mary again.

~
SUNIL
~

Twenty three

Death & Marriage

Ma had done a wonderful job. White and orange flowers hung in long braids around the house and red and white roses entwined over the entrance arch. Twinkling lights brought sparkle to the evening and aromatic spices lingered appreciatively over the guests who had already arrived.

Marriage to Neha meant happiness. I felt blessed and I couldn't wait until I brought her home[167]. I'd left behind the recent past few days that had haunted my days and nights. I could now focus on the upcoming joy.

I smiled in the sun, I smiled in the rain and I couldn't stop. I'd daydream about our prefect day and see Neha's shining face. I'd hear singing and see dancing.

My house was filled with flowers – orange, white, green and yellow, weaved into blankets and hung over the veranda and the courtyard walls – a celebration.

'Sunil, you are to sleep in the front room until your wedding day,' said *Moti-Ma*. 'We will need to decorate it, understand?'

I stayed away but impatient to peer. How would it be? I'd heard from others that it would be a marital haven – my bed would be turned into a four-poster and flowers would hang from the frame, creating a perfumed curtain. Candles would be lit and a fragrance so sweet would swirl from an incense stick around the room.

My bride would wait for me on the bed; her veil draped over her face. I would lift it and she would look away – bashful. Our bodies would entwine in marital bliss, beginning life as husband and wife.

Oh– how I wish my wedding day would come sooner. I embraced myself and sighed.

Tau and *Moti Ma*, my grandparents from Ma's side, distant cousins whom I'd met once or twice, my uncle and his wife and three children were just a few of the guests to have arrived. Leelu *ben* from across the road was always around, helping Ma with whatever she needed doing.

---

[167] ***Bringing the bride home***, In Indian marriages, the bride is married into the groom's family and is expected to live with them.

Although a Christian, Ma wanted to follow the Hindu ceremony (against grandma's wishes).

'It will make Govind very happy, mother. If he were here today, he would have been proud,' Ma sniffed. Grandma rolled her eyes behind her back and muttered something that sounded like "your grandmother would turn in her grave!" I muffled a laugh.

Ma asked *Moti Ma* to oversee the rituals and practically handed the other preparations over to *Tau*. She allocated other duties to herself – like organising the sleeping arrangements for all the guests whilst attending to Meera's demands.

'I have done my chores; can I play with Geeta now?' Meera whined.

'You know this is a big week for *Bhai*, so I need you to be good and helpful. You can play later,' Ma chided.

Meera glumly stayed in the house. Some of the guests asked her to entertain – they had heard about her dancing. She lit up. Meera loved any opportunity to show off her dancing; with a house full of guests, it was perfect. Happily, she put dancing bells on her ankles and began the graceful dance of *bharat natyam*[168]. Everyone stopped to watch this harmonious synchronisation of body and soul as she performed the love between Lord Krishna and Radha. Each beat would see her step in rhythm and rhyme, matching her expression and hand choreography perfectly.

The clapping was thunderous and Ma, who had also stopped to watch, wiped her tears of joy.

'That was brilliant, Meera – you see, you will touch the stars someday,' I said proudly.

'Thank you, *Bhai*,' she said, her eyes twinkling. She kissed me on the cheek.

Dev and Amit were my guards; they were to stop me overindulging myself on forbidden foods – on the chance I may get sick and to stop me from sneaking away to see my bride-to-be.

'Sunil, there you are!'

'Hello Dev,' I said.

---

[168] *Bharat natyam*, a classical dance that commenced from Tamil Nadu – a South Indian state.

'Didn't *Ma-ji* tell you not go wandering off by yourself? What are you doing here?'

I had been standing by the village well for an hour and staring into it. It was dark and frightening, even for me. I couldn't imagine anyone jumping in.

'Nothing, just thinking,' I said.

'Are you thirsty?' he asked, puzzled by my behaviour. He looked down the well.

'No. Dev... remember when I went to Jaipur?'

'Yes, you told me you had a good time.'

'I didn't tell you about the...dead girl.'

'What are you talking about, Sunil? Did you have a bad dream?' Dev asked looking at me strangely.

I shook my head. 'No, listen.' I plunged into my story, occasionally being interrupted with gasps and exclamations from Dev. 'She was only young, why did that man do that to her? She was forced to commit suicide.'

We heard rustling and we looked around. A cat walked out from amongst the trees.

'Who was this man?' Dev asked.

'The villagers were almost certain it was a white man. He visited the family on many occasions – just stopping by. He began to court her secretly I heard and then...'

Dev's face hardened. 'They just can't leave us alone.'

'But what if the villagers were wrong and it was someone else? What if it was someone from their own village? I cannot imagine why a white man would do such a thing.'

Dev smiled sadly. 'Not everyone is like Officer Stuart. He is one of a kind...now listen, it's happened and not you or anyone can do anything about it. Let's pray to *Eeshwaar* that whoever did this is in jail now. It is your wedding and that is the only thing you need to be thinking about. Neha is the most important person right now so clear your mind and let's go home. It's time for the *haldi*[169] rituals.

---

[169] *Haldi*, a pre-marriage ceremony where the bride and groom are lathered in a paste; a mix of milk, oils, sandalwood powder and turmeric which is applied to the face, arms and feet. This is to obtain a flawless complexion for the wedding day.

I stood in my room, looking out of the window, dressed in my wedding attire. Today I was bringing my wife home. I smiled. Amit rushed in excitedly.

'Chameli has been transformed, she is so beautiful. You wait and see,' he said. I was to ride on Chandu's horse to Shankarji's house where the wedding was to take place and no horse was better than Chameli. From Amit's tone, I believed every word he said.

Pooja whistled when she came to see me. 'My *Bhabhi* is so lucky!' she teased.

I touched her face. 'You look stunning.' Pooja coloured red and playfully smacked my hand. I remembered how she looked when I saw her in Bombay. Today, she glowed. She was dressed in a lilac, sequined sari and had applied *mehndi* [170]to her hands. Pooja squeezed my hand and turned to go downstairs. She stopped abruptly.

'Dev,' she said.

Suddenly the atmosphere became tense. Dev gazed into Pooja's eyes passionately and she didn't look away. Moments passed and I began to feel as if I was intruding. I was perplexed – what was going on here? Were they in love with one another...? No, of course not – Pooja was married and Dev was soon to get married to Payal. *Oh Sunil, you are so silly!*

Dev cleared his throat. 'Hello Pooja, it's nice to see you.' He was always polite.

'It's been a long time...you have long hair now. It's nice, I like it,' Pooja commented.

'Nothing matches your beauty,' Dev said then immediately turned to me. 'Sunil, you look handsome. Neha is a lucky girl.'

Did I miss something? 'Er...thank you.'

Amit came in. '*Chalo, chalo.* It's time.' He looked at Pooja and Dev and something changed in his eyes but was gone in an instant. This was very odd. What was happening here? But I would ask Amit later on. Right now, I was getting married.

Dev added the last garment on my head – a *pugri*[171] and led me outside to the dazzling sunshine. The guests stood in their fine clothes, talking and laughing. Somewhere music was playing. Chameli

---

[170] **Mehndi**, a paste made from crushed henna leaves. This is applied to the bride or groom's hands and feet, sometimes in a pattern or just plain dye. In some cultures both women and men apply mehndi and in some, only women. It is thought the deeper the colour, the deeper the love.

[171] **Pugri**, Turban worn in weddings.

stood amongst the crowd, proudly dressed in gold sequins and a red and gold saddle made of velvet. She swished her silver braided tail, announcing her importance. I fed her an apple and she neighed, I thought, appreciatively.

'You look beautiful,' I said to her and she neighed once again.

I was hoisted on and she stamped in approval. Amit came to stand on one side and Dev on the other; both were smartly dressed in white *Shalwaars*[172]. The *baraat*[173] began to dance and lead the way to Shankarji's house.

It was agreed that the house was spectacularly decorated and no expense had been overlooked. Like Ma, Shankarji had perfected everything, from the entrance, the welcoming and the *nashta* to the cool sherbets. I was greeted with love and respect as I stepped down from Chameli.

A sigh rose from the crowd as Anjali walked towards me holding a tier of decorated pots on her head. She marked my forehead with red vermillion and rice grains and then playfully pinched my nose. I was then allowed into the house.

I eagerly waited for my bride as I sat under the canopy of red and white flowers, criss-crossed and weaved into a "blanket" that rested on four white pillars, decorated with spiralled ribbons.

'Amit,' I whispered. 'When is she coming?'

'So much impatience!' he laughed and I hung my face, quite embarrassed.

'Look, here she comes,' he winked.

Neha floated down the stairs; a heavenly image of white, red and gold. Her beauty radiated and dulled even the exuberant of dressers. There was no contest. Whispers of appreciation and happy exclamations went around as she glided towards me. Ma put her hands on her chest and sniffed and *Moti-Ma* wiped her eyes.

A joy like no other, exploded within me and I could just about contain myself, for I longed to shout "Thank you" to the heavens. I couldn't stop gazing at her beauty.

---

[172] *Shalwaar*, an Indian wedding suit.
[173] *Baraat*, a wedding party made up of guests from the groom's side.

The rituals began. *Ghee*[174] and rice seeds were offered to the holy fire and *Lord Ganesh's* blessing was pledged for. I then led Neha around the fire three times, promising her protection, love and an heir and she took the fourth round, coming in front, promising me that if death came for me first, she would willingly take it instead. But a life without Neha wasn't a life worth living and I promised if God took her before me, I would not be far behind.

Finally, I adorned Neha with vermillion and a *mangal sutra* and completed the marriage rituals. Neha was now my wife and I, her husband.

Neha clung to Shankarji and wept. 'I will never forget you, Papa. I will always be here when you need me.'

'Sunil's home is your new home now, *beta*. Always listen to your *sasu-ma*[175], and look after your new family. That's all I ask for,' he advised his daughter gently. 'I will not be here much longer. Promise me you will look out for Anjali when I am gone.'

'Oh Papa, don't say such things,' sobbed Neha. She clung to him harder.

Shankarji smiled. 'I have one last ritual to perform.' He took out a box and opened it. It was his wife's necklace.

'You remembered.' Fresh tears spilled down Neha's face as she bowed her head. Shankarji clasped it around her neck.

'There, you are now complete.' He kissed her forehead.

Neha and I touched the feet of our elders, receiving their blessing and then it was time to take my new wife home. Ma guided Neha towards the *doli*[176] and I climbed back onto Chameli. The *baarat* was going back home with a new member of the family.

Neha hardly slept through the night, for she turned in her dreams, weeping silently, sometimes calling for her father. I held her and rocked her trying to ease her heart. However, my reassurances fell on deaf ears.

---

[174] *Ghee*, Clarified butter
[175] *Sasu/Sasu-Ma*, Mother-in-law
[176] *Doli*, a bridal carriage, carried by four men to the groom's home. The bride sits inside after being wed - a veil covering her face.

'If something happens, Anjali will tell us,' I told her at one point when she was calm but I knew she didn't believe me. Finally, an hour before dawn, she fell asleep. I let her be.

Ma looked up as I came to the kitchen – alone. I told Ma about Neha's worries.

'Oh darling,' she said. 'She will be alright. All girls miss their families after marriage. Give her time.'

'I miss Papa,' Neha said. 'I am very worried about him.'

'You know you can go and see him anytime,' I said.

'Can we go and see him this afternoon? We will only be there for a little while, and then we will come home. Will Ma mind? My responsibilities lie here and I accept them...I will not forget that.'

I turned her face towards mine. 'Your father is my father. We will go and see him this afternoon. Please don't worry.' I kissed her forehead and she gave me a watery smile. 'First, you must have something to eat.' She looked at my empty chai cup and plate. 'I was hungry,' I said defensively and Neha laughed, relieving my heart.

Neha was dressed and ready to go. I took her hand.

'Don't look so worried,' I said. 'Please smile – for me.' Neha did smile but it didn't reach her eyes. 'God will make everything alright.'

The wedding decorations had not been taken down yet. When yesterday the atmosphere was joyous, today it was empty...the house was really quiet. Neha let go of my hand and rushed inside. Anjali was by Shankarji's side, pressing his temples gently.

'*Bas, bas, beta.* It won't help.' His voice was shallow, like he was gasping for breath.

'Papa.' Neha took his hands. 'What happened? Why didn't you call for me?'

Shankarji's eyes flickered to my face. 'Sunil *beta*, it's good you came...'

'I will call the doctor,' I said in an urgent tone. My heart was suddenly heavy.

Shankarji coughed, putting up a frail hand. 'It is no good; the doctor can do nothing for me now.'

295

'I wanted to come to you, *didi*. Papa wouldn't...let...me,' Anjali hiccupped. 'He began to feel ill early this morning. I knew something was wrong but Papa...'

'Anjali *beta*, I have been called for. *Eeshwaar* does not call without reason. I have but a few minutes. Neha and Sunil are here, you are with me...I can say my goodbyes. I...aaah,' Shankarji touched his chest.

He closed his eyes for a second and was still for a few moments. We were still too and dared not breathe...then, he opened his eyes. We relaxed when he spoke again.

'Sunil *beta*, I worry for Anjali. She is still so young...'

Still so young...the words caught in my throat...Sarika had been "still so young"...no one could protect her... that mistake will not happen again.

'No!' I said aloud and all three looked at me. I stepped forward and knelt down beside Shankarji's bed. 'Anjali is my responsibility. I will look after her, she is my sister now.'

Shankarji's eyes filled. 'I must have pleased *Eeshwaar* to give me a good, honourable son. I cannot thank you enough, *beta*. You have given me peace; I can go happily.'

Neha buried her face in his shirt. 'I cannot live without you, Papa. Sunil, please, call the doctor.' She searched my eyes – she wanted to be assured. I shook my head and she hung her head, large drops splashing her cheeks.

Shankarji put his thin hands on his daughter's'. 'God bless you...I love you very much.' He closed his eyes for the last time.

~
DEV
~

Twenty four

Pooja or Payal?

Gunwant-ji and Payal came back to Rajkot to finalise the wedding. They resided at our house on Ma's insistence – Payal was already a daughter-in-law to her. I greeted them as expected and welcomed them warmly but I couldn't help feeling trapped. I couldn't understand how it all happened – Payal and Gunwant-ji knew I loved Pooja, then how?

Payal was a lovely girl but I didn't love her. I would only be marrying her out of convenience. I'd heard that marriage was a joining of two hearts, how could I give my heart when it was already Pooja's? *But she is married, she can longer be your lover – just a friend, Let her go.* But how could I when my heart said no.

Payal never questioned me or tried to persuade me to talk to her. She observed me from afar and did things a wife would. She brought me *chai* every morning, looked after my trivial needs such as looking for a lost sock or getting my clothes out and she helped Ma in the kitchen. She proved to be an excellent cook – a perfect wife and daughter-in-law. I accepted her help with grace, knowing she was trying very hard for me to love her but I couldn't do it.

I woke up one night – I had been dreaming of *Bhai*. I didn't want to wake up; it was such a pleasant dream. I closed my eyes and searched for him, but he didn't come back. I sighed and threw the covers aside and walked out to the veranda.

Bhai and I were talking under the mango tree. He was telling me he was looking out for me in heaven and he was proud of me. I had grown into a fine man and looked after my responsibilities very well and that he was happy to see me take care of our parents. We talked about other things too but I don't remember them...

Payal came up behind me ever so softly that I didn't hear her. 'Are you troubled, *ji*?' I jumped. 'I'm sorry; I didn't mean to scare you. Are you troubled *ji*?'

Since our future relationship was agreed on both sides of the family, Payal began to call me "*ji*", as most wives did. I couldn't get used to it.

'No, I am not troubled. Why are you awake? Please go back to sleep,' I said. 'It's late.'

'How can I when you cannot?' She came to stand next to me. The moon's pale light lit her face – she was breath-taking. She looked at me, her eyes questioning. I looked away.

It was cooler than average at this time of night, Payal rubbed her arms. A shawl lay on a chair and I put it on her shoulders. She smiled shyly.

'I hear you every so often,' she spoke. 'Those dreams you have...you talk about them to someone. Maybe I don't have a right to know but I worry.' She looked up at the moon.

'I speak to *Bhai*, well, his spirit.' I don't know why I trusted her to admit this; it was a strange feeling. 'It sounds like I am mad, doesn't it?'

'Not at all. It helps you,' she said.

I smiled at her. 'You know something? You are different now, very grown-up.'

'Life dictates our persona,' she said. I was impressed and admired her. She truly had outgrown the Payal I knew not so long ago. The slight breeze turned chilly.

'We'd better go back in,' I said. 'And Payal, thank you.'

She smiled and went in. I looked at the moon one more time and went inside too.

I began to go to the veranda more frequently. Sometimes, I hoped to see Payal, to be able to talk to her alone. She made me feel secure and a surprising and happy feeling entered my heart. She would tell me stories of her childhood at times and other times, we would not speak much at all. Just her presence made me feel content. Slowly, I began to trust her and my feelings towards her began to grow. I began to see her as more than a friend and it frightened me. Was I leaving Pooja's love behind? Was I betraying her?

My *sagai*[177] with Payal was set to be in three weeks time and then marriage a week after. But first, I needed to speak to Pooja. I needed to clear things...to apologise and explain. I wanted to make things right between us but she was always with her husband or with someone else. I needed to see her alone.

I saw Pooja at Sunil's wedding. She was even more beautiful. I didn't expect to see her in Rajkot and I was overjoyed. For

---

[177] *Sagai*, Engagement

a moment, I forgot everything, the past few months – Simla, Payal and my imprisonment. It was temporarily erased from my mind and we were again back by the river talking about our marriage.

But then her baby cried and reality slapped me in the face. I saw her with a family of her own and I was left standing in the dark. My heart plummeted and I was jealous – hot and scathing. Pooja should be mine. I was resentful and I hated her husband! But there was nothing I could do.

I tried not to think about her; I tried avoiding her but she was always there, in front of me, either at the bazaar, in the temple or just with Amit and Sunil. I couldn't be where she was – even if it meant being away from my friends. It just hurt too much.

But now, I had to accept Payal, for her destiny was joined with mine. She was going to be my wife, my future and I had no right to think of Pooja anymore. There was only one thing I had to do first, and that was talk to Pooja, just once. I owed it to Payal – to make sure I was doing the right thing by marrying her.

My chance came one early morning when I decided to go for a walk. It was two days before my marriage to Payal and I wanted to clear my head. Amit and Sunil wanted to come with me but I was adamant that I would be alright – nothing would happen to me. They were a few yards away from me, hiding behind some trees. I pretended I didn't see them. The fools, I laughed silently. I walked up the hill, past a small stream and through a thicket of trees. There was a clearing where I wanted to rest and think. The sounds of birds chirping, the scent of the wood and the gentle sway of the trees made me feel calm. But what I didn't expect was to see Pooja. She was sitting alone, on a thick branch which lay low on the ground. She turned suddenly as I came near and she put both hands on her chest.

'Dev!' she exclaimed.

'Sorry, I didn't mean to frighten you,' I said.

'What are you doing here?' she looked around suspiciously. 'Are you alone? Are you spying on me?'

'No, I was just out, walking...Pooja, can I speak to you?'

She seemed unsure. 'Well, if you must.' She fidgeted with her wedding ring. I didn't waste time and asked her.

'Pooja, what happened to us?' I said.

'How do you mean? I am happy, *bas*.'

'You didn't answer my question.'

301

'Whatever happened was God's wish, Dev,' she said. 'We cannot change that.'

'Do you love your husband?'

Pooja looked at me sharply. 'How dare you ask me such a question? He is my husband!'

'But you didn't say you loved him,' I pressed.

'Listen Dev, it's none of your business. I have to go now, Radha will be hungry.'

'Radha?' I asked.

'Radha is my daughter.'

We stared at each other for a long time. 'Ah, yes, you have a family.' I sounded bitter.

Pooja sighed. 'Look, Dev, whatever happened between us was a long time ago. *We* didn't happen, so let it be.'

'I wish I could...can I say something before you go?'

Pooja nodded.

'I want to say that I am sorry for not being there with you when...Amit told me about Satish. I am sorry – I should have been here for you, married you... then you wouldn't have had to marry that old man and be a mother to his children before your time. You deserved better.'

'It doesn't matter now. It is very late,' she said quietly. 'Besides, I love my family, Dev.'

'Why didn't you write to me, to tell me what happened at the Chatterji's? I would have come back straight away and you know that.'

'Would you have married me? A disgraced girl?' There was doubt in her eyes. 'I had no choice and nor did Papa. I'm sorry Dev but maybe this was how it was supposed to be.'

'It doesn't change my love for you, Pooja.'

'Please don't say that.' I saw pain in her eyes.

'It breaks me to see you like...this.'

'Then tell me what you want me to do? Leave my husband so I can run away with you?' Pooja's eyes flashed. 'That's what you want, isn't it? You can't see my happiness, you are jealous!'

'Yes I am, because I want you! Why can't you understand that?'

Pooja began to walk.

'Wait, I'm sorry.' I ran after her. She took a deep breath and her face cleared. She put a palm on my face and looked into my eyes; I couldn't breathe.

'It has been a difficult journey for both of us. I lost you when you stepped foot on Simla's soil and you lost me when Satish entered the Chatterji house. Dev, my love for you has never faltered once but we cannot change our fates. I cannot leave Amar or any of my children anymore than you can leave Payal. It is your wedding in two days, you haven't sent me an invite – didn't you want me to share your happiness?'

I put both my hands on her face and closed the gap between us – we were almost touching. Her breath quickened and my heart thudded faster.

'I was scared - if I saw you there, I wouldn't be able to marry Payal,' I whispered. 'I am scared now...I won't be able to forget you or forget how to love you...'

'But now is the time you have to forget about me. Payal is your future. You must accept it.' Tears sparkled in her eyes and she stepped back. 'You must go now before someone sees us – there will be trouble for you and for me. Go home Dev, it's the only way forward.'

'Pooja, I love you.' I began to cry and I wasn't ashamed. She took my hand.

'I love you too Dev and always will. Till I die.' She was crying too. 'Will you promise me one thing? Will you still be my friend?'

'Whenever you need me...' I said.

'Whenever you need me...' she repeated.

'We shall always be friends,' I finished the sentence.

I walked away, tears refusing to stop. Amit and Sunil silently stepped in line with me, wrapping their arms around me. They didn't talk and we went home in the quiet.

~
ALL
~

Twenty five

Partition

Sunil

I turned the radio off, closed my eyes and sighed. Five thousand people dead in Calcutta; fifteen thousand wounded. Muslims had slaughtered Hindus in the Noakhali district of Bengal and in Bihar, Hindus attacked back, killing thousands of Muslims – just after four days of Jinnah[178] proposing partition of India. He didn't want a Hindu to rule India, no; he wanted his own country – a Muslim country. I banged my fist on the wall.

'Don't think about it Sunil, it will only give you a headache,' Neha put her book down and took off her glasses.

'How can I not? India is on the verge to be partitioned, Neha – two religions against each other. It makes me sick....all those brave men, Rakesh *Bhai* amongst them, fought for a united free India. They sacrificed themselves for *one* country. There will be trouble now, no one will be safe.'

'I cannot ignore it either and I am a little scared too,' said Neha. 'I've noticed the change – our village is changing; the segregation and the hostility towards one another is growing.'

'Where are Anjali and Meera?' I asked, suddenly aware that they were not at home.

'They are at Kajal's house. Don't worry, I have told both girls to come home before it gets dark and during school time – to stick together and come straight home after it finishes.'

'But it's getting dark; they should be home by now. I don't like this.' I put on a shawl. It was getting a little cold. 'I'm going to pick them up.'

'You are right, I will come with you,' said Neha.

I put a hand on her arm. 'Stay here with Ma. No one should be alone, even in the house.'

---

[178] Jinnah - Muhammad Ali Jinnah – a Muslim lawyer and politician, later the first Prime Minister of Pakistan.

'But Sunil, maybe you should take someone with you...maybe Dev or Amit...'

'Kajal only lives a few minutes away. I will be fine, don't worry about me.' I kissed her forehead. 'I won't be long.'

I pondered over the girls as I walked and I had to admit, I was frightened. I'd heard what happened to a Hindu girl in another village – abducted and raped by a Muslim man. She cut her wrists and was found dead by her father in the house. The father killed the Muslim man in revenge.

Anjali is the same age as that girl...just sixteen. I walked faster, praying all the while that *Eeshwaar* keep my family safe.

We watched Mrs Ali coaxing her twelve year old son to eat. I was with Dev and Amit, eating at the *Dhaba*.

'*Chal*, eat quickly, you will grow tall and strong like your *Abu*[179],' she said. I laughed silently – her son didn't need encouragement for his plate was almost finished. I looked at the boy's heavy frame. What was she trying to do to him?

'*Ami*[180], I'm still hungry. Is there more?'

Mrs Ali looked at her son adoringly. '*Chokré*[181], bring more *vaada-pav*[182]!' she snapped her fingers.

Her son began to clean his plate with his podgy fingers and we all burst out laughing. Mrs Ali turned her attention towards us and gave us a look of loathing, like we were cockroaches.

'Why are you laughing? My *beta* is hungry!' she barked. '*Chal* Ahmed, stop eating now. You are so fat, still you eat and eat!' she said. '*Chal*, it's getting late.' She yanked his arm, causing him to drop his *vaada-pav* onto his plate. He moaned to his mother as he scrambled to his feet. 'As soon as this country is divided, we will move to Pakistan. These Hindus are troublesome and I don't want you mixing with such people!' she said aloud.

'Let's go too, Shabnam,' said a Muslim man to his wife who were eating at another table. They left promptly.

---

[179] *Abu*, Muslim word for father.

[180] *Ami*, Muslim word for mother.

[181] *Chokré*, Boy (a young waiter is sometimes called "boy" by customers).

[182] *Vaada – pav*, spiced potato cooked in shallow oil and sandwiched between baps.

308

Taking this lead, some other tables cleared as well; only the Hindu families were left seated. I and the others finished eating in silence but we didn't taste the food.

The sun turned crimson on our way home and began its descent over Rajkot; darkness setting in gradually. It was only six o'clock and the streets were emptying; no one was lingering to talk and nervous men and women walked home in groups of their own kind – either Hindu or Muslim. In every corner, groups of people were found pointing and whispering. The division had already begun.

'You two go home, I am going to see Khan *Bhai*,' said Dev.

'At this hour? Payal *Bhabhi* will be worried,' I said.

'Can you tell her I will be late? I won't be long,' he said and headed off.

'He is stepping on unwelcome ground,' I said watching Dev's retreating back.

'How do you mean?' asked Amit.

'Khan *Bhai* is alright, it's his sons whom I don't trust.'

Dev

I wanted to talk to Khan *Bhai* about partition and what it would mean for the both of us. I didn't want to lose a dear friend. I arrived quicker than I thought and heard shouting from within the house.

'This is our home. Rajkot, the people – they are our family!' That was Khan *Bhai*'s voice, I was certain of it. But I had never heard him so worried, so frustrated.

'*Abu*, India is no longer home to us. When this country is partitioned, there will be a new independent country, Pakistan – where our people will live. It is where we will belong. Just think *Abu*, our people, our land.' That was his first son, Nawaz.

'He is right; there is nothing here left for us. It's all over,' his youngest son – Tariq spoke. He said this with a distinct hatred which surprised me. It was a little unnerving.

'What's happened to you two? I can't believe what I am hearing. Salma, you make them understand!'

'*Ami*, *Abu* doesn't know what he is saying,' said Nawaz.

I assumed Khan *Bhai*'s wife, Salma, couldn't speak, torn between her husband and their boys for I heard not one word from her.

309

'Just remember one thing,' said Khan *Bhai* his voice now full of pain. 'If this country is partitioned, I am staying here in Rajkot. You can go if you want to *your* new country, but I am not going.'

After these words, there was silence. Then, a door slammed. I decided I would talk to Khan *Bhai* another time.

Later that evening, I was still thinking about what happened at Khan *Bhai*'s house. I was proud that he thought of India as his own, yet, to decide to be divided from one's own family – I couldn't understand that. With the loss of *Bhai*, my family was torn in two and nothing could fill that void, not even today.

The next morning, soon after I opened the garage, Khan *Bhai* arrived. We sat listening to the All India radio station and sipped our *chai*.

'Khan *Bhai*, forgive me. Yesterday I came by your house to see you and I overheard your row with your sons...'

'Times are bad, *beta*. I am deeply ashamed of my son's' behaviour. They do not understand and will not try to either. The *Musalmaan*[183] want to free India for a new identity of their own – a new country called Pakistan. Why? I am a Musalmaan but I cannot think of moving to a new country, whether it be a country for Muslims or not. We all have lived together for years next to each as brothers. I just don't like it, Dev.'

'It hurts me too that our Hindu brothers are now turning against our Muslim brothers but what can we do except pray that they come to their senses. It's still early, if the *Raj* doesn't pass the bill, then we have nothing to worry about.'

Khan *Bhai* drained his chai. 'Come home with me, there is something I need to collect and I may need your help.'

Whatever he needed help with was forgotten as when we arrived, so did Nawaz and Tariq.

'What's he doing here?' said Nawaz. He eyed me with disgust.

'Nawaz, show some courtesy and respect, he is older than you,' said Khan *Bhai*.

'*Abu*, he is a Hindu and they are not welcome here anymore,' his son replied folding his arms.

'Tariq - do you feel the same way?' asked his father.

'No *Abu*,' he said. Nawaz threw him a glance of fury but Tariq

---

[183] ***Musalmaan***, Muslim person

ignored him.

'This is my home,' said Khan *Bhai*. 'Everyone is welcome to enter my house whether they are Hindu, Sikh, Christian or Musalmaan. If you don't like it, you don't have to stay.'

Nawaz stormed off into the house. Tariq went to follow, but changed his mind.

'*Abu*, you are right. I'm sorry for speaking out of term last night. Dev *Bhai*, I apologise for our behaviour.'

'There is nothing to apologise for. But thank you,' I said. 'Khan *Bhai*, we will need to go back to the garage. We have an important customer coming at noon.'

Khan *Bhai* turned to his son. 'You are a good boy Tariq and I am proud to have you as my son. Make your brother understand. He is too angry and that will do him no good.'

We left for the garage in a sombre mood, completely forgetting the reason we came here.

Pooja

The news wasn't welcome. It was an unforgivable suggestion. How could we divide our mother in two? Was India just a mere country that had no face, no familiarity? They wanted to divide her. What had she done to deserve this betrayal? I threw the paper aside.

'What have I done to deserve such anger?' Amar asked as he finished tidying his papers. He put them in his briefcase. It was one in the afternoon – time for him to go back to the office.

'I'm not angry at you but at the people of this country. Are they idiots, can't they think for themselves?'

'You are talking about the partition,' he said calmly. 'Pooja, we cannot control what they think or their actions. We just have to live with it.' He leaned over and kissed me. I smiled as I felt the light ignite again which had all but been diminished. I had begun to love my husband again.

'I have to go,' he said.

I grabbed his arm. 'Be careful. I don't know why but I am scared.' I was uneasy. Since the Noakhali massacres, everyone was living in fear. Our neighbourhood had changed. I was very frightened.

'Nothing will happen to me. I will only be at the office for a few hours and then I will be home.'

311

I finished writing my letter to Ma. Since Papa passed away, Ma was alone most of the time. Arjun had moved to Nepal – the wage is good there, he said. The girls had grown up a lot since and they helped Ma with the housework. They were well behaved girls and I was proud of them. Ma was worried, especially now.

I wrote a letter to Amit and asked him to keep an eye on Ma, to look after her. Being so far away, I was helpless but I was satisfied, knowing that Amit would not disappoint me. Indeed he didn't, for he made trips twice a day to make sure she was alright and if she needed anything – he was there to help. Amit had somewhat adopted my family as his and kept a close eye on the girls too. When Arjun came home during his vacations he doubled the effort Amit put in. He felt guilty for leaving Ma but he promised her that once he had made enough money for the girl's' marriages, he would come back. I hoped he would keep that promise.

Since the news of the partition, I began to worry about Ma. I asked Amar if she and the girls could come and stay for a while until it all calms down; he thought it was a very good idea. He went one step further and arranged for their stay himself. He booked the train tickets and they were to arrive in a weeks' time. I couldn't wait.

I looked at my husband and his love washed over me. Tears pricked my eyes; my Amar had really come through for me. Since my arrival back in Bombay, we had slept in separate beds. I began to trust him a few months later and with his compassion, for me and my family, he showed me he wasn't selfish anymore. He showed me his love with every opportunity and I my love for him came back. But I was scared – what if he began drinking again? What if he began to bring women home again? I kept my distance but he didn't falter. He was patient and kept on loving me.

Amar always brought me a hair garland – white, my favourite. He never forgot. I fingered the one he tied on me yesterday and smiled. Today I would ask him to share my room and my bed again. Today, we will be husband and wife once more.

I leaned back into my chair. It was quiet and serene. Radha was asleep, Veer was at the neighbours and Kamla and Rakhi were at the theatre, so I was left with little to do.

Suddenly there was a shout.

'*Memsahib*!' Ram *kaka* appeared at the door. '*Memsahib*,' his voice was barely audible and his face was ghostly pale. 'Please come quick!'

I followed him, my heart thumping wildly. Was it Kamla or Rakhi? Visions of my rape came back to me and shook me. Or was it Veer? Had something happened to him? Radha...but she was asleep in her room. I should check.

'*Memsahib*, where are you going? You have to come now, this way!' Ram *Kaka* pulled me away from Radha's room.

'Ram *Kaka*, please tell me, what's happened. Is it one of the children?'

'No *Memsahib*,' he said. He led me to the open front door.

My world slowed and I saw him. I couldn't breathe. '*Nai, Nai,* Amar. No, wake up, who did this? *Nai,* please...' my sobs came thick and fast. Amar's eyes were far away and his front was washed in red. My tears fell on his face and his eyes flickered to me.

'I was unfortunate...I'm sorry...'

'*Nai*!' I shrieked. 'Amar, no, open your eyes!'

He managed to open them and he looked into my eyes and said the words that broke my heart. 'I love you very much.' His eyes closed and his right palm fell open to reveal a hair garland, once white...now red.

I sobbed and clung to his bloodied shirt. I couldn't let him go, I wouldn't! He was mine...he was mine!

Amit

I hadn't seen Chandu in a few weeks so I decided to find him at his house, knowing that he usually finished his work by this time. I'd taken a bag of apples for Chameli and medicine for his ill father.

Chameli was tied to a fence. She called me when I arrived. Her cart was stationed beside her. I looked around but couldn't see anyone; this was strange. I went inside the house calling Chandu's name but no one answered. Suddenly, I felt anxious.

I went further in looking for his father, whom I expected to be asleep but he wasn't in his bed. A half-drunk tumbler of water sat on a bedside table. It seemed like it was left in haste. Somewhere in the back of my mind, I remembered Chandu telling me that his mother and sister were coming back from Noakhali. I couldn't recollect the date, was it today? That would explain why they were not at home but then why was Chameli here? Chandu would have taken her to the train station, would he not?

I went outside and took the apples out of the bag and fed her.

'I wish you could tell me what happened, Chameli,' I said. She whinnied affectionately. My mind flashed with the possibilities but I shook them away. After making sure Chameli had her fill, I climbed back onto my bicycle. Just then, a small boy came running.

'*Bhaiya*!' he stooped to catch his breath, then handed me a note with Chandu's scrawl on top that said "Amit".

'How did you know I was here?' I asked. I opened the note.

'Chandu *Bhai* said you might come sometime, I kept a look out.'

I took a rupee out of my pocket and gave it to the boy. His eyes widened and his smile broadened and then he went away, running. I scanned the note and frowned. Then, I read it again.

Amit,
We are going to Noakhali. Ma and Avantika are hurt. Please look after Chameli...I will explain later. Chandu

I folded the note and put it in my pocket. I lifted the cycle into the cart and untied Chameli. She let me sit on her and I took her home. Ma and Papa were surprised and I told them what I knew.

'We have to believe it is all good,' said Ma. I knew she was thinking of the Noakhali killings.

'No, it has to be something else, Ma-*ji* and Avantika couldn't have been there when it happened,' I said but I was very worried.

Two weeks later, Chandu came home. He took Chameli but said nothing. I left him alone, knowing he would speak when he was ready.

It was a dark day. Clouds had gathered but there was no rain. The air was damp and still. I was outside in the back courtyard, tending to some plants when I heard Chameli's hooves. I couldn't mistake it, it was Chandu.

314

'Let's have *chai*,' I led him inside. We drank in silence and I waited. Then, he told me.

'It was a mistake, I shouldn't have allowed it. *Bapuji* shouldn't have allowed them to go to Noakhali...but they were adamant. It was my cousin's engagement, it would look bad otherwise. Ma and Avantika went to the bazaar to buy clothes. *Maasi* was with them when it happened. There was no warning, they came wanting murder. Kill the Hindus, kill the Sikhs! They murdered everyone standing in that bazaar.

'Ma and Avantika were barely alive when they were found. *Maasi* was already dead. Ma died on the way to the hospital but Avantika held on.' Chandu wiped his tears on his arm.

'A telegram arrived from *Maasa*[184] and we left in a hurry. We went straight to the hospital from the station. Avantika smiled at us and then...she was gone...she only stayed to see us one last time.' This time huge tears spilled on his face and I took him into my embrace, holding him tightly.

'I'm sorry...' my voice sounded unnaturally loud.

Chandu wiped his face. 'Thank you for looking after Chameli,' said Chandu. 'I will be going home now.'

'If there is anything I can do...'

'Thank you my friend,' he said.

Chandu got into his cart and left. My resolve broke and I cried like a man does when his family has been denied him, when a neighbour who is also your brother leaves you, when the world has turned dark.

---

[184] *Maasa*, Uncle (Mother's sister's husband).

~ POOJA ~

Twenty six

The Attack

For a short while, everything was perfect. *Eeshwaar* gave me my husband back and the child that wouldn't accept me. He gave me a sweet daughter and a son to whom I was already their Ma. Then, he gave me another girl. I was finally happy.

Then my life shattered. He took away my world – my husband. For months, I wasn't there, not in spirit, no. I saw to the children, helped them with their school work, attended to the servants, looked after the house but that's where I stopped. Happiness was somewhere far out of reach.

News travelled quickly as it does – who told them, I didn't know or care. I remember Ma arriving with Arjun, Reema and Ritu. I held onto them and sobbed. My heart was aching and I wanted it to stop. I cried until I no longer could.

Ma gave me a white sari to wear and took away my green and red bangles. She smudged my chandlo and vermillion off. White was my only colour. I was a widow.

Dev arrived with Payal, Sunil with Neha and Amit. I thanked them for coming but didn't really see them. Prayers were said for Amar's soul, to give him peace and sanctuary wherever he would be. I sat through the rituals and stared at my husband's picture, feeling empty and bitter. I didn't cry when he was taken away to be cremated.

'It will take time but she will cry. That's when she will need you,' they told Ma and Rakhi.
My children were with me all the time. They cried and clung to me. I gave them kind words, reassuring them that I would be there for them. I didn't know then that I wouldn't be able to keep that promise in the coming months.

I ate and drank when I was told to. I smiled when I was supposed to and I spoke briefly when spoken to but I couldn't cry. During the nights, I would lie on our bed and stare at the ceiling, watching the fan spin around, coaxing me to sleep. It always came near dawn.

Ma and the girls stayed with me for a while. Arjun apologised but he had to go back to Nepal. I looked into his brown eyes and remembered when we would play together in the mud. During *holi*[185], he used to spray coloured water in my face and I would scream to Ma to tell him off. He would take me to school and look out for me.

Then I cried. I sank to the floor. I curled up in a ball and cried and cried. A long while later, Arjun picked me up and gave me a big hug.

'I won't leave you, *bena*. I will stay.'

Ma was relieved that my tears had finally come. 'This is good for you,' she said and took to looking after me and my family. Arjun was determined to stay with me but I told him to go – Ma was with me.

'If you need me, I will come back,' he said. I nodded and embraced my dear brother.

Reema and Ritu talked to me and played with their nieces and nephew. I felt better most days but other days I couldn't get out of bed and felt like my life was slipping away. Eventually Ma came to me. 'Pooja, you have to stop this now.' She looked angry.

'What do you mean?' My gaze did not shift from Amar's picture. He looked so handsome and his smile was generous as he gazed into my eyes. Ma snatched the frame from my hands.

'Ma, give him back to me!' I cried.

'You are not going to feel sorry for yourself. You are going to take charge of your children, of this house,' she said calmly, placing her soft, warm hands into mine. 'You are a strong woman.'

'I'm not sure I can Ma.'

'I knew a girl who was assertive and responsible. She looked after her family. I can still see her in you, *beta*. Don't forget you have four children – they are your life now and they need you.'

---

[185] *Holi*, a Hindu festival of colours. Men, women and children throw coloured powder and coloured water into the air and onto each other. There would be dancing and singing. A festival to mark good over evil.

320

I did take control. I shook myself out of my depression and I became the proprietor of this house. I looked at the finances and to my surprise, found they were in order. Who had paid the bills and the servant's their wages? I didn't recollect signing any cheques or paying anyone. Had I been so far away from everyone and everything that I was hardly alive? I shook my head, what had I done?

That first morning, I got up very early, washed and dressed myself in a crisp, clean sari. I put on gold bangles and earrings and looked at myself in the mirror. I was every inch a *Memsahib* and now solely responsible for this house and the children. It was time to behave as one.

I opened the door of the bedroom and found Ma there, her fist against the door as if to knock. She was very surprised to see me.

'Are you alright?' her tone suggested a deep concern.

'Ma, I feel good. I feel right.' I smiled and kissed her cheek.

I walked on with a determined air and Ma followed, almost running to keep up. The servants stopped what they were doing as I passed and stared. My smile broadened. Today was going to be a good day.

'Welcome back!' the cook had tears in his eyes. 'I will make you your special *nashta*!' he said and set about cooking. I was suddenly very hungry.

The rest of the family were gathered in the kitchen now and I could tell by the relief in their faces that the worst was over. Oh God, what had I been like?

'Ma,' I said.

'Yes, *beta*,' she said.

'It's....nothing. It can wait.' I began to eat and everyone joined in, talking and laughing. It was good to be back.

After breakfast, when everyone was doing something and Radha was asleep, I took Ma to my room.

'What is it beta? What is troubling you?'

'I need to see the accountant and I want to speak to Amar's business partners. I am worried about the money...Rakhi has studied to a high level, she is very clever. I will want her to come with me but where is she?'

'Your daughter is indeed very clever and smart,' Ma said, smiling. 'These months, she has been the one looking after everything. You don't remember, do you?'

I shook my head.

'After Amar's passing away, Rakhi went to the accountant. Amar had a lot of money saved. He also invested in shares and stocks. Rakhi thoughtfully spent wisely on the house bills. She paid the servants their wage and paid the bills for the children's school.' Ma put a hand on my head. 'I remember a girl just like her.'

I couldn't believe it. My Rakhi had become responsible. She was just like Amar. Tears sprang to my eyes and I went into Ma's arms. 'I can't live without him Ma. I miss him every day.'

'Shhh, I know, *beta*, I know. When your Papa left me, I didn't know what to do, where to go – how to live. I still love him today but I can see the future now. You, the girls and Arjun have been my strength, even dear Amit beta. I cannot be more grateful to him.

'You will see; your children will be your strength. Now go and wash your face and let's go downstairs. Today is the first day of your future!' Ma kissed my forehead.

That afternoon I went to find Rakhi. She was reading a book in the garden. She looked up as I approached her and she stood up from her chair.

'*Nai*, sit, sit.' I pulled up a chair next to her.

'What is it, Ma? Do you need anything?'

I put both my hands on her face. 'What have I done to deserve you? Your nani told me everything beta. She told me how you took control of the money – the bills, the wages, the schooling fees.... I can't thank you enough, I am so proud.'

'Oh Ma, I didn't do anything. Papa was wise to think of the future – our life as a family. I only did what I had to.' She began to play with the pleat of her sari. 'I was frightened for a while, for you Ma. You wouldn't eat or drink...you fell apart. After so many attempts, I could do only one thing, do you remember?'

'You gave me your Papa's promise.'

'I knew you loved Papa very much and you would do anything for him. Without you we all would have been lost.'

'But I didn't do anything, *beta*.'

'No Ma. You were here and that's what helped us get through this.'

I stepped off the bus holding a bag of medicine and dry foods. The road was silent apart from the shrubs and trees rustling in the wind. It was getting stronger.

I wanted to travel by bus – it made me feel free. It stopped me from worrying about things that didn't need worrying about, like the hallway needed sweeping, Radha's hair clip was lost and needed finding, Rakhi needs new clothes, Veer needs a hair-cut and Kamla is studying too much. These things were too trivial to worry about but still, I don't know why...I was troubled.

I had been in the house a lot. Ma made me see that I needed to go outside, maybe away from here, go to places and see the city. She made me promise before she and the girls went back to Rajkot.

'I am satisfied, you have found your path,' she said. 'You have shown me you are able to carry on and take care of your family but beta, if you need me, I will be here for you.'

'I'm going to miss you very much.' I hugged her tightly but she let me go before we both cried.

'No more tears,' she said.

One of the maids had fallen ill and her family were poor. She needed medication. I could have asked the driver to go and deliver it for me but as Ma made me promise to go out, see the 'outside', this was for me to do. So, here I am now, on a windy day, standing on a deserted road.

I began to walk. Soon I came upon a few small dwellings, a shop that sold biscuits and other items. A young boy sat on the footpath, polishing shoes. Passing them, I walked through dense trees and then came to an opening of a narrow road. This led to Ramkumari's village.

Ramkumari was a sweet girl and I found her quite by accident. It was before Amar's passing away. The poor girl was told to go from her previous employment, wrongly accused of theft.

323

Rumours flew to all the wealthy households and so she was unable to find a job anywhere. Nobody wanted a thieving servant.

One day, as I was walking, I saw her sitting on the street, trying to sell hair garlands. Without thinking, I went to her.

'*Bena*, can I have a *gajra*?' I asked her. 'It has to be white...my husband always brought white ones for me.'

The girl held one out to me.

'How much?'

'Whatever you want to give *Memsahib*,' she said.

I took out two rupees from my purse and went to put it in her hand and that's when I saw her properly.

'Your name is Ramkumari, isn't it?'

'How did you know?' she gasped.

'These are fine,' I said as I looked at the *gajra*. 'Beautifully made. You are quite skilled. Tell me Ramkumari, are you still looking for work?'

'Yes *Memsahib*, but no one is willing to hire me...' her eyes were cast down.

'Why is that?' I pretended to not know.

'They think I am a thief but I am not *Memsahib*. I have never stolen and never will.'

I made a quick decision. 'Ramkumari, whether anyone sees this or not but I do. I see honesty in your eyes. I want to ask you, would you like to come and work for me?'

Her face lit up and she began to speak but then looked down and shook her head.

'I will not judge you,' I said. 'I can see it in your eyes – you are good and an honest worker. Please reconsider coming to work for me.'

Ramkumari nodded.

'Good,' I said softly. 'I live – '

'I know. You are Pooja *didi*...sorry, *Memsahib*. I know where you live. All the working people know you. They say you are a very nice *Memsahib*.'

I laughed. '*Chalo*, I'm glad to hear that.' A thought came to me. 'Ramkumari, I want you to call me Pooja *didi*. *Thik ché né*[186]?'

---

[186] *Thik ché né?* Is that alright? (Gujarati)

I finally arrived at her house, exhausted. I was scratched and managed to slip on the way. Mud and leaves clung to my arms and clothes; I must look a state.

'Is someone there?' I called. There was some rustling and banging from within. Then, a slim, attractive woman opened the door. She was carrying a baby on her hip who stared at me with enormous eyes.

'Who are you? Who do you want to see?' she asked politely.

'I am Pooja. Ramkumari works for me; I have come to see her.'

The woman's eyes widened. 'Please forgive me. Please come in.' The woman gestured me in with her free hand. The baby continued to stare at me. I smiled at her and she looked away.

The house was large but basic. Some children were playing in the dusty yard. They stopped to stare at me and then laughed.

'*Chup*! It's rude!' the woman snapped at them. 'Go inside and make yourself useful!'

The children went inside obediently; I was impressed.

'Come in, *Memsahib*.'

As I went in, I touched my face and some dried mud came off. 'I fell,' I said apologetically.

'It happens.' I saw her lips twitch. 'The road can be slippery. I will give you something to wipe down with.' She put the baby down and went into the back.

A man dressed in a dull vest and *dhoti* was lying on a bed. He was unshaven and his hair clung to his forehead, it was slick with oil. His eyes lingered on me; a horrible smile playing on his lips as he looked me up and down.

'I am Ramkumari's *Babuji*. How are you?' he asked. 'What's in the bag?'

'How is Ramkumari? Is she any better?'

'No, not better. Worse.' His eyes darkened and he shifted so he was looking out of the window. How strange.

Around eleven people walked in – it looked like the whole family was here. They positioned themselves at various corners of the room and took to watching me, perhaps waiting for me to give them a speech. The silence seemed to press down on the room and I fidgeted, feeling very nervous.

'I like to read,' a young child smiled, showing her teeth. She held her book towards me. I turned the thin pages and was pleased and

325

amazed to find nothing torn or scribbled on. It was old but much loved and it seemed as if she had read this book many times. I handed it back and she cradled it to her chest. I made a mental note to buy her some new ones.

I noticed other things too: the saris and blouses the ladies wore were sewn-patched in different places, where it had either ripped or was worn out. The saris were old; dulled and faded by the scorching sun. I remembered my life before Amar and it had not been much different.

I listened to their woes as I waited for Ramkumari to emerge from her room.

'My husband is working in a factory. I see him after long, long hours in the night. He is always working very hard, you see. His employer is white people, you know. They make him work hard and give little money,' said one of the women.

'My daughter is thirteen,' said another woman. 'She is of age to get married but look; she is dark and too thin. Husbands want fat girls. And look, she has no charisma, no one likes her.'

The woman just described herself and I felt pity for the girl. She was not as her mother described her. In fact, she was fair and very beautiful. She seemed charming too. I pitied the mother for having such a dimmed view of her daughter and was angry as well. There was indeed, some story to this.

'I'm sorry but if Ramkumari is not able to come here, can I see her by her bed?' I asked hopefully.

The family glanced at each other, very nervous.

'*Memsahib*, she will come in now. I will go and call her,' said the woman with the baby.

At that moment, Ramkumari burst out of her room and ran outside where she vomited loudly. I dropped my bag and rushed to her. The other women followed me with faces of alarm and shame.

'*Eh Baghwaan*! I told her stay inside, but no, she doesn't listen! The whore!' the father said loudly from inside. I was shocked. The women shrunk away a little.

Ramkumari stopped vomiting. Her face was ashen and her hands shook. I helped her inside. No one came forward to help this child. I didn't understand why, surely her mother should...what was going on here? Ramkumari lay down on a straw mat. Her mother seemed to be afraid of something. We sat facing one another and I waited for some explanation. I hoped it wasn't what I had guessed already.

'Will someone tell me what is happening here? Ramkumari hasn't been to work for a week now. You say she is ill...'

The women remained silent.

'How far along is she?' I said finally.

'*Memsahib*, please forgive us...' said Ramkumari's mother.

'Four months!' shouted the father. 'She has disgraced us. We found out - five days it's been like this. She cannot keep her clothes on!' Her father spat on the floor. '*Besharam*[187]!'

'It wasn't her fault that she was raped, *ji*. She is your daughter,' whimpered the mother.

'*Chup kar*[188]! I told you to marry her off to that man. He's got a big house, a big family and a lot of money but you do not listen!'

'He is forty-five years old, *ji*. How could we marry her, she is only sixteen!'

'Tch!' the father got up and went outside.

'Ramkumari, why didn't you tell me?' I asked.

'*Didi*, I was scared that you will not want me anymore,' Ramkumari said. 'I am sorry.'

I did a quick calculation. 'Is that why you were told to go from your last employer?'

Ramkumari didn't answer.

'*Memsahib*, my daughter is very unfortunate. She was raped by her *Saab*...*Memsahib* didn't believe her and made up a story that she was stealing!' her mother said.

I felt sick to the stomach as my past came back...I had not yet forgotten what had happened to me at the Chatterjis...I had been a maid too.

'You won't let her go, will you *Memsahib*? Without her wage, we will be desolate. We will have no hope of feeding or clothing the family,' said another woman. She seemed like she was eighteen and newly married.

'You just got married?' I asked her.

'*Ji*, I am Meenu, Ramkumari's *Bhabhi*. This is my husband. He works in the white man's factory, that *Mata ji* told you about.'

'Ramkumari, you rest now. Go to your room,' I said.

---

[187] *Besharam*, Shameless
[188] *Chup Kar*, Be quiet

327

'I am not to come back to work for you, is that what you will tell me next?' she said, fright in her eyes.

'Not at all. You will come back to work for me but not until you are well enough. Now, don't worry, everything will be alright.'

I saw that the sun was low in the sky. Everyone at home would be worried about me.

'I have to leave now but before I go, let me leave you this little gift.' I opened the bag and produced dry lentils and nuts. I left the medicine inside. Ramkumari would not need it now.

'This is too much, no *didi*, we cannot accept it,' said Ramkumari.

'You call me your sister but you won't take a gift from me?'

'*Shukriya*[189],' she said.

'*Chalo*, look after yourself.' I put a hand under her chin and lifted her face. 'Now, don't worry, *Eeshwaar* is with us.'

'*Didi*, take some *Prashad*[190] before you go,' she got up slowly and went to the little temple. She picked a sweet from a dish and closed her eyes, saying a prayer and put in my hand.

I lifted it to my eyes and thanked God for the blessing and said a prayer for Ramkumari. I put it into my mouth.

'Meenu *beta*, Shamu, take *Memsahib* to the road. Is that where your automobile is?' asked Ramkumari's mother.

'*Nai*...I came by bus.'

'But why?'

'*Kaki ji*, I come from a family just like yours. We didn't have much money either and I worked as a maid, just like Ramkumari. I will not forget that now. I travelled by bus to keep me from forgetting my past.'

'You say the truth. Money is neither here nor there and one must not forget themselves. I thank *Eeshwaar* for bringing such a wonderful *Memsahib* to my Ramkumari. May *He*[191] keep you blessed. Go Meenu, Shamu, take *Memsahib* to the bus stop.'

Meenu and Shamu took me down a shorter route to the main road.

'The bus stop is over there, I will go myself, you don't have to wait,' I said.

---

[189] *Shukriya*, Thank you
[190] *Prashad*, Food offered to the Gods and then given to people to eat, as a blessing.
[191] *He*, God

'No *Memsahib*, we will feel better knowing you have got on the bus safely. It is late and a lady shouldn't be here alone,' said Shamu.

As we waited, three more people joined us. It was very dark now and Shamu lit the oil lamp he so wisely brought with him. The surroundings became easier to see now.

The bus came at last and I began to relax. Meenu and Shamu bid me goodbye and I stepped inside. They didn't leave straight away but waited patiently until the bus moved on.

The bus wasn't full and I settled myself down at the back. I put the bag down that now only contained the medicine that Ramkumari didn't need. I closed my eyes, thinking of her.

Her life reflected my past. Whereas I was fortunate, she was not. She was with baby...who will marry her, give her the support that she needs? I was frightened of her father's reaction. What will happen in the following months when the neighbours begin to notice, when her stomach would swell? There would be widespread insults. How would she and her family be able to cope? I had heard of families burning their daughters or killing them...the kinder ones told their daughters to leave the home. Even so, how will Ramkumari eat and feed her child? There was only one way forward.

It is none of your business, stay out of it. She is nothing to you. Forget about her.

No, I cannot forget about her. She is still a young child and she needs help. I will help her! I will talk to her family, it is the only way.

The bus lurched to a stop and I found myself hurled from my seat and I crashed to the floor. Everyone was screaming and shouting and I couldn't make sense of anything, what was happening?

'Kill the Hindus! Kill them all!' someone was shouting.

My focus sharpened and I saw men rip people with their swords. The screams became high pitched.

'*Nai!*' I screamed. My heart thudded wildly as I looked at the masked men.

'Take her!' one shouted.

I scrambled on my knees and tried to get away but he was too fast. He grabbed my arms and dragged me off the bus, throwing me onto the ground. He slapped me across my face and my eyes watered.

'Amar! Amar!' I screamed. All around me there was noise and something sticky clung to my forehead. I seemed to be falling into darkness...I came back to this hell and saw the man laughing, standing before me. He began to undo his trousers. I stared at his face in horror.

'*Nai, Nai*, please, let me go...' I cried.

He began to rip my clothes with the tip of his sword. I turned my face and found a rock. With all my strength, I threw it at him and hit his face.

He yelled and fell backwards, his head hitting the ground.

I got up but then I felt something sharp slice my stomach...my focus went again...

The man looked familiar and he smiled. I smiled too. I was dressed in my wedding sari and I was beautiful. I was at the temple with Amar. We were getting married. He held out his hand and I took it. From the top of the temple stairs we could see the city; it was white and stunning. The sun shone brightly on us – it hurt my eyes. I turned to look at Amar instead.

'You are beautiful. I love you very much,' he said. 'But it is not your time yet.'

I tried to find the meaning of his words but he was fading...he let go of my hand...

I opened my eyes and sunlight engulfed me. I was pleased; I was still with Amar, in heaven.

'Pooja *didi*?' an anxious voice said.

'Her wound has been treated and she is out of danger, but she needs a lot of rest. She was very lucky,' said a voice I didn't recognise He came into focus. 'Pooja, I am Dr. Kothari. You are in hospital How are you feeling now?'

'Doctor, where is Amar?'

'Who is Amar, *beta*?' he asked.

'Doctor *Saab*, she is thinking of her husband, my father. He is no longer with us.'

I moved my head and saw the room was full. Around me were the people I loved; Rakhi, Kamla, Veer and...Ramkumari, she was holding Radha. Meenaxi Ba was there, Ramu *Kaka* too.

'Ma, please, don't talk,' Rakhi put her hand on my head and I drifted off to sleep; I wanted to see Amar again.

I was watering the garden today, something I enjoyed. It gave me peace. The gardener was on the other side, weeding and humming happily.

It had been two months since the horrific incident. I hadn't been allowed to travel alone again and if I wanted to go somewhere, I was to be driven. These were strict orders from Rakhi, Kamla and Ma.

I'd nearly died, had it not been for Meenu and Shamu. They heard the screams and came running back. Other neighbouring people came to help but it was too late. The driver was dead as were the other passengers. I was just breathing. They took me to the local doctor. He did what he could but advised with urgency to take me to a hospital for my pulse was weak, although my bleeding had stopped. It was nearly too late for me, the doctor said.

Was it God's wish or my children's pleas that helped my heart going? I was grateful to be alive.

Ramkumari came outside. She took my hand and helped me stand. I wasn't quite right; my wound was healed but it had weakened me. I smiled at my new daughter. She was now six months into her pregnancy and she was looking very well. I took her into my family after she was thrown out of hers - by her father. We talked about her baby and she agreed to give him or her up for adoption. I was glad to see she understood.

So now I carry on, without Amar but with the love of my family. I have been very lucky.

~
DEV
~

Twenty seven

The New India
14 August 1947

'At the stroke of midnight hour; when the world sleeps, India will awake to life and freedom.'

Pandit Jawarlal Nehru
14 August 1947

The day finally arrived that everyone was waiting for – the day of Indian Independence. After decades of living under the rule of the Raj, our mother was now free. But at a price.

Since the news for partition the country was restless. Many riots took place; many people were murdered. Then for a while there was silence. Now, Pandit Jawarlal Nehru – one of the leaders of the Quit India movement, announced the day of Indian Independence and everyone rejoiced. A few things happened to us – I, Pooja, Amit and Sunil. This movement had brought us happiness, fear, worry along with pain and loss and of course love.

Amit was married after Stuart left for Calcutta and moved to Hyderabad with his wife. He still loved his *Memsahib* and couldn't bear to be near their house that brought back memories. The house that once was Mary *Memsahib* and Stuart *Saab's* residence was taken up with another white family. It felt alien to him. Amit wanted to move forward now and that meant to move away and begin a new life.

Pooja – what can I say? That I am proud of her? Yes but it is more than that. Life played a cruel hand but she came back stronger. Taking Amit's advice, she began a business making spices. The business soared.

But that was not all Pooja did. She set up an orphanage for children and called it *Amar Prem*[192] – meaning Love always. To this date she has seventy children. Some are adopted and some are not but she pledged she would do whatever it takes to make those children smile. In the last year she married her eldest daughter, Rakhi and it was an extravagant wedding.

She was still my Pooja underneath that exterior and she was still my best friend.

Nothing very exciting happened for Sunil but he was married and happy. Ah yes, I forgot. He was going to be a father! Neha was soon to give birth! The smile on Sunil's face widened every day but he became protective and overbearing too. Poor Neha was miserable of his constant fussing but she took it with grace.

And then there was I.

I married Payal but I couldn't love her; I still loved Pooja. I had ashamedly neglected Payal's needs, her dreams and expectations were broken by my lack of commitment. After Amar died, I saw my wife properly. I berated myself for being selfish and then I made a decision: to love my wife as a whole. I concentrated on making her happy and took her on a vacation to a hill station, where I showered her with love She became happier and more devoted than before and I returned it.

Today, we were all here, together, in Delhi to witness the change of government. India's freedom – the unfurling of the Indian flag.

We walked to the grounds of the Red Fort. Here, our new prime minister, Pandit Jawarlal Nehru was to address the nation. All around us, people talked excitedly and sang songs of freedom. Every man, woman and child were euphoric. Exhilaration exercised the minds and bodies as they shouted,

VAANDE MATARAM[193]! *HINDUSTAN ZINDABAD*[194]!

---

[192] *Amar Prem*, Love always
[193] *Vaande Mataram!* A freedom cry amongst Indians. In later years it was sung in schools and organisations as a national anthem.
[194] *Hindustan Zindabad*, Long live India

336

We joined joyful faces from all sides; a throng of people filled with pride, marching towards Red Fort. Finally, we arrived at the grounds and waited for the Independence speech to begin; a speech that was to become one of the most famous speeches ever made.

At exactly 12am, 15th August 1947, India became Independent. A new country – a new land of its own. No longer was it chained to the *Raj's* iron clad hand. Yes, she was free!

My eyes were wet as I watched Pandit Jawarlal Nehru unfurl the flag: saffron orange, white and green. The twenty-spoke wheel took leadership at the centre of the flag in blue. The British Union Jack was lowered to be replaced by the new Indian flag.

A deafening roar filled the air and we stood – clapping and wiping away tears, embracing our neighbours. We sat down and immediate silence reigned as the speech began...

I thought of *Bhai*. He should be sitting with us, shouting in happiness. His handsome face would be erased of all the creases of stress and anger; the *Raj* was out and his revenge would be justified. But he wasn't here to see his dream.

'He should be here,' I whispered hoarsely. '*Bhai* should be here.'

Payal squeezed my hand and I was surprised to feel her head on my shoulder. I hadn't expected her to hear for I said it mostly to myself.

'*Bhai-ji* is still part of this celebration. He made this happen.' Her voice was musical and it calmed me. 'He is rejoicing with us now.'

'Thank you,' I said, caressing her face.

I looked over to see Pooja with her head on Amit's shoulder. His wife - Anuradha was sitting on the other side of Pooja, whom she adopted as a sister and had Radha in her lap. Radha was now three and very beautiful, like her mother. Anuradha was crying into a handkerchief as the speech unfolded.

Sunil wasn't really paying attention to the speech but was gazing at his wife as she concentrated on Nehru. I suppressed a laugh, it was just like him. I imagined his stomach grumbling – he hadn't eaten in the last two hours!

I turned my face sharply towards the stage. *Bhai* suffered, he sacrificed...he secured freedom...but he was not here.

Payal took my arm and smiled. She had become my companion and my rock. She looked after my many needs and took things calmly. She made me understand when I refused to listen. She rubbed my palms and rested her head on my shoulder and my anger vanished. I felt peaceful and closed my eyes for a second, focussing on my wife and her sweet scent. I felt free of the chains...

The speech ended and tremendous applause erupted from the crowd. The celebratory party began and was carried through the streets. Fireworks were set off and the children cheered. Lights burned in memory and salutation to the martyrs – the brave ones. It was a celebration that went on throughout the night. The singing and dancing died around dawn as tired but happy Indian citizens made their way home. This day would never be forgotten.

The next day saw the English begin to move out of India.

Partition had begun.

1.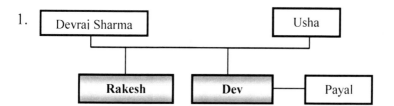

2.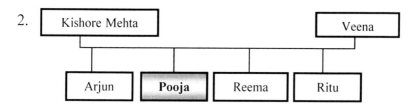

3.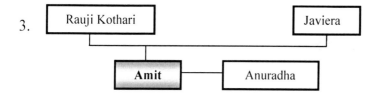

4.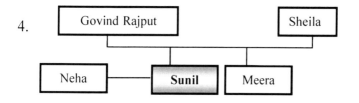

339

5.
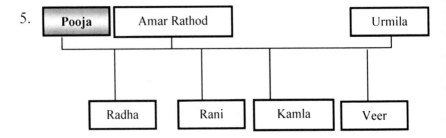

Other characters

1. Shankarji (associated with Sunil)
    Anjali

2. Khan Bhai (associated with Dev)
    Gunwant-ji

3. Grandmother Chatterji – Nani (associated with Pooja)
    Rama
    Mangal Ba
    Shivraj

4. Stuart   (associated with Amit)
    Mary
    Tom

5. Rai   (associated with Sunil)

6. Chandu   (associated with Amit)

Glossary

All words are Hindi words unless specified. Hindi was and still is a unifying language in India used commonly between different castes.
The Indian language is colossal in which many tongues incorporate words from one language to another, for example: *baraat* and *chai* are both used in Hindi and Gujarati (aswell as other Indian languages such as Punjabi).
Some words/sentences in this book are in Gujarati which is clarified.

A

Aacha , Alright
Abu, Muslim name for Father
Achar, Condiments
Ahimsa, To not harm body/mind/soul
Amar Prem, Love always
Ami, Muslim name for Mother
Anglo-Indian, People who are from mixed Indian and British descent and British people who were born or living in India during the times of the Raj.
Angrezi, English
Aré, Oh
Avu chu, I am coming (Gujarati).

B

Ba, Grandmother
Babu, Man
Babuji, Father
Bapu, Mohandas Gandhi was known as Bapu (father) and also as "Mahatma" meaning Great.
Baraat, a wedding party made up of guests from the groom's side.
Bas, That's all/stop/that's it
Ben/Bena, Sister
Besharam, Shameless
Beta, said in the context of son or daughter.
Bewakuf, Idiot
Bhabhi, Sister-in-law (brother's wife)
Bhagwaan, God
Bhai/Bhaiya, Brother (Elder)
Bhai-ji, Uncle (father's elder bother)
Bhaiyo, Brothers
Bhajiya, Savoury vegetables coated in Gram flour (made from ground, dried hick peas) then fried.
Bharat natyam, a classical dance that originated from Tamil Nadu – a South ndian state.

Bhuddu, Silly
Bhojan, Food
Brahmin/ Brahman, a Hindu caste ranking the highest position in the hierarchy of Indian society/Hindu caste system.
Bringing the bride home, in Indian marriages, the bride is married into the groom's family and is expected to live with them.

C

Chai, Tea
Chai lélo, Take some tea. Young boys and girls roam the streets and train stations trying to sell tea for a living).
Chal, Come
Chalo Batcho! Come children!
Chapals, Sandals
Chana dal, Lentils used in a soup like curry, which is served with rice.
Chandlo, Gujarati name for Bindi. A red dot painted on the forehead of married women (Now a fashion statement and worn by girls and women alike, married and unmarried. The chandlo now comes in an array of colours and designs).
Chokra, Boy (Gujarati word)
Choro, Leave me
Chotti, Young/Small
Chotti Memsahib, Young Memsahib (the elders are always Memsahib or Saab and the children are referred to as Chotti Memsahib or Chotté Saab).
Chottu, Younger brother
Chowkidaar, Guard
Chudi-wallah, Bangle seller
Chudla, Gujarati word for bangle
Chup, Quiet
Chup kar, Be quiet
Coolie, Indian porter

D

Dadi , Paternal grandmother
Dadu, Grandfather
Dayan , Witch
Dever , Brother-in-law (The wife calls her husband's younger brother "Dever").
Dhaba, a small restaurant which sells "quick" snacks and refreshments such as chai/juice aswell as hearty meals.
Dhoti, White wraparound sheet worn instead of trousers.
Didi, Sister (elder)
Dikra, Son/daughter (Gujarati).
Divo, a divine flame used in holy Indian rituals and ceremonies. Also used to give peace to the deceased.
Diwali, a Hindu festival celebrating the return of Lord Ram & Sita to Ram's kingdom after fourteen years of exile. A path was lit to welcome them home.

Doli, a bridal carriage, carried by four men to the groom's home. The bride sits inside after being wed - a veil covering her face.
Dupatta , a multi-purpose scarf, worn over the head as a veil or over ladies' Indian suits.

E

Eeshwaar, God (also Baghwaan)
Eh Baghwaan, Oh God
Ek , One
Ek dena , Give one

F

Faiba, Auntie (Father's sister)

G

Gajra, a flower garland, worn by Indian ladies, in buns or in braids. Usually made with jasmine.
Gali , narrow street/alley
Gandhi, Mohandas Gandhi (also known as Bapu and Mahatma Gandhi (the Great one). He was known to begin the Quit India Movement.
Ganesh, Hindu God – the elephant God – worshipped at the beginning of Hindu rituals and when commencing new beginnings – a protector against bad tidings.
Ghee, Clarified butter
Goonda-giri, a gang who like to terrorise, steal and fight – sometimes leading to worse victim endings.
Goré, White (man)

H

Hai Baghwaan, Oh God
Haldi, Turmeric - an anaesthetic ingredient used in the form of powder or paste, for many purposes, including healing minor cuts and colds and used in Indian cooking such as *daals (lentils)* and *sabzi* and fried *puri* and *thepla* (like roti but deep or shallow fried). Also used during pre-marriage ceremonies where the bride and groom are lathered in a paste; a mix of milk, oils, sandalwood powder and turmeric which is applied to the face, arms and feet. This is to obtain a flawless complexion for the wedding day.
He, God
Hé Ram! Oh Rama (Hindu God).

Hé Ma, Oh God (referring to female Gods such as Sri Laxmi, Durga Ma, Sita, Saraswati, Parvati) – calling them Mother.
Hill station, a vacation point for Indians and the English alike.
Hindustan Zindabad, Long live India.
Holi, a Hindu festival of colours. Men, women and children throw coloured powder and water into the air and onto each other. There would be dancing and singing. A festival to mark good over evil.

I

Inquilab Zindabad, a Hindi phrase used during the Quit India movement which translates into "long live India".

J

Jai Hind, a common salutation used during the Quit India movement in speeches and communications – a translation of "long live India/victory for India".
Jaldi ben-ji, Quickly sister
*Jaleb*i, a sweet delicacy made of flour and water, dipped in syrup.
Ji, Wives did not call their husbands by their first names and substituted with 'Ji in respect.
Jijaji, Brother-in-law (sister's husband).

K

Kabadi, an aggressive Indian game played by men, seven on each side. The goal is to tag or wrestle the player sent from the opposite team before he reaches their home base. Tagged members are out. When all members of a team are out, the other team wins.
Kai to Ché, There is something (Gujarati).
Kaka, Uncle (father's younger brother) but also used to acknowledge elderly men in respect (Gujarati word).
Kaki, Auntie (father's younger brother's wife – Gujarati word).
Kamini/kamina, Evil (Person)
Kankoo, red powder – vermillion. Used as a symbol of marriage or for holy Hindu rituals.
Karenge Ya Marenge! Will Do or Die, The words of Mohandas Gandhi during a passionate speech when Quit India was called for: 'We shall free India or die in the attempt!'
Kem Cho, Faiba?, How are you, auntie? (Gujarati)

Khabar ché? Do you know? (Gujarati)
Khaman dokla, Gujarati savoury dish made with Besan flour.
Khanna, has several meanings - food/lunch/dinner.
Kismet, destiny.
Kurta Pyjama, a long shirt and pyjama style trouser worn by Indian men.
Kuthé , Dog.
Kya, a Hindi word which translates into "what".

L

Lagan, Wedding
Lassi, a sweet or salty yogurt drink.
Lathi, Baton
Log, People
Lord Krishna & Radha, Lord Krishna and his devotee Radha. Krishna is a well-loved Hindu God, who got up to mischief in his early years and later became a hero, defeating villains. Also a story of love and devotion between Lord Krishna and Radha. Lord Krishna is known by many names – Kishen, Gopal, Murali and Kanhaiya being some of them. Their story is known by generations of Hindu worshippers and relayed in plays and books around the world.

M

Madhubala, a famous Indian actress.
Ma-ji, Mother (directed to one's mother-in-law or to another's mother, out of respect).
Mari chokri, My daughter
Masterji, Professor
Maasa, Uncle (Mother's sister's husband)
Maasi, Auntie (mother's sister). This word is used to address ladies, even though not related. Sometimes also called "Kaki" in respect of them being elder.
Marajh, Indian priest
Mata, refers to "mother Gods". The Tulsi is seen as a mother.
Mané khabar ché, I know (Gujarati).
Mané Shu Thayu Ché? What's happened to me? (Gujarati).
Mangal Sutra, a necklace worn by married women to symbolise their marriage, whose husband is alive.
Maro dikro, My son (Gujarati).
Marajh, Hindu priest
Mari Ma, My mother – said in the context of being sarcastic, like 'Yes, my dear!' (Gujarati).
Maurat, holy period of time.
Mehndi, a paste made from crushed henna leaves. This is applied to the bride or groom's hands and feet, sometimes in a pattern or just plain dye. In some

cultures both women and men apply mehndi and in some, only women. It is thought the deeper the colour, the deeper the love .

Mela, India fair
Méré bharat mahaan! Long live India!
Musalmaan, Muslim person

N

Na/Nai, No
Namasté, Greetings
Nashta, Breakfast
Nasta layaw, Bring some refreshments.
Nuker, corner

O

Oh re my baap, an exclamation in Hindi or Gujarati – oh my, my father – also meaning 'Oh my God'.

P

Paan, Betel leaf
Pai lago, an action to touch *one's feet to show* respect.
Paisa, Money
Parie, Angel
Parotha, Indian flat bread (shallow fried)
Petticoat , an undergarment tied at the waist to allow saris to be kept in place.
Phool-wallah, Flower seller
Prashad, Food offered to the Gods and then given to people to eat, as a blessing.
Pugri ,Turban worn in weddings.
Puri, Deep fried Indian bread
Pyar, Love

R

Rajkumar, Prince
Ram Ram, saying Lord Rama's name "Ram Ram".
Raj, Meaning King (Raja)The British Government during its reign.
Rickshaw, this has many meanings – a two-wheeled vehicle pulled by a man; a cycle-rickshaw or an auto-rickshaw. In the days of the Raj, the first two were common.

Roti, Leavened bread
Rupaiya, Rupee

S

Saab, Sir
Sabzi, Vegetables
Saaché, Really (Gujarati)
Sagai, Engagement
Saru tu avigayo, Good, you came (Gujarati)
Sasu/ Sasu-Ma, Mother-in-law
Sepoy, a native of India employed as a soldier during the Raj.
Shahid, Martyr
Shalwaar, an Indian wedding suit
Shu, What (Gujarati)
Shu ché, What is it? (Gujarati)
Shukriya, Thank-you
Sitar, an Indian string instrument made of gourds and teak.
Spinning cotton, Mohandas Gandhi used the spinning wheel to defy the Raj, to create his own clothes. This was a unifying element for all Indians who followed his example. It was seen as economic and the boycotting of all foreign goods followed shortly after.

T

Tabla, Indian drums
Thaali, a dish made of steel/brass/silver.
Thik ché né? Is that alright? (Gujarati)
Tonga, a vehicle drawn by horse or bullock.
Tonga – wallah, Tonga driver.
Tulsi tree, a holy basil tree, sacred and worshipped by Hindus. This plant is seen at temples and in Hindu homes and is offered water and prayers. The Tulsi is likened with various Indian Gods and Goddesses and is considered auspicious.

J

Ullu ka Patha, Fool

V

Vaada – pav, spiced potato cooked in shallow oil and sandwiched between baps.

Y

Yaar, Friend
Your feet are heavy, a saying in the Indian language, meaning you are pregnant

Notes

Gandhi

In India Mohandas Karamchand Gandhi was known as 'Mr Gandhi' and later as 'Mahatma' or 'Great Soul', then, more familiarly, as 'Bapu' or 'Grandfather'.

His childhood was uneventful. He was born into a Hindu family and had a venerable old father whom he loved and respected and a pious young mother whom he adored. The young Gandhi was deeply attached to the world around him and used to climb the mango trees in the garden and bandage the 'wounded' fruit. `

He may have been a model child, but as an adolescent he went through rebellious phrases like any other – styling himself on English youths, smoking in secret with a Muslim friend, seeing girls other than his wife and eating meat (forbidden to strict Hindus).

Then in South Africa, where he went to earn a living as a shy young lawyer, Gandhi came into contact with apartheid and everything changed. The future Mahatma was already showing his colours as the champion of truth and freedom through non-violent resistance (*satyagraha*).

Since his death Indian schoolchildren have been taught to think of Gandhi as the father of the nation. India was still part of the British Empire when he was born in 1869; by the time he died, in 1948, India was a free country, thanks to him.

The Salt March

On 2 March 1930 Gandhi warned the viceroy that a *satyagraha* was scheduled for nine days' time. No one yet knew what he had in mind.

On 12 March Gandhi set off from Sabarmati armed with a pilgrim's stick and accompanied by seventy members of his ashram.

As he walked he preached his usual messages about spinning, about *khadi*, child marriages, alcohol – and, in passing, told people to ignore salt laws – and for an hour each day he and his companions worked at their spinning wheels.

Villagers flocked to join them as they passed; three hundred village heads abandoned their duties in the name of non-cooperation, and when they arrived at the coast, at Dandi, the marchers were several thousand strong.

They had been walking for eighty days, but Gandhi had refused to ride the horse brought for him for his use, or to resort to a cart like some of the others.

The Quit India Movement

On Monday 13 April 1942 – on a day of silence therefore – his inner voice dictated the watchword: 'Quit India'. In August Gandhi decided to act upon his intuition and launched an appeal for a final act of disobedience, declaring 'Freedom has to come not tomorrow but today.'

He appealed for open rebellion, a comprehensive, non-violence revolution, and gave himself three weeks to negotiate with the viceroy and explain his decision.

By dawn, instead of the hoped-for freedom, Gandhi found himself - along with all the leaders of the Congress – confronting another set of prison cells.

A word from the author

Freedom of the Monsoon is a work of fiction based in India in the early 1940s. Although the characters are fictional, what they went through reflects on events that have occurred in India - in Indian cultures and society over the years.

Some events are taken from real life situations such as _The Salt March – a history on its own._ You will come across Indian values and beliefs, its customs and languages during the course of the book. With India being a diverse nation, rich in colour and culture, I have tried to bring out the "flavours" with little references – the _gajra_, the _Tulsi tree_, the Gujarati wedding traditions – are some of them.

I wrote this book to bring the readers the other side of the story. I believe the feeling, the consequences of the Quit India Movement are seldom shown and I hope this book brings that to the forefront.

Thank you

I am grateful to Thames and Hudson and the author, Catherine Clement for permission to quote material from *Gandhi: Father of a Nation*.

I thank Veena Sharma, who gave me invaluable, first hand insight of Simla. I thank my friends and family who have encouraged me through the years of working on this project and I profoundly thank my brilliant editor, John Hudspith, for pointing me in the right direction and guiding me through ***Freedom of the Monsoon***.

Finally, I thank my husband, Chetan, for supporting me along this long and most challenging journey, whom without, I wouldn't have been able to complete this book.

Lightning Source UK Ltd.
Milton Keynes UK
UKOW020836080212

186869UK00001BA/6/P